THE STRAIGHT WAY

Bob Williston

The Straight Way
Copyright © 2023 by Bob Williston

Library of Congress Control Number: 2023922111
ISBN-13: Paperback: 978-1-64749-964-8
          Hardback: 978-1-64749-965-5
          ePub: 978-1-64749-966-2

All rights reserved. No part of this publication may be reproduced, distributed, or transmitted in any form or by any means, including photocopying, recording, or other electronic or mechanical methods, without the prior written permission of the publisher or author, except in the case of brief quotations embodied in critical reviews and certain other noncommercial uses permitted by copyright law.

Although every precaution has been taken to verify the accuracy of the information contained herein, the author and publisher assume no responsibility for any errors or omissions. No liability is assumed for damages that may result from the use of information contained within.

Printed in the United States of America

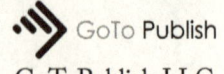

GoTo Publish

GoToPublish LLC
1-888-337-1724
www.gotopublish.com
info@gotopublish.com

CONTENTS

Dedication v
Thanks.. vii
Preface... ix
Chapter 1 1
Chapter 2 11
Chapter 3 25
Chapter 4 33
Chapter 5 41
Chapter 6 53
Chapter 7 61
Chapter 8 67
Chapter 9 77
Chapter 10 89
Chapter 11 99
Chapter 12 111
Chapter 13.. 121
Chapter 14 131
Chapter 16.. 145
Chapter 17 157
Chapter 18 179
Chapter 19.. 191
Chapter 20 201
Chapter 21.. 209
Chapter 22 219
Chapter 23 227
Chapter 24 235

Chapter 25 247
Chapter 26 257
Chapter 27 265
Chapter 28 275
Chapter 29 285
Chapter 30 293
Chapter 31 299
Chapter 32 305
Chapter 33 317
Epilogue 319

DEDICATION

The Straight Way is dedicated to my grandsons Jacob and Michael. Both of them, as pre-school children, had been given inordinate attention by suspected predators, one of them a pastor. We denied them access to our children, and we are now thankful because our suspicions have proven to be valid. Abuses cannot be undone.

THANKS

Special thanks to Cherie and Chester who read, proofread, and edited me through this project. Their contributions and encouragement were much appreciated. This is not to forget the many others who followed my progress with interest and encouragement.

PREFACE

In the small northern California town of Espadín there is a congregation of an obscure Christian sect commonly called the Way. Among those who know members personally, they have a reputation for strict morality and modest living. Way members are not distinguishable from the rest of society by any peculiarity of habit or dress, but two points of doctrine separate them from mainstream Christian churches. One is that they hold their weekly worship services on Thursday evenings in the homes of their local bishops. The other is their ritual of foot washing, which is performed during their Thursday evening worship service.

The Way was organized somewhere in the Midwest in the 1880's by a man named John Campbell. Campbell had become seriously disenchanted with the mainline church he had been attending, so he began having his own Bible studies with a few of his friends. Before long attendance had grown to 15, and Campbell was encouraged to go out recruiting others for their group. By 1900 he had become a traveling preacher. Others who wanted to go preaching also would do so under Campbell's tutelage. As the preachers became trained, they spread out and an organization emerged to manage the affairs of the budding ministry.

However, this not so distant history is never mentioned among the members. In 1901 it was discovered that Campbell had been having a five year affair with the wife of one of his converts, so the senior members of the group ousted him from his position and expelled him from the organization. To distance themselves from the shameful reputation of their founder, the new leadership decided never to mention his name again. But the sect continued to grow. Today small congregations have been established throughout all of the United States, as well as in many other countries of the world.

The Assembly at Espadín

The Townspeople
Carl and Marge Waterman
George and Marion Patten and Joey
Herb and Sharon Fitch and Sally
Rodney and Carla Sturm and 3 children
Floyd Armstrong
Mr. and Mrs. Dan Spinner
Maggie Price and Aggie Cutter
Helen Sawyer and Adam
Ana Castro and Maria
Lidia Gomez and Jason
Floyd (heavy equipment operator)
Floyd (tire salesman)
Pablo

The Students
Amy Frost and Jesse Weber
Floyd and Jenny Gilmore
Janet and Melissa

Marty Spinner

CHAPTER 1

Who sends their son or daughter to college in Espadín? What greater world experience is to be gained in such a faraway environment? Nothing ever happens there. Perhaps it's a place to find both a quality education and the love of one's life. Espadín is an enchanting, romantic hamlet, after all.

But then, it's not just students who go to Espadín. And truth be told, one person has gone there with the intention of disrupting others' lives – albeit for the betterment of all. However, every messenger has a secret – this time it's an appetite that, if nurtured, will destroy not only his victims, but a whole community. Who can sustain his dreams through such disruption? We will see.

Amy and Jesse met in a class on the history of the English language when they were sophomores at Espadín State College. They had claimed seats beside each other and held onto them through the semester.

Jesse used to glance at Amy, and shock himself every time he discovered he had missed something important in the lecture. Amy wanted to be a teacher, as did Jesse. She was sure she wanted to be an English teacher. Occasionally she talked about being a librarian, but she had decided she could settle on one or the other in her junior year. She was bookish, but neither a prude nor a geek. She was tall and slim. She looked like a young athlete. Her light blond hair and fair skin announced her Scandinavian background. And Jesse loved her smile.

Both Amy and Jesse were enamored with ESC, as everyone referred to the college. It was a small college nestled in a beautiful oak grove in the sleepy little town of Espadín in the Sierra foothills of northern California.

Espadín had been settled by a small band of Mexicans who wandered there when California was part of Mexico. No one seemed to know what drew them to that area, because the town was established before the gold rush occurred. But even the gold rush evaded Espadín. It remained a quaint foothills hideaway. College students came to Espadín, did their four years, and then went away. A majority of the locals commuted to Sacramento or some other city in the Sacramento Valley for their work.

Jesse was from San Bernardino. He was raised by his natural parents in a modest home, and considered his upbringing enviable. The worst tragedy of his life had been the death of his four year old sister from a rare blood disease when he was 14. He believed it changed his life by making him more concerned for the welfare of others.

All his life his parents had been devout in following their faith, the Way. They were not manipulative parents, and pushed nothing on him. But some of the people in the faith's assemblies would make it clear that the Way was the only right way, and all others were condemned to hell. Jesse did not subscribe to that notion fully, because he used to listen to his parents discussing people who had been expelled from the Way. He gathered that they believed each person who had been expelled was closer to salvation than the ones who expelled him. His parents spoke of God being able to keep people when others rejected them. That was a great comfort to Jesse, because he was always quite afraid of certain preachers when they came to his home to visit.

Jesse wanted to be a teacher, like his father. He sometimes thought he wanted to be an elementary school teacher, but he felt more inclined to be a high school science teacher. Physics was his favorite subject. He also had a secret fantasy of going to the Olympics and winning a swimming medal. Since he had come to ESC he had really taken his swimming seriously. The coach of the swim team had begun encouraging him to go as far with the sport as possible.

Amy had quite a different background. Her father had been in the military and they had moved frequently. When Amy was in high school her father retired and moved to Eureka where he opened a coffee and souvenir shop.

Amy always thought her parents were super religious, but when she was about 10 they just stopped going to church. She had frequently heard her father criticize the pastor. He was always talking about the pastor's involvement with politics, and complained that people treated the collection plate like a prize game at the circus. The collection was a freewill offering, but people always watched to see what others donated. They either praised the donors for their sizeable offerings or criticized them for being stingy. The prize was salvation, of course, so the contest could become a serious concern among the congregation.

Interestingly, Amy had a brother, Andy, who was 10 years older than she. He'd been her hero from an early age, always her great protector. Because of the 10 year difference in their ages Amy frequently made a small joke of the fact that Jesse would treat her so gallantly because he also had a favorite little sister who had been 10 years younger.

When the professor in the English class had told everyone to find a partner for an exercise, Amy and Jesse had paired up. They considered themselves friends ever after. The exercise was to write a paragraph in King James English. They each wrote one, and then Jesse had laughed when he had proofread Amy's passage:

> *Thee ist a good friend of mine. Shouldst I asketh thou to doest me a wee favor? I hath been awaiting the arrival of mine father from yon marketplace, and me fearest he dideth befallen in an accident. Canneth you takest me there to seeth what have happened to him?*

After a lot of chuckling, Jesse edited it for her. He commented that King James English was easy once you were familiar with it, to which she had replied, "How come you know all about this?"

"Well, in the church I attend everyone uses that form of English."

"No kidding? That must be cool."

"Well, maybe so."

"What church do you go to?"

"It's not a church, really. We just have meetings in houses."

"What's it called?"

"We just call it the Way. I think that was what it was called in Jesus time."

"Has it been around that long?"

"I think so. I don't know really, but I can ask someone who might know."

"No bother. That's OK."

Over the next couple of months Amy continued to ask Jesse questions, and when he learned that there were going to be gospel services in Espadín he invited Amy to go.

The gospel services were being held in the old Greek Playhouse. The building had long since been abandoned by the Drama Department at the college, and the city council now rented it out to any group who needed a place to meet in public. It was becoming dilapidated, but Amy and Jesse found it full of people.

Amy was anxious. They were almost late, but Jesse led her to two empty seats in the second last row. A few people turned their heads to see who had come in. The first thing Amy noticed was that everyone seemed to be silently meditating, and thought they had to be a peaceful congregation.

Then she noticed the pretty little girl sitting beside her was watching her intently. When Amy looked at her the little girl smiled widely and retreated shyly. She looked at her mother. Amy guessed it was for whatever approval the little girl needed for her exchange with Amy. The mother smiled at both of them and went back to reading her hymn book.

A quiet sound of footprints preceded the appearance of two men who made their way to the front of the theater. Amy determined they were the preachers. One was very young, and appeared somewhat nervous. He appeared to Amy to be the same age as she and Jesse, which she thought unusual. He was clean cut, preppie looking, and had a friendly smile.

The older man appeared to be in his forties. He was tall, well-built and well groomed. He had a confident step, and when he reached the front of the theater he waited while the younger man sat down in one of the chairs in front of the stage. He immediately announced that they would sing *Tell Me The Story of Jesus*.

Jesse handed Amy a hymn book, and they found the number. Amy was immediately impressed with the singing.

> Tell me the story of Jesus Write on my heart every word
> Tell me the story most precious Sweetest that ever was heard
> Tell how the angels in chorus Sang as they welcomed His birth
> Glory to God in the highest Peace and good tidings to earth

It took a couple of lines for the singing to reach full volume, but everyone sang. Amy recognized strong four part harmony, and when they reached the chorus she began to sing with everyone else. The hymn's message was simple and clear. She had never realized that hymn singing could be so beautiful.

When the hymn was finished Amy whispered to Jesse, "You're a good singer."

"Thanks," he replied. "You too."

The younger preacher announced he would pray. He used *thee* and *thou* throughout his prayer, and Amy found it quite fascinating. The thought crossed her mind that this old version of English was charming, and wondered if the young preacher were making grammatical errors that she could not recognize.

The prayer was short. It was a humble supplication for God's guidance in the messages he and his fellow preacher were about to deliver. Amy was very impressed that everyone had respectfully bowed their heads while the young man prayed.

When he had finished his prayer, the young preacher began to deliver his sermon. He read something from Jeremiah about God thinking about His people, and seeing to it that they came to an expected end. He encouraged people to develop their own personal relationship with God, because that was how individuals came to the expected end. He never said that the expected end was heaven, but it was not difficult to know what he meant. Neither did he make any mention of what happened to people who did not come to an expected end.

Amy related to his explanation of how people can spend their whole lives not knowing what their end would be. She had always wondered how her own life would unfold. The preacher assured people that God's words are true, and advised them to keep pursuing their relationships with God.

It was a short message. Amy was surprised, but a bit relieved as well that he had switched to modern English. When he finished, he sat down and the older preacher announced that they would sing another hymn.

> *Is there a heart that is waiting, Longing for pardon today?*
> *Hear the glad message proclaiming Jesus is passing this way.*
> *Jesus is passing this way, This way, today.*
> *Jesus is passing this way, Is passing this way today.*
> *Is there a heart that has wandered? Come with thy burden today.*
> *Mercy is tenderly pleading, Jesus is passing this way.*

The words were touching, and again the message was simple and clear. Amy found these messages very positive. She remembered again that her father had been offended because his political leanings were quite contrary to the pastor's. Amy decided that if nothing political was mentioned in the service she would have to tell her father about this church.

> *Is there a heart that is broken, Weary and sighing for rest?*
> *Come to the arms of thy Savior, Pillow thy head on His breast..*

What kindness! Amy thought. She had expected the theme of the service to be give up your sin, but she found this message more inviting and much less threatening. It made her think of so many times in her young life that she had felt lost in the great universe. By the time the hymn finished, she was anxious to hear what the second preacher had to say.

He began by reading a few short passages of Scripture. Then he closed his Bible and began: "This is a gospel service. The word *gospel* means good news, and the purpose of this meeting is to announce good news to anyone who will hear it." Amy liked his British accent. It made him sound more sophisticated, learned, maybe even suave.

The preacher explained that the Jewish nation used to be the only place to find salvation. The Old Testament Law had to be obeyed, whether one wanted salvation or not. He explained that all the Law provided for at best was punishment for anyone who disobeyed it.

According to the preacher, it had been promised many years before Jesus was born that He would come to the earth to show man a better way to salvation. The Jewish Law was not to be the means of salvation. Instead, people were to follow Jesus' teachings, and believe in Him. That would be their salvation, and that was available to anyone who would hear and believe. "This," he said, "is the good news of the gospel that man no longer need to depend on any man's exercise of law to be saved."

And then they sang another hymn.

Under the burdens of guilt and care Many a spirit is grieving,
Who in the joy of the Lord might share, Life everlasting receiving.
Life! Life! Eternal life, Jesus alone is the giver.
Life! Life! Abundant life, Glory to Jesus forever.
Burdened one why will you longer bear Sorrows from which He releases?
Open your heart and rejoicing share Life more abundant in Jesus.

When the singing ended, the British preacher prayed briefly, and the service was over. Everyone was thanked for attending and invited back for the next service.

The congregation began standing and greeting each other with handshakes. As they moved to leave the theater, Amy listened to what everyone was saying.

"It's good to see you."

"Wasn't that a good sermon!"

"Where has your husband been?"

"How are things down in Sacramento?"

"Did you hear that Muriel had a heart attack?"

"Are you enjoying this nice weather?"

Then Jesse was introducing Amy to the little girl who had been sitting beside her. "Amy, this is Maria."

"Hi, Maria. You're a very pretty little girl."

Maria smiled shyly, then said, "You're a pretty lady."

As they emerged from the theater Jesse introduced Amy to the preachers. "Amy, this is Howard and Scott."

The British preacher, who was obviously Howard, said to her, "Nice to meet you. Thank you for coming."

And Scott said, "Nice to meet you, Amy."

On the sidewalk Amy and Jesse were surrounded by a group of young adults. Jesse announced, "Guys, this is my friend Amy. I'll let you all introduce yourselves." There was Floyd, Melissa, Gary, another Floyd, and a half dozen more whose names Amy could not remember.

Then one of the girls said to Amy, "I've seen you before. You used to come out of a classroom while I was waiting to go in."

"I'm sorry I didn't recognize you," Amy said. "Do all of you go to ESC?"

One of the Floyds laughed loudly. "No, I sell tires." He pointed to another guy. "And he digs dirt." Everyone laughed.

"But they have a lot more money than any of us students," Jesse added.

The visiting lasted only briefly. When the lights in the theater were turned out, everyone began leaving. As the young people were separating, one of the girls invited Amy to play tennis with all of them next Saturday. Amy accepted gladly.

On the way home Amy said, "I liked that service a lot."

"That's good."

"Those kids from the college are all nice. They seem like really good friends."

"They are."

"Do you play tennis with them?"

"Sometimes, but not always. I more often go swimming on Saturdays."

"I like that guy Howard's accent. He's a good preacher."

"Yeah. He's from England. He's kind of new in California."

"The other preacher. What's his name?"

"Scott."

"He looks like a little boy. How old is he?"

"I think he's 21. I don't know for sure. I think he was always a grade ahead of me in school."

"Is he from San Bernardino too?"

"No. He's from Yreka or somewhere up there."

"How did you know him when you were in school?"

"We knew most other people in the Way in the state because we have semiannual retreats that everyone goes to."

"Oh," Amy said. Then she commented, "Those preachers only use thee and thou when they're praying."

Jesse laughed, still tickled about Amy's problems with old English.

On Saturday Jesse took Amy with him to the Zócalo, where they were to meet anyone else who wanted to play tennis that day. The Zócalo was a huge park in the center of town. Word had it that it was the site of the original town when the first Mexicans settled there. As time passed the businesses slowly pushed the residents out of the area and for a couple of decades it was the town's business district.

When the Americans began flowing over the Sierra Nevada into California, the businessmen of that quiet hidden town became frightened, and the better off ones packed up and left. The little town struggled on. The business center declined, and by the time Californians discovered it as a retirement paradise it was an eyesore in the otherwise tidy community and idyllic countryside. So a new business area was designated and the business slum was razed for a park, the Zócalo, which would be more becoming of the town's elegance. Legend had it that it was named for the great Zócalo in Mexico City.

The only person at the tennis court was Melissa, whom Amy had met at the gospel service the previous Sunday night. They greeted each other, and Melissa suggested she and Amy have a game while Jesse waited for someone else to arrive. Jesse was pleased that Melissa was being so cordial with Amy.

In a few minutes Scott, the preacher, showed up. Melissa called, "Hey, Scotty." Scott waved back and the girls played on.

"Good to see you, Scott," Jesse said.

"Good to see you," Scott replied. "And it's good to see your friend. Is it Amy?"

"Yeah."

"I saw Melissa over here by herself, so I decided to just walk around until someone else came along," he joked. "It wouldn't look good for me to be out here alone on a Saturday morning with a girl."

They both laughed. "Let's play," Jesse said.

None of them were great tennis players, but they had fun. Every bad move brought a laugh, and it wasn't long before both matches lost track of the scores. After half an hour Melissa decided she was too tired to continue, so Jesse suggested they go to the coffee shop across the street.

"It's too bad no one else showed up this morning," Jesse said.

"I think everyone's studying for their midterms this weekend," Melissa thought.

"Maybe so," Amy agreed. "I only have one this semester."

"You're lucky," Jesse said.

Scott spoke up. "Do you think Marty's studying for his midterms?"

Melissa guffawed. "No, he just sleeps in. He's such a spoiled brat, he never studies. He just knows everything."

There was a pause while the coffees were served. Then Scott said, "Did you hear there was a new girl who confessed in Eureka last week?"

"No. Is it someone I know?" Melissa asked.

"Maybe not," Scott explained. "She had no connections in the Way. She just met Carol Street somewhere and she brought her to gospel services."

"I'm from Eureka," Amy said. "What did she confess to?"

There were a few puzzled glances among the other three. Scott blushed slightly, and said, "In our faith that's what we say a person does when he, uh, becomes a member of our group."

"Confess?" Amy asked.

"Yeah," Jesse said. "I don't know if any others use the word that way."

"What do you have to confess to?"

Jesse couldn't answer that. Scott rescued him. "You don't have to confess to anything, really. I think what it means is that the person more or less confesses to the previous error of his ways and is going to do better from now on."

"Oh." Amy thought about that. Then she asked, "How long have you been a pastor?"

Scott chuckled. "It's only been about four months. Since last summer."

"Where did you go to college?"

"Oh, I didn't go to college. I just began preaching with Howard."

"That's interesting," Amy commented. "I thought all preachers went to college."

Jesse explained, "Scotty is doing onthejobtraining."

"Yeah," Scott agreed.

"So Howard is teaching you how to preach?" Amy asked.

"I guess so," Scott said. "That's how it works, really."

"How long are you going to be here learning how to preach?"

"Probably for a while longer. At least two months, but it could be up to a year or more. Or until Howard's sent somewhere else."

"I liked your sermon the other night. It was very positive."

"Thank you," Scott said.

Before long Scott excused himself, explaining that he and Howard had some visiting to do in the afternoon. As they were leaving, Scott turned to Jesse and said, "Say hi to Kyla for me."

Jesse stammered, and managed to say, "Yeah, I will."

When Scott and Melissa were out of hearing, Amy asked, "Who's Kyla?"

CHAPTER 2

When she heard the rap on her door, Maggie expected it would be Jesse returning from the supermarket. To her surprise it was Aggie.

Aggie was the Way's only spinster in Espadín. She had been in Espadín longer than anyone could remember. She was obviously wealthy, because she lived in a lavish condominium and had a full time maid. Everyone found that amusing, because she was perfectly capable of caring for her own household. Instead she spent every day, except Sundays of course, walking around Espadín with a step more suggestive of a military drill than a relaxing stroll.

"Come in," Maggie said. "It's been a long time."

"Yes, Maggie. I've been missing you at assembly." Assembly was the word used by members of the Way for their Thursday evening worship services.

"I know. I've not been able to get out at night for a while. Winter's coming, and winters are starting to be hard on me."

"And you haven't been to gospel service for nearly a month," Aggie admonished.

"No. My arthritis is really bothering me."

"You should make an effort to get out. Howard will be coming by to check up on you."

Maggie took that to be a somewhat veiled threat. "I'd like to have a visit from Howard."

"Can I get someone to call for you so you can get to the services?"

"That's not necessary. I have a ride any time I need one."

"I'd like to see you getting out more often."

"Oh, Aggie. Wait til you get twisted up with arthritis and you'll know how it is to get out."

"I hope I'd still do whatever possible to get to services."

Ah, Maggie decided. *Aggie has come to touch me up.* Maggie didn't like the way the conversation was going, but Aggie didn't intimidate her. Maggie would just not bother to reply when Aggie became too pushy.

Aggie moved on with her newssharing agenda. "I see that girlfriend of the Weber boy is continuing to come to the gospel services."

Everyone had begun taking an interest in Amy's attendance at the gospel services. No one asked, but most people assumed she and Jesse were romantically connected.

"Yes," Maggie agreed. "Isn't that nice! We haven't had anyone confess in this town for a long time."

"But she's such a trollop!" Aggie exclaimed. "Why do the servants approve of him hanging around with her?" *Servants* was the word used for the Way's ministers.

"Why do you say that? She looked quite respectable to me."

"Maggie! Did you not see the pants she wears to the services? What is this world coming to? No one seems to know how to dress decently any more, not even for church services. It's a wonder the Weber kid doesn't tell her not to wear pants."

"I don't imagine Jesse would think it's any of his business."

"And the trouble with Howard is that he doesn't straighten people out when they get off the straight and narrow. If he stays around here I can just imagine other girls will want to wear pants to assembly too. And her hair! Can you imagine the nerve of her prancing into a service with those Pharisee braids?"

"Well, Aggie, if she is properly convicted and makes a confession, I would expect the Holy Spirit to tell her what she should do. Actually, I thought she had beautiful hair."

Aggie was silent for a minute. She was always irritated when Maggie made positive comments about people she didn't like.

Then Aggie continued. "There you go again, waiting for the Holy Spirit. I'm afraid the Holy Spirit doesn't speak to college students these days. The servants just have to tell people what they need to do. And Howard's just too slack in that respect."

Maggie chuckled. "You should tell Howard that the Holy Spirit needs a little push."

"Maggie, you're terrible."

"I like Howard very much. He's so kind to people. And he has a very positive message in gospel services. I'm glad he's here. Maybe when spring comes I'll be able to attend more of his services."

"I've never heard a servant that I didn't enjoy listening to. The spirit of their messages is all just wonderful. I can't really get enough of it. Wouldn't it be wonderful if he continued to have gospel services here in Espadín through the whole winter until next summer?"

Maggie didn't respond. She always thought Aggie went a bit far with her adoration of the servants, but she knew better than to try to convince her of that.

Maggie was the classic little silver haired lady who was acting grandmother to all her friends in Espadín. She was 88. She thought she was the same age as Aggie, but Aggie would never tell anyone how old she was.

Some of the little kids in Espadín thought Maggie and Aggie were real sisters and called them the Baggy Sisters behind their parents' backs. It caused them problems, though, because when they relied on the nickname for both of them they got so they didn't know which one was Maggie and which one was Aggie. And they knew it was not polite to call either one of them Baggy Sister to her face.

Maggie had come to Espadín 20 years earlier, when her husband had retired and decided to fulfil a longtime dream of living in warm California. He never liked the cold North Dakota winters. Unfortunately he died suddenly a year after they had established their new home in Espadín.

Maggie was stoic about the loss. She decided she would have to take in children for day care to support herself, but before she got organized to do that she learned that her late husband had left a more sizeable provision for her than she had imagined. It put her on a comfortable enough budget that she sold their house and bought a small condominium apartment where she could live without working for an income. She decided to stay in California. Her children had all moved away from North Dakota and she had come to love life in Espadín.

Aggie had another topic to discuss. "Have you heard what Rodney Sturm's problem is?"

"No, I haven't. Does he have a problem?"

"I'm sure he does. But no one seems to know what it is. I saw him having a very heated discussion with Howard after the gospel service last Sunday night."

"I haven't heard a word."

"You have to get out more often so you'd know what's happening to people."

Maggie sighed. "Sometimes I think the less I know the better off I am."

"I should call Rodney and ask him what it was all about. I didn't get close enough to hear what they were talking about."

"I wouldn't do that," Maggie advised. "I'm sure he'd tell others if he wanted them to know."

"Well," Aggie explained, "some people just wait for other people to tell the news so they won't have to tell everyone themselves."

"We should have a gossip column editor for the Way."

Aggie took her seriously. She said, "I don't think that would be good. I think the way we spread the news among us now is much better. It's more like talking to friends than reading about strangers in the newspaper. It is such a sweet fellowship to be able to sit and have such wonderful brethren to consider."

Maggie laughed. She was always amused by Aggie's skill at rejecting any suggestion she might be a gossip.

There was another rap at the door. "That'll be Jesse," Maggie explained.

"You're expecting him?"

"Yes. Can you get the door? Please."

"Sure."

Jesse came in with a number of shopping bags hanging from each hand. "Hi Aggie. Hi Maggie."

Maggie said, "Jesse, thank you so much again. You're such a good young man."

"It's a pleasure, Maggie, as usual."

"Do you do this often for Maggie?" Aggie asked in her investigative tone.

"Occasionally," Jesse replied.

"You're too modest, Jesse," Maggie explained. "You come here every week to get a shopping list for me."

"That's thoughtful of you."

"Thank you."

"Just put them on the table, Jesse. I'll put it all away." Jesse set everything down and sat with them.

Aggie had a burning question. "What does your friend think of the gospel services?"

"She likes them," Jesse replied.

"Do you think she'll be ready to confess soon?"

"I have no idea, Aggie."

"You should ask her."

"Aggie," Maggie chastised. "You can't ask people anything like that."

"Why not? She should know by now. She's been to a few gospel services already. Someone should be encouraging her to confess."

"She gets a lot of encouragement," Jesse said. "She's made friends with all the kids who go to the college."

"I'd like to know what she's thinking," Aggie said.

"OK, I'll ask her." Jesse laughed.

"Maybe I should ask her," Aggie persisted.

"No," Maggie warned. "Don't do that. I think it would sound too pushy."

"Shouldn't we impress her with the urgency of being saved?"

Jesse was visibly worried that Aggie might do just as she said. "I wouldn't do that, Aggie. Amy's a really private person, and she doesn't talk about her feelings to strangers."

"Oh." Aggie accepted the correction. "But don't ask her to come to assembly until she confesses."

"Why not?"

"The servants don't recommend it. Things get said in assembly that might be improper for her to hear."

Jesse was puzzled. "You mean we shouldn't let people see our footwashing?"

Maggie was becoming distressed.

Aggie explained, "Yes. Some people don't care for that if they've not come to a confession. They don't understand the need for it."

"And some people are offended when they hear us making negative comments about other religions too," Maggie interjected.

Before long Aggie decided to go on her way. Both Maggie and Jesse were relieved.

Maggie asked Jesse to stay for a cup of tea. It was their routine when he delivered groceries. Maggie poured and sat down with him at the table.

"Jesse," Maggie began. "Don't take Aggie too seriously. She's terribly nosey and bossy."

Jesse laughed. "No worry, Maggie. I have her number. And I'll keep Amy away from her."

"Good idea." Maggie was smiling. "I think she's jealous that I have someone deliver groceries for me and she doesn't."

"Oh, that's funny."

"But I wouldn't repeat a thing she tells you." She paused. "You also have to be sure you know exactly what you've said to her. Stories get twisted, you know. I just don't tell her much."

"That's a good idea," Jesse assured her.

"But she's a really good hearted person. She has everyone's interest at heart, and I'm very sure she's generous with the servants. They visit her often."

"Ah." Jesse made a mock gesture of sudden understanding. "Is that how you tell who's tight with the servants?"

Maggie just cast him a smug, knowing glance.

When he was leaving, Jesse kissed her on the cheek and said, "I'm going to bring Amy to see you one of these days."

"I'd love to meet her."

"Who's Kyla?"

Jesse didn't know what to say. He hadn't expected Amy to ever ask him that, or he'd have decided what to say when she did. It surprised him that he suddenly didn't want Amy to know much about Kyla.

"Kyla's a friend of mine in Riverside," he said.

"Oh. Is she your girlfriend?"

That was the precise question he didn't want to answer. "I don't think so." *What a lame answer that was!* He thought.

Amy smiled. "I see. She used to be, huh?"

"Well, kind of. We weren't all that.... you know, serious about each other."

"She'll get over it."

How could Amy know enough to make such a statement? "I didn't love her that much." Jesse realized he was bumbling.

"There are lots more fish in the sea," Amy said. "My Mom always says, 'If you're not fussy you have to take leftovers.'"

They laughed.

Kyla was a year younger than Jesse, and she went to assembly with him all the time they were growing up. There weren't many other young people in the Way in their area, so they found themselves together frequently in social gatherings with their parents.

After Jesse got his driver's license he began taking her with him to see other young Way friends in Orange County. He didn't think of those outings as dates, because they often took Kyla's younger brother with them. But somewhere along the line it came to be understood that they were boyfriend and girlfriend.

In the beginning Jesse wasn't sure he liked being her boyfriend because he didn't find her that attractive. He thought she was good looking, but she didn't share much of his interests. He always wanted to go to college and be a professional, and Kyla just wanted to get out of high school and get married. That's what bothered him. It wasn't because he wanted a wife with a career, it was because she didn't share his enthusiasm for intellectual pursuits.

Despite all the time they'd spent together, all they'd ever done was hold hands when they went walking somewhere together and Kyla was trying to keep pace with him. Kyla's brother used to tease them about kissing and hugging, and Jesse had found it embarrassing because they didn't have that kind of relationship.

It wasn't until Jesse and Kyla went to Disneyland one Saturday after his graduation from high school that they actually kissed for the first time. Kyla had been clinging to his arm, and when they got on their first ride she threw her arms around him and kissed him on the lips. He hadn't expected it, and he realized his part of the kissing was really awkward. On the next ride he knew what to expect, so he was more prepared to get it right.

It was fun, even exciting. Rather than hold hands the rest of the day, they walked around with an arm around each other. That evening when he took her home they kissed around the corner from her house so her brother wouldn't see them, and then he dropped her off in front of her house.

Before two weeks passed, Jesse heard from his friend Daryl in Orange County that it was rumored that Jesse and Kyla were engaged to be married. Jesse denied it, of course, but Daryl didn't believe him. He told Jesse he might as well come clean about it because once he got married everyone would know about it anyway. Daryl promised to throw him a big party with all their friends before he got married.

Jesse was worried. He worried about it all summer. He had asked Kyla out for dinner the following Saturday evening, so he decided to tell her what he'd heard.

"I heard a rumor about us," he said.

Kyla smiled. "Tell me what it was."

He thought he was going to faint. "Someone told me they heard you and I were getting married."

"Oh," she said. "Word sure travels fast."

"Did you hear the same thing?"

"Actually, no. But I'm not surprised about the rumor."

"What do you mean?"

"It's hard to hide things, you know."

She thinks we're getting married, he thought. *I don't want to get married. How did this get started?* "I don't think I want to get married," he blurted.

She looked shocked. "You don't? Why not?"

"I want to go to college and get an education and establish myself in a career."

"Can't I help you do that?"

He was silent. Kyla stopped eating. Finally she said, "Couldn't we do that?"

"I don't know," he said. "I never thought about that."

There wasn't much of a kiss that night when he took her home. And the next week was torture for him. He realized she'd interpreted the whole day at Disneyland as some kind of an engagement ritual, and he kept saying to himself, *I don't want to get married. I want to do a lot of things before I get married. She'd get pregnant and I'd have to quit college and go to work. Worst of all, he decided he didn't love her enough to throw away all his plans for her.*

Through the rest of the summer things didn't improve for him. He never mentioned the marriage thing again, but Kyla's kissing got more and more ... intense. By the end of the summer he'd made up his mind that he didn't care for her as a girlfriend, that the relationship was over, and that he'd look for another girlfriend. By the time he went to Espadín he was looking forward to getting out of the situation.

He didn't give Kyla his address in Espadín, but a week after he arrived there a letter came from Kyla. He didn't read it. Under a sickening cloud of guilt he threw it in the trash. He felt wretched because he wasn't leveling with her, but he didn't know how to go about getting rid of a girlfriend. In fact, it still embarrassed him somewhat that he still didn't know how to go about getting a girlfriend in the first place.

He received a couple more letters from Kyla, and threw them in the trash too. He just wanted it all to go away.

In hindsight, he wondered why he'd ever considered settling for such a relationship. He realized it was because his selection of possible girlfriends in the Way was quite limited. And he knew how frequently it was rumored that marriage to someone outside the Way was a very dangerous decision to make.

November came, and Amy had not missed a gospel service. Jesse faithfully tended to his Saturday morning swim routine, and most Saturday afternoons he and Amy spent studying in the college library.

Amy had grown quite fascinated with Jesse's friends at the college. It amazed her that they could all get together and just have fun. The guys were most respectful of the girls. They treated Amy much like her older brother had treated her, and she was comfortable with them.

There were differing and conflicting personalities, of course. But she noticed that the hyper, superciliousness of Marty, the group clown, was no indication that he was disrespectful of anyone. She noticed that the prissy, pokerfaced Janet was not really the annoying person she looked like. None of the guys had ever asked Amy out. She suspected it was because they thought she and Jesse were going together, despite the fact that they'd never given any indication that they were.

Amy's most amazing moment with them was the day the girls took her aside and asked her if she and Jesse were an item. She said they weren't, and one of the girls said, "Cool. He's up for grabs, girls."

Another girl informed Amy, "And you can have any one of the other guys you want. None of us want any of them."

And another one commented, "And everyone wants Jesse." They all laughed wildly. They had bonded.

Then there came a very memorable gospel service. It was the last service before they all dispersed for the Thanksgiving break. Amy had a haunting sense that this would not be like the other services. She was greatly moved by the first hymn they sang.

Jesus is standing in Pilate's hall,
Friendless, forsaken, betrayed by all.
Hearken, what meaneth the sudden call!
What will you do with Jesus?
What will you do with Jesus?
Neutral you cannot be.
Someday your heart will be asking:
What will He do with me?

Amy sang heartily, but she was taking the message personally. She needed a personal answer to the question in the hymn, and she'd never given that much thought. It was troubling to her. She suddenly realized that by not dealing with the question she would by default be rejecting Christ. That was a very sobering thought.

Jesus, I give Thee my heart today
Jesus, I'll follow Thee all the way

Gladly obeying Him, will you say?
'This will I do with Jesus.'

It was a good verse for the hymn to end with. It was the resolve to the question. She determined the better option for her would be to follow Jesus.

Amy didn't hear much of the first prayer. She was greatly worried about her need to follow Jesus. She decided she'd have to ask someone, probably Jesse, what following Jesus involved.

The next hymn was equally troubling.

Life at best is very brief Like the falling of a leaf
Like the binding of a sheaf Be in time
Fleeting days are telling fast
That the die will soon be case
And the fatal line be passed Be in time.
If in sin you longer wait You may find no open gate
And your cry be just too late Be in time
Time is gliding swiftly by
Death and judgment draweth nigh
To the arms of Jesus fly Be in time
O I pray you count the cost Ere the fatal line be crossed
And your soul in hell be lost Be in time

Wow, Amy thought. That's an ultimatum. It was frightening to her that it still wasn't clear what to do to avoid hell. She'd surely ask Jesse how you accomplish that, because he appeared not to be troubled by this singing at all.

Sinner heed the warning voice
Make the Lord your final choice
Then all heaven will rejoice
    Be in time
Come from darkness into light
Come, let Jesus make you right
Come, and start for heav'n tonight
    Be in time

Amy had become so troubled by the end of that hymn that she hardly heard anything Scott was saying. It was his usual short and anecdotal style of sermon.

And then they sang a third hymn.

Softly and Tenderly Jesus is calling
Calling for you and for me

See, on the portals He's waiting and watching
Watching for you and for me
Come home, come home
Ye who are weary come home

At this point Amy realized she was trembling. She attempted to calm herself, but was not completely successful. At least with this hymn she was beginning to think the answer to her question was soon to be revealed. She still couldn't imagine how it would become apparent, but she'd come to depend on Howard telling them something relevant to their concerns.

Time is now fleeting, the moments are passing
Passing from you and from me
Shadows are gathering, death beds are coming
Coming for you and for me
Oh! for the wonderful love He has promised
Promised for you and for me
Though we have sinned, He has mercy and pardon
Pardon for you and for me

That hymn was a perfect reflection of all of Howard's preaching over the past couple of months. He talked a lot about the wonderful things that were available through the gospel. She always felt he had a great message of hope, one she envied and wanted for herself. But tonight she found she couldn't concentrate fully on Howard's message. He was as convincing as ever, and it bothered her that she might not remember everything he said as she usually did.

Finally his sermon was over. It was then she found out what was different about this service. Before Howard announced what the hymn would be, he made a brief speech.

"We feel there may be someone in the service tonight who has been concerned about their soul, and is ready to make a commitment to follow Jesus. We'd like to give any such person the opportunity to make a public expression of this decision by standing to his feet while we sing the last verse of this hymn. This expression would not mean you are joining a religion, and the expression in itself is not a saving gesture. Rather, it is a step one can take to demonstrate to our friends an acceptance of the wonderful gospel message."

Amy listened with mouth open and eyes unblinking. That was the answer she'd been waiting for! She'd decided some time ago that Jesse's attractive attitude and integrity had something to do with his religion. She considered that she'd have nothing to lose, since she wasn't joining a religion. It amazed her that Howard's kind of gospel message had nothing to do with a church. She decided that she wouldn't put off telling her father about this Way any longer.

And then they sang.

A hand all bruised and bleeding is knocking at the door
Is knocking at the door of your heart
It is the hand of Jesus who long has knocked before
Though oft you have told Him to depart
O don't you hear Him knocking, knocking at the door
He's knocking at the door to come in
He wants an invitation to cross the threshold o'er
Then Jesus will save you from all sin

Amy didn't want to make the mistake of standing at the wrong time. Worse yet, she was afraid she might get mixed up and the hymn would end before she stood up. So she held her finger by the fifth verse. When the time came, she stood up.

Why will you keep Him knocking? Why don't you let Him in?
He'll fill your pathway with delight
That hand so torn and bleeding will wash away your sin
O welcome the Savior in tonight

When the hymn was over she looked around and there were two other people standing as well. Howard said, "Thank you. You may be seated." Howard prayed, and mentioned the people who'd been standing. The service was over.

People flocked to shake Amy's hand, and express their delight with the decision she'd made.

"I'm so happy for you."

"You'll never regret your decision."

"I'm so pleased to have you in this family."

"I hope you get to come to my assembly. Do you live here in Espadín?"

"Hi. I'm Agnes. People just call me Aggie. Welcome to the Way. You will find this to be the most important decision of your lifetime. And this is my friend Maggie. She doesn't come to services a lot, but she is a very nice lady."

"Hi, Amy. I feel like I know you already. Jesse delivers my groceries to me, and I'm so appreciative of that. He's such a fine young man."

"Ah," Amy said. "You're Maggie. I'm so pleased to meet you. Jesse has mentioned you a few times."

"Good things, I hope," Maggie said.

"Only the best," Amy assured her.

As they were leaving the theater, Howard and Scott shook their hands. Howard expressed his happiness that Amy had made a decision. He asked whether they could arrange to have a visit with Jesse and Amy, and it was agreed they'd have dinner at Jesse's apartment two evenings later.

By the time they were on the way home Amy felt quite besieged by the number of people who'd taken time to speak personally to her. There wasn't much conversation. They were both left speechless, Jesse because he'd never expected Amy to confess, and Amy because she'd never dreamed she'd get such attention from complete strangers.

Jesse dropped her off at her dorm. She had a test the next morning and wanted to study some more.

But when she was alone she decided she was unable to concentrate on her studying, so she went to bed and decided to worry about the test in the morning. Her mind spun with the questions of what would happen next, and wondered how she was going to fit in with all the others in this very close family. That, she'd learned, was what the people in the Way liked to call the group.

CHAPTER 3

In Santa Monica, dinner was ready in the Shipman household. Clay kissed his wife and son and took his place at the table. Nancy set a steaming casserole on the table and took her seat. They all bowed their heads and Clay said grace.

"So how was your day?" Clay asked Dennis.

"Good. I got an 'A' on my Math test."

Nancy was smiling. Clay said, "All right, little scholar! For that we'll have some Dairy Queen later on."

"Can I have a banana split this time?"

"Why not? It's hard work getting an 'A'."

"Well, not in Math," Dennis said. "Everything in Math is easy."

"Tell Daddy how you came to my rescue at the store today," Nancy suggested.

Clay laughed. "You did a SpiderMan stunt?"

"No," Nancy said. "It was a mathematician stunt."

"Tell me," Clay said.

Dennis hesitated for a while. "Oh yeah. The lady in the store was going to make Mom pay $7.92 for three packs of cards, and I knew it was wrong because they were only $1.98 each."

"Did you multiply $1.98 in your head that fast?" Clay asked.

"No, I didn't have to do that," Dennis explained. "I know that 98 cents is two cents down from a dollar, and so three of them would be six cents down from a dollar. And the lady was down to 92 cents. That was too many cents down."

"Wow!" was all Clay could say.

Dennis continued. "She said she made a mistake on her cash register, but Mom didn't know she did it."

"Saved me about $2.00," Nancy added. She exchanged an amused and proud glance with Clay and went back to the kitchen to get a pitcher of cold drink.

"That's great," Clay commented.

Dennis was quiet for quite a while as he dug into his dinner. Then he turned to Clay again. "There are kids at school that don't like you. I'm kinda scared of them."

"Really. Why is that?"

There was a long pause. Then Dennis said, "They told me bad things about you."

"Such as?"

"Tyler told everyone in the class that you let a bad killer off. They told me he's going to go and kill someone else now."

"Are you talking about Mr. Chen?"

"Yeah. I don't want Mr. Chen to come and kill us now."

"Not to worry, Dennis. Mr. Chen likes what I did for him, so we're safe. And we'll take care of the bad kids at your school."

Dennis did not necessarily understand, but he trusted his father.

Clay was a midthirties criminal defense attorney and partner in the Katz, Berry, & Shipman law firm in Santa Monica. The firm specialized in criminal defense, and Clay was rapidly rising to celebrity reputation for his ability to handle complicated and controversial cases. His most recent accomplishment was the acquittal of a Mr. Chen who was accused of murdering three members of a family.

Clay grew up as an only child in Kearney, Nebraska. His father was an oldtime grocery store operator, making a modest living from providing the necessities of life to their tightknit community. When the era of big supermarkets arrived in Kearney he saw the writing on the wall and purchased a fast food franchise.

The family were faithful followers of the Way and from time to time were subjected to friendly jabs from their customers. The most frequent difficulty for the clients was the grocer's refusal to sell tobacco products. He always told people it was a matter of conscience with him. Clay remembered his father mentioning to his mother when they moved on to the fast food business, "At least no one will be asking us for cigarettes and beer anymore."

As Clay grew up he was always fascinated with the great trains that sped through Kearney. He felt awed at the powerful and unstoppable roar as they passed through town. It occurred to him that Kearney would possibly be unable to consume the contents of a single train in a whole year. There were obviously great numbers of hungry and needy people at both ends of the railroad. Early on Clay would wonder what kind of social structures would be found in a place where strangers were all squeezed into small areas. Kearney was anything but a big city. He had tried to discuss that concept with someone once, and their response was a simply "Who needs to know?"

Clay became the valedictorian of his high school class. He had always expected to work for what he achieved, so a scholarship for fully paid tuition at the University of Nebraska at Kearney came as an unexpected windfall. His father had hoped he would get a degree in agriculture, but Clay had insisted on a liberal arts program. That worried his parents, because they couldn't think of anyone who made a good living with what you learn in that kind of program. But they had made no effort to dissuade him from his decision.

They did object when he informed them in his senior year at UNK that he was going to study law. Among all their friends in the Way, attorneys were the proverbial slippery crooks of society. They simply did not believe a member of the Way could be a lawyer. They told Clay what he expected them to tell him about that. But Clay insisted that it was an honorable thing to defend the down trodden. They settled for that. That summer they went with him to Los Angeles where still another scholarship allowed him to have a small apartment and full tuition paid.

It was in law school that Clay became passionate about the law, and he soon decided he was going to be a criminal defense attorney. That was the top of the heap, as far as he was concerned. And by that time he had become convinced he had the ability to get there. He had been quite selfconscious of his rural Great Plains background, so he volunteered to have his IQ evaluated by a post graduate student in psychology. When he learned what it was, he left all his doubts about his ability to compete behind him.

It was also while at law school that he met Nancy. He was drawn to her first by her attractive smile, then by knowing her roots were also east of the Rockies. On their first date Nancy asked him what he was studying and he told her he was going to be a criminal defense attorney.

Nancy looked at him, stunned. "Wow! What do the servants think about that?"

"I never asked."

"Didn't they find out before you came here?"

"No one said a thing. I think my parents were concerned about what people would think, so they didn't tell anyone."

The Straight Way

"Yeah," she thought out loud. "That's what happens. They were smart not to tell."

Clay wondered what she was thinking. He had already decided that she was his kind of girl. Back home country and looking for a life that would require a lot of adrenalin. He didn't have to ask the important question, she volunteered it.

"You're the neatest guy I've ever met. You are passionate about something that is very important."

"Like the law?" he asked.

"Yeah. And you don't bother looking for advice from incompetent people."

"Like the servants?"

"Yeah." Then she blurted. "And you're so gorgeous to look at." She had embarrassed herself.

Clay turned fiery red, and Nancy said, "I'm sorry. I shouldn't talk like that. I don't know what happened. I just never thought …."

"That's OK," Clay said. "I wish I weren't so shy so I could share how I feel too."

Then they were both quiet. Clay decided she was waiting to hear how he felt, so he said, "I, uh… you're, you know, so beautiful."

That was the turning point. They were madly in love from that day on.

His parents were in Los Angeles for his graduation from law school. When the ceremony was over he surprised them by asking them to Las Vegas with him and Nancy for their wedding the next day. He and Nancy had decided to refuse any advice from either set of parents, so that invitation was the only forewarning his parents got. Yet they were not totally surprised. By then they knew how Clay would run his life, and they had expected he and Nancy would be married anyway.

The date was set when Clay and Nancy received the news that Nancy's parents agreed to meet them in Las Vegas on that date "for a graduation celebration," they said.

It turned out to be a very romantic occasion. Nancy and Clay left the next morning for a honeymoon and their four parents had to find something to do in Las Vegas for a few days before they went back home.

Now Clay was a successful criminal defense attorney. He had defended Chen in a long and widely publicized trial, and just the day before the jury had delivered a not guilty verdict. Clay had not given a lot of thought to what his son might think of the publicity he had gotten.

"I knew that was going to happen with Dennis in school," Nancy lamented.

"I'm sorry, Dennis." Clay was curious. "Were there other kids who said things like that?"

"They all talked about it. And they told Mrs. Freeman too."

"What did she say?"

"Nothing. She just looked really shocked and never said anything." He took a few more bites of dinner, then asked, "Did Mr. Chen really kill those people?"

Clay was quick to answer. "Actually I'm quite sure Mr. Chen did not kill those people."

"Why was he taken to court?"

"It looks like someone else did it and pretended it was Mr. Chen instead."

"Oh." Dennis thought about that for a while.

Nancy said, "Honey, do you think it would be worth our while to put Dennis in a private school?"

Clay scratched his head. "This will blow over in a couple of days."

"I worry about him all the time," she said. "You get a lot of controversial clients these days."

"I know," Clay acknowledged. They had briefly discussed this scenario a few times. "Maybe we have to consider that."

"There are some advantages for kids like him in the right private schools," Nancy said. "And I don't like what I hear about the kids in middle schools these days."

"I'll ask Nathan tomorrow what school he sent his kids to." Nathan was one of Clay's law firm partners.

"I can't go to law school yet," Dennis protested.

Clay and Nancy laughed. Nancy explained, "Don't worry. It would be a normal school. You might like it more than a public school, though. We couldn't take you there until after summer vacation this year anyway."

Clay said, "I'm not sure I like the 40 to one studentteacher ratio in the middle schools anyway."

Dennis was listening intently, knowing the conversation was about him. "I just want to go to a school where I can have some friends."

"You can have good friends at any school," Nancy assured him. "You know how to pick good friends."

"OK," Dennis consented. After a pause, he asked, "Daddy, why do you get criminals free?"

"I don't really get them free. That happens only when the judge and jury believe they should go free," Clay explained. "It's the judge and the jury who decide whether a person is guilty. I just make sure the prosecutor doesn't tell lies about the person on trial."

Dennis absorbed that information. "That's good. I think you have the most important job in court, don't you?"

"I think I do. I make sure the prosecutor actually proves a person did something. If he can't prove that, I tell the court that the person has to be let go because he is not guilty."

"So you rescue people who have been harassed by the police," Dennis concluded. He had heard all about how the police could harass people, and considered it heroic of his father to be helping victims. "You're as good as SpiderMan," he announced.

Clay and Nancy laughed.

When they finished eating, Nancy asked, "Do I understand that dessert is at Dairy Queen tonight?"

Dennis piped up, "Yeah. Let's go right now."

After Dennis was tucked into bed for the night, Clay said, "What do you think? Should I opt out of criminal defense work until Dennis gets out of school?"

"Absolutely not." Nancy was firm. "You have invested too much in your career to drop it now. There isn't anything else you really want to do, is there?"

"I don't want to make life any more difficult for Dennis than necessary."

"He'll have to learn to cope. We can't shelter him from everything. And children do learn to cope. I'm sure other criminal defense lawyers' children know about this. If he really does want to become a lawyer, he should know about this aspect of the work."

"Yeah."

"I know what he feels like because I get a cool shoulder from some of the women at assembly."

"Really? Who does that?"

"Mona and Diane mostly. I just don't like those women at all. Diane even asked me once why the servants ever allowed you to become a lawyer. I just told her that you never asked their permission. She looked at me like I had three heads."

Clay laughed. "That woman hasn't had an original thought for a long time. I'll bet she calls the servants for permission to fart." They both laughed.

"She's probably stuck herself shut with super glue so she won't commit a fart at all." They laughed even harder. Nancy continued, "Why are there so many of those old fogies in the Way?"

"They get to kiss up to the servants."

"Aren't the servants aware of what these kinds of people are doing to them?"

"Sure," Clay said. "But have you ever heard of a servant complaining about all the fawning."

Nancy mocked the common reprimand. "Shame on you, talking about the servants that way." Then she asked, "What would it take to change their attitude about lawyers?"

"They'll change their opinion when someone in the Way comes to me for a defense."

"That'll be the day!

CHAPTER 4

Howard and Scott arrived for dinner just as Amy arrived. There were handshakes all around, and Jesse offered each of them a seat by the table. "I don't have much furniture, you know."

There followed friendly chatter about the general poverty of students, and the conclusion was reached that it was all worth while in the end. Amy found Howard an engaging conversationalist with a good sense of humor. She found Scott charmingly shy, and quite good looking, but she suspected he did not date girls as part of his commitment to his ministry..

Jesse proposed that Howard say grace, which he did, and they began eating. Jesse had prepared a roast chicken and baked potatoes. The vegetables were from a can. Amy studied Howard and Scott carefully, and they seemed comfortable with Jesse's catering abilities and ate with gusto. That helped her relax.

After a while Howard changed the conversation to Amy. "We're so glad to have you with us," he said.

"Thank you."

"Has Jesse told you about assembly?"

"Just briefly. He told me the gospel services were to get the public interested in the Way. But I'd like to go to some of those assembly services too."

"Of course. You can go to assembly with Jesse. There's a nice group of people who meet there, and you should be very comfortable with them."

"Can I ask you a question?"

"Sure." Scott and Jesse were not contributing to the conversation.

"Why do you have these assembly services on Thursday night?"

Howard smiled. "That was the time of the week that Jesus washed His disciple's feet. It's usually referred to as the Last Supper. Jesus told them they had to have Him wash their feet or they'd not have any part with Him. So we've been keeping that ever since."

"Oh, I see." Amy mulled that over in her mind. "I really don't know much about the Way."

"It's quite simple, really. I'm sure Jesse can answer any questions you have. What do you think, Jesse?"

Jesse gulped. "Well, Howard, I'll do my best."

Howard turned again to Amy. "Jesse has a fine reputation, and we know that he has a good understanding of the Way."

Jesse blushed. "Thank you."

Jesse served chocolate ice cream in bowls of four different styles. More jokes were made about him being a poor student.

When dinner was over, Howard and Scott announced they had another visit to make that evening. They shook hands again, and left.

While they were washing dishes, Amy asked, "What is this thing about washing feet?"

"Oh," Jesse said. He seemed a bit sheepish. "At assembly the bishop washes people's feet, just like Jesus instructed."

"Will I have to do that?"

"No. At least not to begin with." Jesse had never been called upon to explain foot washing before. Actually, he had avoided telling people about it because he did not think most people had even heard of the practice, much less understood the meaning.

"I don't want to make a fool of myself at this assembly," Amy said. "Tell me everything I'm going to have to do when I go."

"Nothing, really. Just observe a few times and you can begin to participate when you feel comfortable."

"Cool."

When the dishes were put away, they sat down to the Physics assignment they were working on. Amy was sorry she had signed up for the course, but she liked being in class with Jesse and he was a great tutor. They got through the assignment, but Amy's mind was on a lot of other things. And that night it was even more difficult to concentrate on the assignment.

Of course, she had a lot to think about. She accepted the idea that she had not joined a church, but she felt that she did in some manner belong to the Way. That was comforting to her. Still, she wondered what the demands of her commitment to the Way were going to be. But she reasoned that if Jesse wasn't overwhelmed by such a commitment, neither should she.

The Thanksgiving holiday was coming right up. In her mind she was also rehearsing all the ways she could tell her father that she had joined the Way.

When the Thanksgiving break was over, Jesse and Amy met at the coffee shop in the Student Union Building. Anyone who wanted to meet anyone needed only to sit around in the Student Union Building until that person showed up!

"How was San Bernardino?" Amy asked.

"Forever the same," Jesse replied. "It's really not an exciting place. How was Eureka?"

"I had a really good time. A lot of my high school friends were around, and we had a great time."

Jesse was curious. "So did you tell your father about your new faith?"

She sobered. "I tried to, but I didn't make a lot of progress."

"Maybe he thought you were trying to convert him."

"Oh, he's not convertible. At first, when I told him this wasn't a normal religion, he about flipped his lid. He told me if I'd joined a cult he would regret ever sending me to college. He warned me that cults recruit at colleges."

"That's a pretty common reaction."

"It is?"

"Yeah. I know a number of people who had a really difficult time with their families when they came to the Way."

"When I explained to him what it's all about, he seemed to calm down a lot. I told him about how nice everyone was to me, and how uncomplicated the rules are. He actually told me he was pleased I was reading a Bible." She laughed. "I always used to tell him it was too boring to read."

She chewed on her sandwich and continued. "He told me he'd like to meet someone from the Way. Could you come home with me some weekend so he can see you?"

Jesse laughed. "I guess so. You just say when."

The next day Jesse and Amy were having lunch at the coffee shop again when someone interrupted their conversation. "Can we share your table with you?" Five students whom Amy had seen at the gospel services had just arrived.

"Sure," Jesse said. "We can all squeeze around here."

The guy Amy recognized as Floyd said, "Hi Amy."

Jesse asked, "You know everyone here today, Amy?"

"I know Floyd and Melissa and Janet."

"There are two Floyds here. This guy is Floyd Armstrong, and this is Floyd Gilmore. You know Melissa, and Janet. And this is Marty Spinner"

They all shook hands. Amy asked, "How many Floyds are there?"

"Hundreds," one of the Floyds replied, and everyone laughed but Amy. She didn't get the joke.

"There are Floyds all over California," Janet explained. She cast a glance at Floyd Armstrong and added, "And they're not all normal either."

Floyd replied, "Ah, come on. You're just jealous because you don't have the assets necessary to be a Floyd too."

"I'm sure they're all named for Uncle Floyd," Melissa explained.

Amy didn't understand. "Are you all related, or something?"

"Oh, no," Marty said. "Uncle Floyd's no one's real uncle. He's just the big cheese. He's the top servant for California. All the mommies get brownie points for naming their kids after him." He snickered. "Kind of flattering to have someone named for you, though."

"Marty, you're rude."

"And you!" Melissa said. "You're only hope of fathering a Floyd is if you can find a wife, and then maybe convince her to call him Floyd Marty." Everyone laughed.

The conversation was jovial. It was clear everyone had been rejuvenated from the long weekend.

"Oh! Did you hear what happened to Howard when we were gone?"

"What happened?"

Marty emulated Howard's British accent. "Why, he had a nervous breakdown!"

Amy said, "Poor Howard. He didn't seem like the kind of person who would have a nervous breakdown."

"Well, it's not necessarily all that serious," Marty assured her. "Probably Uncle Floyd just told him he had a nervous breakdown. You'll get used to that. When servants disappear they all have nervous breakdowns."

"Pay no attention to Marty!"

"Why?" Amy asked. She didn't know what else to ask.

"I don't know. I guess it keeps the gossip down."

"Amy, what probably happened is that Howard had a problem with Uncle Floyd, and Uncle Floyd sent him away."

Amy became still more concerned. "Does he do that a lot?"

"I think it's every time he takes the notion."

Janet did not like the tone of the conversation. "You shouldn't talk that way about the servants. You know that Uncle Floyd will ask anyone to go wherever he needs them to go."

"What do you think happened, then?"

"I really don't know, but I was told he had cancer or something," Janet protested.

"I guess the only way we'll ever find out what happened to him is to find him and ask him ourselves."

"Don't laugh," Marty warned. "We've got a real problem now. Bart is here."

"Oh, no. I know him. Brutal Bart!"

"What's he like?"

"He loves the 'L' word." A couple of them laughed.

Jesse asked, "What's the 'L' word?"

"Lasciviousness."

"Yeah, I remember he used to always be talking about the evils of lasciviousness."

"I've heard he's a really cranky old man."

"Is Scott still going to stay here? I really like him."

"For sure. He wasn't married to Howard, you know!"

"Scott didn't have his nervous breakdown yet."

Marty got serious. "I still think a nervous breakdown would be better than getting a wrong spirit, though."

"Yeah, you really go far away when you have a bad spirit."

Janet spoke up in a sharp, critical tone. "What do you mean by a bad spirit?" Amy had decided Janet was at least a bit prudish.

Marty explained. "That's when Uncle Floyd gets ticked with one of us and sends us packing."

"I don't want to have this conversation," Janet said. She got up and left, throwing what was left of her lunch into a trash can.

As though nothing had happened, Marty said, "That girl's probably short a few brownie points with Uncle Floyd. I'll see that he hears about her defense of him."

"I'd be careful," Melissa warned. "She's apt to tell Bart everything you said."

"I'll cross that bridge when I get to it."

After they'd all gone to class, Amy commented to Jesse, "I hope they're a bunch of jokers."

Jesse assured her they were. "But I'm curious about what happened to Howard."

"He's was such a good preacher and seemed to be so relaxed."

"I hope we find out what happened. I liked Howard too."

Amy was fascinated with her first assembly service. She and Jesse rode together to the home of the bishop. She was amazed that they just opened the door and walked in. The first thing Jesse did when they arrived was sit on a chair near the door, kick off his shoes, and expose his bare feet. There was a large bowl with water on the floor in front of the chair.

Amy watched fixedly as the elderly, kindly looking man kneeled on the floor in front of Jesse. With a wash cloth in one hand and one of Jesse's heels in the other, the man gently washed the foot and then dried it with the towel he had tucked into his belt. He put the first foot on the floor and repeated the ritual with Jesse's other foot. When he finished, Jesse slipped his feet back into his loafers and stood.

Taking Jesse's lead, Amy took a seat beside him in the living room. There were a dozen other people in the room, but no one spoke. Most appeared deep in meditation. Amy noticed Maggie, and when their eyes met they both smiled impulsively.

The room filled with people, and the service began. There were hymns. A number of people prayed. A number of people gave short sermons, including Jesse. She didn't keep track, but she thought the people who gave sermons were all the same people who had prayed. She decided to ask Jesse about that after the meeting.

Near the end of the service, there was a passing of bread and wine. Someone said grace for the bread, and the bishop passed it to a number of attendees who each broke off a piece and handed it back. The routine was repeated with the wine glass, and the bishop handed the glass to the same people who got the bread. Amy had another question for Jesse.

"What do you think?" Jesse asked her after the meeting.

"It's totally WOW!" she said. "That all seems to make a lot of sense to those people. It's far less complicated than church." She paused a minute. "Well, not less complicated. It's just that everything is so humble and sincere." She groped for the words.

"Yes, that's right," Jesse assured her.

"Did it tickle when that man washed your feet?"

Jesse laughed. "He doesn't have the tickle touch."

"How do people decide to have their feet washed or not?"

"It's not difficult," Jesse explained. "You have to be baptized before it is appropriate to have your feet washed."

"Baptized?"

"Yeah. Dunked in the river."

Amy was amused. She continued, "And why does the bishop pick certain people to have bread and wine?"

Jesse was becoming uncomfortable. Amy was coming up with questions he wasn't sure he knew how to answer. He explained, "The people who can't get their feet washed can't have the bread and wine. It's symbolic. If your feet aren't washed, you aren't clean enough to have the bread and wine."

"Not clean enough?"

"It's just symbolic of being cleansed from sin."

"WOW!" There was a long pause. Then she commented, "I guess I should be baptized now. How do you go about that?"

"I think you'll have to talk to Bart. He'll tell you if you're ready, and we'd have a baptism for you."

"I don't like that man. I think he's as brutal as someone said he was. I only saw him once, but I can tell."

"He wouldn't be unkind to you, I'm sure. He's probably a lot kinder than he looks."

"I hope so," Amy said confidently.

Jesse didn't want to discourage Amy, but he really felt the same way about Bart. He remembered that when he was 12 and had confessed, he'd waited until there was a servant in the area that treated him kindly and then he asked to be baptized. He would never have asked anyone like Bart.

Over the years he'd been afraid of a lot of the servants, especially some of the older ones. He wasn't sure why, but he knew it had something to do with the way they talked to him about adult concerns on a childish level. Sometimes he resented their delving into topics he preferred to discuss only with his parents. By the way his parents would talk to him after those little visits, he was sure they were trying to make everything palatable for him and still maintain respect for the servants. Occasionally his parents would tell him a servant had some wrong ideas about some matter. That had bothered him a bit because he understood that you were supposed to believe everything the servants said.

Jesse was genuinely worried that Amy was so enthusiastic about her new faith that she would go straight to Bart and be shocked at his refusal to let her be baptized. It baffled him, however, that Amy had sensed Bart was brutal. He'd expected her to find him sober, maybe wise, but never brutal. On the other hand, he was pleased that Amy was comfortable with all the people he was comfortable with.

Deep down, Jesse felt uneasy. He wanted to think well of all servants, but his childhood fear of the scary ones still remained. It wasn't that he was afraid for himself he felt he could avoid confrontations with the servants. What worried him most was what might happen to Amy if she began talking frankly with Bart. And he didn't know how to go about tutoring her on how to talk to servants.

CHAPTER 5

Maggie's phone rang. It was Aggie. "Maggie, are you going to be home this afternoon?"

"I'm always here, Aggie. Are you coming over?"

"Yes. I'll be right there."

Aggie was upset, and Maggie was surprised at Aggie's tone of urgency. Aggie didn't normally call before she came to visit.

When she arrived, Aggie went straight to an easy chair and asked, "Did you hear what happened to Howard?"

"No. I know he went away."

"I was told Uncle Floyd sent him to the Bay area."

"I guess he wants him down there."

"Probably so. I wish I knew why, though. I think it has something to do with Rodney Sturm, but I don't know what it is. And I also learned that the police have visited Helen Sawyer."

"Aggie! Are you sure about that? What was it about?" Helen was a recently widowed single mother of a young boy whose nickname was Spike.

"I know they were at her house, but I don't know what they were doing there. And that Spike, whatever his name is, is a bad kid."

"Yes, he's a problem. It's a shame his father passed away. Poor Helen!"

"But I'll tell you something, Maggie. Howard has one fault. He's too easy on these slack people. I think Uncle Floyd must be upset because he's not cleaning this area up." She paused, then continued. "You know, Rodney Sturm had a problem too. I don't know what it was, but I saw Howard trying to calm him down. Howard should just tell people like that to behave and not coddle them so much."

"Who knows how decisions get made for the servants?" Maggie thought out loud. "Maybe Howard was the problem."

"Maggie, don't go spreading rumors like that about a servant of God. That would be terrible."

Maggie smiled. "Yes it would."

"I wouldn't tell anyone that if I were you. It must be Spike who misbehaved. Poor Helen."

Maggie was amused, because it was Aggie everyone thought of as the Espadín gossip.

Aggie continued. "I read in the newspaper not long ago that a kid in Sacramento called the police and told them her father was molesting her, and they arrested the father. The mother claimed the girl was mad at the father when she called the police, and that girl did it to punish her father. Children these days have no respect whatsoever. Imagine how the poor man felt. They put him in prison."

"I hope that's not what Spike did to poor Helen. But you know, there's a lot of child molestation taking place, Aggie."

"Children just have to be taught first of all to obey their parents, no matter what. If they don't learn that, how can anyone expect them to submit to the servants?"

Maggie was silent. Aggie continued. "It used to be that children were to be seen and not heard. I think it made them better adults when they grew up."

Maggie was still silent, and it was beginning to annoy Aggie.

"Maggie, don't tell me you think it's OK for a child to report his parents to the police?"

Maggie was troubled about the possibilities. "Would you want someone molesting your child?"

"No, probably not. But children have to be in submission to adults, especially their parents."

"A lot of people feel like you."

They had tea, and Aggie decided it was time to go. "Now don't tell anyone what I told you, Maggie. The servants don't want things getting whispered around."

I'm sure I missed the point of that whole visit, Maggie thought. She couldn't think of anything Aggie had told her that would be of any interest to anyone else.

A couple of days later Jesse and Amy arrived at Maggie's door.

"Oh, Jesse. I'm so glad you brought Amy with you."

"She wanted to come, Maggie."

"You know, this is so wonderful of you." Maggie turned to Amy. "Jesse helps me so much. He takes my grocery list every week and does a perfect job. I just wish I weren't all old and creaky anymore."

"This is what friends do for each other," Amy said.

Maggie almost cried. "My dear, you're a fine young lady." She pulled a shopping list off the pad on her table and handed it to Jesse.

Maggie was fulfilling her wish to have Jesse and Amy for dinner that evening. Amy and Jesse both kissed her on the cheek when they returned with the groceries. They'd developed a great affection for Maggie, and had talked frequently to each other about her kindnesses to everyone.

Amy brought her a box of candies. As she presented it to Maggie, she noticed a redness in her eyes. "Have you been crying, Maggie?"

"Oh no, dear. Don't worry about me."

Amy wasn't convinced, but took her word for it. The apartment smelled of oven roasting.

First they visited about their plans for the summer. Jesse had applied to have a tutoring job. Amy was going home to Eureka. Summers were busy in her father's souvenir shop, so she didn't have to go looking for summer employment. She had no intention of being in town for the summer semester. The Central Valley in summer was too hot for her liking.

A buzzer went off, and Maggie jumped to pull a seasoned pork roast from the oven.

"Can I help you with something," Amy asked.

"No, dear. I'm really doing the easiest thing I can for dinner, if you'll pardon my laziness. As soon as the potato scallop is ready we can eat. I might get Jesse to cut the roast then."

"You bet," Jesse said.

Until the buzzer went off again, discussion revolved around the outing planned for the next day on Espadín's Zócalo.

Maggie made quick work of putting the food on the table, and they sat down. Jesse said grace, then sliced the roast.

When they finished the meal, Maggie brought out dessert. It was then that Amy asked Maggie if she'd tell her how she'd been introduced to the Way, and Maggie was glad to tell her the story.

"It was when I was 16," Maggie began. "I was this poor country girl who got her parents to let her go to a big town and see what she could accomplish. My uncle lived in Chicago and told all these wonderful tales of the big city, so I begged him to take me there. When I got there I was just overwhelmed with the sights. It looked to me like the Great Depression had never happened in Chicago.

"I got a job working as a maid in a rich doctor's house. They also had a nanny to look after their children, and we got to be really good friends really fast."

It was going to be a long story, so no one rushed with their dessert.

"The nanny's name was Lizzie. We never got out of the house much because, you know, two young girls in that big wild city were not safe. But usually on Sundays we would have some time to go out and walk around before I needed to get the family's dinner.

"One Sunday afternoon we heard singing, so we walked around the block until we found where it was coming from. There was this gathering there on the side of the street, and some preacher was standing on a box. When the singing stopped, the man started to talk. Lizzie wanted to hear what he was talking about, so we went closer.

"I thought he was a politician, but he wasn't. I didn't want to get too involved, but Lizzie insisted. It turned out the man was preaching, not giving a political speech. He was the first servant I ever met."

"Do you remember what he was preaching about?" Amy asked.

"Oh yes. Well, I don't remember what all he said, but he was talking about glorious freedom. I'd never heard of that before, and he was so enthusiastic about it. Whatever he said made me feel that he had something I didn't have." Amy was enjoying it.

"You see, we didn't go to church much when I was small, but I do remember that the preacher there was so boring. All I ever seemed to hear was how we should shape up and behave and whatever so that we could earn our way into heaven. I often wished I could die young and get the whole thing over with fast. A whole lifetime of being good, you know, was not my cup of tea when I was just 16 years old." They had a good laugh.

"When he was done preaching, they sang another song, and some people in the audience were singing too. It sounded so nice, outside like that. After they sang, he said he was going to be back the next Sunday. I didn't plan then to go back to his next service, but I thought all week about that freedom he'd said. And I had all these memories of everyone I'd feared growing up, and all the people I thought would like to push me around. I guess today they would call me a feminist, or something." She laughed.

"Anyway, when it came Sunday afternoon again, it was me who drug poor Lizzie off to hear the street preacher. Frankly, I don't remember much about what he said. What I really got to understand was that we really weren't serving God while we were satisfied with the grip of tradition. But he wasn't telling us that we had to revolt against our traditions. Just follow Jesus and be free. It was a wonderful message to me as a young girl. And he never asked for money from the audience. That was a miracle to me."

"That sounds like Howard," Amy commented. Jesse nodded agreement.

"I don't know how many weekends we went there. Lizzie pretended never to like them that much, but before long she was depending on me to explain it all to her." Maggie got a wide smile on her face. "I'll never forget the day I confessed. The preacher announced that if you raised your hand during the hymn you would belong to God's family, so I raised my hand."

"You raised your hand because you were all standing anyway?" Jesse asked.

"Yes. You see, all the servant brought to the street was a box he could carry. He'd open it up and take out his Bible and some hymn books, I guess, and then stand on it to preach.

"Anyway, when we were about to leave that day, this young man ran up to us and stopped us. He was so handsome. He introduced himself, and asked us if he could show us to the Thursday evening assembly. I had no idea what he was talking about. But I gave him our address and he said he'd come by on Thursday and take us to the service so we'd know how to get there after that.

"On the way back to the doctor's house, Lizzie said to me, 'What do we do now?' And I said to her, 'We?' And she said, 'Yes, I raised my arm too.' It was so funny. I was so concerned about myself that I didn't even know she'd confessed too."

"How funny!" Amy said.

"I bet the guy showed up on Thursday evening," Jesse joked.

"Oh yes, he did. I'd kind of forgotten about it, and I was really surprised when he showed up. I didn't know what to say. Lizzie suggested he come back the next week and we would know by then whether our employer would let us out for the evening."

"And he was anxious to come back to your house again, wasn't he?" Amy quizzed.

"Oh yes, dear." She laughed. "I shouldn't tell you this, but I was very pleased with myself. Lizzie wanted him really badly." She hesitated. "But he asked me to marry him."

"I knew it," Jesse laughed.

"What a sweet story!" Amy mused, and kissed Maggie on the cheek. "Did your employer let you go out on Thursday evening?"

"Yes, he did. He came to an agreement with us that if I'd have dinner prepared and Lizzie would have the children ready for bed, then we could go out on Thursday evening. It was because we were going to a religious service. But he lowered our pay by ten percent for the inconvenience. We didn't care. I got a chance to see John twice a week that way, and besides, I was totally engrossed in the newfound joy I had with the people of the Way. They were such a good and fun group of people. I felt perfectly safe with all of them."

"What happened when you were married? Did you continue to work for the doctor?" Amy asked.

"Oh no, dear. The doctor didn't want a married maid. But John's father was old and he wrote him a letter and told him he'd like him to come home and take over his farm because he couldn't operate it any more by himself. So we were married in Chicago and had our honeymoon way out on the Great Plains with his Mom and Pa. What a wonderful time it was!"

"Were his parents in the Way?" Amy asked.

Maggie lost the excited tone in her voice. "No, dear. They never confessed. That was our only problem. They were very devout Lutherans and they kind of blamed me for taking John away from the church. I'd hear John downstairs arguing with them sometimes late at night. But we just valued our freedom so much that we just stuck to it.

"After a couple of years, the servants came to a little town near our farm, and we got to go to their gospel services there. It was romantic in the sleigh in the moonlight, except when it was so cold you almost froze to death.

"There were four people in that town who confessed at the time, and the oldest guy volunteered to have assembly meetings in his house. We were overjoyed, because we hadn't seen anyone in the Way since we had left Chicago, and now all of a sudden we had an assembly there."

"That's a wonderful testimony," Jesse commented. "I like to hear those kinds of stories."

"Everything was the same then as now," Amy concluded.

"Oh yes, dear. The Way never changes. The whole world changes, but the Way is sure." Maggie paused. "But I liked those times a lot more." Then her eyes welled up with tears.

"What is it, Maggie?" Amy was concerned.

"I worry about what's happening," she said.

"What's happening, Maggie?" Jesse asked.

"I don't know," she said. "Aggie is really upset about something these days. She thinks the police have something to do with Spike." They were quiet a minute. "Oh, I don't know, dear. I think something's wrong. I know Aggie's nosey and all, but sometimes she upsets me with some of the things she busybodies into." She wiped her eyes with a napkin.

Amy and Jesse waited while she got her composure. Finally she said, "I guess I shouldn't get into that. Gossiping, you know."

"If it's among us, Maggie, it's not gossip," Jesse suggested. Amy nodded agreement.

"You're such kind and mature kids."

There was a lengthy pause. Then Maggie said, "I hope you kids have a good time on the Zócalo tomorrow."

"Would you like to join us?" Jesse asked.

"They won't want an old lady out there with them."

"But I think there's a nice old lady who'd like to be out there with them." Amy smiled.

"It's going to be a nice warm day," Jesse said. "And we'll come and get you."

"We'll come and get you in the morning and bring you back any time you want," Amy said.

"What a wonderful idea. If it's OK I'll take you kids up on that offer. I just love the kids that come here to college."

On the way home Amy asked, "Why could she be so upset?"

"I don't know. She's old, you know. Maybe she just worries about things."

"Maybe so."

It turned out to be a beautiful Martin Luther King Day weekend, and the annual get together of the young Way friends arrived. About midmorning people started showing up on the Zócalo. Over the next hour the ones from Espadín were joined by a few carloads of students from Chico. There were even a couple of cars from Sacramento.

When Jesse opened the door to help Maggie out, someone yelled, "Hey guys! Here comes Maggie!"

Everyone turned, and about half of them ran to the street to greet her. Maggie was in her glee, and Amy marveled at the attention they were all giving her.

"Oh, I'm so glad to be here with you all," Maggie said.

Amy climbed from the back seat, pulling a folded beach chair behind her. Jesse announced, "Everyone, this is my friend, Amy

Foster. She just confessed before Thanksgiving. You can all introduce yourselves to her."

Amy was surprised that there were so many people there, probably 30 altogether. The best part for her was that, as they arrived, they all jumped into the excitement like family getting together after being apart. All of them approached her individually and introduced themselves. She regretted that she couldn't remember all the names she learned. But she did remember one name in particular, Trevor. He was the nerdy computer science student from Chico. An intelligent geek, she decided. She was amazed that he had anything in common with the rest of them. The fact that he appeared so comfortable with the rest of them told her he could trust them not to ridicule him.

They were all happy to have Amy with them. One girl said, "I'm so glad to meet you. We heard about you in Chico." One of the girls even asked her to go and visit her sometime in Sacramento. Amy immediately felt like family.

"Where's Scotty?" someone asked.

"Marty asked him to join us, but he didn't think Bart would let him."

"Scotty has to be a good little boy." There were smiles.

"I wish he could be here. He's such a really great guy."

"Who wants to start the barbecue?"

"I'll do it." Two guys grabbed the charcoal and gas and began preparing the barbecue grill.

"How have you been, Maggie?"

"Just great, dear," Maggie replied. "And today will make me feel even better."

"It's going to be nice and warm too."

Melissa crowed, "Look at this, girls. Oh how I love to watch men cooking."

There was a show of bulging biceps, of sorts, around the barbecue grill.

"Not exactly the Mr. World contest, is it, Melissa? Let them cook." There was a burst of feminine laughter.

Marty'd been quiet, with somewhat pained look on his face. "Why aren't you helping them, Marty?"

"I can't move. I have cramps."

"You're turning green!"

"He has diarrhea."

"Don't bend over, then."

Janet, of course, was horrified. "That is so rude!"

"Where's Scott?"

"Bart and Uncle Floyd are both in town. He's not allowed out."
"What did he do?"
"Nothing. He just went in the service and got assigned to Bart." A few laughed.
"Bring over the burgers. The charcoal is ready."
"What's new, Jesse?"
"Our swimming coach has decided to coach me for competition."
"Hey, way to go. I heard you were a great swimmer."
"You should see him in a competition."
After a few minutes Trevor asked, "Where's Marty?"
"Check the restrooms first." Everyone turned toward the restrooms just as Marty emerged from the entrance.

When Marty saw everyone staring at him, his impulse made him reach down and check his fly. Everyone roared laughing, Maggie included.

"Here are the sodas."
"These patties are much better than those little things we ended up with last year."
"Do you like hamburgers, Maggie?"
"Of course."
"Where's Tanya today?"
There was a pause. "Tanya doesn't come to assembly anymore."
"I'm sorry to hear that."
"I see her in class once a week. She's a good girl."
"There's a new girl in the Eureka, I heard."
"Yeah. I met her. She's cool."
"She was kind of a biker chick or heavy metal freak, something like that. She met Carol Street in a flea market, or somewhere, and they got talking."
"The first time she went to a gospel service she had purple hair and a big hoop through her nose. The servant about ran away when he saw her."
"We'll have to meet her."
"Hey! Do you all remember that mountain man dude who showed up at retreat a couple of years ago? The one with the suspenders on his shorts."
"It's funny to see weirdos come to retreats."
"Was that the one with the woman with the big bazookas?"
"Yeah. They took him away and got him to put on some long pants."
"They didn't take Bazooka Lady away, though. What a sight! She was all ....."

"You guys are disgusting! Did you go to retreat to check out the women?"

"No, but she just happened to drop in." Everyone laughed.

"Hey, here comes Gilmore and Jenny."

"Why so late?"

"They're always late. They're getting more like Siamese twins every day."

"But Siamese twins have to be the same sex," Trevor explained.

"Just an expression, Trevor. They're always sticking together."

"Oh, I see."

Conversation slowed when the burgers and dogs were ready. Amy was pleased at how well everyone waited on Maggie. She was also impressed that Maggie was enjoying herself so much.

"These are the greatest people," Amy said to her.

"Aren't they, dear?"

"No one is drunk, or cussing, or fighting."

"I know. I love every one of them. They are all a credit to their parents."

When they were finished eating, someone suggested they have their ball game.

"I can't play ball. I'll clean up this stuff."

A few balls, bats, and gloves were rounded up from their cars, and the game started. There was humorous commotion over picking sides, and there were reminders that they try not to hit a ball into the traffic around the Zócalo.

"Marty knows that it can be costly, don't you Marty?"

"What happened to Marty?" Trevor asked.

"See that big house over there. The one with the huge window on the front. Marty sent a ball through that window."

"You should've seen the look on his face when he saw what happened."

By mid afternoon the heat had caught up with them, so they decided to disband.

"Why don't some of you come to the gospel service in Sacramento tomorrow night?"

"I can't. It's too far from Chico. Maybe some time through the summer."

There were hugs all around, and a few kisses. Maggie got her share. Before long the last car pulled away, and the Zócalo returned to a sedate city park.

"I haven't had so much fun in years," Maggie said as they helped her into her apartment.

"We'll take you again next time," Jesse promised.

"We'll see. I'm an old lady, you know."

"You're very young inside," Amy assured her.

"You're both so kind."

CHAPTER 6

Nathan was the Berry in the Katz, Berry, & Shipman law firm. Nathan and Clay had great respect for each other, having been at law school together and sharing many mutual societal concerns. They were both passionate in their views of the use and misuse of the law.

When Clay asked him about a private school, Nathan said, "Take your kid to the César Chávez Leadership Academy. You'll never regret it."

"It sounds good all ready," Clay said. "I like the name." César Chávez was the great activist for the rights of itinerant farm workers, who were primarily Mexicans. His leadership in the style of Mahatma Gandhi and Martin Luther King Jr. precipitated strikes, boycotts, and even fasting in the 1960s and 1970s, but his efforts brought about groundbreaking legislative reform in California. Nathan and Clay had convinced Tony Katz, their other partner, that Chávez' photograph needed to be displayed in their front office with their other greats.

"Dennis will just become more and more bored in public school. At César Chávez he'll not be homogenized with the rest of the population. He's too sharp to miss out on the kind of an education he'd get there."

"Yeah, he's a bright kid." Clay was secretly proud of Dennis.

"He'll begin doing his own research the day he arrives," Nathan explained. "If he wants to be a lawyer he'll never get a better preparation anywhere else."

"He does want to be a lawyer. He just doesn't want to go to law school until he's big. I guess he thinks he'll miss all the kid fun in the meantime." They laughed.

"I'll assure you, at César Chávez he'll have all the fun without all the middle school garbage."

Clay and Nancy went to the Academy to check it out and were greatly impressed. Part of the education process there involved the tutelage of each middle school student by a high school student. The dean explained that this served two great purposes, individualized guidance for the younger student and training in communication and leadership for the older student.

The school was expensive, but by the time Clay and Nancy arrived back home they'd quite decided the benefits were worth the cost.

"Can we pay for this?" Nancy pondered.

"We will," Clay assured her. "I'd do without one of my paralegals to pay for it if I had to."

Ten minutes before the Academy closed for the day, Clay called back to make an appointment to take Dennis for an interview. That evening he completed the application for admission.

Among the literature given them was an elaborate booklet written for fifth graders who were prospective students of the Academy. It took Dennis the whole evening to absorb the information, and before the evening was over he was sitting right up on the table watching Clay complete the application.

When they tucked him into bed that night, he said, "Are you sure I can go to that school?"

"No, we aren't sure yet. But we'll make sure you're name is on the list, and if they have enough room they'll let us know."

"Good," Dennis said. "Can we go and see that school tomorrow?"

"Sure. Time to sleep now."

Back in the dining room, Nancy was sitting at the table with a few stray tears running down her cheeks. "What is it?" Clay asked.

"I don't know if I can live up to that kid's expectations," she said. "Where does he get all that drive for a 10year old?"

Clay smiled. "You have nothing to worry about. Dennis is going to be doing all the work. You don't even have to push him, he's raring to go. He runs full time on imagination, challenge, and adrenalin."

"I'm glad we don't have two of him," Nancy said.

"Poor little Nancy," Clay cooed and kissed her. "You are the world's best mother to him. And don't forget that."

She sighed. "Mom and Dad won't know what to think of this."

"Don't tell them," Clay said. "That's my motto."

"How could I forget?"

"I only ask for advice when I'm willing to consider the response."

"What a rebel!"

"And you love it." Nancy giggled.

The next day was Saturday, so Dennis begged to see the Academy as soon as he got up. Clay drove past it for him.

Dennis was not overly impressed with the building, but he did see a playground of sorts.

Oh good," he commented. "I'll be able to play at this school too."

"It looks like you can at least play tennis and basketball," Clay explained. "Probably more, but we can't see everything from the street."

Dennis was satisfied.

On Sunday there was a fellowship gathering in Inglewood. Nancy made one of her popular pot luck dishes and Dennis planned on having fun with Alexander, his friend from their assembly. When they arrived Alexander was already there, so he and Dennis went off to the monkey bars in the back yard to play while the adults visited around the house.

"I'm not going to a school next year," Dennis proudly announced.

"You can't do that," Alexander said. "The police will come and get you and make you go to school."

"I'm going to go to an academy instead."

"What's an academy?"

"It's like a school, but it's a special place to learn all the things you like to learn," Dennis explained. "And you don't have to put up with gangs there."

"Do you have gangs at your school?"

"Not really. But in middle schools there are gangs. All they do at my school is sell some drugs outside the gate."

"Really? I don't think they do that at my school. Maybe next year I'll see them doing stuff like that in middle school. But I'm not going to have anything to do with them. They're bad kids who do that."

"I know." Dennis was hanging upside down. "I'll be going to the César Chávez Leadership Academy next year. What school are you going to?"

"I don't know. They never told me what it's called. I guess it's just called middle school."

"I want to be a lawyer when I grow up. What are you going to be?"

"I don't know. Maybe I'll work somewhere fun like Disneyland, or somewhere like that. I think it would be fun to fly airplanes, though. My Dad told me those guys make a lot of money."

"I'm just going to be a lawyer like my Dad. That's all I want to do."

"Your Dad is a lawyer?"

"Yeah."

"No, he can't be a lawyer. Lawyers hang out with bad people."

"Well my father only hangs out with good people. I know it. He has a very important job."

Alexander was concerned. "Do the servants know he's a lawyer?"

"I don't know," Dennis said. "Maybe not. I don't think he talks to the servants much."

"He has to talk to the servants." Alexander was astounded. "My father always asks the servants what to do."

"Why?" Dennis asked.

"Just because he has to, I guess. They know what he's supposed to do."

"That's weird. How come he doesn't know what to do by himself?"

"Because he ... you know. I don't know why. People are just supposed to do what the servants tell them. Doesn't your father do that?"

"I don't think so." Dennis had never been told about that.

"You better tell him that."

"Why can't your father do what he wants?"

"I think it's because he's afraid he'll do something God doesn't like him to do."

"Well my father doesn't do anything God doesn't like him to do," Dennis assured him.

"Then he must be asking the servants what to do all the time."

Dennis didn't know what to think of that. So he asked, "Do you ask the servants what to do?"

"Yeah, sometimes."

"What do they say?"

"They tell me all the right things to do."

"Like what?" Dennis didn't know what that would be.

"They tell me things like that I'm supposed to do what my parents say. And I have to do what the servants say. And I'm not supposed to do bad things?"

"Don't your mother and father tell you not to do bad things?"

"All the time. But sometimes I don't do what they say. That's when I get in trouble."

"I just try to do all good things," Dennis assured him.

"But you must do bad things sometimes. Everyone does."

"I don't know. I don't get in trouble very much. What do you do to get in trouble?"

"I'm in trouble all the time. I was chasing Tammy all around the house last night and she ran into a chair and hurt herself, and I was in big trouble for that." Tammy was Alexander's little sister.

"How did you know you were in trouble?"

"They made me sit in a time out chair for a long long time. I was afraid I'd get a beating, but I didn't get one that time."

Dennis was very puzzled about these revelations. "Do your parents beat you?"

"All the time," Alexander said. "Don't yours?"

"No."

"They're supposed to," Alexander explained. "You'll grow up to be a gang member if they don't."

"Who said that?"

"Everyone tells me that. Didn't you know that? Your parents are supposed to beat you."

Dennis was worried. He'd never been told that before. He didn't want to grow up to be a gang member, but neither did he want any beatings. "I wouldn't want to get beatings," he said.

"Neither do I. They sting and sometimes I really howl."

Dennis was horrified. "Do they really hurt?"

"Yes stupid. That's why they beat you."

"That awful. That's bad. You better not let the police know that your parents beat you."

"Why?"

"They'll arrest your father."

"Man, Dennis. You're sure crazy. I'd like it if I didn't get any beatings, but I think I'll be getting them for a long time yet, until I grow up, at least."

Dennis was distressed now. "If your father gets arrested, I'll tell my father and he'll get him out of jail. That's what he does, you know."

"Really!"

"Yeah. That's what lawyers do, you know."

Alexander thought about that for a long time. Then Tammy showed up, so he said, "Let's get out of here. I don't like to play with girls."

"OK."

Before long lunch was ready and everyone gathered around. Alexander and Dennis waited patiently while the adults did their bread and wine ritual. Dennis was quite amused that Tammy wanted some of the bread and wine too. But he couldn't laugh out loud because he knew you had to be quiet at that time. Tammy would learn that too, sooner or later.

A lot of the conversation that day surrounded the arrival of a new servant to the Los Angeles area. His name was Chester something, but Dennis had never heard of him. Everyone seemed to think Chester was a most wonderful person. Dennis wondered if he'd ever get to see Chester. He was glad to learn that Chester was a very good person, because he didn't want to be asking mean people questions about what he should do.

Dennis and Alexander helped themselves to all the good food. When they were finished, they went off to play some more. As usual, Tammy caught up with them every time they moved on to another activity. By mid afternoon everything had been cleaned up and it was time to go home.

On the way home Dennis was quiet most of the way. Then he said, "Daddy. When are you going to start beating me?"

"Beating you?" Clay asked.

"Yeah. Alexander said you are supposed to beat me."

Clay and Nancy laughed. Then Nancy said, "No one is going to beat you. Why would we beat you?"

"When I'm bad."

"You're not bad," Clay insisted. "And no one is going to beat you."

Dennis was confused. He didn't understand why Alexander had to have beatings and he didn't. He decided he'd just be thankful he had the parents he had and certainly not complain.

Then he asked, "Am I supposed to be asking the servants about everything I do?"

"No," Clay said. "Why do you ask?"

"Alexander said I was supposed to do that."

"You can tell Alexander that you are not supposed to ask the servants what to do. As long as you're a kid and we're your parents, we're the ones you need to take your concerns to first of all."

Dennis was relieved. He'd had a lot of fun playing with Alexander, but he was certain he didn't want to ever go and live at Alexander's house. He considered that someday he might do Alexander a favor and get him to come and live with him.

When they got home, Dennis got out the booklet from César Chávez Leadership Academy again and reviewed it one more time. It got him over his worries about all Alexander had been telling him.

That night, after Dennis was in bed, Nancy announced, "Irene is interested in our religion." Irene was an artist who displayed her work at the same gallery as Nancy.

"Really?"

"Yeah. She started asking me a lot of questions. I guess she's not too well pleased with the church she goes to now."

"What church does she belong to?" Clay asked.

"I don't know. I never asked. But she doesn't think the people there are all that friendly."

"I suppose if she likes to go somewhere on Sundays she shouldn't be stressed to go to fellowship with us."

"I've been thinking of asking her to gospel services, now that Chester's in the area."

"That would be good."

"They say Chester's a good preacher, too."

"That's what I've heard."

"I get kind of nervous when she starts asking me questions because I'm not sure what I'm supposed to say about things. I'd sooner have her ask the servants the questions, but they're never around when you need them."

"You'll tell her the right answers," Clay assured her. "Surely she won't want to know anything you don't know."

"I'm just going to ask her to gospel services and let Chester answer her questions. I just don't want the servants to tell me I told her something wrong."

"Ask Chester to go to the gallery to meet her some day you're both there."

Nancy laughed. "Oh no. I don't think that would be a good idea."

"Why not?"

"I'm not sure Chester would like some of her paintings."

"Oh, you mean the ones of naked men?"

"Yeah," Nancy said. "I'm not sure a servant would visit a gallery with nudes on display."

"How do you know Chester wouldn't enjoy that?" Clay laughed. "Tell Irene that Chester might even be interested in posing for her!"

"You don't worry about anything, do you?"

"Yes, I do. But you can also tell her that we'll take her to the service with us. By the way, where does she live?"

"Simi Valley," Nancy replied.

"On second thought, forget that offer."

Nancy joked. "I changed my mind. She lives here in Santa Monica."

"Then tell her I'll provide transportation to services if she brings paintings with her."

"I wish I could ignore you."

"Seriously, though," Clay said. "I've never taken a stranger to a gospel service."

"Neither have I."

"Maybe we'll be able to find someone after all."

"Wouldn't that be nice?" Nancy said.

Clay yawned, stood up, and headed for the bedroom. "Yeah, that would be nice. And speaking of male nudes, you'll probably be able to find one for yourself in the bedroom sometime within the next ten minutes."

"Then I'll call Irene and get her to come on over with her paints and canvas."

"Tell her to leave the canvas at home," Clay called back.

"You're a crazy man," Nancy said when he was out of sight.

CHAPTER 7

"Why so blue?" Amy asked Jesse while they were waiting for class to start.

"Is it that obvious?"

"Yeah."

"I've been dumped."

"You've been dumped? How have you been dumped?"

"It's my old girlfriend ... down in Riverside. She wrote to me to tell me it's all over between us."

"I thought you said you were done with her already."

"I was. I guess she had to make one more swat at me or something."

"That can make you blue. I'm just curious. Did she say why she was getting rid of you?"

Jesse cringed inside at the *getting rid of you* phrase. "Yeah. She told me she'd found someone better."

"Oh," Amy scoffed. "I have to meet that guy."

"What do you mean?"

"It's just that ... you know, you're an all right kind of guy. She has to be stupid. Or is this new guy a number eleven?"

"Oh!" *So maybe Amy thinks I'm a ten*, Jesse thought. "I know who he is. Maybe he is an eleven. I think he has a lot of bad attitude, if that means anything."

"Her loss!" Amy confirmed. "Here comes Mr. Physics. What a drag this class is. I know I won't be taking another physics class, even if you're in it." They both laughed.

When the class was over, Amy said. "You know, I was thinking during class. Why don't you come home with me next weekend?"

"Yeah, I'd like that. I've never been to Eureka."

"And can we ask Maggie to go with us?"

"Would your parents want two of us there at the same time?"

"Sure. I'll just tell them they're having company. You can sleep in Andy's room, and Maggie can sleep in the guest room. It would really calm my Dad's suspicions about the Way for two very sane people to visit with him."

"We can ask Maggie. She has a lot of aches and pains in the winter."

"I'll beg her. I just love that little old lady."

"We got her to the Zócalo. She might go to Eureka with us too. You ask her."

"I'll do that. And you can forget that what'shername in Riverside. I'll find you someone a lot better."

Jesse blushed, and thanked her with a chuckle.

In his mind he'd begun to think he should maybe make some moves to date Amy. When he first met her, he admired her. She was very attractive and she was fun to study with. Besides, she didn't have a boyfriend that he had to compete with for her time. He'd never considered that she might confess someday, but she did; and recently he'd been considering asking her to date him. The problem was, he didn't know how to convert their relationship from one of studying companions to dating steadies.

Maybe, he thought, she's making her own moves on me. Maybe inviting me home with her is just a move to get me to fall in love with her. I'd like to go along with that, but I don't want to make a fool of myself by making some moves of my own and then find out I was misinterpreting her gestures. He'd come to think that he'd never learn how to socialize and date like other people his age because he'd been in the Way. It was comforting to know that Amy was now in the Way and she'd understand why he wasn't like everyone else.

To their great pleasure, Maggie decided without much coaxing that she'd go with them to Eureka. She had her small overnight bag packed and was ready to go when they went to pick her up at noon on Friday.

"It's been years since I left town for anything except retreats," Maggie announced as they drove away from her apartment. "Thank you so much for inviting me along. I'm very much looking forward to meeting your parents, Amy."

"My Mom was really surprised when I told her I wanted to take you with us, but she was pleased about it, really."

"I suppose I'm the first old lady you ever brought home with you for a weekend."

Amy laughed. "Yes, you are."

Jesse added, "And who better for us to introduce to Amy's parents to give them a favorable impression of the Way?"

"Oh my," Maggie said. "I'll have to behave myself now, won't I? Did you kids hear that there's going to be a big snow storm in the mountains up north?"

"My Mom told me to make sure I had my snow chains and blankets in the trunk. That's why I'm having Jesse drive today. Do you suppose Jesse can drive in a snow storm?"

"Sure," Maggie assured her. "Anyone can drive in snow. I guess when you live in North Dakota most of your life you just believe that anyone who can drive a car has to know how to drive in snow."

"I've never been in a car in a snow storm," Jesse said. "We saw a lot of snow in the mountains from San Bernardino, but we only got the rare flakes of snow in the valley. I don't think my Dad ever drove a car in the snow. Aren't you afraid I'll take us all into a ditch?"

"Oh no," Maggie assured him. "We'll do fine."

Before they reached Redding, Amy called her mother who told her they would definitely need chains in the mountains between Redding and Eureka. Maggie insisted they stop and let her get them something hot to eat before they headed west over the mountains. When they got back in the car, Amy indicated to Maggie that the blankets in the back seat were there in case they would have to spend the night in the car.

Maggie was amused... "My dear, we aren't going to have anything like one of those old fashioned storms we used to get in the Dakotas. I'm kind of excited, because I haven't been out in a big storm in years."

Jesse was nervous because it was rapidly turning to night and the snow was beginning to build up on the highway. When they started gaining altitude they were stopped and required to install their chains. Amy tutored Jesse on their installation, and he was impressed that she knew all about chains. While they installed them she told him about a police officer of questionable intelligence who once tried to make her father put his chains on the rear tires of a vehicle with front wheel drive.

Jesse felt a bit stupid because he'd never even considered which wheels would need the chains. "I guess the officer must have been from southern California like me," he laughed.

"You're pretty smart about this for someone who hates physics," Jesse said.

"Oh, don't worry, I'm not stupid." They laughed.

Maggie began relating stories about notable storms she and her husband had traveled through when they lived on the Great Plains. Amy and Jesse found them interesting. By the time they passed the chains off point, Jesse realized he'd been so interested in Maggie's adventurous stories that the slow traveling hadn't seemed so long and tedious after all.

Amy helped him take the chains off, and Maggie continued to exclaim about being out in a snow story. "I haven't been in a snow storm since I came to the Central Valley," she said.

Jesse felt quite accomplished, having driven for the first time in the mountains in a snow storm. *I'm going to call Dad and tell him as soon as I get back to Espadín*, he thought.

Mr. and Mrs. Foster were gracious and welcoming hosts, and Maggie immediately hit it off with Mrs. Foster. Jesse thought Mr. Foster had a good first impression of him. They talked only briefly before they all retired for the night.

On Saturday morning everyone met in Mr. Foster's shop for coffee and sweets for breakfast.

"Maggie's from North Dakota," Amy told her parents.

"I've been here in California for quite a while now," Maggie said.

But Mr. Foster had his own serious agenda that couldn't wait. "Did you belong to this faith when you were in North Dakota?" he asked.

"Yes. I found it as a young girl in Chicago before I was married."

"What have you given up for this group?"

Maggie thought for a while. "I don't think I gave up anything, really. I didn't have much to start with, but I've had a good life and made a lot of friends. My dear late husband was truly wonderful to me. We had a big farm in North Dakota."

"Amy assures me that this isn't a cult."

"Oh no," Maggie assured him. "This isn't a cult. It's just a group of people who want to follow the Bible and have fellowship together. Everyone lives in their own houses and they all work at normal jobs and raise their own families. It's nothing at all like those poor people in Jonestown or Waco."

"How do they treat their women?" Mrs. Foster asked.

"I can tell you that the women are well treated," Maggie replied. "The men in the Way are noted for their good manners and morals, and they're often told to treat their wives with great respect. I think Jesse's as good an example of our young men as you can find."

Mrs. Foster appeared satisfied. Jesse blushed.

Amy said, "We're going to a fellowship gathering Sunday morning. Would you like to go with us?"

"Here in Eureka?" Mrs. Foster asked.

"Yeah."

"What kind of service would it be?" Mr. Foster asked.

"It's not a service," Jesse explained. "We just get together to enjoy fellowship with each other. It's more like a pot luck dinner."

"Interesting," Mr. Foster said. "You mean there won't be anyone preaching or anything?"

"No," Amy said. "It's for fellowship, not brainwashing."

Mrs. Foster looked at her husband. "You remember, dear, that your objection to religion was all about the preacher running the show."

"That's true," he said. "You know, folks, I have a very serious disapproval of religion. After all my years of going to church I decided it was all politics and money."

Amy said, "You can come with us tomorrow if you want and see what happens. I'm sure you'd be welcome." She looked to Jesse for his approval of the invitation.

"Yes," he said. "I'm sure you'd be quite welcome. People like you usually find our gatherings are better fellowship that everyone sitting in rows in a formal church."

"So will you come with us?" Amy asked.

Her father hesitated. "Maybe not this time. I have to think about this a lot more. But I may take you up on the invitation again someday."

Jesse was relieved that he'd not been put too much on the spot. He was a lot more comfortable just living his life as an example than telling people about it. It sometimes worried him that he wasn't being a lot more aggressive about looking for converts to the Way, but he knew it wasn't his nature to want to influence anyone in a way they didn't welcome.

When they'd finished their coffee, Mr. Foster suggested he take everyone for a ride to Redwood National Park, and Maggie was delighted. The weather had cleared and the sun was shining brightly. She found the coast spectacularly beautiful. She exclaimed over the big trees, and marveled at how different this part of the world was from the Great Plains where she lived most of her life.

That evening Mr. Foster invited them all to dinner in a seafood restaurant to give them a good taste of the ocean. They visited until everyone was tired.

The Straight Way

On Sunday morning Mrs. Foster prepared a sumptuous breakfast, and Mr. Foster asked for the address of the house where Amy was going for the gathering. Early in the afternoon Amy, Jesse, and Maggie returned to the Fosters' house and gathered their bags to return to Espadín.

"Do come back again," Mrs. Foster said. "I enjoyed our visit so much. It was just too short a time. And Maggie, you come with them too."

"Thank you. You've been most gracious hosts." She handed a small parcel to Mrs. Foster. "Please accept this little gift for your wonderful hospitality. And please feel welcome to come to my house any time you come to Espadín to see Amy. She's a really wonderful little girl."

Mr. Foster shook Jesse's hand warmly. "It was good meeting you. Amy's talked a lot about you and it's all been good. Come back any time you want."

"Thank you,"

And they were gone.

"No snow this afternoon," Jesse announced. "We'll make much better time today."

"And I have to tell you something," Amy began. "My father is really pleased with you and Maggie. And he thinks the Way is worth investigating."

"Cool," Jesse said.

"You'll never guess what he did this morning while we went for fellowship. He went and parked where he could watch the house and see what was going on."

"Really!" Jesse was surprised.

"What did he see?" Maggie asked.

"He said he saw some people walking by the window with plates of food in their hands. And he also saw some of the kids running around in the yard."

"What did he think about that?" Jesse was curious.

"He thought it was the proper way to take children to church, or whatever it's called." She laughed. "He was always upset with Andy and me for having sore butts in church. I can remember that myself."

"So he didn't see anything that scared him," Maggie concluded. "That's good."

"Yeah. And he told me he'd like to go to fellowship next time I come home for the weekend."

"All right!"

CHAPTER 8

"Quick," Nancy said when Dennis came in from school. "Go and change into long pants and a nice shirt. We're having company for dinner."

"Great. Will there be a kid?"

"Not this time. It's Chester, the new servant."

"Oh. They said he was nice, didn't they?"

"Yeah, they did."

"All right!"

Dennis disappeared into his room and came back out just as the telephone rang. It was Chester calling to be let in the apartment building.

Chester was a short, balding, middleaged man with a jovial manner and a ready handshake. He graciously shook hands with both Nancy and Dennis. Nancy suggested that Chester and Dennis visit in the living room while Nancy finished preparing dinner and until Clay arrived home from the office.

At dinner conversation came easily, to begin with. Chester told Clay he was from the Napa Valley, but had been in South America for many years as a missionary for the Way. He was enjoying being back in California, and in Los Angeles in particular. He had two unsaved siblings in the Los Angeles area, and he was hopeful that he could contact and possibly entice back into the Way.

Chester told some stories of his time in South America. He explained some of the difficulties faced by missionaries in differing cultures, and some peculiarities of foreign cultures that made people suspicious of the Way. He was modest about his successes at gathering in converts, but dropped numerous names of people who had become devout followers. One of the names he dropped was César.

At the mention of César, Dennis interrupted. He asked his father, "Daddy, was César Chávez a Communist?"

The question startled Clay, and Nancy's eyes darted from Dennis to Clay and to Chester. "No," Clay answered. "César Chávez was not a Communist. Why do you ask?"

"Chester told me he was a Communist."

Nancy immediately busied herself with getting something else from the kitchen. Chester sat smiling widely and said nothing. Clay repeated, "No, Dennis, he was not a Communist."

Chester said, "I think you would find that despite his claims to the contrary he was in fact a Communist."

Dennis was watching Clay expectantly, and Clay felt challenged. He said in a subdued voice, "It's not like a person who is politically active to hide his agenda."

"Yes, that would seem difficult to believe, to the average person. But considering all the problems he caused for the government and the people of California, it was really apparent what his agenda was. From a servant's point of view we get to see that Communism is the main force of evil in the world that is really devoted to destroying the Way. We must learn to identify that evil in all its forms. Satan's aware that people in the Way are the most difficult of all people in the world to deceive, so he presents himself to us in ways that even we'll not recognize him. Communism is a very deceptive doctrine." Chester was smiling widely and speaking patiently.

Clay chewed on some food, thought a while, and then said, "I gather Dennis told you he's planning to go to the César Chávez School in the fall."

"He did. And he said it's a private school. I was surprised that one of our friends would want to indoctrinate their children with any of these strange doctrines."

Clay absorbed the comment. Dennis was still watching his father in expectation. Clay asked, "What do you know about César Chávez Leadership Academy?"

Nancy had returned and was glancing nervously around the table.

"I don't know anything," Chester admitted. "But I know from the name that I'd not want to know anything about the place. It's obviously a private school for some reason."

"I told him all about the academy," Dennis interjected. "And he told me I shouldn't be a lawyer."

Gutsy move, Dennis, Clay thought. "Don't worry, Dennis. You can be an attorney if you want."

Chester's smile began to wane. Clay said to him, "I guess little boys like to be like their fathers."

"I was really surprised myself to learn that you're a lawyer. I don't know of anyone else in the Way who is. Do you not find yourself in conflict with your commitment to the Way?"

"What conflict do you see, Chester?"

"I've been told that you caused a lot of discomfort among our friends by getting that criminal off scot free."

"But I asked you what conflict you see?" Clay insisted. His adrenalin was kicking in and he realized he'd have to remember he was not in court.

Chester was losing his composure. "Are you not concerned that it bothered a lot of people that you received so much publicity?"

"No," Clay said. "I'm still curious, though, about the conflict you find between my two professions."

Chester stumbled to find an answer. "I would think it's not becoming of a Christian to let a criminal go free."

"I don't let anyone go free," Clay explained. "I'm not a judge, I'm an advocate."

Chester's face was flushing pink. Nancy's eyebrows were raised worriedly, and her movements were becoming nervous.

"Christians should not be associating with such low life as that Chinaman, don't you think?"

"Do you know Mr. Chen?"

"Well, no. But I read all about him in the newspapers."

"I think what you read in the newspapers was what people were saying about Mr. Chen."

Chester took a long pause, then he said, "Christians have a responsibility to present a Christ like example to the world."

"What would be a Christ like stand to take in a courtroom?"

"I would expect that a good Christian would prefer to see justice served."

"How would he do that?"

Chester thought for a while, and said, "I guess he would be honest and acknowledge that the criminal did what he did."

"Is that in line with Jesus' example?"

"Of course. Can you imagine Jesus' out fighting for criminals?"

Clay smiled. "If I remember correctly, Jesus was known for His gospel." He glanced at Nancy, and she shot him a horrified glance.

"What do you mean?" Chester asked.

"Well, the meaning of gospel is good news. Jesus' good news was that he set sinners free. What is that verse? The Lord sets prisoners free."

"Oh! You mean The Lord looseth the prisoners."

"I guess so."

"Well, you see, in the Bible what it means by prisoners in that sense is people who are prisoners of sin, and prisoners of false religion. Prisoners of deception. God would never have intended that Jesus should let all the criminals in the world go free. It would create anarchy. God loves order. No, criminals should not go free, do you think?"

"I don't know."

Chester did not respond. He looked like he did not understand Clay's response.

Clay continued. "I guess I just expected prisoners to mean people in prison, not sinners. Why would it say prisoners if it meant sinners?"

"All prisoners are sinners, you know," Chester said.

"True. But not all sinners are prisoners. It seems to me like there has to be something for prisoners too, or it would say sinners not in prison."

Dennis spoke up. "My Daddy makes them prove that a man is a criminal before they lock him up for good."

Chester looked at him in surprise, then turned back to Clay. "These are difficult things for most people to understand. You have to be in the right spirit when you read these passages to know what they really mean."

"Really?"

"Well, of course, Clay. Servants have been specially called to interpret these things for people."

"Interesting. Now where does the teaching of the Holy Spirit come in? We're supposed to be taught by the Holy Spirit, so would that not help us to understand when we read?"

"In a sense, maybe," Chester stammered. "It would be reasonable to expect, though, that the Holy Spirit would particularly teach our friends to be obedient to the servants and give the servants special insights to guide folks like you."

"Really?"

"Well, uh, yes."

"I was interested in knowing what your thoughts were in that respect."

Nancy urged everyone to take seconds. Then Clay announced, "Nancy has a friend that she's planning to invite to your gospel services."

That's wonderful," Chester said. "Tell me about her."

"Her name is Irene," Nancy said. "She's been a good friend of mine for a few years now."

"And she's an artist," Dennis added.

"An artist!" Chester remarked. "Interesting. How did you meet her?"

"She sells her art at a gallery not far from here," Nancy said.

"Well!" Chester said. "It's unusual to meet someone in an art gallery who has any interest in spiritual matters, I would imagine."

No one responded, so Dennis said, "She paints really pretty pictures."

"What kind of pictures does she paint, Dennis?" Chester asked.

"I like the one of the man sitting on a rock by the river the most."

"He must have been a fisherman," Chester suggested.

"Oh no," Dennis replied. "I think he was going swimming because he had nothing on. But I think he just saw the goose instead, and decided to feed it or something. It's a really big Canada goose."

Clay watched Nancy nearly choke, and winked at her.

Chester continued. "Artists are so difficult to save because they are so interested in sensual and carnal matters. It really destroys any interest they might have in spiritual matters. It prevents them from being able to respond to the Holy Spirit."

"How so?" Clay asked.

"They are really seriously at odds with God's plan for human beings. The Holy Spirit wants to lead people into good, moral, upright living, and the art world is notorious for hindering that work, even destroying it. They see nothing wrong with flaunting naked bodies. They call it art, but think of the damage it does, especially to children. It's no wonder the world has become so polluted with pornography."

Dennis watched Chester, wideeyed.

Nancy fidgeted.

"Nancy's a professional artist," Clay said.

"Oh," Chester replied. "Well, I guess I could be assured that she doesn't have anything to do with any of the immoral art."

"We have a statue of a naked couple in our bedroom," Clay said.

Nancy had agonized enough. She said, "Maybe we should all go to the living room and have our coffee now."

Chester looked relieved. "That would be nice, thank you."

They all stood. Chester and Dennis went to the living room. Clay excused himself to help Nancy clear the table.

When Chester was safely out of hearing, Nancy said, "What are you trying to do?"

Clay laughed. "What do you mean?"

"You're making him mad."

"But he's not supposed to show it." Clay laughed. "He's a servant."

"I was afraid he was going to ask you if I'd ever painted a nude."

"And I'd love to have told him we were keeping that information a secret."

"Why don't you just agree with him and let it go?"

"No way. Dennis is listening. I'm not going to let anyone bamboozle my son, servant or no servant."

"I declare, between you and Dennis you're going to scare me into an early grave. Do you want him to expel you?" *Expel was the word used in the Way for excommunicate.*

"Don't worry. He'd have to find a reason before he did something like that."

Nancy was exasperated. "He could find a reason if he needed to."

"He doesn't need to yet, though."

She waved him away and said, "Go in there and talk to him, and change the topic of conversation."

Clay took her in his arms and kissed her. "You make the best coffee in the world."

"Go in there and talk to him, and change the topic of conversation."

In the living room, Chester turned the topic to the weather, and noted that the winter days were beginning to lengthen. He admired the view from the apartment window. The sun had just set on the Pacific Ocean.

Nancy served coffee, and Chester announced his plan for gospel services in Inglewood. He was being ambitious. He was having three services a week, Sunday, Tuesday, and Wednesday. Of course there would be regular assemblies on Thursday evening and the fellowship gatherings on Sundays.

Nancy apologized that she probably could not be there every night because Dennis needed to be in bed early on school nights. Chester related stories about people he knew in South America who frequently kept their children up late because they wouldn't deprive their children of any opportunity to be in a gospel service.

Clay looked at Nancy, and the look on her face said it all. *Yeah,* Clay thought, *Nancy gets shot down again.*

Dennis ran off to his bedroom at one point and returned with a hand held computer game. Clay reminded him to keep the volume down. And Chester told stories about how people in South America would make their children put their toys away and sit up and listen while the servants were visiting in their house.

Dennis interrupted to comment, "Man that must be awful boring for the kids."

Nancy gulped visibly, and Clay chuckled.

When it was time to leave, Chester thanked them profusely for their hospitality and declared the visit to be quite wonderful. And he was gone.

"I thought he was supposed to be nice," Dennis said as soon as he left.

"Isn't he nice?" Clay asked.

"No. Well, maybe he's just stupid. He didn't want to hear anything about you being a lawyer, did he?"

"That's not a big deal, Dennis. He just has some funny ideas."

"And I don't think he likes Mommy, either. I know what he meant all the time he was talking."

"Well, just remember Dennis, this is our house, not his. OK?"

"OK. But am I going to have to put my toys away when he comes here to visit?"

"No," Nancy said. "You are very polite and quiet, and that's all you need to do."

"Good. My butt gets sore when I have to listen a long time."

Back in the kitchen, Nancy said, "It looks like we're in for a hinting good time. He sure knows how to drop hints."

"We'll get him over that soon enough," Clay assured her.

"You'll get yourself in trouble."

"He needs to be respectful when he comes into someone's house. There's nothing wrong with the way we run our lives here."

"Is it me, or am I getting old or just losing something? Why am I constantly feeling threatened by the endless dropping of hints? Do I have to live the rest of my life dealing with this kind of thing? I'd like to just have the servants come here and visit and talk to us like we were all right.

"My Dad always said, they only come around when they think you need some guidance."

"I don't know what men think, but I know what I think. All this hinting around about all the good things other people do that are opposite to what I do I get insulted. I'm not so stupid that I don't know what they're doing. And I'm not so childish that I couldn't handle it if they came out and told me exactly what they thought of me. They just say it so that you can't defend yourself without accusing them in some way. I'm not some kind of slave or prisoner who has no right to speak for myself."

"He'll go away sooner or later. We'll just have to see that he doesn't get a chance to pump Dennis again. Maybe we'll get a civilized servant next time around."

"Don't you feel threatened, Clay? He comes to your house and drops all these hints. You know he expects you to conform. You're an attorney, he knows you're not stupid. He can't possibly think you don't get the hint."

"You're quite right. And have you noticed, he doesn't like it when I ask him questions straight up. You know why they do that?"

"Why?"

"It's because they use suggestive talk that gives them leeway to make it mean something else if they get a response they don't appreciate. It makes you mad, doesn't it?"

"I would not want to have you cross questioning me in court."

"But I love it when you squirm." He laughed.

Nancy shook her head. "Where do you get the nerve to talk to him that way? You know, they expect people to just agree with everything they say, no matter what. I get so nervous. You didn't even answer all his questions."

"I don't have to answer his questions. He didn't answer very many of mine either. You could have played judge and ordered him to answer my questions," he joked.

"No thanks. And Dennis is no better than you. He says exactly what he thinks. You're both so hardnosed I never know what to expect."

Clay laughed. "Like father, like son. But we'll survive. We've been around servants like that before."

"I just feel weird sometimes criticizing the servants. Mom and Dad would never allow us to say a negative word about the servants. It just got to be taboo."

"They're all just humans. We're not responsible for their idiotsyncracies." That was Clay's favorite expression for a person's eccentric behaviors.

"You're going to say that in court someday," Nancy predicted.

"Oh no. I behave very well in court." He laughed.

"So how did you do in jail today?"

Clay laughed hard. "I have to tell you this. There's this guy in there complaining because they want to add time to his sentence. They found him conducting an illicit business in his cell. He was charging other inmates for five minute sessions with his girl substitute."

"A real entrepreneur. You should have told Chester about him! How much money has this guy earned, anyway?"

"I have no idea. They took his toy away from him, but he probably has enough cigarettes now to last him for the rest of his time in the slammer."

"You should write a book," she said.

CHAPTER 9

Aggie came back to Maggie's apartment the next Saturday afternoon. Maggie knew she'd been quite agitated for some time, and it was because she could never get any insight into Rodney Sturm's problem.

People had remarked that Rodney had been missing at assembly. That in itself was not an indication of a real problem, because Rodney was quite new as a convert and it was to be expected that he may not yet have grasped the urgency of always being at assembly. But people did know Rodney had been confronted by Howard about something, and that was a significant indication there was a problem. There was the suggestion going around that Howard was too tenderhearted to handle Rodney's impassioned outbreaks.

The real indication of a serious problem was Uncle Floyd's sudden appearance in town without any previously announced agenda. Aggie learned that he'd arrived at the Bishop's house with a stranger, and that was most curious. Aggie couldn't restrain her curiosity. She went straight to Maggie's apartment.

"Maggie," she said. "You weren't here last weekend."

"No, I wasn't. I went on a little vacation."

"Really?"

"I went to Eureka with Jesse and Amy. I had the most wonderful time."

"It must be getting very serious between them."

"You mean Jesse and Amy?" Maggie asked.

"Yes."

"I don't think there's anything going on between them, Aggie. I think they're just really good friends."

"That's a relief. I'd hate to see him get tangled up with her before she has a chance to prove herself."

"You get impatient," Maggie suggested.

"Maybe you're right." Aggie paused, then said, "I still don't know what's going on with Rodney Sturm. He's missed another assembly and fellowship gathering. I wouldn't be surprised if Uncle Floyd is here to deal with him. Uncle Floyd is in town, you know."

"No, I didn't know that."

"He was seen at the Waterman's house with a stranger, but no one seems to know why. I have my hunches, though." Carl Waterman was the bishop of the Espadín assembly.

"Well," Maggie said, "I don't expect it has anything to do with either you or me."

"I should hope not. You'll never guess what I got to do this morning."

"What's that?"

"I got to talk to a journalist for the Sacramento Bee. He wanted to know about the Way. Isn't that wonderful?"

"I'm sure it was. What did he want to know?"

Aggie had been out early that day, and she'd gone first to the little mom'n'pop's restaurant where she frequently ate her meals. Her favorite booth was taken, so she found another.

"How are you this morning, Aggie?" the waitress asked.

"Chipper," she replied.

"Glad to hear it. The usual this morning?"

"Why not?"

Her breakfast came right up.

When she was about finished, an eccentric looking young man came into the restaurant. He stood and looked around, then turned to the cashier and said loud enough for Aggie to hear, "How can I meet someone in this town who is a member of the Way? It's a religious group."

Aggie grabbed the opportunity. She jumped from her seat and approached him. "Sir, I've been in the Way for over 60 years. Can I help you?"

"Maybe so," he said. "I've just heard about this religion and I'd like to know more about it."

"I'd be most delighted to help you. Come and join me at my table." She turned to a waitress and asked, "Can I have my table cleared and talk to this man?"

"Of course," the waitress replied.

As they were sitting down, the man commented, "I can tell you're very enthusiastic about this church."

"I am," she confirmed.

"Ma'am, I have to tell you something," he apologized. "I'm a reporter for the Sacramento Bee."

"Does that mean you'll write something in the paper about me?"

"Not really. I may write something about your faith, though."

"That's wonderful. Where do we start?"

"I guess I'd like a brief sketch of your principle beliefs."

"I can do that." She preened. "Well, we're not great in number, but we're very faithful to the teachings of the Bible. We believe in keeping them all. I think you'd find that the Way is perfect, even if some of the people aren't."

"I can appreciate that. Is there anything that is critically unique about the Way?"

Aggie thought. "Yes, I think there is. We even keep the foot washing that was instituted by Jesus."

"That's fascinating."

"Yes, we believe that we must be washed in order to be clean."

"That's quite understandable. What kind of a clergy do you have?"

"We have a very quiet and compassionate ministry, and they are totally devoted to doing God's work."

"I think what I meant was how your people are organized. Kind of who does what."

"Oh, I see. Actually that is very simple. We have no organization at all. We have our lay people, and we have our preachers. We call them servants. And they are led by God to go preaching in needy places."

"Do they have a superior?"

Aggie paused, and seemed not to know the answer. Then she said, "We are all equal. Everyone has their own relationship with God. We all have our own place to fill."

"But do you turn to someone when there is a problem?"

"Certainly. The servants are always diligent in helping us."

"And what about your servants? Who do they report to?"

"God," she said. Then she thought a minute. "Well, we have a head servant here in California. Maybe that's because there are so many things that the other servants don't have the time to address."

"Does this head servant give direction to the servants? Does he manage their work?"

"No, no," she assured him. "They're all directed by God. I can see why some people wouldn't think that, but we are people who are very serious about correct order. You know, who is supposed to submit to whom. People in the world don't submit to anyone anymore, and I'm so thankful that we've not lost that."

"So who submits to the head servant?"

"I'm certain all the servants do."

"And who submits to the servants?"

"Well, everyone else. Probably I should say that the bishop really is next in the chain of command from the servants. I'm sure they are."

"Who are the bishops?"

"They're the men who have our assemblies in their houses. They are carefully selected for their roles, because the rest of us submit to them." She chuckled a bit to herself. "Well, not everyone really. The men all do. The women submit to their husbands, but I don't have to do that because I was never married." They both laughed.

"I'm sorry," the reporter remarked.

"It's OK. God has blessed me as a single person. His will is best, you know."

"For sure, Ma'am. Now, what involvement do the servants have with families?"

"I'm glad you asked. No one cares about the families much anymore. The servants are very helpful to families."

"How so?"

"They regularly go to their houses for visits, and they can advise parents on how to raise their children. They're just wonderful for the children. We're so fortunate because we've read so frequently in the newspapers that in other religions the ministers are always molesting children. And the people still continue to go to those churches. I'm sure Satan has something to do with that, or they'd all be looking for something better. Something perfect."

"You're very convinced of this, aren't you?"

"Oh, yes. I've lived long enough to see all the fads and fashions come and go, and the only thing, mind you, the only thing that has not changed in my lifetime is the Way."

"But you don't appear to be an oldfashioned person. I mean, your style of dress pardon my noticing is quite normal, as opposed to some groups such as the Amish and others."

He thought she was flattered by his comment. "Well, you know, we have no rules about any such things. The Holy Spirit leads us to appear modestly. Young people have no examples of modesty these days, except in the older ladies of the Way, like me."

The reporter studied her for a long while. "What would happen if one of your ministers were to molest one of the children?"

"I have no fear of that happening. Unlike other religions, our servants give their whole selves to God to be an example of perfection in the world. They would never be tempted to do anything that was improper."

Aggie noticed that the reporter was becoming impatient, so she said, "Is there anything else I can tell you?"

"Yes, maybe so? One more question. How many of your faith are there in Espadín?"

"Probably between 30 or 40 people, counting the children."

The reporter moved to get up. "I hate to do this, but I have a very busy schedule today and I have to be going." He pulled a card from his jacket pocket and handed it to her. "Here is my business card, Ma'am. And I thank you sincerely for talking to me. It was a real pleasure"

"Any time," she assured him. "It was a great privilege to talk to you. The Way is the joy of my life. And please take my name and phone number and call me if there is anything else you want to know. I'd be greatly pleased."

Aggie was so insistent he decided he would more easily get away from her by accepting her name. He took another card from his pocket, handed her a pen, and said, "You're so kind. Put your name and phone number on this and I'll save it."

Aggie beamed. She used her finest script and handed it back to him.

"I hope he writes something good," Aggie said.
"Yes, I hope so."
"And then I went to see Sharon Fitch before I came here."
"How is Sharon today?"

It was nearly half a mile from the restaurant to Herb and Sharon Fitch's house, but Aggie always walked everywhere. She considered that Sharon would probably be home, it being a Saturday morning.

Aggie sometimes thought Sharon avoided her. Half the time she went to visit Sharon would talk to her for a mere two minutes and then tell Aggie she had something to do that Aggie wouldn't be participating in. This was one of those times.

Aggie observed immediately that Sharon had been crying. She asked, "Sharon, are you not well?"

"Have a seat, Aggie. I'm OK. I just have this terrible attack of hay fever."

"I'm so sorry to hear that."
"I have to go to the clinic in a little while."
"They'll fix you up. So what's new in your household?"

The Straight Way

"Nothing new, Aggie."

"I see that Uncle Floyd's in town."

Sharon made no comment, so Aggie continued. "We weren't told he was coming to town. I wonder if he'll be visiting around."

"I have no idea," Sharon sighed.

Aggie thought of another question. "Is there something important happening in town this weekend?"

"I've heard of nothing."

Aggie made her visit short and left.

"So you see, I didn't get any news from Sharon at all," Aggie said.

"Well, I have no news either," Maggie apologized. "But I'll have to watch the newspaper to read about you."

"I hope he reports it all correctly," Aggie said. "It would be good for the Way if he makes some good comments about us."

They briefly discussed the weather, and Aggie went on her way.

The next morning there came an early message that everyone in the Espadín assembly should meet at Dan Spinner's house for Sunday Fellowship. Everyone knew that anyway. Months before their regular fellowship potluck schedule had already been set. The urgent part of the message was that everyone was to be there. Apparently Bart had something he wanted to address with the whole assembly.

Amy and Jesse arrived together. When they walked up to the door, Jesse just opened it and waved Amy to go on in.

"Didn't you forget to ring the doorbell?" Amy asked.

"We don't have to ring the doorbell here either," he explained.

"This is neat." She was surprised at how the Way members would just walk into each other's houses.

"They're expecting us," Jesse explained. "Otherwise their doors would probably be locked."

"I should hope so."

Inside was a small crowd, all of them people Amy had seen at the gospel and assembly services. The gorgeous little Mexican girl, Maria, was there, and there was an empty seat beside her. Jesse suggested Amy sit beside Maria, and he would stand. Maria always wanted to sit beside Amy.

There was one person present that Amy had never seen before. He was a disheveled looking middle aged man. He stood out. He was not quite as clean shaven as the other men, and he wore jeans instead of slacks. He was shaggy haired, with no indication of a hairstyle like the other men. Everyone called him Pablo, but no one introduced him to her.

The room was curiously silent. It looked to Amy like it was going to be another service of sorts. Bart occupied a prominently placed chair, and Scott sat beside him. Scott looked like a frightened rabbit in a snare.

Jesse was standing with Marty in the corner of the room. Marty whispered to him, "What have you done now?"

"Nothing I can think of."

"I think you're about to find out." Marty snickered under his breath.

"Maybe you're the offender," Jesse suggested.

"It's not me. I'm always in trouble. They don't call meetings like this to talk about me anymore."

"They've given up on you, huh?"

"Yeah."

"What's this about, anyway?"

"Darned if I know," Marty said. "Maybe Bart just wants to scare us all in case we have any ideas about trying anything funny while he's around here. You're lucky you showed up."

"Why?"

"Bart's taking roll."

Jesse looked, and Bart was indeed making some marks in a small notepad.

Marty continued. "Poor Scott looks like he's about to shit a brick."

They both laughed.

Suddenly Bart stood and began to speak. "The reason I wanted everyone together this morning is to make you aware that we have a gossip problem to deal with. It has been brought to my attention that people are speculating about why Howard was moved away. Someone has even been telling that Howard has been molesting children."

Amy scanned the group. Everyone was sober and attentive.

"I'd like to nip this rumor in the bud," Bart continued. "We cannot have people telling things like this about the servants. It's not profitable for the service to be subjected to this kind of gossip. Uncle Floyd has asked me to see that these rumors get corrected."

"So why was Howard moved away?" Rodney Sturm asked.

Bart looked stunned. "Uncle Floyd didn't say why he was moved."

"But do you know why?" Rodney persisted.

Bart clearly did not like the question. "I think if I told you anything it would be gossip. If you're patient I'll be telling you everything you need to know."

To the astonishment of everyone, Herb, Sharon Fitch's husband, spoke up. "Would you tell us if Howard were in fact a child molester?" Sharon cringed and dropped her head.

"You're children are safe," Bart said.

"But you didn't answer my question," Herb shot back.

"Careful, Herbie," Mart whispered in Jesse's ear.

"This ministry does not put your children in danger," Bart stressed.

There was a quiet unease sweeping throughout the room. Some showed signs of shock, some disbelief, and a few were agitated.

Rodney continued. "Can I ask you a question?"

"You don't seem to need permission," Bart said. He was no longer able to mask his annoyance.

"Sounds like Herbie and Rodney are both bad boys today," Marty speculated.

Jesse tried to shush Marty, but Marty's comments definitely eased the tension.

"A hypothetical question," Rodney began. "If one of the servants were messing with children, would you tell the rest of us who to watch out for?"

"The Bible tells us that these are things that should not be mentioned among us."

"Then in that case, I would call the police," Rodney said.

"The Bible forbids us to take our brother to the law," Bart said.

But Rodney had not finished. "If one of the servants murdered someone, would you call the police?"

"These are questions we don't need to answer," Bart assured him. "I've never heard of a servant killing anyone."

Rodney glared at Bart. Bart said, "I'm very disappointed with the bad spirit you're demonstrating by addressing me in that manner."

"And I'm disappointed that you can give me no assurance that you'd warn us if there were a child molester among us," Rodney said.

"We need to end this discussion because it's going to disturb people," Bart urged.

Herb spoke again. "We don't need to discuss this anymore anyway because it's already been reported to the police."

That comment startled the group more than any of the previous conversation. There were audible catches of breath throughout the room. Even Marty dropped his jaw.

Bart's face turned red. He looked at Rodney and was almost stuttering. "Shame on you for exposing the Way, and a servant especially, to the law."

"Who said I told the police?" Rodney looked around the room. "Did anyone hear me say I reported anyone to the police?"

There was dead silence. Then in a low, calm voice Herb said, "No, Rodney. We will all recall that you did not tell anyone you called the police."

"We'll talk about this later," Bart concluded and looked around the room. "Well, now that we have cleared that little problem up, the ladies can put things in order for our pot luck."

No one moved for several minutes. When people began standing and milling about, many of them looked startled, some dazed, many frightened. It was clearly going to be an uncomfortable gathering. Bart began circulating and shaking hands as though nothing were out of order.

Amy was freaked out. She said to Jesse, "Does this kind of thing happen often?"

"I've never seen anything like this before."

"What's going on here anyway?"

"It sounds like someone thinks Howard is a child molester."

"I'd be worried about what would be done about a child molester. Surely they wouldn't just let him go, would they?"

Jesse shrugged. "Unfortunately I think that's what happens. I've heard of that happening, but I've never been anywhere when it happened."

In the oversized dining room the women loaded the large table with food. There were salads and casseroles. Someone had contributed a roast, and there was a paper tub of fried chicken.

When the table was ready, Bart spotted Rodney and Herb quietly talking to each other in a corner. As he approached them they stopped talking. Bart said, "I'm going to ask you two fellows not to partake of the bread and wine today."

"Why?" Rodney asked.

"It's because of your attitude," Bart said.

Rodney looked at Herb, who shrugged his shoulders and turned away. Rodney decided to take Herb's lead and said nothing.

"Thank you, fellows," Bart said. "I appreciate your compliance with that request."

When Bart moved on, Rodney said, "He's crazy."

"Be careful," Herb warned. "Bart's not a compassionate guy."

Everyone who was going to participate in the sacramental routine gathered in the vicinity of a small table set with a small loaf of bread and a goblet of wine. Everyone else stood back. Dan Spinner asked

Bart to return thanks for the bread, which he did. Then Dan picked up the loaf and it was handed from one to another until all those standing around had taken a piece of it.

Dan then asked Scott to return thanks for the wine, and the wine glass was passed among those participating. When that was finished, Dan drank what was left of the wine and left the room with what remained of the loaf.

"Time to eat!" Mrs. Spinner announced. A queue formed at the table and conversation picked up. Everyone appeared to relax, and the visiting even became pleasant. It was early afternoon when people began drifting away from the gathering.

On the way home, Amy said, "That has to be one of the freakiest things I've ever seen. I'm amazed, no one got offended and left. Are they always that complacent with the servants? And who decided who gets the bread and wine?"

"They tell people not to take it if they have not been baptized," Jesse explained.

"Oh, I see. I'm going to be a long time getting these things all sorted out."

"You'll get it," Jesse assured her. "It's probably more confusing right now because it's all new rather than overly complicated."

"You're probably right."

"And you'll have to remember that Rodney gets a bit hot under the collar quite easily."

"It sounds like he thought he had a good reason," Amy said.

"Who knows?"

That afternoon when everyone went home, a few of them retreated to their usual read of the Sacramento Bee. Some missed it, but others found it on the second page of the Del Rio supplement to the Bee. *One modest headline read, Clergyman to appear in Del Rio Superior Court Monday morning.* That court was in Espadín, because Espadín was the county seat for Del Rio County.

For any of the Way friends who read it, the startling news was that the clergyman named was Howard Barnes. He was even identified as the leader of the local assembly of the Way, which was an obscure sect with some curious practices. Worst of all, he was accused of several incidents of child molestation.

Probably the most horrified of readers that Sunday evening was Aggie, who discovered that she had been quoted by the reporter as either denying or ignoring the fact that her spiritual guide could have been arrested on such serious charges. What humiliated her most was that the reporter had written that the lady he interviewed came across as more fanatical than factual. Her only consolation was that he had not used her name.

If anyone in Espadín did not get the news on Sunday, they surely did on Monday morning. The Monday edition of Espadín's 8page *Town Crier* carried the blaring front page headline that read *Espadín Clergyman Molesting Local Children*. For half the town's people it was a sensational break from the rag's stream of mundane notices of the appearances in court of rowdy and drunken college students. But for the members of the Way it was very shaming and frightening.

As the story went, Howard Barnes had been arrested without incident on the weekend in the Bay Area. It was expected that he would be brought back to Espadín to be charged. None of the victims were named, but it was mentioned that he was suspected of molesting at least four children of elementary school age.

Interestingly, there was virtually no mention about such news among the Way friends in Espadín that week. The truth was that no one dared say anything until they knew exactly who was who and what was really going on. Of course, Bart had warned them not to speak about it, so most of them had the personal discipline to avoid the temptation to gossip.

Aggie suffered most. She felt like she'd been fired from her unofficial role as comforter to God's people, and it was another of Satan's attempts to divide and conquer. What burned most was her need to learn the identity of the stranger who reportedly delivered Floyd to the Waterman's house. But she couldn't find out. She kept herself literally locked in the house with her maid the whole week. She dared not go out in case someone saw her and wanted to talk, and for the first time she realized she wanted desperately to read the Town Crier, no matter what Bart thought of it.

Her greatest dread was that the servants would find out she had any connection to the newspaper. She was sure many of them would understand her sincerity, but she suspected Bart was one who frowned on all aspects of the media.

The next Sunday fellowship potluck had previously been scheduled to occur at the Sturm residence. Someone, whoever decides such things, decided that it should not be moved because a lot of them kept the schedule on their kitchen bulletin boards and would be upset if by some means they showed up at the Sturms' to find the location had been changed without their knowledge. So everyone went to Sturms.

Bart appeared also. When he arrived, Rodney took him aside and asked whether it would be appropriate for him, as owner of the house, to handle the bread and wine that day. He was not sure how long Bart's prohibition on him was to be in effect.

Bart looked at him like he had completely forgotten the incident of a week earlier. He said, "Yes, this is your house. Anyone who objects to sharing the bread and wine with you didn't have to come here this morning." And he moved on.

Rodney was frustrated. He was expecting Bart to tell him it was acceptable for him to handle these sacraments, but what he got sounded to him like a onetime clearance instead.

Floyd was not at the potluck. It was possible that many of them did not know he was or had been in town, but no one dared mention it. But everyone would be concerned for him because he was now very old and the weight of the recent publicity would be taking its toll on him.

They had entered a period of anxious waiting.

CHAPTER 10

The quiet problem that had suddenly exploded on the Way friends in Espadín had actually been uncovered weeks before. Herb Fitch had made a telephone call to Floyd.

"Uncle Floyd, this is Herb Fitch in Espadín."

"Herb! It's good to hear from you. How are things in Espadín?"

"Not good, unfortunately."

"I'm sorry to hear that."

Herb launched right into his complaint. "That's what I'm calling about. Howard Barnes has been molesting my daughter and I want something done about it."

"Oh, dear, Herb." He sounded quite helpless. "Has your daughter been trying to attract him? You know how young girls can be."

"My daughter is eight years old, and Howard is a 45 year old man. No, she wasn't trying to attract him."

"Did you talk to Howard about this?"

"No, I didn't. Child molesters never admit it, and I'm not going to have him lie to me."

There was a pause on the line. "Herb, I'm surprised at your suggestion that he would lie to you. How could you feel a servant would lie to you?"

"Because he is a child molester."

There was another pause, longer this time. "You know, Herb, these young girls sometimes say people have abused them just to get attention, and they have ruined a lot of good people. Is there any evidence of this except her word against him?"

Herb was becoming furious. "Like what?"

"Well," Floyd considered, "there would probably be some injury to the girl if he had actually been molesting her."

Herb did not answer for a long time. "What you're telling me is that if my daughter doesn't have any physical injuries, you aren't going to do anything about this."

"Basically, yes. There'd be no other way to prove anything, and I can't be doubting the servant's word about things. I have to defend the servants. They're noble servants of God bringing salvation to people, and there aren't nearly enough of them. If I can't defend them against the works of Satan, what will become of all of you? We have to defend the Way at all cost. Can you imagine how damaging it would be for a servant to end up in court about a child molestation? Everyone would believe he'd done it, and the Way would be known everywhere to harbor a child molester. We can't have that. God wouldn't be pleased if we let the standard down. It's an evil world out there." As an afterthought he added, "And you need to worry about your daughter's reputation. What boy in the Way would want her for a wife if they knew she'd already been molested?"

Herb listened in disbelief. To be as pointed as he could and still maintain some semblance of respect, he said, "You know, Floyd, my daughter is not merchandise. If she'd sustained physical injuries, Howard Barnes would be in jail right now. I just want something done about this. That's all." He hung up abruptly, without any closing respects.

A couple of days later the Post Office delivered several notes in Espadín from Floyd Toner. One was addressed to Herb Fitch. It read:

Dear Herb,

I have been talking to Carl Waterman and according to him no one has had any complaints about Howard, so I think your worries are quite unfounded. But to calm your worries, I have taken care of this with Howard.

In His service,

Floyd

Herb read the note several times, and passed it to Sharon.

She read it and asked, "So what agreement did he make with Howard? He hasn't done a thing!"

"Who knows? He just looked after it." Herb sat stunned.

"In that case, I'll be driving Sally to school and everywhere else so that man will never be alone with her again. And I'll do that until he gets moved to another area."

"That could be a couple of years."

"I know. But Sally's more important to me than he is. I'll do whatever I have to."

Another note from Floyd was delivered to Howard Barnes. It read:

Dear Howard,

I would be pleased if you could go to San Jose and be of a help to the folks there. They will be expecting you there for next weekend.
In His service,

Floyd.

After he read it, Howard announced, "Well, Scott, I guess I'll be leaving you."

"Oh," Scott said. "I guess that's the meaning of this note I got." Scott held up a note he had received from Floyd.

"What did he say?" Howard was worried.

"All he said was that Bart Stanley will be joining me here in Espadín."

Howard relaxed. "Bart'll keep you in line."

"Well, I guess that's part of this work, getting used to Bart," Scott said. "He always used to scare the dickens out of me all the time I was growing up."

"Good luck. I'll be thinking of you."

Then a couple of days later Carla Sturm called Sharon. Carla was as new in the Way as her husband Rodney, and she had adopted Sharon as her adviser when she had questions.

"I have a question," she said. "Have servants been known to molest children?"

Sharon was shocked. "I suppose it's possible." Her mind raced. She realized her nonresponse was a practiced attempt to protect the servants and the Way from gossip and possible scandal. She felt sick that she had to choose between her daughter's safety and the reputation of a child molester. "In fact, I know at least one who has molested at least one child."

"I didn't know a servant would do such a thing." Carla said.

"They're just human," Sharon explained.

"They're supposed to be servants of God."

"Yes, I agree with you."

"I'm really upset by this, because I was led by everyone to believe the servants would never do anything wrong. I don't want any of them bothering my kids."

The Straight Way

Sharon decided Carla needed some help. "We don't allow Sally to go anywhere by herself." She did not know what else to tell her without crossing the line of gossiping about a servant. "It's a good policy, you know, even with a servant, I guess. You never know what kind of weirdo will decide he wants to mess with your kids."

"You're right. But I thought we'd have a bit of respite from that kind of problem when we came to the Way. What should I do if one of them molests one of my kids?"

"I really don't know. There's not much we can do except watch our kids. If it weren't for the Way I suppose I'd call the police immediately."

"I'm thinking I'd call the police."

"I'm not sure I'd do that," Sharon cautioned her. "We don't take one another to the law. The servants wouldn't approve, and you might get yourself in trouble with them."

There was a long pause. Carla sighed loudly, and said, "I really need an answer to this question. I'm really worried. When I think about it some more I'll get back to you."

"Sure."

Carla did call back. She told Sharon, "Rodney decided to call the police."

Sharon had to make better sense of what Carla was talking about. "Are you talking about Howard?"

"Yes. We don't want him around our children, so Rodney called the police. We'll get a restraining order if necessary."

There was a breathless pause. Sharon's heart was pounding and skipping beats. "Oh. Did he bother any of your kids?"

"No, they say not. But we're not going to give him a chance."

"Why do you think Howard would do such a thing?" Sharon asked.

"My kids told me that Howard bothered someone else in our assembly."

Sharon's mind was spinning. She had never expected to have to deal with anything like this happening in her lifetime, and she dreaded what catastrophe was in the offing. *Could the whole town know that my daughter was molested by a servant?* She thought. At the same time she was greatly relieved that someone had done something. She felt guilty for being relieved that Howard had been reported, and glad it wasn't her who had called the police.

When Herb came home from work Sharon told him immediately what Carla had shared with her. And Herb had more news for her. "I heard at the garage today that Howard just went to San José."

"Is this all related."

"That's probably Uncle Floyd's way of dealing with it," Herb said. "I'm going to see the police too."

"Oh no, Herb."

"Yes, I am. Rodney's a good honest man and I'm not going to let him get beat up alone for this defense of Sally."

"But Herb...."

"No, don't change my mind. Sally did nothing. Howard did everything. We can't sacrifice our children for the perverse pleasures of some sick servant. I'll be back." He pulled his jacket on and was gone.

He was gone for two hours before he returned, and Sharon began to panic. She expected he would tell the police everything he knew, and she worried that the servants would learn that he had reported Howard. It crossed her mind that Herb could be arrested himself. In the event that the police would not believe a clergyman would do such a thing, she imagined they would investigate Herb instead. She was greatly relieved when she heard his car pull into the driveway.

"I told them everything they wanted to know," he said. "And I'll sleep very well tonight."

Sharon was stunned. They were both very quiet through the evening, and Herb went to bed early. After Sally's homework was finished, Sharon put her to bed and joined Herb, who was already asleep.

But she could not sleep. She fully expected Herb would be expelled from the Way for what he had done, and she considered all the eventualities if he were. She wondered how embarrassing it would be for her to go to assembly meetings without him. She wondered if she would be expelled with him as an accomplice, as sometimes happened. She knew it would devastate both of them. And she wondered what they would do with the rest of their lives, given that their fellowship with all their good friends would be gone.

Herb was up and gone to work on time the next morning. Sharon got up long enough to give Sally breakfast. Then she told her to play upstairs in the house all day and not to answer the door or the telephone. And Sharon slept all day.

Nothing more was heard about Howard once he left Espadín. Bart Stanley arrived in town, and it appeared he would continue to have gospel services where Howard had held his. From all appearances, it seemed the molestation issue had disappeared.

But the police had been provided with a list of all the individuals who were under 18 and attended the Espadín assembly. Investigators quietly interviewed each one.

The Straight Way

The night Howard was arrest, Floyd had been comfortably resting at the home of Victor Bergman in Bakersfield.

Victor was the owner of one of the largest meat packing operations in the Central Valley. He claimed he had been in the business already for 50 years, and showed no signs of retiring. He and his wife lived in a spacious but unpretentious tract home in an upper middle class neighborhood. It was obvious he was very wealthy. There was no one in California who had not seen the name Bergman on an eighteenwheeler.

It was after midnight when the telephone rang, and Victor was annoyed. He expected it to be just another wrong number, but it turned out to be John, Howard's new young companion preacher in the Bay Area. He said he urgently needed to talk to Floyd.

Victor had to wake Floyd. When the conversation was over, Floyd emerged from his room and was visibly shaken.

"We have a very serious problem," Floyd began. "Howard Barnes has been arrested."

"Whatever for?" Victor was horrified.

"John says that the police mentioned something about molesting children."

They sat silently for a time. Then Victor asked, "Is it true, or is it some kind of misunderstanding?"

"I don't know." Floyd was agitated. "There've been a number of complaints about Howard, but I don't know that any of them have had any merit."

Victor asked, "Is there something I can do to help you? Howard's going to need some legal advice."

"Isn't there some kind of lawyer who defends people in court when they have no lawyer?"

"There's the public defender for people who can't afford to hire a lawyer."

"I suppose he could go to that person." Floyd sighed deeply.

"In any case he'll need bail immediately," Victor explained.

"I don't know much about these things," Floyd admitted. "But I suppose I should at least go up there and see what can be done for him."

"I'll go with you," Victor offered.

"Thank you so much."

That Monday morning found Floyd and Victor in Del Rio Superior Court in Espadín, where Howard was making his first court appearance. No one else of the Way was there. Floyd was quite relieved.

He was very concerned about the negative publicity this situation was going to bring for the Way.

The elderly judge was quite devoid of emotion. By the time Howard was to be taken back to his jail cell, the judge had set his bail at $500,000. He noted that Howard had tried to avoid arrest by leaving the county, so he instructed that if Howard could raise bail he would still not be allowed to leave the county. He was forbidden to be in any place where there was any person under the age of 18 years. He told Howard to get himself legal counsel.

Howard complained that he was penniless and couldn't pay for an attorney. The judge proposed that he provide Howard with a public defender. Howard's response was that he wouldn't consider a public defender. He said he'd been told they were the cheapest attorneys the courts could find, and they didn't care whether their clients got a proper defense or not.

The judge listened patiently. When it appeared Howard had finished, he said, "Mr. Barnes. You are free to provide yourself with appropriate legal counsel. Otherwise, I will appoint counsel to defend you. My advice to you is that you not attempt to defend yourself on these very serious matters."

When Howard was gone, Floyd looked at Victor as if to say, "What do we do now?"

"Let's go and take care of his bail," Victor said.

"We can't do that," Floyd said.

"Yes. Let's go."

"Who has a half million dollars? It won't hurt him to sit in jail."

"Uncle Floyd, I don't think you understand. I'll provide his bail so he can prepare a proper defense."

"That's very kind of you."

When they finally got to speak to Howard privately, Floyd suggested he let the judge appoint an attorney for him. He explained, "You'll be creating an unnecessary expense by hiring your own lawyer."

Howard was adamant. "I don't want a public defender. I'll defend myself before I let a judge tell me who will defend me."

Victor interrupted and patted Floyd's arm. "I'll take care of it."

Floyd's expression showed that he had no grasp of the situation except that it was going to be extremely expensive and far beyond his ability to deal with it. He turned to Howard and said, "We'll get back to you, Howard."

On their way back to Bakersfield, Floyd was very quiet. Only once did he mention Howard's predicament. "The man's pretty demanding considering the predicament he's in. I should have sent him home before he could bring this shame on the service."

Victor asked, "Can we go to L.A. in the morning?"

"Whatever for?" Floyd asked.

"We'll go and see Clay Shipman."

"Oh," Floyd said. "I know that man."

"He's a criminal defense lawyer."

"Do we want him involved? He doesn't have such a great reputation among our friends."

"From what I've heard he's probably the best defense attorney we can get. The people who hire him seem to have good reason to trust him. Right now we need someone like that."

Floyd breathed a heavy sigh. He took a long pause to watch the fields and orchards slide by. "Let's do that. I'll take your guidance on these matters. We'll just not tell anyone he's one of us."

All the Way students showed up together that day for lunch in the college cafeteria. Not surprisingly, the conversation soon turned to Howard.

"Did anyone go to court yesterday?"

"You mean to see Howard?"

"Yeah."

"I don't think anyone was there."

"Someone should have been there to support Howard," Janet said.

"I think a lot of people would go just to see what happens to him," Floyd Gilmore added. "Jenny thinks they should throw the book at him."

"That's terrible," Janet protested. "He's a servant of God, and that's no way to treat such a person."

"Why don't we all just go to the court the next time he appears," Marty suggested.

"Marty Spinner's organizing another protest!"

"Anything to get out of class," Marty chuckled.

"When is he going to appear again?"

"I don't know. You can find out on the Internet, I'm sure."

"Who called the police on him, anyway?" Janet asked.

"One of the parents, probably," Melissa said. "Someone told me there were three or four kids he was messing around with."

"That's the end of his preaching career."

"What's going to happen to him now?"

"They send those people away for life, or until they get murdered in prison."

"See what happens when you turn a servant over to the police," Janet said.

"Janet, we can't let people molest our children."

"But you don't have to report them to the police," Janet protested.

"Then what's the answer."

"I know," Marty said. "A really big sharp butcher knife."

"That wouldn't work. That's not what makes a person molest."

"How do you know?"

"I read it in a book."

"I know," Marty said. "It's a mental disease. Cut his head off."

Janet was aghast. "Marty, you ought to be ashamed of yourself."

"Well then you'll have to find another solution," Marty said.

"Just send him away," Janet offered.

"They've already done that."

"Yeah, they sent him all the way to San Jose."

"No, they sent him here from Colorado."

"And they sent him to Colorado from Iowa."

"Who told you that?"

"Just pick the kids you want him to mess with and send him there, I suppose."

"What if he didn't do anything?" Janet asked.

"Then he can plead not guilty and they can sort it out in court."

"We shouldn't be talking about this," Janet said. "Bart told us not to talk about this."

"What Bart doesn't know won't hurt him," Marty offered.

"I'm kind of embarrassed by this," Amy said. "I don't want my father to find out that this was the preacher who convinced me to join the Way."

Everyone became quiet.

"There are preachers in every church who molest children. Tell him that."

"I could never tell my father that I supported such a person," Amy said. "He'd be furious about that."

"What's he supposed to have done, anyway? Someone told me he didn't rape anyone. What's the big deal?"

"What business does he have doing anything with little kids?"

"But if he didn't hurt any of them, what's the problem?"

"You're really annoying me now," Melissa said.

"But why lock someone up for years if he never hurt anyone?"

"Would you like Bart making advances on you?"

"Not really. I'd just say no."

"You're not going to get anywhere with him," Melissa said. "That's the mentality that lets these creeps carry on at their sickening games."

"What would you do if someone killed your mother?"

"I'd call the police."

"And then, if the police find out it was Bart who killed your mother, what would you think then?"

"It wouldn't be my fault if I didn't know who did it."

"See what I said? You'd let someone molest your kids and you wouldn't call the police."

"But I'd know ahead of time that it was a servant. And you shouldn't report servants to the police."

"But you'd call the police if it were your neighbor who molested your kid?"

"I sure would."

"So a servant child molester is OK and any other child molester has to be put away."

"I don't get it," Amy said. "How do you think we should deal with servant child molesters?"

"They'll get severely whacked at the pearly gates," Marty chuckled.

"Oh Marty, be serious."

"I am serious. Don't you think it's silly for us to sacrifice our children until God gets around to removing these characters?"

"We have to protect children," Amy said. "What could we expect our children to think of us if they realize we didn't do anything to protect them from molesters?"

"I agree."

"I'm going to class," Janet said.

"Are you going to tell Bart what we're talking about?" Marty asked.

"I'll think about it," Janet said as she walked away.

"I have to go to class too."

"Me too."

CHAPTER 11

Clay was at his desk nursing his morning coffee when the phone rang. It was the receptionist, and she informed him that a Mr. Floyd Toner would like to see him.

Clay was surprised. "Send him in."

"No, I'm sorry. He doesn't have an appointment," she said.

"It's okay," Clay assured her. "He's a friend of mine. You can send him in."

Clay was uneasy. *What is Floyd Toner coming to my office for?*

Floyd had Victor Bergman with him. Clay had frequently met Victor at retreats and had enjoyed talking to him.

There were handshakes, and Clay offered them seats in front of his desk.

Floyd began. "I won't take a lot of your time. I know you're a busy man. But we have a problem, and you've been recommended to help us."

"You know I only work on criminal defense cases?"

"Yes, I know. Unfortunately Howard Barnes has been arrested for molesting children."

Clay had never met Howard, but he'd heard him preaching at a couple of retreats and found him helpful.

Floyd continued. "Our problem is that he won't have a public defender, and he isn't going to plead guilty. I think he should just tell them what he did and take his punishment. It would be a lot easier on everyone. But he's insistent that he needs a very good attorney."

Clay studied the old man sitting before him and felt great pity for him in his present dilemma. "It really doesn't matter whether anyone's guilty or not. Everyone in a criminal court needs an attorney. There's such a thing as being shafted in the justice system."

"What does that mean?" Floyd looked puzzled.

"It means that if an accused person is not properly represented he may be sent away for something he's not legally responsible for."

"Oh."

Victor was sitting silently and attentively beside him.

"Where is Howard?" Clay asked.

"He's in Espadín. He's out on bail, and he's staying at the studio up there with Bart and Scott." In the Way, when someone mentioned the studio, they were referring to the studio apartment provided for the servants while they were working in the area they were assigned to.

On impulse Clay smiled and commented, "That might be punishment enough in itself."

Floyd was not impressed, so Clay restrained his humor. "I'd need to talk to Howard."

"He's been banned from leaving the county where he is," Floyd explained.

"I'll go to see him."

He'd never taken a case before he'd talked to the accused person, but this case was different. He was hauntingly reminded of having discussed this very possibility with Nancy.

He thought for a moment that he should just donate his services for the sake of the Way, but changed his mind. *I can always change my mind and do it pro bono if the accusations turn out to be too outrageous.* He apologized to Floyd that he'd need a retainer, to which Floyd responded by pulling a check from his pocket, asking for an amount, and filling in the amount Clay suggested without hesitation.

Clay was shocked. He'd never heard of a servant writing a check, and certainly not for that amount of money. He briefly examined the check, and found it had been signed by Victor. *A client backed by the integrity of Floyd Toner and the finances of Victor Bergman should never embarrass me,* he decided.

Clay wanted to know more. "What do you think, Floyd? What was he doing?"

"I don't know, but he must have done something." Floyd had a weary tone in his voice, something Clay had never detected in his preaching at retreats. "I'm afraid some kids may just have twisted up some innocent move on his part. I don't know any details."

Clay realized he was not going to get anything more from Floyd. The old man was distraught about the whole situation.

"I'll do what I can for him," Clay said. "I won't know what to tell you to expect as an outcome until I see Howard and study his case.

I can't promise to get him acquitted, of course, but I can see that he doesn't get punished unnecessarily."

"Is there any way we can keep this out of the news?" Floyd asked.

"There's not much chance of that," Clay explained. "Everything that happens in courts is public record. For sure this will get some negative attention in the news."

"Even if he changes his mind and says he's guilty?"

"I wouldn't be surprised if it's already been in the news," Clay said. "Reporters hang out in courtrooms to get all the news they can."

"This is going to be terrible," Floyd said. "Howard's not my greatest concern. The worst part of this is the damage the publicity will do to the reputation of the ministry."

Clay thought about Dennis, and wished Floyd had mentioned Howard's victims.

"This could be difficult. How are you handling it?" Clay asked.

"Oh, it doesn't really matter too much about an old man like me. This is undoubtedly just another plot of Satan to discredit the Way."

"You may be right."

"As the end nears these kinds of things will happen, you know. Satan wants to scare as many people away from the Way as possible because his time is getting short."

Clay checked his appointment book, and proposed that he meet with Howard in two days in Espadín.

"That's good," Floyd said. "I'm going back to Espadín and I'll tell Howard." When he was leaving he said, "I appreciate this so much. What would we ever accomplish without the good will of our friends? God is a great provider, isn't he?"

"He most certainly is," Clay assured him.

Victor's face came back to life. On the way out of the office he turned to Clay and whispered, "In the future, please send any bills to me."

"I'll do that."

Victor pulled out a business card and handed it to Clay. They gave each other knowing, if somewhat embarrassed, smiles. And Victor and Floyd went their way.

Clay sat for a long time, stunned and amazed. He felt exactly like he'd felt the day Chen's wife came in and asked for his help. *What am I getting myself into?* he thought. When he realized he'd been sitting at his desk staring into space long enough, he called Nathan and told him they needed to have lunch, as soon as possible, and right across the street.

"Clay," Nathan said. "It's only ten o'clock."

"It's urgent."

"Okay. Can you give me twenty minutes?"

"Sure."

While he was waiting for Nathan he took a brisk walk around the block to digest the bombshell challenge that had landed in his lap.

As soon as they'd ordered, Clay said, "Okay. Now for the advice."

"Go ahead."

"There's this preacher in my faith who's accused of molesting children. His superior just came to visit me this morning and wanted me to represent him – I mean represent the accused preacher. I've basically agreed to take his case, but I'm worried about the advisability of defending someone from my own group."

"Is he a personal friend of yours?" Nathan asked.

"No. I've not even met him in person."

"What's the problem? You took the case without even meeting him? That surprises me."

"Yeah, I know," Clay said. "But I have a very strange feeling about representing him – same faith, all that. You know."

"We all defend people of our own faith all the time," Nathan said. "I see no conflict of interest here. Anyway, you have the right to defend them."

"True," Clay agreed. "You're right. But you know, in a small group like ours the dynamics can be more complicated."

"Do you have any conflict of interest?"

"No."

Nathan waved away any concern. "They should appreciate having Mr. Acquittal on their side."

"I'm Mr. Acquittal now, am I?

Of course. Ever since the Chen trial. I'll never forget how you screwed the truth out of those guys. I put work aside to watch that on TV. If you can handle that case, you'll do just fine with this one."

"Thanks, I appreciate that." Clay took a long slow sip of his drink. "Unfortunately we have to prove a bit of a guy's innocence, don't we, if indeed he is innocent. But I'm not sure what I'm getting into with this. I don't know exactly what he did yet. I'm not meeting the man himself until the day after tomorrow."

"You've never had a case like this."

"No."

"I'll tell you what to do. Use the case to educate yourself. Use the preacher to educate yourself. Child molestation cases have to be some of the most difficult. The education you get will be valuable to you, unfortunately at his expense. Where is this guy you want to defend?"

"He's in Espadín, in Del Rio County north of Sacramento."

"I've know that place. Notorious for sloppy investigative work there. Nothing really ever happens in that county. It's mostly drunk and disorderly conduct by students at the State College. There's nothing else there, I've heard. My sister went to school up there. My parents have a vacation house in the Sierras not far from there."

"I've never been there," Clay said.

"Here's your opportunity to put this little village on the map."

I know what my concern is, Clay thought. *I'm going to get to see how much truth I can screw out of a servant and any number of the Way friends!* "I'm nervous," he admitted.

"No, you're not," Nathan said. "You know, from time to time you give us such brilliant lectures on the necessity of the defense attorney to force the prosecution to prove the case. That's your forte. You'll do fine."

"Thanks, Nathan. In moments like this I need to be reminded of my strengths."

"I'm always amazed at how humble you are as a person while you're racking up these courtroom accomplishments."

"If I were trying to be flamboyant in the courtroom it wouldn't work so well."

"And another of your quotes goes: The truth does not necessarily reside in the flamboyant defense."

"Don't quote me too much," Clay laughed. "Most of my words of wisdom come from my thinking out loud. Anyway, I expect this guy has seriously messed up. People in this group are notoriously protective, even secretive, concerning the preachers. For someone to report him has to mean it's really, really over the top."

They had a good lunch of pasta and salad, and a visit about their wives and kids.

"Thanks for the talk," Clay said. "I can always depend on you. We'll have to have our families together for dinner, real soon."

"Say when. We're a team, man!"

Clay always talked to Nathan before he launched into any difficult case. Nathan always seemed to know just how to ignite his energy and enthusiasm for a case.

Clay visited Howard at the studio in Espadín. He had to ask Bart and Scott to leave while they talked. Bart seemed reluctant, but Scott was quite relieved to be sent away.

Howard began. "Thank you for coming to my help. I appreciate this so much. I've been refusing to talk to anyone about this. Is that appropriate?"

"That's probably best."

"I suppose there's a world of gossip floating around about me by now."

"I don't know. I hear Bart has forbidden people to talk about you."

"It would be interesting to know who that directive was to protect," Howard said.

Clay thought about that for a while. "Who do you think it was to protect?"

"Him and all the other servants. Their reputation, you know."

"Surely they won't try to manipulate the process. They know they could be prosecuted for that."

"I'm not sure they know what you can be prosecuted for. They circumvent the law themselves whenever convenient for them."

"I'm here to take care of that for you."

Howard relaxed.

They discussed the charges being brought against Howard. Howard maintained that he was not going to plead guilty to anything. Clay didn't try to dissuade him. He acknowledged that most of the evidence they had to deal with was of the hesaidshesaid kind, unless more were discovered.

"Isn't that to our advantage?" Howard asked.

"It can be," Clay agreed. "It'll probably depend on how the prosecutor makes his case. Anyway, I'll be questioning the evidence to find the holes in what's been presented. People can even lie in court, you know. It's my job to see that you're treated fairly. But I also need for you to tell me everything I need to know to defend you. What do you want to tell me?"

Howard sat for a long time. Then in a somber voice he said, "I don't have any idea what to say."

Clay was puzzled. "Nothing at all?"

"Nothing." And he sat quietly for a long time.

"I need to know any explanation you have for any of these charges," Clay urged.

"I have no explanation for anything."

Clay studied him for an expression, and Howard sat expressionless. *You are the most frustrating client I've ever interviewed,* he thought. "When I've studied all the discovery I'll review it with you. And you'll have to give me some idea what it's all about. I need something to argue with. Can you do that for me?"

"Okay."

That was the general summary of Clay's meeting with Howard. But a preliminary review of the charges against him suggested a rather varied and frequent indulgence into the taboo with at least five prepubescent children in a short period of time. *Our gossip mongers could salivate for months over this stuff,* Clay thought. He was, in fact, shocked at the magnitude and scope of the alleged activities.

On his way back to Los Angeles he began wondering how he'd break this news to Nancy. *In what unmelodramatic way can I announce to her that a servant has been molesting the Way friends' children?* he thought. He knew she'd become anxious over the reaction of the Way friends to his involvement in the case, so he thought of a way to reassure her: *At least I shouldn't have to worry about being expelled as long as Uncle Floyd has hired me to do the job!*

When he opened the door to their apartment, Dennis ran and jumped on him and threw his arms around his neck and his legs around his waist. Nancy was standing nearby, smiling widely, and announcing, "I haven't cooked dinner. Can I treat you to dinner out? I have two surprises for you."

As they pulled from their parking garage, Clay said, "Okay. What's the surprise?"

"I don't know if it's that important, really, but a scandal is a scandal." She lowered her voice to prevent Dennis from hearing. "There's a servant in major trouble."

"Really?"

"Yeah. Howard Barnes. You know, the one we saw at the last retreat." She braced for a right angle turn at the intersection. "He molested a child."

"Where did you get that information?" Nancy was not a gossip.

"A little birdie told me."

Clay did not respond.

"What do you think?" Nancy asked.

"I'm surprised," Clay answered.

Nancy laughed loudly. "Nothing blows you away, does it?"

"Not anymore." He thought how ironic it was that it turned out to be Nancy telling him the news about Howard.

Nancy did not give him any chance to announce his involvement in the case. She just continued. "I didn't really get you out for dinner to tell you that." Clay pulled into the restaurant parking lot. "There's a surprise in here for you too."

"I like surprises."

They were escorted to the table reserved for Shipman. The surprise was already seated. It was Clay's mother and father, and Clay was surprised.

Everyone got hugs, but Dennis got them first. He almost choked his grandparents with his hugs. In their excitement they missed the amused glances of the other diners.

"What brings you to town so unexpectedly?" Clay asked.

"We're going on a cruise tomorrow from San Pedro," Grandpa said.

"Yes, Grandpa got a last minute ticket just a couple of days ago," Grandma explained. "They were going cheaper then. The boat must not have been full."

"What a pleasant surprise!"

"Can I go too?" Dennis asked.

"Not this time, sweetheart," Grandma apologized. "But I think one of these days you'd like that, wouldn't you?"

"Would it be on one of those really big ships?"

"Oh yes."

"Wow. I can hardly wait."

"How have you all been?"

"Just fine, dear. And appreciating a break from the winter weather already."

"There was snow on the ground when we left Kearney."

"Are the big grasshoppers still there, Grandma?"

"They're all gone for the winter, dear."

"I like to watch them, but I won't touch them. They look at you with those spooky eyes."

"Kids, did you know that Pete Winnie passed away?" Pete was a centenarian widower that was dearly loved by everyone in the Kearney assembly.

"No." Clay showed concern.

"Yes, about a month ago. He just passed in his sleep. Old age, you know."

"It's nice to see such a kind old man passing so peacefully."

The news from Nebraska flowed. Then Grandma asked, "So what's new here?"

Nancy and Clay glanced at each other, and Grandma continued without pausing. "Is it true what we hear about that servant here in California?"

"Which one?" Nancy asked.

"The one who's been raping children."

"You mean Howard Barnes?"

"Howard Barnes, my dear. He's back in Colorado, isn't he?"

"Oh no," Clay said. "He came to California last year."

Grandma became somber. Quiet Grandpa spoke up. "Are you feeling all right, dear?"

"Yes, why?"

"You got awful quiet."

They laughed.

"I had a terrible thought," Grandma said. "Howard was abusing children in Iowa before they sent him to Colorado."

There was another pause in the conversation. Nancy said, "Do you suppose that's why they moved him from Iowa to Colorado."

"I thought God moved them," Dennis interjected. Everyone looked at Dennis, surprised that he was even listening.

"He does," Clay explained. "But sometimes they misbehave and someone else has to help them go away."

"Servants don't misbehave. Alexander told me so."

"Well, maybe not," Nancy assured him. Dennis went back to making designs with his green beans before eating them.

On this turn of conversation, Grandpa came alive. "I always said they were doing the wrong thing when they sent those people to another state."

"Yes, I agree," Grandma said. "When they go wherever they go they just keep on where they left off."

"It makes me worry about him," Nancy said, glancing at Dennis who was still preoccupied with his beans.

Feeling assured that Dennis was too occupied to follow the conversation, they continued. Grandma said, "I've known Howard for maybe 15 years now. He used to come around for retreats, and he was such a great preacher. So uplifting. We old ladies just marveled at how he escaped the clutches of some pretty girl and stayed in the service."

"He's not bad looking," Nancy said.

"It's too bad about this other thing. But what can we do about it?" Grandma said.

Grandpa burst out. "Call the police."

Grandma gasped. "My dear no! Call the head servant, maybe."

"Bah!" Grandpa had a conviction. "The head servant only sends him to another state. I tell you this, and it's true. You've already lost your case when you pick up the phone to call the head servant."

Grandma gasped again, then relaxed. Grandpa continued. "On the day some head servant reports one of his servants to the police, I'll change my mind."

"But Ship!" Grandma always called him Ship. "You don't take your brother to the law."

"Nonsense. If you take the servants' advice, you'd call the police. Every time they hear that one of the Way friends is being bothered by someone, they tell him, 'Call the police, the police are our friends.' If I feel unsafe I'll take their advice and call the police. If you don't cooperate with the law you have no protection."

There was another pregnant pause. Then Grandma said, "I'm so thankful I don't have to make those kinds of decisions. I give such matters to Grandpa to deal with." She took another bite.

Grandpa smiled. "She does that so when my decision backfires she can excuse herself from any guilt."

Everyone laughed.

Grandma looked at Clay. "So what's going on in the legal business today, dear?"

"Well," he pondered. "I just finished a long murder trial."

Grandpa chuckled, and said, "I haven't read the newspaper so much in the rest of my life as I did this past six months."

"I know," Grandma said, excitedly. "You've made us kind of celebrities in Kearney."

Clay smiled broadly.

"You caused more fights in Kearney in the last six months than you ever did when you were living there," Grandpa said. "All those old men that sit around in the feed store didn't talk about anything else for months."

"So what are you working on now?" Grandma asked. She made it sound like crimes could be planned around Clay's work scheduled.

"Well now that you ask, I do have a new case. I have just today begun working on a case that will much surpass the Chen case in your sphere of interest," he smiled.

"See," Grandma said. "He even talks like an attorney."

"What's this one?" Nancy asked.

"I've just been retained to defend Howard Barnes." He tried to hide his amusement at the shock that hit them.

Grandma even dropped her fork. For an instant no one moved.

Dennis broke the silence. "Are we going to have dessert?"

Nancy shook her head, then said, "Yes, of course. Anything you want." She looked at Clay and said, "I'm speechless."

"Can I get dessert now?"

Grandma said, "I don't know what to say."

"That happens every so often," Grandpa joked.

"Do they have good apple pie here?" Dennis was ignored again.

Grandma was recovering. "What are you going to do?"

"I'll defend his legal rights before the court."

"Don't let him off," Grandma said.

"Mom," Nancy explained. "It's not Clay who lets anyone off. He just has to convince the judge to let him off."

I have the whole family trained to speak for me, Clay thought.

"Let him off?" Grandma was horrified. "You finally get one of those creatures in jail and then let him off. They'll send him back to Nebraska." She looked to Grandpa for help.

Clay said, "A better way to explain it is to say that I'll be attempting to protect him from false accusations, so he won't be abused by the legal system."

To Grandma, one explanation was as good as another. She thought a while, then burst out laughing. "Can't they just, you know, kind of.... cut some things off and let him go?"

"It's entirely possible that he never even used his things." Clay joked.

"Clay, you're bad!" Grandma said.

"I finished my beans," Dennis announced.

A gleam came to Grandma's eye. She leaned over to Nancy and said, "Remind me to tell you something I know when those two guys aren't around."

Dennis stopped conversation again. "Are you guys talking about that improper touching stuff?"

"Yes, we are," Nancy said.

"I know all about that," Dennis said. "They told us all about it in school. Boy, was I glad to learn about that stuff. I sure don't want any nice people doing bad surprises to me."

"Sex Ed," Nancy whispered to her mother in law.

"That's good," Grandma said.

CHAPTER 12

"Thanks again," Maggie said as Jesse put the groceries on her table.

"My pleasure," Jesse assured her. "How've you been doing this week?"

"I'm a bit down. It's been a difficult week for me."

"It's because of Howard, is it?"

"Yes," Maggie said. "This is depressing." She was already pouring their tea.

"I just try to remind myself that we're all human, and we shouldn't be distracted by the mistakes of others."

"That's true."

"There'll always be people who fall off track and mess up. We shouldn't really put our faith in people."

"You're right, Jesse," Maggie agreed. "We're always told that the Way is right but the people are all human. I think we just expect that the servants are going to be perfect for some reason."

"I know why," Jesse said. "It's because people think we owe our salvation to the servants, or to the servants' approval. I don't think my parents believe that but I know a lot of people do."

"That's right," Maggie agreed. "You had wise parents. You know, Aggie just worships the servants. I think if they told her to stand on her head and spit nickels she's try."

Jesse laughed. "I can just see her trying that."

Maggie chuckled. "I haven't seen her for a while. I wonder why."

"She must be trying not to talk about Howard."

"That'll kill her." Maggie laughed.

"We should do something fun again," Jesse suggested.

"Don't waste too much time on me. I'm hoping to visit my daughter when she and her husband move to southern California next summer."

"I wish I could have you meet my parents too. I think you'd get along really well with them."

"I'd love to meet them."

"Next time they come up here I'll be sure to bring them to see you."

"Wouldn't that be nice!"

"Can I do anything else for you today?" Jesse asked.

"You've already done plenty," Maggie said. "As well as bringing me some groceries you were able to cheer me up again."

"You get a bit lonely, don't you?"

"Yes, I do. I don't know what I'd do without all the students who come here to Espadín. They're so good to me, and they're so young in spirit. It's really refreshing. I don't do well with old fogies."

"They all think the world of you, Maggie. You're their surrogate Grandma here in town."

"Isn't that nice! I think if it weren't for them I'd move somewhere to be close to my kids. It's just that my kids keep moving around all the time with their jobs."

Their tea was gone, and Jesse decided to go.

"I'll remember what you told me about all people being human," Maggie said. "You're a wise young man. You study well because you deserve to get good grades. And swim hard. Maybe I can see you in a contest sometime."

"I'd like that."

It pleased him that he'd been able to help Maggie on a difficult day. She'd helped him too. She made him realize the small things he could do for her were important to her, and he felt good about that.

It was Thursday, so that evening Amy and Jesse went to assembly, and gave Maggie a ride. Howard greeted them at the door, and Amy waited while Jesse had Carl wash his feet.

A number of people were absent. Herb Fitch was there, but Sharon and their daughter Sally weren't. Aggie was there, as were all the college students. Marty Spinner's parents were there, but Rodney Sturm arrived alone; his wife Carla and their three children weren't with him.

Then George Patten arrived with his son, Joey. George's wife, Marian, wasn't with him. Amy noticed that none of the school age children were present, except Joey. She assumed that the mothers were at home with the children.

Because there were fewer people in the room than usual, Amy had no difficulty taking her turn making a short prayer and offering some spiritual thoughts. She was beginning to feel more relaxed about that. She used the other students as models of what might be expected of her.

Amy observed that when the time came for the bread and wine to be shared, Carl didn't offer them to either Rodney or Herb. She guessed they were still being punished.

It was usual when assemblies were over for everyone to circulate and greet each other, but Rodney just got up and left. Amy watched, and noticed that Herb did stay and speak to Howard. She guessed it must be Rodney's children who had been molested, and maybe not Sally.

As they were leaving, Jesse turned to Aggie and asked, "Are you walking?"

"Yes, I am."

"Let me give you a ride."

"I like to walk."

"You shouldn't be walking alone at night," Amy said. "I didn't know you did that or I'd have stopped you before now."

"Well, thank you." Aggie accepted the offer. "But this is really a very safe town, you know."

Except for the occasional child molester, Amy thought. She was trying to understand why, despite the absence of so many members and Rodney's hasty departure, everything had gone so smoothly. *Can these people not be upset about anything?*

In the car, Amy said, "Those people who didn't get the bread and wine. Were they the same ones who didn't get their feet washed?"

"Yes," Aggie said.

"Why didn't they get their feet washed?"

For a while there was no answer. Then Jesse said, "I think probably Bart told Carl not to wash their feet."

"That's probably why," Maggie agreed.

"Where were all the kids tonight?" Amy wanted to know.

"We were told that Howard wasn't supposed to be around anyone under the age of 18. The judge ordered that," Aggie explained.

"Oh, I didn't know that," Amy said. "But Joey Patten was there."

"Yes, I saw that," Aggie said. "I guess George decided not to let the judge run his life. I hear he's been very supportive of Howard. That's good."

"But won't that get Howard in bigger trouble?" Jesse asked. "If he's not supposed to be around kids, he could get arrested again."

"I'll have to tell him," Aggie said. "See what happens when the law gets involved in the Way. Terrible, I say."

"Tell me," Amy said. "Why doesn't a servant wash people's feet? It sounds like something a servant should do."

"In God's way servants are not underlings," Aggie said. "They're above that."

"But they're called servants. Who are they supposed to serve?" Amy wondered.

"They serve God," Aggie said. "Only God."

"Shouldn't we be called servants too, then?" Amy asked. "We serve God too."

"Oh no," Aggie said. "The servants are much closer to God. That's why we must submit to them."

"Could we wash each other's feet, then?"

"No," Aggie assured her. "Only bishops can wash feet."

"It sounds like I'm trying to find out who the untouchables are," Amy giggled.

"They're the ones who can't let Carl wash their feet," Jesse laughed.

"We shouldn't laugh," Aggie chided. "It's a sad situation not to be able to have your feet washed."

Amy didn't respond. *I wonder if she thinks I'm that bad off*, she thought.

"Where was Bart tonight?" someone asked.

"He went to Yuba City." Aggie had all the answers.

After they let Aggie out, Amy asked, "Did she have all that who'swhointheWay correct?"

"I think she did," Maggie said. "I don't care too much for all that talk of order. I might be wrong, but I think people get too carried away with their rank. But that's the way things go."

"We don't see much of Scott anymore," Jesse said.

"Poor little fellow," Maggie said. "I hope he can handle it until he can be sent somewhere else. Bart's not a kindly old man, that's for sure."

"We'll just have to hang in there until all this is over," Jesse said.

Amy and Maggie agreed.

The next Sunday fellowship gathering was moved from the Fitch residence to the Sturm residence. The reason given was that Sharon Fitch was not well, and would not be able to have the gathering at her house.

There was some curiosity about how the Sturms would accept Howard at their house, and how they would accommodate the children should Howard show up. But Howard wasn't there, and all the children were. Bart and Scott were also there.

Everything was going very smoothly, and the visiting was cheerful. Shortly before the meal was ready, Bart announced that he'd like to have everyone's attention for just a minute.

"It appears that a large number of people were absent from the Thursday evening assembly," he began. "I presume that was because Howard was at the meeting." No one spoke, so he continued. "I have a suggestion to make. We should just all go to assembly and take our children with us. That would be good for everyone."

"I don't think so." Herb interrupted. "That's not legal."

"Well, who will know?" Bart asked.

"Everyone in Espadín. Everyone knows by now where Howard is staying, you can be sure."

"Well," Bart suggested. "Maybe then all the adults should come to the meetings and you can hire baby sitters for the children."

"Why do we have to leave our children home?" Rodney protested. "Why should we punish our children to accommodate a child molester?"

"He's a servant of God," Bart said.

"Only until he's expelled," Herb said.

"Well, I can't expel him," Bart said. "We'll just have to accept him until he's expelled."

Rodney was upset. "I think as long as nothing's going to be done to keep Howard away from our kids we'll obey the court and babysit our own children."

Bart was annoyed. "You make it very difficult for God's servants, Rodney."

"I think it's Howard who makes things difficult for us. And I think you're not helping us either."

"This is your house," Bart said. "You can say what you wish. But in matters of the Way one must give the servants their rightful place and respect." He turned to Herb and said, "I see that Sharon's not here today."

"She's not well," Herb said. "Otherwise this gathering would be at our house."

"She's not well enough to come for fellowship?"

"It's her nerves, Bart. This whole matter has been extremely difficult for her."

"Sally's here," Bart remarked. "It looks like your daughter's doing much better than your wife, and it was your daughter who thought she was molested."

Herb paused a minute, then said, "I don't want to ever hear of you speaking about my wife and my daughter like that again. And I'm not staying here today. My wife needs me more right now than anyone here."

Bart was shocked, and for a change was speechless. Herb turned to Sally and said, "Do you want to come home with me or do you want to play with the other kids?"

"I want to play with the other kids," she said.

"Okay. I'll come back and get you later."

Carla intercepted Herb as he was leaving and said, "You don't have to come back today, Herb. I'll take Sally home when she's ready."

"Thank you so much," Herb said.

When Herb had gone, Bart spoke up again. "Does anyone know where Gilmore and Jenny are today?"

No one knew. One of the students said, "They may have gone away for the weekend."

"Together?" Bart asked.

"Probably," Marty said. "They're always together."

"I see," Bart said, and was quiet. "I guess it's time for us to eat now."

Marty got Jesse aside and confided to him, "I heard Bart telling my Dad he was going to clean this town up. We better be careful."

"I guess so," Jesse agreed.

On Monday the students all met as usual in the cafeteria for lunch. There was news.

"Did you hear about Gilmore and Jenny?"

"No. What?"

"They got married at Lake Tahoe on Saturday."

"What?"

"Yeah, they just ran away and got hitched. I called Gilmore last night to see where he skipped out to, and that's what he told me."

"Wow!"

"We'll have to have a party for them."

"But that's not the end of the story. Bart showed up at Gilmore's apartment this morning and expelled both of them on the spot."

"No way!"

"He sure did."

"Why?"

"I guess he thought they were indulging in the L word or something."
"Was Jenny there?"
"Yeah. She slept with him last night."
"Bart probably thought they were fornicating."
"Too bad. They can't fornicate anymore!"
"Did Bart know they were married?"
"I don't know. Gilmore called me this morning and told me he had to stay with Jenny today because she was so upset."
"Is she pregnant, or something?"
"I don't know. No one said she is."
"So what if she is? They're married anyway."
"Can you get pregnant that fast?"
"Oh Janet, don't ask questions like that."
"I think we need to do something to cheer them up."
"Can we have dinner at a restaurant for them? No one has a place big enough for everyone."

It was decided they'd all meet at the Cantina Dos Gordos, and Marty undertook to make the reservation and get back to them all.

Everyone was generous in their congratulations. A lot of jokes were made about their elopement, and some were even made about how they'd dodged Bart to do so.

"Did he really expel you?"
"Yes, he did." The conversation got serious.
"Why?"
"He never said why. He just waited outside in the parking lot and came at us when we came out yesterday morning to go to class."
"I'll bet he thought you were fornicating."

Jenny blushed. Gilmore looked a bit sheepish, and said, "Well, he didn't accuse us of that, but he probably thought we were when he saw the two of us coming out of my apartment this morning. Bart doesn't ask a lot of questions."

"And he doesn't let you say very much either," Jenny said, a touch of anger in her voice.

"Does he think you're pregnant?"

"He never said. My father's going to call him today and see what made him so mad. I just thought he lost his mind. I've never seen a servant carry on like that."

"So does that mean you can't go to assembly now?" Amy was curious.

The Straight Way

"I guess so," Gilmore said. "He didn't really say all that much. He just said he was expelling us because we were just dirty spots on the carpet."

Jenny started to cry.

"I told you he was a mean man," Amy whispered to Jesse. "I feel so sorry for them."

"You have to tell us if your father accomplishes anything with him," Melissa said. "This is terrible. I'm going to call my parents when I go home and tell them what happened. This makes me really angry."

"You know what my parents have often said," Jesse offered. "They say the people who get expelled are probably closer to God than the people who expelled them."

"You'll just have to live with this," Janet advised. "Bart's a servant, and you shouldn't even dispute what he tells you to do."

"Oh Janet, you don't really believe that, do you?"

"I sure do."

"So do we just all go to hell if Bart doesn't let us go to assembly?"

"Don't talk so foolish."

"It's not foolish," Jenny said. "It's offensive. What can I do now?"

"Let's order dinner. And Jenny and Gilmore, you guys can still hang out with us no matter what Bart says."

"You guys are so kind," Gilmore said. "Thank you so much."

At that point Marty staggered in, towing a string of paper. "I'm sorry it took me so long," he said. "But I think I still have this banner in one piece. It unrolled on me when I tried to open the front door."

One of the waitresses showed up with some thumb tacks and helped them put the banner on the wall. It read, *Congratulations, Mr. and Mrs. Floyd Gilmore.*

The students met again in the SUB after the next Thursday evening assembly. That was so they could spend some time with Gilmore and Jenny.

Jesse and Amy were the last ones to arrive, and it was apparent that Amy had been crying.

"What's the matter, Amy?"

Amy couldn't answer.

"Bart took daggers to her after assembly," Jesse explained.

"Oh no! What did he do?"

"I was asking him if I could be baptized," Amy explained. "And he just laughed at me."

"That's rude."

"Did he say yes?"

"No, he told me I wasn't ready yet. He told me I hadn't demonstrated enough spiritual growth, and I felt so stupid because I didn't know what he was talking about. I asked him why he thought that, and he laughed again and told me he'd seen me going to class wearing pants."

"He's such a prude."

"Well he has to make sure people know what they're supposed to be doing," Janet reminded them.

"What does wearing pants have to do with spiritual growth?" Marty asked.

"The spirit will teach us that women shouldn't wear pants," Janet stated emphatically.

"We all wear pants to class," Melissa said.

"Oh no, we don't," Janet protested. "I never wear pants to class."

"I don't understand," Marty said. "How come Melissa can be baptized and wear pants to class and Amy can't?"

"Bart wasn't here when Melissa asked to be baptized."

"Can you unbaptized someone?" A few people laughed.

"No, but you can be expelled."

"I feel like I'm not getting anywhere," Amy said. "I just get comfortable and then something comes up that knocks me down somehow."

"It's Bart, Amy. Don't let him get you down."

"But I'm supposed to obey him and I never know what he wants. I don't want him yelling at me all the time."

"Just avoid him until he goes away."

"That's what I do."

"I just don't want to be the next person to get expelled."

"We'll go to bat for you," Marty said.

"Thank you," Amy said.

"So what did Bart tell your father, Jenny?"

"Nothing helpful," Jenny said.

"What did your father say about you two getting married?"

"The first thing he said was 'Are you pregnant?' I said 'No.' Then he said, 'Congratulations. Just stay in school.'"

"Good. But what did Bart tell him?"

"The first thing Bart said was that we had been fornicating. My Dad told him we were married, and Bart asked when we'd been married. Dad told him that we'd been married on the weekend. Bart wanted to know if Dad knew ahead of time that we were getting married and he said no. So then Bart went into this big long sermon about not getting married that way."

"What's his problem with your wedding?"

Gilmore explained. "According to Bart there are moral ways to get married and immoral ways. I was supposed to ask Jenny's father for permission to ask her to marry me, and then if she said yes we were supposed to talk to Bart about it. He said if we didn't keep to that order of things it made people think that we had to get married, and that made a shameful statement about the Way."

"Oh what a crock!"

"So now if you're married, is he going to unexpel you?"

"Oh no. He said that as long as it looked like we had to get married because we were fornicating we should not be permitted back."

"This is incredible. I can't believe it."

Janet was her usual straitlaced self. "Why did you run away and get married anyway?"

"I just figured my father didn't need the problem of getting my family together for a wedding," Jenny said. "My Dad and Mom are divorced, and my Mom doesn't want to have anything to do with him or any of his family at all. I didn't think it would be kind to put him through that kind of an exercise."

"Oh," Janet said. "That does make a bit of sense."

"Well, Bart doesn't think so. I really think he's just ticked off because we didn't ask his permission," Gilmore said.

"Are we supposed to get his permission to get married?" Amy asked.

There was a short chorus of *no*.

"But it doesn't hurt to ask," Janet said.

"Why ask?" Marty said.

"Because if you're not meant for each other the servants can tell you so."

"How would they know?" Marty asked.

"They know things we don't," Janet protested.

"Hey, I'm going to marry whoever I want and the servants can butt out, especially the ones like Bart. Babbling Bart."

A few people laughed, and Janet protested.

But the dinner was fun. And Amy liked their company.

CHAPTER 13

Nathan studied the view from Clay's window. "It's going to rain."

"Who cares?" Clay replied, without looking up.

Nathan turned to him. "You've scratched your head. This indicates a deep matter indeed."

Clay dropped his papers and looked up, laughed, and relaxed.

"So how's your molestation case going?"

"Difficult," Clay said. "No wonder molestation cases are so hard to prosecute. I've decided they're equally hard to defend."

"Does he have a defense?"

"Nothing I can get a grip on."

"So he has to have done something."

"Oh yes," Clay said. "But I can't really get his side of the story. He's playing dodge ball with me."

"That's an integral part of a child molester's *modus operandi*, isn't it?"

"Whoever said that is right on target. This guy! I don't know what to think of him. He comes across as really cooperative much of the time, but he has these lapses into nervous chatter. I certainly don't want the prosecutor examining him."

"Is he schizophrenic or anything?"

"He has a very uneventful psych profile. The only notable mention is that he has great concern for spiritual matters. There's no history of mental disease. He has no criminal record."

"What do you think?" Nathan was interested.

This is crazy, but I get a sense that he's using this situation for something. Deep down he's seriously angry and can't speak about it. Alice is doing some research on these kinds of guys for me." Alice was Clay's paralegal. "I'm trying to understand the guy, but he won't communicate. Denial, denial. And evasion and evasion."

"And here we are spending our lives in the pursuit of the truth."

"A fine selection of terminology," Clay smiled. "Everyone wants the truth until it comes to the whole truth and nothing but the truth."

"I know your devotion to this group," Nathan said. "I hope you're getting paid."

"Yes. I have no concern in that respect."

"I was afraid you'd take the case pro bono. I hope this man realizes how fortunate he is to get this kind of support from such a small group. I read in the paper that he's out on a half million dollars bail."

"Yes, half a million. The judge considers him a flight risk. Actually he was sent away by his superior in an effort to hide him and it didn't work."

"Never works, does it?" Nathan commented. "Anyway, good luck."

"Thanks."

Nathan was quizzing Clay because he knew Clay had been in Espadín the day before. And Clay had a frustrating time with Howard.

"Now what about Maria Castro?" Clay asked Howard. "She says you got her to take her panties off on the street."

Howard looked shocked. "On the street? I'd have been arrested."

"What were you doing on the street with Maria?"

"I met her at school and walked home with her. Ana appreciated that because she wasn't free to go home from school as soon as Maria was." Ana was Maria's mother, and a teacher at Maria's school. "Usually by the time we got to her house, Ana would be there."

"Did you make any stops along the way?"

"A couple of times she stopped to play hopscotch on the Zócalo. Then we'd go on."

"Did she go into the restroom there?"

"No."

"Tell me why a woman could find a little girl's panties on her lawn."

"Maria was always throwing things away. I even told her once that she might get arrested for littering, and she just laughed. She may be spoiled, you know, such a pretty little thing."

"Did you ever see her throwing panties away?"

"I got so I never paid any attention to what she was throwing away. She could have done that."

Clay paused. Howard slowly rolled his thumbs over each other.

Then there were the allegations that he had molested Sally Fitch. "Tell me what happened with Sally Fitch," Clay suggested.

"I was sleeping in a bedroom at the Fitches house, and she had the bedroom next to mine. There's a door between the two rooms."

"So you went to her room after everyone was asleep?"
"No, she called me over to help her."
"So you did go into her room at night."
Howard looked blank for an instant, then said, "I did."
"What did she need help with?"
"She'd had a nightmare and couldn't settle down. I talked to her for a while and she soon went back to sleep."
"What can we tell the court to convince them that was the case?"
Howard thought for a while. "I don't know. It never crossed my mind that it would turn out like this."
Clay looked in Howard's eyes. "Did you tell her parents about the nightmare?"
"No." He faltered. "Well, yes I did. I told them in the morning that I thought I heard her crying. And when no one else came, I opened the door to help her. They thanked me for helping her."
Then, of course, there was Jason Gomez. Like Ana Castro, Jason's mother, Lidia, was a single mother. Unlike Ana, who had Maria as an unwed mother, Lidia had been married at the time of Jason's birth. Her husband just disappeared one day and had never been heard from since.
Clay began. "Tell me what happened in the garage with Jason Gomez."
"In the garage, right?"
"Yes."
Howard thought. "Well, Jason has half the garage for himself, so all his play things were out there. He always wanted me to go out and play with him, so I did. I thought it would be good for him to have a kind of surrogate father figure." He smiled. "As it turned out, he had a lot of parts for an electric train set, and I have this love of trains. So I spent a lot of time putting together an elaborate railroad system there. He was elated with it."
"What was the secret corner in the garage?"
That startled Howard.
"The claim is that you took him into the secret corner and molested him there," Clay explained.
"That must be …. Oh yes. I do remember the secret corner."
"What went on there?"
Howard tried to snicker. "There was a place in the corner of the garage where Jason told me he kept his secret things from his school friends."
"Did he show you into it?"

"Yes. He told me I was able to see it." He thought for a while, then added, "The place smelled just a bit of urine. I asked him why, and he said his best friend from school used to go in there and pee. He said that one time his friend went in there and took out his penis while Jason watched. I guess the idea was that he'd show it to Jason in there in case Lidia came out and caught them."

Clay wrote on his pad: *Neighbor kids not allowed in secret room – but kid showed Jason his penis there.???*

Then Clay asked, "What happened with Joey Patten?"

Howard was quiet a long time, so Clay prompted him to respond. "What did you do with Joey?"

"He had a ...." He paused. "I was sleeping in the spare single bed in his room. He got up a couple of times to go to the bathroom. Then he got up once and when he opened the door he banged his head badly on the door frame. He fell down on the floor, so I got up to see if he was okay. Then we discovered that in the commotion he'd wet his pajamas because he hadn't made it to the bathroom."

Clay made some notes while Howard paused.

"We had to get dry pajamas from his closet. He changed in front of me, and felt a bit embarrassed." There was a pause. "You know, Americans are much less casual about things like that than Europeans are."

"Aren't the British supposed to be conservative?"

"Not since the Americans decided they were going to be the conservative ones."

He's clever enough when he wants to be, Clay thought. "Can you tell me how urine got on the bed sheets? Surely he didn't wear the wet pajamas back to bed."

"Really?" Howard was surprised. "Yes. Now I remember. He didn't want to go to the bathroom to put them in the dirty clothes basket. I thought he just put them on the floor, but they were in his bed when he left for school the next morning. He must have put them there."

"Did this happen more than once?"

"Yes. A couple of times. He's a really nervous child. I think his father's outrageously severe with him. That's probably what makes him so nervous. He's scared of absolutely everything he sees. I became really afraid to be staying there so much because, well, this is what happens when you leave yourself open to these kinds of accusations. You can't prove you didn't do something wrong."

"Did you touch him?"

There was a pause. "Yes, I guess I did. I helped him off with his pajamas, so, yes, I would have touched him."

"Did you touch his privates or his buttocks?"

"I don't think so. All we had was a night light, so I couldn't see that well."

They continued on to talk about Adam Sawyer, or Spike, as Adam insisted he be called.

"I did not molest him." Howard was emphatic.

"The claim is that you performed fellatio on him."

"No, no, no," Howard protested. "That's where everything went wrong." He stopped abruptly.

Clay waited.

"In fact, he raped me," Howard said.

Clay continued calmly. "Tell me what happened."

"He held my head and penetrated my mouth."

"Did you protest?"

"No. He said if I didn't let him do it he'd call the police. I know, everyone knows, he's a really bad kid. I shouldn't have gone anywhere with him. What could I do? Can you imagine the scandal if he were to call the police and tell them what he did?"

"That's where we are right now," Clay said, looking Howard in the eye.

Howard didn't respond.

Clay concluded Howard was having difficulty understanding that the public wasn't going to be sympathetic to him. Throughout the interview, Clay watched Howard's eyes, and they remained steady. Either Howard was innocent and was framed, or he was a most accomplished liar – in any case, accomplished at circumvention.

On impulse, Clay asked him, "Did you molest children in Iowa and Colorado?"

Howard blinked, and gulped. "No."

"You'll have to excuse me, Howard. We don't want anyone in the court surprising us by bringing out any skeletons from your closet."

"We can't have that, can we?" Howard smiled. "You know, I'm quite sure now that it must have been Spike who called the police on me. The other parents in Espadín all complain because he's such a wild kid. I suppose he has these strange fantasies and thinks all the other kids are like him."

Clay listened, but didn't respond. Howard continued to offer explanations while Clay made some notes. *You're talking a lot but you're not answering questions well,* Clay thought.

Clay was meditative on the plane back to Los Angeles. He was feeling the pressure of his professionalism not to tell Nancy all about the case. He and Nancy always shared what they knew about the servants. They could joke between themselves about them like they could never do with the other Way friends. It's because no one dares to admit they recognize anything uncomplimentary about a servant, Clay guessed. There was very little comic relief to be had with Nancy these days at the expense of the servants, especially Howard.

Of course, everyone would acknowledge that the servants aren't perfect. *So how come no one can tell the real reason why some of them get sent packing?* Clay wondered. He pondered, again, as he often did, how so many of the Way friends could actually give the impression that they believed none of the servants ever did anything wrong. *Surely, they've heard about old Anthony!* he thought. Anthony was a servant who had been banished from the Way when it was found that he'd gotten three high school girls pregnant. Can they really think, just because no one ever reported anything to the police that no one knows what happened?

By the time his plane landed at LAX he'd settled on what exactly he'd tell Nancy this time. He'd say, *Children should never be left alone with a servant.* It wasn't profound, but stated with the right tone of voice she'd know exactly what he meant. And he wouldn't mind if she quoted him to other Way friends.

Then he thought of Nathan. This is really weird. I can say what I want about the servants to him, but I can't tell Nancy.

Midway through the afternoon a few days later Clay's telephone rang, and it was Nancy. "Can you be home for dinner for six o'clock?"

"I guess so. Is it urgent?"

"Chester wants dinner at six o'clock."

"Chester wants dinner!" Clay laughed. "He liked your cooking so much he wants to come back so soon."

"I guess so. I wasn't planning to have dinner until seven, but he suggested six, so I guess I can handle that. I'll get a chicken when I pick up Dennis from school."

"In that case, I'll be sure not to be late for dinner," Clay assured her. "It's Friday anyway."

When Clay arrived home by 5:30, Chester was already there. He was in the living room talking to Dennis.

"Welcome," Clay said.

"Thank you," Chester replied. "Dennis is a charming host."

"Thank you. Maybe I'll see if there's anything I can help Nancy with in the kitchen."

"Sure."

In the kitchen they listened to the conversation in the living room.

"So have you started going to your new school yet?" Chester asked.

"Not yet," Dennis said. "I won't start there until the sixth grade."

"I see."

"That's not until August," Dennis explained.

"So you're in the fifth grade now."

"Yeah. But I don't like the fifth grade anymore. It's kind of boring."

"Really?"

"Yeah. We don't do enough Math or Recess. I like them the best."

Chester laughed.

When Nancy called them all to dinner, Chester turned the conversation to his gospel services. "I've been having some very good interest in my gospel services. There's been quite a number of strangers who've come to them."

"That's nice," Nancy commented.

"How much is quite a number?" Dennis asked.

"Five or six," Chester said. "That's very good for these times."

"I'm going to be in town on Sunday evening, so I'm planning on going to your gospel service," Nancy said.

"That'll be good," Chester said. "Will you be able to bring your friend, Nancy?"

"I haven't had a chance to invite her yet," she explained.

"You haven't seen her?" Chester asked.

"Well, I've seen her, but I haven't had an opportunity to invite her."

"We should take full advantage of all our opportunities while we have them," Chester said. "Time is passing, and people's souls are at stake."

Clay watched Nancy, but she didn't look up when responding to Chester. Clay said, "Nancy didn't have the opportunity yet."

"Oh," Chester replied. "I thought she said she'd seen her."

Nancy glanced at Clay, then said, "Yes, I saw her, but I wasn't talking to her."

"She'd probably appreciate your asking her," Chester said.

Nancy didn't reply.

Chester continued. "I've been waiting for you to come to my gospel services. I haven't seen you yet, except for the first Sunday."

"We have a very busy lifestyle," Clay apologized.

"Yes, before we know it our lives will all be over and we'll realize how many important things we've neglected."

"Neglected?" Clay asked.

"Well, yes. We put our lifestyles ahead of the Way, when actually the Way is more deserving of our time, for our own benefit."

"Are you prone to that too?" Clay queried.

That startled Chester. "Well, probably I do," he smiled.

"We'll have to work on that, won't we?" Clay said.

Nancy promptly got up and went to the kitchen for something.

Chester waited until she returned, then said, "I was glad to see when I came to your assembly last night that you were there."

"We always go to assembly," Clay assured him.

"So your bishop has told me," Chester agreed. "I was particularly looking for you at the gospel service on Wednesday evening."

"I was out of town," Clay explained.

"It would have been nice if Nancy could have been there."

"Why Nancy?" Clay asked.

"Well, she'd have taken Dennis with her, and he needs to hear the gospel," Chester explained.

"I don't drive to Inglewood alone at night," Nancy said.

Chester didn't reply.

"Actually, Chester, that's not the only reason Nancy wasn't there on Wednesday evening. She went out to a meeting of the Parent Teacher Association at César Chávez."

"Oh," Chester said.

Nancy was visibly nervous. *Don't worry, dear*, Clay thought. *I'll take care of him.*

"Is César Chávez in a good area of town?" Chester was looking directly at Nancy.

"Chester," Clay said. "If Nancy had not gone to the Parent Teacher meeting she'd have been at home making sure Dennis had his homework done and got to bed at a decent time."

Chester didn't respond. For a while he savored his food, then spoke again. "How are things going with Howard's case?"

"We're working on it."

"It's unfortunate that we have to deal with such matters," Chester said.

"Yes, it is," Clay agreed. "But it's a common enough crime."

"Really? Do you get a lot of these kinds of cases?"

"No, I don't."

"It'll be good for him to be found not guilty," Chester said.

"Do you suppose he will?" Clay asked.

"Well, what do you think?" Chester asked.

"I'm not sure I should comment."

"Well, he's in good hands."

"Thank you," Clay said.

"It's unfortunate that innocent people have to pay so much to defend themselves."

"That's a refreshing understanding of the justice system."

"Why do you say so?" Chester asked.

"The most common complaint is that money can buy an acquittal."

"Maybe the righteous will prevail this time," Chester smiled.

When dessert was finished, Nancy asked Dennis to go and get his homework. "I'll clean the table for you," she said.

"It would be nice for Dennis to visit with us for a while," Chester suggested.

"I think he'd better do his homework," Clay insisted.

"Does he have school tomorrow?" Chester asked.

"No," Clay said.

There was a long pause. Then Chester asked, "Couldn't he do his homework tomorrow?"

"We have other plans for tomorrow," Clay said, and smiled to himself. *I wonder if he'll ask what we have planned for tomorrow.*

But Chester didn't ask.

When they settled in the living room, Chester asked, "Do you have any questions for me?"

"Questions?" Clay asked.

"Yes. About spiritual matters, of course."

"I don't have any at the moment," Clay said.

"What have your meditations been about today?" Chester asked.

"I've been trying to figure out how to defend Howard in court."

Chester sighed. He visited but contented himself with small talk for another hour, and then decided to leave.

"Poor Chester thought I was going to talk about Howard," Clay said when Chester was gone.

"I'm weary," Nancy said.

"I'm tired. He asks too many questions. I'm going to bed."

Nancy burst out laughing. "'Are you prone to that too?' I can't believe you asked him that."

"It was fun, wasn't it?"

Clay fell soundly asleep right away. But when Nancy came to bed she thought about Chester's visit for a long time before she went to sleep. I worry too much, she thought.

CHAPTER 14

Finally Howard's trial was less than a week away. Clay admitted to Nathan that he was more anxious about this trial than he'd been about the Chen trial.

A couple of times Clay had encouraged Howard to reevaluate his not guilty plea, but Howard remained insistent. It was especially frustrating that Howard's explanations for all the incidents were either flimsy or nonexistent. For that reason Clay was relieved that he didn't have to convince Howard not testify in his own defense. In fact, he was relieved that Howard seemed not to expect any convincing defense at all.

"I can't make you plead guilty," Clay told him.

"Thank you," Howard said. And he seemed satisfied with that.

Floyd Toner, on the other hand, was quite anxious to speak on Howard's behalf. Clay had tutored him on the questions he'd ask him in court, and the kinds of questions the prosecutor would ask him on cross examination. But Clay was in a quandary – he had not explained unambiguously to Floyd why he was going to let him testify.

Clay's intention was to show that the style of ministry in the Way made servants vulnerable to any kind of serious accusation. He was sure Floyd didn't understand that. He agonized about using Floyd's testimony in a way Floyd would not appreciate, but he reasoned that he could leave it to the prosecutor to interpret Floyd's testimony any way he wanted.

The most frustrating thing about Floyd was his apparent inability to separate what was legally factual from what would be necessary, in his mind, to protect the ministry from shame. The rumor throughout California was that everything would to go well for Howard in court, and that calmed the fears of most people in the Way. Rumor also had it that Floyd was very proud of the manner in which the Way friends in Del Rio County had set aside their differences and pulled together for the good of the Way. Some people had even begun to speak about the trial as an occasion for non-believers to be impressed with the integrity of people in the Way. But none of that encouraged Clay.

A number of people had expressed an interest in attending the trial, but Bart had advised them that wouldn't be necessary. The thought had crossed Clay's mind that Floyd might be just shrewd enough to keep the Way friends from hearing all the dirt that was going to be pulled out from under the carpet.

Wednesday night after dinner Nancy said, "I have something to tell you."

"What is it?"

"I have it from a credible source that Uncle Floyd's been tutoring the kids in Espadín on what to say in court next week."

"Where did you get this information?" Clay asked.

"A little birdie told me," Nancy smiled. "I'm afraid if I told you either you or I or the little birdie'd be in trouble."

Clay laughed, then sobered. He knew the little birdie was Nancy's cousin Yvonne in Santa Rosa. "Thank you for that information," he said. "I need to know that."

When Nancy went off to help Dennis with his homework, Clay called Floyd in Espadín. "Uncle Floyd," he said. "Something has come up and I need to talk to you about it."

They agreed to meet at the Watermans' house on Friday morning. It was a good place for them to meet, because the house had a comfortable den where Clay and either Floyd or Howard could close the door and have privacy. Marge Waterman catered to them, but otherwise didn't disturb them.

When Clay announced he was going to leave earlier than planned for the trial, Nancy immediately asked if she could have the weekend with Yvonne.

Aha, Clay thought. I knew it!

"Goodie," Dennis said. "I can play with all the kids all the time I'm there."

If the truth were known, few in Espadín cared for what had been rumored throughout the state about them. Bart had told them not to gossip, of course, but there seemed to be no clear sense of when information about someone changed from news to rumor to gossip. So quietly, everything became known among them.

In any case, the standard etiquette on sharing news was meaningless in the present situation. Everyone knew the purpose of suppressing discussion was to shelter guilty persons from embarrassing exposure and scandal. But this time the scandal couldn't be kept under the carpet – it was all in the newspapers. That had never happened to them before. Furthermore, parents had become horrified at the magnitude of their discovery.

As expected in a crisis, Floyd Toner was in town soon after Howard's arrest to conduct his own investigation. The first person he visited was Aggie Cutter, but no one ever heard what was said during that visit.

Floyd's second visit was to Maggie Price, and as with Aggie, he had Bart present as his witness. Maggie had the reputation of never gossiping about anyone, so no one even bothered asking her about the visit.

The next visit was to George Patten, Joey's father. George was a very highly respected member of the Way. Someone once mentioned that George's great grandfather was the first person in that family to confess, and the family had gained the reputation of being old faithful among the Way friends. George had three cousins who had gone into the service, and one of them was sent to a foreign country to preach.

When George learned Floyd was in town, he immediately called him and told him he wanted to talk to him. Floyd set a dinner appointment with him and his family for a Wednesday evening. Bart went along.

Conversation around the table was quiet and polite. They discussed news from George's three servant cousins. Floyd quoted a verse from the Bible that he'd been meditating on, and he expounded on it while everyone else listened and watched him attentively.

When dinner was over the men and Joey retired to the living room while George's wife, Marian, cleared the table. When she finished she joined the men and George introduced his concern. "I think this is a tragedy, one of the servants being prosecuted in court."

"Yes," Floyd said. "This'll reflect badly on our whole ministry."

"Is it proper for a Christian to take a servant to court?"

"According to the Scriptures it isn't. But you know, sometimes we have people among us who don't follow the Scriptures on all points."

"Yes. I suppose so. My real concern is what to do if this case goes to trial. You see, Joey's been telling things to his mother that he shouldn't be mentioning. I've tried to correct him, but you know how children are. They lapse and forget easily. I was wondering what I should be doing to prepare him for court, if it comes to that."

Joey sat poker stiff and silently on a chair beside his father.

"I'm sorry to hear he's doing that." Floyd pondered his answer. "I suppose he should tell the truth, or it might look bad for Howard. I'd hate to hear of him saying anything too disrespectful of Howard. We have to keep as much of the negative out of the newspapers as possible. And our poor dear friends here in Espadín won't want to be shunned by the town's people. A terrible thing for our testimony to the world!"

"I told Joey he shouldn't be telling his mother all these things he thinks Howard's done to him. I've continually told him he can't talk that way about the servants. But he's been telling his mother all kinds of nasty things."

"Children are like that with their mothers," Floyd agreed. "And you know, it's a most difficult thing to get the mothers to stop spoiling the children in that respect. You've given him good advice."

George turned to Joey. "Now you remember what Uncle Floyd has said, okay." He turned back to Floyd and said, "Yes, Uncle Floyd, I have the same concern as you. We need to be sure the Way is properly represented in court. We know this is a great occasion for Satan to turn people away from the Way."

"That's true, and we have to do what we can to prevent that from happening. But who knows? This may be a privilege in disguise. It's entirely possible that someone in the town will be drawn by the spirit of the Way friends through this experience. God works in mysterious ways, you know."

"Joey, you hear all that?" George asked.

"Yes, I do," Joey squeaked.

"In fact," George said. "I'll be sure to be in court with him if he has to go, to be able to help him with his testimony. You know that children tend to get confused and tell things that aren't true. I've been trying to teach Joey not to do that, but he falls back sometimes."

Joey cast George a frightened and embarrassed look.

Floyd said to Joey, "Your father's a very godly man. I fully recommend that you take his advice. We have to live godly lives, no matter who disagrees. If people give us a bad time, we just have to remember that God knows the good we've done, and He'll remember that."

When the visit ended, George was satisfied he'd received the spiritual support he needed. Like everyone else in town, he'd heard the rumor that Howard wasn't going to plead guilty, and that was going to force the county to hold a trial.

Floyd was generally pleased with the response he was getting from everyone in Espadín. But he wasn't prepared for the conversation he was to have with Herb and Sharon Fitch.

When Floyd and Bart visited the Fitches, Floyd began. "We're here today to talk about the trial of Howard, seeing that he refuses to confess to anything."

Herb responded quickly. "Are you going to tell us what to say if we end up in court?"

"Well, no, Herb. But I do want to remind you how Christians should treat one another. It's just not appropriate for a Christian to take his brother to the law."

"Howard's brethren aren't taking him to the law," Herb explained. "Howard committed serious crimes, and the state is charging him with those crimes, not his Christian brothers. This isn't a civil matter of people suing one another in court"

Floyd thought a minute. "I see. Interesting. I didn't know it worked that way." He thought a while more. "Then there's no danger that the children will have to accuse him in court."

Herb didn't know what to say. "I don't understand."

"Well, if the state is going to prosecute him, maybe none of God's people will need to be in court."

"Not really. The prosecutor will subpoena any person he thinks he needs to prove the charges against Howard. And the victims are more likely to be subpoenaed than anyone else."

"But they're just children. Can they make them testify without their parents' consent?"

"I'm afraid they can."

"What would happen if they just didn't appear in court?"

"Then I'd worry that the judge would issue a warrant for someone's arrest. Either the child or the parents."

Bart looked like he wanted to have his part in the conversation, but he let Floyd continue.

Floyd sighed. "This is going to be very difficult. I'd hate to see one of the children exposing Howard to the court."

"What would you most like to see at this point?" Herb asked.

"I don't know. We should probably just tell our children not to tell anything about Howard and get it over with."

"It's too late now for that. Anyway, the kids will be cross questioned to find flaws in what they say."

"That shouldn't be a problem," Floyd assured him. "We have Clay Shipman to defend him."

"The Clay Shipman we know in L.A.?"

"Yes. He's a very good lawyer, and I think he'll do what is right for us."

"I've met him at retreats," Herb said. "And he's been in the news a lot recently."

"Ah," Floyd said. "You've read about him in the newspapers. Well, for now we're very fortunate to have him. We'll do what we can to help him."

"Floyd, I'm still concerned that you appear to be trying to manipulate the trial, if it happens."

"Now Herb, you must remember that anything Howard did to your children is far less damaging than the court proceedings will be."

"Aren't you putting the reputation of your ministry ahead of the safety of my child? Do you know what that man is supposed to have done to the children?"

"No, but it was probably the usual. Kids quickly forget things like this."

There was a long silence. Sharon had begun to sob quietly in a tissue.

Finally Herb spoke. "Floyd, you don't have proper respect for the innocence of my daughter. Furthermore, you're really trying to manipulate witnesses. That's a crime, and you could be prosecuted for that. You could also be prosecuted for not going to the police when you heard what Howard had done. Clergymen are required by law to report every suspected child molestation they learn about, you know. You need to think about that." After a short pause, he said, "I'm not even sure it's proper for us to be having this conversation at this time. We should wait till the trial's over."

Floyd was visibly shaken. He turned to Bart and said in a very low voice, "I think maybe we should go."

Bart nodded in agreement and stood up. They exchanged handshakes. Floyd said, "You folks have a good day. It was nice meeting you." And they were gone.

Sharon said to Herb, "This is really disgusting."

"I'm glad it's the justice system that's going to sort this out."

"They'll excuse a servant's felony crimes but expel a college student who gets married without their permission."

"Straining at a gnat and swallowing a camel."

On the surface, everything looked normal still in Espadín. The Way friends had continued their assemblies at the Watermans' house. It had been decided that, to disrupt fewer people's routines, Howard would leave the Watermans' house on Thursday evenings and stay at the studio until everyone had left the meeting place.

As anticipated, Floyd had arrived back in town for the trial. Also, it didn't go unnoticed that Friday morning that Clay was in town. Ironically, the Way friends in Espadín weren't telling anyone that Howard's attorney, the recently famous Clayton Shipman from L.A., was one of them. They weren't sure they wanted the rest of the town to know it was one of them who had defended a man of Mr. Chen's reputation. They did speculate about who was paying Clay, if indeed he was getting paid.

When Clay arrived at the Watermans' house, he was surprised that Mark Volpe was there with Floyd. Mark was a high ranking servant, in his sixties, and frequently rumored to be heir to Floyd's position.

"Uncle Floyd," Clay began. "Something concerns me greatly. I've been told that you've been exerting pressure on the prosecution's witnesses, asking them not to tell all they know about the case." He waited for Floyd to answer.

"You mean the parents of those children?" Floyd asked.

Clay nodded yes.

"I don't know who would tell you that. I told the children to tell the truth."

"What exactly did you tell these people?"

"I encouraged them to tell the truth, of course." He thought for a minute. "Wasn't that okay?"

"Can you tell me the exact words you used with any of them?"

Floyd looked puzzled. "I just told them to tell the truth?"

Clay reworded the question. "What else could you have said to them? This is extremely important, and I have to know about it."

Floyd thought a minute. Mark studied both Floyd and Clay. Then Floyd said, "I expect I told them not to say anything that would bring dishonor on the Way and the servants."

"That's what worries me," Clay said.

"Is there something wrong with that? Our first duty is to uphold our standards, you know."

"How many of them did you give this advice to?"

"I told all of them that. What were there, five of them?"

Clay felt himself cringe. "Uncle Floyd, I need to explain something to you. This matter of telling the truth, I'm afraid you and I have been interpreting it differently."

Mark showed concern. Floyd said, "How can that be? The truth is the truth."

"Yes, Uncle Floyd, you're right," Clay agreed, then proceeded slowly. "But right now what is going to bring dishonor to the Way and the servants is also the truth."

A frown fluttered across Floyd's forehead.

Clay continued. "The highest authority in settling matters in this country is the court system, not God, and the courts and judges are only free to do as they see fit within the limits of the law. They can't set the law aside because it condemns one of us. They can be removed if they do."

Floyd struggled to understand. Clay waited.

Then Floyd said, "You mean that this judge isn't going to respect the Word of God?"

"He's required to obey the law first. He's taken an oath to that effect."

"Oh. That's strange."

Clay waited to let him absorb what he'd explained to him.

"I thought this country's motto was *In God We Trust*."

"That's what they say, isn't it. I think the expression *In God We Trust* is used as loosely as the word Christian. It doesn't necessarily represent our understanding of either God or Christian."

"Oh." Floyd sat with his head back and thought a while. Then abruptly he said, "What a godless world we live in!"

Mark spoke for the first time. "That must be why everyone calls lawyers liars," he chuckled.

Clay smiled, but didn't acknowledge the comment.

Floyd looked at Mark and pointed to Clay. "Don't forget this man's a lawyer."

Mark lost his smile immediately.

At that point Clay decided he'd definitely not have Floyd testify in court. He'd never let himself believe with any certainty that he could have Howard acquitted, and he now concluded that Floyd would be no help to his effort.

Before he informed Floyd of his decision, he decided there was one final test he needed to make. "Uncle Floyd," he began. "I know you're not familiar with the court system. The questioning and cross questioning can be a lot more brutal than one expects. Do you really think you're up to testifying in this trial?"

Floyd took the bait. "I do. I might be far over the hill, but my love for the gospel and truth is more fervent than at any other time in my life."

Abruptly Clay asked, "What would you tell the court if they asked you about the children Howard molested in Iowa and Colorado?"

"I wouldn't say anything." Then the shock registered on his face, and he said, "No one ever said he was molesting children there."

"But you knew it anyway, didn't you?"

It startled Floyd. "That's long in the past now. We've forgiven him for that."

"But I asked you if you knew about it anyway."

"I wasn't told he had molested children. I was told that he spent far too much time with children."

The room was silent. Mark was embarrassed. Floyd was flustered.

"Uncle Floyd," Clay began again. "I'm not going to have you testify in this trial."

"You aren't? Why not?"

"The main reason is that you've been discussing this matter with the victims. In court we call that tampering with the witnesses. It's a crime, and people have been given hefty fines for that."

"Oh."

"There's a reason for that. It's to prevent witnesses from knowing more than their own personal involvement in the case."

"Really?"

"It's critically important because every witness has to swear to tell the truth, the whole truth, and nothing but the truth. No lying or hiding secrets in court."

"I know."

Clay was going to address the whole truth and nothing but the truth topics, but decided against it. He didn't want to offend Floyd any more than necessary. He explained, "In a criminal trial, each side in a case has to be diligent to keep the other side from covering up anything that could relate to the full truth."

"All our friends, are we not all on the same side?"

"No, Uncle Floyd. Not this time."

"Satan has succeeded in dividing God's people again." Floyd shook his head. "Sometimes I think I've lived too long,"

"I'm sorry," Clay said. "I expect you're disappointed."

"We're paying you to present our side of the story in court."

"No, Uncle Floyd. You're paying me to present as honest a defense as I can for Howard, and that includes telling the truth – not skirting around the facts, but telling the whole truth and nothing but the truth. That's the only honorable approach to use."

"Oh," Floyd responded.

"Let me explain what just happened between you and me. I succeeded in having you tell me that Howard has a past. You didn't plan to let me know about that, but I got it out of you. If you were testifying in court the prosecutor would be a lot more brutal than I've been. I don't think you're up to that kind of grilling."

There was a long period of silence.

"Uncle Floyd," Mark interrupted. "He may be right."

"Yes," Floyd consented, "maybe so.

There wasn't anything else to discuss, so they made small talk for another half hour. The conversation was mostly between Mark and Clay, with a few comments from Floyd. Floyd fretted to himself under his breath much of the time, and Mark and Clay exchanged amused glances about it.

As Clay was leaving, he heard Floyd say to Mark, "I think we'd better give Victor a call."

If anyone expected the last weekend before the trial to be nothing more than anxious waiting, they were mistaken. The whispering continued.

"What a terrible thing to have a servant on trial! Shameful, shameful! Someone should be required to pay for causing all this."

"Can you imagine what our neighbors will think of the Way? We've worked all our lives to make a good impression, and now this!"

"I hope this doesn't do poor old Uncle Floyd in. He's so old and feeble, and we need him. I can't imagine the Way without him."

"They go easy on ministers, I'd expect. And if we go there to show our support for him, they'll see that."

"Howard's such an encouraging preacher and spirit filled man. What a shame!"

"Who called the police anyway?"

"It's too late to do anything. Satan has him in the hands of the justice system now."

"Who's paying for this trial anyway?"

"I'd expect some rich Way friend is donating the money to the service."

"I think the servants have a huge stash of money somewhere."

"Howard could have a public defender for free."

"He should have just pleaded guilty and left the rest of us alone. Now all of us will have to endure the shameful publicity of a trial."

"Gossip is just flying around this town, and they'll be blaming all this on the Way."

"Some of you people make me really groan. Who's the victim here, Howard or the innocent kids?"

"You shouldn't be so ready to talk that way about a servant."

"I heard some women in the supermarket talking about this."

"Are you not praying that God will save the Way from this thing? There'd be no truth in the world if everyone got scared away from the Way."

"You know, God might do the right thing on His own."

There were also letters to the editor of the Espadín Town Crier. Most of the writers were outraged at what was happening in their cozy community.

"What is this man doing walking through our streets?"

"What kind of cult is he working for?"

"This is not the kind of town where we want a child rapist running free."

"The man should be locked up and tortured for as long as he lives."

"Is there not some legal way to get these people out of Espadín?"

"Espadín to become another Waco."

"People in this town have to take better care of their kids. I see little kids coming home from school and just opening their unlocked doors to get in the house. It's a sure way to attract predators to molest their kids."

"How are the rest of us to know that these people are not molesting their own children just like their pastor is doing?"

All the excitement surrounding Howard's case was punctuated for Amy and Jesse with a visit from Bart. He said he especially wanted to meet with Amy, so they met at Jesse's apartment. As usual, Bart had his witness with him, but this time it was Floyd instead of Scott.

Fear rose in Jesse as he let these two powerful people into his apartment. He was sure they were going to be reprimanded.

"We're here to discuss Amy," Bart began.

Amy turned red, but remained calm.

"We'd like you not to participate yet in assemblies."

"Okay," Amy agreed. "Is there some reason why I shouldn't?"

"We just notice that the spirit hasn't moved you sufficiently to make it look good for the Way if you were to participate in the assemblies."

"How do you mean?"

"It'll be revealed to you in good time."

Amy had no idea what he meant. She wanted to ask Jesse, but she could wait until after they left.

Bart continued. "I'm not all that comfortable discussing outward appearance with young ladies, but maybe Jesse could help you in that respect. I know his mother well, and she's a very godly woman. For sure she's been a good example for Jesse."

As they were leaving, Amy said, "Thank you. I'll do my best." Both Bart and Floyd appeared pleased with her remark.

When they were gone, Amy asked, "What was that all about?"

Jesse was embarrassed, she could tell.

"What are they talking about? How would they know whether some spirit had moved me or not?"

"I think I can explain," Jesse said. "They probably don't like your hair in braids."

"So why didn't they tell me that?"

"I think they're both a bit weird. They're so old they're nervous about so many petty things."

"So if I don't braid my hair it'll be okay?"

"They'd like that, I'm sure." He paused. "They'd consider it a sign that the Holy Spirit has been working in you. I think it says somewhere in the Bible not to braid your hair."

"I don't get this at all, but I'll work at it."

"You're okay," Jesse assured her. "You'll find that there are some really weird people in the Way. I just avoid them if I can."

"I guess every religion has their share."

What no one expected that weekend was the demonstration that erupted in front of the Watermans' house on the Sunday evening before Howard's trial was to begin. Someone in a motor home parked across the street and displayed a banner that read: *You are harboring a child predator.*

Several people arrived carrying placards reading *Child molesters are not welcome in Espadín*, and *Take your cult and leave*. It was all peaceful, and the demonstrators confined themselves to the sidewalk.

Marge noticed them first, and she called Carl to see them. They were startled, and not just a bit embarrassed that they'd been selected for such a demonstration in their quiet neighborhood. Howard came out from his room and found what they were looking at.

"Just draw the curtains," Marge said. "You don't need to see this."

"Don't worry about me," Howard said. "I'm going to call the police."

"Oh no," Carl said. "We don't want the police to be involved."

"We don't need to be subjected to this," Howard said, and he went straight to the telephone to call the police.

It was only a matter of a few minutes until a police car arrived. By then a couple of the Watermans' neighbors were out on the sidewalk arguing heatedly with the demonstrators.

"These are fine people. Take your demonstration somewhere else and leave us alone," one of the neighbors was yelling. Shortly there were fists flying, and one of the demonstrators fell flat on the sidewalk. The other demonstrators turned all their attention to the neighbor who'd knocked their fellow demonstrator down, and were only restrained when the policeman turned on his flashing lights as he pulled to a stop beside them.

About that time the Town Crier's main reporter showed up with notepad and pen in hand.

A second police car arrived, and the officers engaged themselves in heated discussions with everyone on the sidewalk.

Eventually the Watermans' neighbor friend was handcuffed, put in the back seat of one of the police cars and taken away. The demonstrators remained on the sidewalk. The driver of the motor home went and sat in his vehicle, but didn't leave.

One of the officers came to the door and spoke to Howard. "Unfortunately we can't keep these people from carrying their signs on the street," he said. "We've warned them to stay off your private property. Hopefully no one else will get hurt, but you can call us if they get out of hand again."

CHAPTER 16

Marty met Gilmore and Jenny in the lobby during the break. "Guess what?" he said as he hung up his cell phone. "Carl Waterman's in the hospital with a heart attack."

"Really!" Gilmore and Jenny replied together.

"They don't think he's going to survive."

"This is sudden."

"You know they had a demonstration in front of his house last night."

"No."

"Yeah, and one of his neighbors was arrested for assaulting one of the demonstrators."

"Because of Howard?" Jenny asked.

"Yeah."

"What all did Howard do, anyway?" Marty asked. "It sounds like all he did was look at smooth little girls."

"Well, that's illegal," Jenny said.

"But would someone in the Way report someone to the police for doing that?" Gilmore questioned.

"It doesn't sound like anything I'd expect anyone to report," Marty said. "Something else must have happened. We've only heard about Maria so far."

"Poor little Maria," Jenny said. "I think if I were her mother, I'd go after him with a hay fork."

"Gosh, Gilmore," Marty advised. "You better not try anything funny with this girl. She sounds pretty vicious to me."

Gilmore laughed.

"You better believe it," Jenny assured them.

When they returned to the courtroom the prosecutor called Olga Berger to the stand. She was the supervisor of the latchkey program at the school where Ana was a teacher and Maria a student.

"Mrs. Berger, do you have Maria Castro in your care in the latchkey program?"

"Yes, I do."

"Can you tell us why you have her in your care after school each day?"

"Her mother told me she wanted to leave her in my care because there was a man who was bothering her on her way home from school."

"Did Ms. Castro ever tell you how the man was bothering her?"

"No, not really. I didn't ask, I don't think."

Clay made a move to object, and then changed his mind.

"Did you also have Sally Fitch in your care each day after school?"

"Yes, I did."

"Were you ever told why you were asked to keep her in your program?"

"No."

"But do you know why it was that her parents wanted her in your program?"

"Objection, your honor," Clay interrupted. "The witness already said she did not know why."

The judge thought a minute. "I'll overrule that objection. There are other ways to know things than by being told about them."

"Do you know why her parents wanted her in your program?" Mr. Duncan repeated.

"No. But last fall I did get a visit from her mother and she gave me very strict instructions that Sally was not to leave my care with anyone but her or her father."

"Do you remember when it was last fall that these instructions were given to you?"

"It was just before Thanksgiving, if I recall correctly."

"Was there anything unusual about Mrs. Fitch's instructions to you at that time?"

"Well, yes there was."

"Tell us about that."

"All the parents of the children I care for must provide us with a list of people who are allowed to pick up their children. We make no exceptions to that rule. If anyone who is not on that list tries to pressure us, we call the police to have them removed. We already had such a list on file."

"So you found it surprising that Mrs. Fitch would request that kind of security at that time?"

"Yes. We had Sally in the latchkey program for two years previously, and it seemed to me that Mrs. Fitch was having an emergency ...."

"Objection," Clay interrupted. "This calls for speculation on the part of the witness..."

The judge thought for a minute. "Objection sustained. Members of the jury, would you please ignore that last response. You may continue, Mr. Duncan."

"Thank you, your honor," Mr. Duncan said, and continued with his questions.

Then Clay asked Mrs. Berger. "You told this court that there was a particular man who was bothering Maria Castro on the way home from school?"

"Yes. I'm sure Ms. Castro said it was a particular man."

"Did she tell you who the man was?"

"No."

"Did she give you any indication about who it might be?"

"No."

"Did you have any concern about that man?"

"Well, yes, I did. But I didn't ask any questions."

"Should you have asked?"

Mrs. Berger thought a minute. "No."

"Why not?"

"I didn't think bothering automatically meant abusing, so I didn't ask who. Whoever it was couldn't have taken Maria out of my care, anyway."

"When Maria was in your care, did she show any signs of having been abused?"

"No."

"None at all?"

"No. She was a perfectly happy little girl. I know her mother quite well and I know she's a very diligent mother. No, I saw no indications of abuse at all."

"When Mrs. Fitch was talking to you about Sally, did she happen to mention who it was that Sally may have been fearful of?"

"No."

"Did Mrs. Fitch even give any indication that someone other than she or Mr. Fitch would attempt to pick Sally up from school."

"Yes – well, no. She was just very specific that when anyone else came to pick her up that Sally was not to leave with him."

"Did Mrs. Fitch specifically say him, or was she just referring to a person, not specifically a male or female?"

Mrs. Berger thought a while. "I don't remember whether she made any such indication to me. I don't remember whether it was a him or a her or a person."

"Did you detect in Sally any indication that she may have been abused?"

"She was very quiet. But not unusually so. I did notice, though, that when a man came to the desk to pick up a student that she would always run to the back of the room."

"Could that have been a coincidence, or was it predictable behavior with Sally?"

"It was predictable behavior. She and a couple of other little girls always played near the main door, but she'd run to the back of the room when a man came in. She'd only stay at the front of the room when her father came to get her."

Clay finished his questions at that point.

The next person called was Maybelle Kennedy. She was one of the counselors at the elementary school in Espadín. She reported that part of her assigned duties was to talk to classes about all health and safety issues.

"Did you have classes with Maria Castro in them?"

"Yes."

"In the sex education portion of that course, did you observe Maria's response to the information you were giving them?"

"I remember she was very quiet, but I don't remember that she showed any signs of trauma that might be related to sexual abuse."

"Did you also have Sally Fitch in any of your classes?"

"Yes, I did."

"And what topics do you address in the sex ed. portion of the program that Sally was in?"

"We review the inappropriate behaviors that children should avoid, as well as what they should do about them when they are confronted with them."

"What do you advise them to do when they're inappropriately touched?"

"They're told they have to tell their parents, or some other person of importance or responsibility in their lives."

"In the course of discussions in this class, did Sally ever make any comments to you about being improperly treated?"

"No."

Mr. Duncan's questioning seemed to wither, and Clay began his questions.

"Mrs. Kennedy, what does the sex education module of your health program consist of?"

"For seven and eight year olds the primary concern is their safety, and how to recognize and report abusive treatment. It's somewhat disguised as a lesson in safety."

"Is there anything in the instruction that would entice a child to experiment?"

"No. Unless a child is interested in being abused, there isn't anything in the curriculum to encourage the children to experiment. Unless children at that age have been exposed to sexual activity, they're really too young to have an interest in experimenting. Little boys and little girls still don't like each other at that age."

"Now you told us that Sally never made any comments about being improperly treated. Is that right?

"No."

"No?"

"I believe the question I was asked was if Sally ever made any comments to me about inappropriate activities. But she did make comments to others."

"What did she say?"

"She told a couple of other students that a man had done that to her. I found a way to intervene in that conversation and tell her that she had to tell her parents."

"Did you report this to the authorities?"

"Yes, I did."

"Did you report this to Sally's parents?"

"Yes, I did."

The testimony of Maybelle Kennedy concluded. *I wish I'd never asked*, Clay thought. *I hate it when the prosecutor doesn't ask his own questions!*

Sharon Fitch came next to the stand. She was visibly nervous, and her eyes darted around the courtroom.

"How do you know the defendant?" Mr. Duncan asked.

"He was ... is a minister in my religion."

"What was his relationship with your family?"

"He preached at our services. And he came frequently to our house for visits."

"You'll have to speak a bit louder, Mrs. Fitch, for all the jurors to hear you."

"Okay," Sharon said. "I'll try."

After a number of questions, he asked her, "Did there come a time when you became suspicious of Mr. Barnes?"

"Yes."

"Please tell the jury when that was."

"It was last fall. In October. I don't remember the date."

"What made you suspicious of Mr. Barnes?"

"My daughter complained about him."

"What did she say about him?"

"She said she was afraid of him. She said she didn't like him."

"Did she tell you why she was afraid of him?"

"Yes."

"Tell the jury what she told you that frightened her."

"She said Howard followed her around too much at our fellowship pot lucks with our friends."

"Is that all?"

"No."

"Tell us all the things she was afraid of."

"Objection, your honor," Clay said. "The question is too broad in scope and the answer would be hearsay."

"I'll sustain the objection," the judge said. "Please rephrase your question, Mr. Duncan."

"Can you tell us all the things Sally said she feared about the defendant?"

Clay wanted to object to it as being hearsay, but changed his mind. *I might be able to use it to my own advantage.*

"She told me he came into her bedroom and made her take her pajamas off." She paused. When Mr. Duncan didn't ask another question, she continued. "She told me that he showed her his, uh, penis."

"How disgusting!" Aggie whispered.

"This is why people reported him to the police," Maggie concluded.

"No wonder," Aggie said. "I thought all he was doing was looking at them."

Mr. Duncan continued. "What did you do about these things?"

"We just kept Sally away from him."

"What did you do when Mr. Barnes came to your house?"

"There were two occasions when he was at our house for dinner that we sent her to stay at her friend's house."

"After Sally made these accusations, did Mr. Barnes come back to stay overnight at your house again?"

"No."

"What would you have done if he had?"

"We'd decided that we'd... ."

"Objection," Clay intoned. "This question is about a hypothetical situation that never came to pass."

"Objection sustained," the judge said.

"Why did the lawyer do that?" Aggie asked.

"He didn't want Sharon to answer that question, I guess," Maggie explained.

"I'd like to hear her answer," Aggie said. "I wish he wouldn't do that."

"Oh well," Maggie said, stifling a giggle.

Mr. Duncan ended his questioning.

"Mrs. Fitch, did you call the police about these complaints?" Clay asked.

"No."

"Did you speak to counselors about these complaints?"

"No. Well, yes. The counselor from school called me."

"What was her advice?"

"She said I should call the police."

"Did you speak to other parents about this?"

"No. Well, yes."

"Who did you speak with about this?"

"Well, I didn't talk about Sally. I just talked to Carla Sturm."

"So you talked to Mrs. Sturm."

"Yes."

"But you didn't talk about Sally."

"No."

"So what did you talk about?" Clay asked.

"We talked about what to do if a servant were to molest one of our children."

"But you didn't mention Sally?"

"No."

"Why not?"

Sharon was flustered. "Well, Carla just wanted to know what to do if a servant did such a thing. That's all."

"Did you approach Mrs. Sturm about this question or did she approach you?"

"She approached me."

"Was it a hypothetical question on her part, or had a servant assaulted one of her children?"

"No. She said no one molested any of her children. She just wanted to know what to do in case one of the servants did."

"And you did not tell her about Sally."
"No."
"Why not?"
"I was ashamed."
"I can appreciate that. But does a mother not forego her shame to protect her young daughter from molestation?"

Sharon wrung her hands, and looked desperate. In a shaky voice she said, "I told Carla I didn't believe in reporting a servant to the police for any reason. That's all we talked about."

"Do you also believe that it's not appropriate to tell one of your friends that a servant has molested your child?" Clay asked.

Sharon looked horrified. "Why would I do that?"

"Perhaps to warn her that the servant was a child molester. Would you tell your friend in that case?"

Sharon agonized. "No."

"Why not?"

"I... I think I'm scared of saying anything bad about a servant."

"Would you warn your friend if your child had been molested by a stranger who could also molest your friend's child?"

"Yes."

"Did Howard ever tell you that he helped Sally with a nightmare while he was staying at your house overnight?"

"No."

Clay had no more questions.

The next person called to the stand was Sally Fitch. "How old are you?" Mr. Duncan asked.

"I'm eight."

He questioned her gently, as he had with Maria. Sally paid close attention to his questions and answered precisely.

"What do you think of Mr. Barnes?"

Sally was silent, and glanced apprehensively at Howard. The prosecutor assured her she could tell him the truth without any repercussions, so she said, "He's scary."

"Why do you say he's scary?"

"He always wants to look at me under my panties. I don't like that."

"Has he asked you to do that more than once?"

"Yes."

"Do you know how many times?"

"No. I forget. There were a lot of times."

"Did he tell you why he wanted to look at you there?"

"He told me it was smooth and pretty."

"Did he show you under his underwear?"
Sally hesitated, then said, "Yes."
"When did he do that?"
"When he came into my room at night."
"Tell me about that."
"He came into my room when I was asleep and wanted to see me under my pajamas. And when I showed him he took out his penis and did something to it."
"Did he touch you under your pajamas?"
"No."
When Mr. Duncan was finished, Clay asked, "Did you tell Howard you didn't want to do these things?"
"No."
"Why not?"
"I wasn't supposed to tell him I didn't like it. He told me it was our secret."
"You said that Howard showed you his penis?"
"Yes."
"But did you actually see his penis?"
"Yes. I did."
"What does a penis look like?"
Sally paused, then said. "I know what a penis looks like, but his isn't normal."
"In what way is it not normal?"
Howard's face turned fiery red.
"It has some funny skin all over it that he ... did something with."
Clay had no more questions for Sally.

When they were leaving the court house that day, Aggie said, "I've never heard of anything so disgusting in my life! And that Mr. Shipman – is he really one of us?"
"Yes. They said he was."
"He treated poor Sharon like she was lying. Shame on him. No wonder Uncle Floyd doesn't like him."
"Should we come back tomorrow?" Maggie asked.
"I think we should. I know Bart and Uncle Floyd don't think we should, but, well,"
"You want to know everything that happened, huh?"
"Oh Maggie. You know what I mean."
Maggie smiled.

Clay asked Nathan, "Can you have dinner with Alice and I?"

"I can. I didn't tell anyone when I'd be back to camp."

"Good. It might not be good for me to be seen eating alone with Alice in a restaurant in this town."

"What's wrong with Alice?" Nathan wondered.

"She's not my wife. Nancy's in Santa Rosa, and I don't know how many people of my faith might just see me with Alice."

"Oh, I see. It's a small town too, isn't it?"

"What do you think?" Clay asked over dinner.

"What do you think?" Nathan asked.

"At this point I don't know what to think. It's not an exciting trial, is it?"

"No, it's not. Frankly, I think your client has thoroughly screwed himself."

"I think he knows it, too. I hate working this way. If he were a violent rapist I could work on forensics, but this hesaidshesaid stuff gets slippery. And I really blew it when I asked that kid what a penis looks like."

Alice laughed heartily. "I'm telling my husband that one."

"Don't you ask all your clients if they've been circumcised?" Nathan joked.

"Maybe I should start. They never told us in law school that we'd need to know that."

"And you expected an eightyearold to say she didn't know what a penis looked like," Nathan smiled.

"Caught again," Clay agreed.

"So are you going to move on to defending sex offenders?" Nathan asked.

Clay thought for a long time, then said, "You told me to treat this as a learning experience. I'll tell you what I've learned. I'll not defend another clergyman again. Well, at least one of my own faith."

That evening the demonstrators returned to the street where the Watermans lived. One of Carl's neighbors went out and met them. He informed them that Carl had had a heart attack and Howard was no longer at that house."

Someone had learned where Howard had gone for the night and in barely 15 minutes they all showed up in front of the servants' studio with their placards.

The owner of the house, who'd rented his studio apartment to the servants for many years, was irate and called the police. The police officer, of course, told him there was nothing they could do because the demonstrators weren't on his property and they weren't interfering with traffic. And it wasn't late enough in the evening for them to be charged with disturbing the peace.

After the demonstrators had been there for an hour, they began chanting that Howard was a child molester and a bishop killer. At that point, Howard called Clay in his hotel room and asked him what to do. Clay went to the apartment, and found himself surrounded by angry people on the sidewalk. They wouldn't talk to him, but he felt jostled and was afraid there may be violence.

Clay called the police, and when they arrived the threatening posturing ended. "What's with the bishop killer sign?" one of the officers asked.

Someone said, "Carl Waterman died and we want this fancy L.A. attorney to go back home."

The policeman reminded them that he could do nothing for them, and reminded them that they had to respect the laws concerning disturbing the peace after nine o'clock. And they all slowly dispersed.

CHAPTER 17

Next morning the Sacramento Bee published the following news item.

Cult Bishop Dies during Molestation Trial

ESPADÍN — Carl Waterman, the bishop of the small congregation of the Way in Espadín, died suddenly yesterday afternoon at the age of 88. His death has been attributed to a heart attack. Speculation among the citizens of Espadín is that tensions surrounding the trial of Howard Barnes contributed to Waterman's demise.

Barnes, a clergyman in the Way religion, is on trial in Espadín for a number of charges of molestation and the sexual assault of five young children whose parents are members of the Way. The trial got under way yesterday morning in the Del Rio Superior Court.

The Way is an obscure group of Christians. Members in Del Rio County number approximately 35. They have a reputation in the community for high moral standards and moderate living, but little is known about the internal practices of the group. The members remain secretive and defensive about its workings. The Way is most widely known for its foot washing ritual which occurs each Thursday evening.

Numerous citizens of this normally quiet community have demonstrated in front of the Del Rio Court House and in front of residences where Barnes has been staying. Police have reported one arrest for violence related to the Sunday evening demonstration. Barnes was released on $500,000 bail pending the outcome of this trial. Counsel for Barnes is Clayton Shipman, the Santa

The Straight Way

Monica attorney who defended Lee Chen at his murder trial in Los Angeles.
Barnes, who was a minister to the members of the Way, has been replaced in that capacity by Bart Stanley. Mr. Stanley has refused to communicate with the media.

Maggie was having breakfast that morning with Aggie. "I'm so sorry about Carl," she said. "He was such a good man."

Aggie agreed. "He'll be greatly missed."

"I'm sure he was all upset because of the demonstrations, but people have the right to protest when they want, I guess."

"Yes, but it makes it bad for us when people are allowed to say what they want about the Way publicly."

"I think they're just upset about Howard being here in town. They're not upset with us."

"It's all the same thing," Aggie sighed. "Touch one of us and you've touched us all."

"Aggie, we're not responsible for anything Howard's done. People are smart enough to know that."

"I don't think so. We're all supposed to be the same. We aren't supposed to have someone doing things like that. We don't believe in it. Anyway, we need the servants. There wouldn't be any Way if it weren't for the servants. We have to do what we can to keep them."

Maggie frowned, but didn't respond.

"Did you read the newspaper this morning?" Aggie asked.

"No."

"They said Carl died and there were demonstrations. And they called the Way a cult. Can you imagine that? And they said we're all keeping secrets. It was really bad."

"They get to tell whatever they see, I guess," Maggie said.

"You'd think they'd recognize how embarrassing this is for the Way."

"I'm not embarrassed," Maggie said. "It's Howard who should be embarrassed."

"It's okay for him to be embarrassed, but it does terrible damage to the Way."

"We'll just have to keep living a good example and people will recognize us for that."

"We need a good reputation or no one will pay any attention to us."

"Aggie, we make our own reputation."

"Well I'd like to be able to hold the servants up to the world as a perfect example."

"I was quite proud to hold up a young college student as a good example to a family in Eureka recently."

When they were leaving the coffee shop, Aggie groaned, "Off we go to hear more about Howard looking at little girls."

The first witness called that morning was David Goldstein, a counselor and teacher at the elementary school in Espadín. Mr. Duncan asked him about Jason Gomez. "Did Jason give any indication in Sex Ed. class about being involved in such activities?"

"Yes, he did."

"How so?"

"When I began telling the students about people wanting to get them into their vehicles, Jason volunteered to share what he knew about that. He said they'd take you for a long ride and then get you to do bad things."

"Was there any discussion about what the bad things were?"

"Yes. He said they'd want to play with you for a while and then they'd ask you to take your clothes off."

"Did you report this to anyone?"

"Yes, I did. I told the police."

"Did you discuss this with Jason's mother?"

"Yes, I did. In fact, she called me and asked me what to do about it."

"What did you tell her?"

"I told her to call the police."

Clay had only a few questions to ask Mr. Goldstein. "Did Jason actually say that someone had done these things with him?"

"I don't recall that he actually said it happened to him."

"Is it protocol for a teacher to assume a child has been molested if he can describe such a scenario to the class?"

"No. But it is protocol for a teacher to report such a student for investigation. The law requires me to do that."

"Would it not be appropriate to investigate further before you reported such a juvenile discussion?"

"No. I have no authority to investigate my students. I just have a legal responsibility to report any suspicions of abuse."

"Thank you. I have no further questions."

Then Jason came to the stand.

"What did you do with Howard?"

"He used to take me places in his car. One time he took me to Sacramento. And one time he took me to Yuba City."

Eventually they came to the questions about improper activities.

"In the car, I told him I had to go to the bathroom," Jason said. "And he said he did too. So he stopped by a little river and we peed in the water."

"Is that all you did?"

"Well, no."

"What else did you do?"

"He wanted me to let him see my penis."

"And did you?"

"No. A car came by and we had to go."

Then there were questions about what went on in the garage at Jason's home.

"He was helping me build a train set. And then he wanted me to show him what was in my secret corner. It's a kind of closet in the back of the garage where I keep my things."

"What kind of things?"

"Things I don't want other kids to play with."

"But you took Howard in there?"

"Yes."

"And what happened in there?"

"He wanted me to take my pants down so I could show him my penis?"

"And did you?"

"Yes."

"What happened then?"

"Howard got down on his knees to look at it. And.... he looked at it. He told me I was nice and smooth – down there."

"Is that all?"

"He said he wanted to make it hard so he started, you know, feeling it. He started getting it, you know, hard, and it made me pee." He stopped abruptly, blushed with embarrassment, and lowered his head.

"How often did you do that in the secret corner?"

"Three or four times."

"Did you tell anyone?"

"Yes. I told my mother. I wanted her to tell him not to come back."

"Who else did you tell?"

"I told Spike and the policeman, but I don't think I should have."

"Why not?"

"Howard told me it was supposed to be our secret."

Then Clay had asked, "Did you pee in the secret corner?"

"Yes. I had to. I couldn't help it."

"Did Howard pee in the secret corner?"

"No."

"Did any of the kids you play with pee in the secret corner?"

"No. I don't let any of them in there."

"Did you tell your mother who peed in the corner?"

"I, uh, well, I told her it was Howard who peed in the corner."

"Why did you tell her that?"

"I didn't want to get into trouble."

"But you told your mother that Howard wanted you to take your pants down."

"Yes." Jason paused. "But that wouldn't get me in trouble, if he told me to do it."

"Were you not afraid that Howard would get in trouble?"

"No."

"Why not?"

"Because servants never get in trouble."

Lidia Gomez came to the stand. "Howard took a great interest in Jason," she said. "I thought it was because he was an only child with no father."

"When did you become concerned about that relationship?"

"Jason began wetting his pants. He hadn't done that since he was very young. He was embarrassed about it. Then one day I discovered a urine smell in the garage, and I asked him about it. He said it was Howard who did that, and I became upset. I told him there was something wrong and I needed to know. So he told me Howard was doing bad things with him and he didn't want him to come back to our house again." She began to cry.

"What did you do about that?"

"I called the counselor at school."

"And did you call the police?"

"No. I think the counselor did. The police came to me."

Clay wanted to know if any of Jason's friends ever went into the secret corner.

"No. He kept everything in there that he didn't want any of the neighbors to play with."

"Did any of the neighbor children have access to the garage when Jason was not at home?"

"No. I keep the garage locked whenever neither of us is home."

There ensued a heated whispering at the defense table. "You told me it was the neighbor kids who were peeing in the corner," Clay said.

Howard stammered. "I thought that was what he told me."

"Was Jason telling the truth?" Clay looked him directly in the eye.

Howard was stunned. "Yes."

Clay studied Howard's face, but Howard said nothing more. He flinched, then looked back at the judge. A red flush rose from the collar of his shirt.

Amy's father was going back to Eureka that afternoon, so Amy and Jesse had lunch with him before he left. Mr. Foster said, "You know, that guy's a true pedophile. I'd bet money he's been molesting children for years."

"Why wouldn't he have been caught before now?" Amy wondered.

"It's probably been covered up. Where was he before he came here?"

"Colorado, I think," Jesse said.

"The Way has members there?"

"There are members in all the states."

"That's why he's here in California," Mr. Foster said.

"I thought Howard was the greatest person," Amy said. "He was really good to me."

"I'm sure he was," Mr. Foster said. "He had no prurient interest in you. But religious groups send their child molesters away to protect their own reputation. They're more interested in their own reputation with the public than in the consequences to the victims. They send the molesters away to keep themselves out of the media. The one thing they mostly don't want is unfavorable press."

"But Dad," Amy said. "Aren't they supposed to show that they believe in living morally?"

"Yes, they are, but they have the notion that sending these people away accomplishes that. And it doesn't do a thing for their reputation. They're only fooling themselves – they're not really hiding it. Everyone knows what's going on. Even the people who don't know what's going on suspect something's going on. No one gets yanked from a position like that without notice. What they really accomplish is to implicate themselves as accomplices to the crime."

"Marty knew something was going on," Amy recalled.

Jesse nodded agreement.

"So this is the message they've given everyone," Mr. Foster continued. "They've said that when a preacher commits a crime they're not going to hold him accountable for it, and everyone else will be forbidden to complain about it."

"Yeah. We've been asked not to talk about it," Jesse said.

"That's an attempt to prevent anyone from even hearing suggestions of what happened. In Washington that's called spin control. My guess is that anyone who doesn't comply with the coverup could be treated worse than Mr. Barnes."

"What's worse than what he's getting? He could go to prison."

"Oh! That's what the law is doing to him, not what the clergy is doing. All the clergy did was send him to San José. If you talk too much they could send you to hell."

"Hell?"

"Yes. They could excommunicate you," Mr. Foster said. "It means the same thing to them, really, because they only excommunicate people they believe are evil enough to go to hell."

"I never thought of it that way," Jesse said.

"What do the other members of this group think of Barnes?"

"Some of them think he's not guilty," Jesse assured him. "I could argue every day with some of them."

"Most of the kids who go to college agree he should have been taken to court," Amy said.

"What do you think?"

Jesse went first. "We don't believe in molesting children, and we don't believe in breaking the law. And I don't believe in excusing him of his crimes. I'll just pray for him whatever happens."

"I think he should have been arrested," Amy said. "From all I've learned, that's the only way to stop a child molester."

"I'm glad to hear that," Mr. Foster said. "But I'm still worried about one thing. What's going to happen with your status in this group?"

"What do you mean?" Amy asked.

"The group is divided, apparently. I have no fear of what you two are going to do. But if you're going to be honest with everyone concerning this case, sooner or later you're going to butt heads with someone who doesn't appreciate your integrity. Whatever happens, you're going to be watched to make sure you're in step with the party line, and you'll be in trouble if you're not."

"Well, I'm going to do what I said I'd do," Jesse said. "I suppose if I had kids, I'd have different business with Howard. But in this matter, Howard's responsible for himself and to the law. I don't know what else to say."

"Why do you think this will happen to us?" Amy asked.

"It's how things work in these kinds of religions," Mr. Foster said. "If that doesn't happen, I'll be tempted to join myself."

Back at the court house they were waiting to go inside when Amy and Jesse simultaneously felt someone touch their elbows and say, "What are you doing here?" It was Bart.

"Hi Bart," Amy said. "We're waiting to get into the court house."

"That's what I thought." Bart appeared angry. "I'd like you both to leave and go back to school."

Amy started to say something but Bart interrupted her. "You have no business being here watching this shameful show," he said.

Mr. Foster stepped up to Bart. "Who are you?"

"And who are you?" Bart asked.

"I'm this girl's father. Now who are you?"

"This girl shouldn't be here…"

"But who are you?"

"I'm her spiritual advisor," Bart said.

"Well in that case, stick to giving her spiritual advice and leave her alone on the street."

"Listen, mister," Bart said. "You don't understand. This girl has made a commitment to the Lord and it's my responsibility to guide her in how to conduct her life."

"You listen to me, mister." Mr. Foster was angry. "You just bug off and mind your own business or I'll call that police officer over there to come and shut you up. I'm going to stay right here until these two kids get into the courtroom and I don't want to hear of you interfering with them again. If I do, I'll be back in town to see you."

Bart started to say something, but decided better of it. He looked around and saw the policeman Mr. Foster had been referring to, then turned and walked away.

"What's his name?" Mr. Foster asked.

"Bart Stanley," Jesse said. "I'll apologize for him. He's Howard Barnes' replacement. He's not the nicest kind of guy."

"He's going to be trouble for you," Mr. Foster said. "Amy, if he tries anything like that again, I want to know about it."

"Okay," Amy chuckled.

Mr. Foster turned to Jesse. "I'm going to depend on you to tell me if she doesn't."

"Okay," Jesse agreed.

"It doesn't matter whether he's likeable or not," Mr. Foster explained. "He's on a power trip, and I want you both to stay out of his clutches."

The crowd had moved and Amy and her father exchanged a kiss, and Mr. Foster shook Jesse's hand.

"I love you both," Mr. Foster said. "I want you to take care of yourselves. See you later."

Jesse detected a trace of a tear in Amy's eye. It surprised him that Mr. Foster would include him in his admission of love for Amy. *I wonder if he thinks Amy and I have something going on*, he thought.

Once inside, Jesse asked Amy, "How come your father's so sure about that?"

"I don't know."

"It's scary."

"Why?"

"He might be right. I hope not."

"Bart's already told me not to speak at assembly."

"I know."

The school nurse came next to the stand, and reported that Joey Patten was sent to her by his classroom teacher because he was complaining about sore legs.

"Could you determine the cause of his sore legs?"

"I discovered he had bruises on the backs of his legs and on his buttocks. I also discovered that he had welts, like belt marks. I reported it to the police and to Child Protective Services."

Most of the nurse's testimony was about her determination of the abusive treatment Joey had received and the referrals she'd made. Then Clay had questions to ask.

Did Joey tell you how he received these bruises and marks?"

"No. He didn't want to tell me."

"Did he give you no indication at all?"

"None. I asked him if he'd ever been spanked at home, and he said he had been, sometimes. But he refused to make any connection between these marks and a spanking."

"Was there any indication that Joey had been sexually abused in any way?"

"No. I didn't suspect any sexual abuse."

George Patten was sitting in the front row of spectators. He looked relieved about the summary of the nurse's testimony.

The prosecutor then called a social worker from the Child Protective Services who told the court he also had determined Joey had been physically abused. And he said he'd confirmed his suspicion in a conversation with Joey's mother. He also told the court that he'd taken Joey to the Emergency Service Center at the local hospital, where he learned he'd also been molested sexually.

To the surprise of all the Way friends, the social worker reported that Joey had been placed in a temporary foster facility for three days while Social Services personnel worked with his family to determine whether he could again be in danger if he returned home. Joey had been allowed to return home after three days, and the social worker was still making regular visits to the home to monitor his treatment.

Clay took his turn asking questions as well. "Was it your determination that any of the physical abuse was attributed to my client?"

"I personally didn't suspect any physical abuse by your client, sir."

"Was it your determination that any of the sexual abuse was attributed to my client?"

"I didn't suspect that your client sexually abused Joey."

"Did you ask him who abused him?"

"Yes."

"What did he say?"

"All he'd say was that his father had spanked him."

"Did you ask him about sexual abuse?"

"Yes. All he'd say was that he didn't know what happened to him."

"Did he have no explanation at all?"

"No. Actually, the child was so traumatized by what had happened to him it was impossible to know if he could properly recount what had happened."

Mr. Duncan called Dr. Hung to the stand. "Did you have occasion to examine Joey Patten in the Emergency Service Center?"

"Yes, I did. He was suffering from a number of large bruises to the legs, as well as three lesions that appeared to be caused by being struck in some manner."

"Did he explain those bruises to you?"

"Yes, he did. He told me his father had beaten him."

"Did he tell you why his father had beaten him?"

"He told me his father didn't want him telling his mother things about the family's clergyman."

"What was his complaint about the clergyman?"

"He said the clergyman had asked him to do a number of inappropriate things for him, and that he had attempted to penetrate Joey anally with his finger."

"Did you find any physical evidence of that?"

"Yes, I did. I found that he had a tear in his anus."

"Was that not an indication that he had tried to insert something else into his anus?"

"No, not necessarily. But it was consistent with an attempted penetration with an unfiled fingernail, or with a hangnail."

To the surprise of many, Clay had only one question for Dr. Hung. "Dr. Hung, does such an injury to the anus as was sustained by Joey necessarily mean that he was sexually assaulted?"

"No, not necessarily."

"I have no further questions."

"Mercy!" Aggie gasped. "That was so disgusting!"

"Poor, poor child!" Maggie whispered.

"Why would the man want to do such a thing? I don't believe it."

"This makes me sick."

"We should have stayed home."

Finally Joey Patten was brought to the stand. He made a pathetic scene, sitting in the big chair in front of the whole court. He answered each question carefully, until they came to the details of his activities with Howard.

"What do you think about Howard?"

"He, uh, he's a good man."

"So you liked spending time with him?"

There was a long pause. "Yes," Joey stuttered.

"Did Howard ever ask you to do anything you didn't want to do?"

Another pause. "No."

The judge struck his gavel and interrupted in a loud voice. "Bailiff, would you please escort that man out of the courtroom and have him identify himself for me." He pointed to George Patten.

"Mr. Duncan, can you repeat your last three questions again, please. The individual I ordered out of the courtroom was making signs to your witness while he was answering."

"Thank you, your honor."

The judge explained to Joey that he could safely tell the court the truth.

"Am I going to be in trouble?" Joey asked.

"Certainly not," the judge assured him.

"I don't want to get my father in trouble," Joey said.

"You'll not get your father in trouble."

"Okay."

"Tell us what Howard wanted you to do," Mr. Duncan instructed.

"He wanted to see under my underwear."

"Did you let him see under your underwear?"

"Yes."

"How many times?"

"I forget."

"Was it more than three times?"

"Yes."
"Is that all he asked you to do?"
"No."
"What else did he ask you to do?"
"He wanted to touch me, you know, between my legs."
"Did you let him?"
"Yes."
"Did you want him to touch you there?"
"No."
"Why did you let him?"

Joey looked trapped. "I don't know. He told me I was nice and smooth there. I just did whatever he told me to do."

"Were you afraid?"
"Yes."
"Is that all he did?"
"No. He felt my butt too. And he hurt me." He began to cry.

Mr. Duncan took him some tissues. "I don't have many more questions."

"Okay," Joey sobbed.
"How did he hurt you?"
"He was trying to stick his finger into me, you know, into my butt."
"Is that what hurt?"
"Yes. Really bad."
"Did you tell anyone about this?"
Joey hesitated. "Yes. I told my Mom."
"Did you tell anyone else?"
"No. Well, I told the doctor too."

When Mr. Duncan was satisfied, Clay asked, "Did Howard force you to do any of these things with him?"

"No."
"Did he beat you in any way?"
"No."
"Who was it who beat you before you went to the doctor?"
"It was my father."
"Why did he beat you?"
"He said it was because I'd told my Mom what Howard had done."
"You weren't supposed to tell her that?"
"No. He said I was never to tell anyone anything like that about a servant. He said he'd beat me every time I did."

The atmosphere in the courtroom had grown more tense, and the jury's gaze was fixed on Joey.

"Are you still afraid of Howard?" Clay asked.

"Yes. And I'm scared of my father. I don't want anyone to tell him what I told you, because he'll beat me again."

"We'll do everything we can to prevent that from happening," Clay assured him.

The bailiff accompanied the sobbing Joey to a private waiting room to regain his composure.

Marian Patten came to the stand looking disheveled and terrified.

Mr. Duncan said, "Tell us what the relationship was between your son and Mr. Barnes."

"He was a very good preacher, and I was very disappointed that he didn't get along well with children. But Joey didn't like him."

"Did Joey tell you why he didn't like Mr. Barnes?"

"Yes."

"What did he say?"

"He said he didn't like the things Howard did to him."

"Did he tell you what those things were?"

"The doctor said he'd been sexually molested."

Clay interrupted. "Objection, your honor. This is nonresponsive."

"Objection sustained," the Judge said. He advised the jury to ignore Marian's answer, and said, "Mrs. Patten. Can you please answer the exact questions Mr. Duncan asks you?"

"Yes, sir. I'll try."

Marian studied Clay while Mr. Duncan asked the next question. "Did Joey ask you to check an injury he had sustained?"

"Pardon me, sir."

Mr. Duncan repeated the question, and Marian looked again at Clay as though to beg him to object again. When no objection came, she said, "Yes, he did."

"What was his injury?"

"He had a kind of hurt, kind of a cut, on his bottom. He didn't want to show it to me, but I thought I needed to see it, so he showed it to me. And it was very sore, and he didn't want me to take him to the doctor. My husband doesn't really like to take kids to the doctor because he thinks, you know, that they're always reporting parents to the police. But I wanted to take him to the doctor …."

"Pardon me, Mrs. Patten. All you have to do is answer the questions I ask you."

"Oh, okay."

"Did you ask him how he had sustained that injury?"

"Yeah, I did. He told me Howard had done it, and I was really upset. When I told my husband about it he was furious and he gave the kid a whipping for saying such a thing about a servant. I was really upset, because he does that all the time. He really gets mad when anyone says anything about the servants. I wanted to be able to do something for ..."

Mr. Duncan was about to interrupt her again.

"Mrs. Patten," the judge interrupted. "Please just simply answer the questions Mr. Duncan asks you and do not elaborate unless he asks you to."

"Oh, okay. I'm sorry."

"Continue, Mr. Duncan."

"Mrs. Patten, were you suspicious that someone had molested Joey?"

"Yes."

"Did you report that to anyone?"

"No. But it wasn't my fault. I was scared. I didn't want anything more to happen to either Joey or me and I didn't know what to do. I don't know what to do. I try to be a good mother but ..."

"Mrs. Patten," Mr. Duncan said. "You are not on trial here. It's Mr. Barnes who's on trial."

"I know. I just can't take any more of this. One person hurts my child and everyone else is mad when I say anything about it. It's disgusting. Some days I think I'm going to lose my mind because no one cares what happens to us." Marian burst into tears and for a while could not get control of herself.

Mr. Duncan's frustration was apparent. "Did you notice any change in Joey's behavior?"

"Yeah. He started wetting his bed, and he hadn't done that since he was really small. And he ran away a few times. I'm afraid they're going to take Joey away from me again because he runs away so he won't get another beating."

"This trial isn't about your husband, Mrs. Patten. It's about Mr. Barnes."

"Okay." She looked confused. "But the reason he was getting beatings is because he was talking about Howard."

"I have no more questions."

Clay had some questions for her. "Have you or your husband ever asked Mr. Barnes not to come back to your home?"

"No. George wants to be a bishop some day and he says all the time that if he does anything disrespectful of a servant they'd never let him be a bishop."

"Have you or your husband ever asked Mr. Barnes not to be around Joey anymore?"

"No. We couldn't do that. We have to allow the servants to come to our house when they want and Joey would…. I know why Joey got his beatings, but I couldn't tell Howard not to come to the house."

"I have no further questions, your honor."

The judge turned to Marian and said, "Mrs. Patten, you are free to go now."

"Thank you," she said. She slowly got herself together and left the courtroom.

Dante Stokely, a counselor from the Don Gaspar de Portolá Middle School, took the stand. Mr. Duncan asked, "Did you have occasion to speak with Adam Sawyer as a guidance counselor?"

"Yes, I did."

"Would you please tell the court the circumstances of that visit?"

"Spike – that's what we call Adam – was sent to me by his classroom teacher because he persisted in discussing oral sex with other students in the classroom. The home room teacher said it was disturbing and she wanted me to counsel him about that."

"Is that not a normal thing for middle school students to talk about?"

"It is, really. But I was told it had become an obsession with him."

"Tell us what happened during that counseling session."

"What is discussed in my counseling sessions is privileged communication. It would be unethical of me to discuss that."

"But Mrs. Sawyer told me to ask you any questions I wanted," Mr. Duncan said.

"Mr. Duncan," the judge interrupted. "You know better than this."

"Uh, yes, your honor." Then to Mr. Stokely he asked, "Did you gather from your discussions with Adam that he'd been involved in such activities?"

"Objection," Clay interrupted. "This question calls for speculation on the part of Mr. Stokely."

"Sustained."

Mr. Duncan asked several more questions, but got answers to none of them because of either Clay's objections or Mr. Stokely's refusal to answer.

"Did you report this to anyone?" Mr. Duncan asked.

"I didn't have a chance. I was approached by the police the following morning."

"Why on earth won't they let him tell what he knows?" Aggie asked. "I thought this trial was supposed to give us all that information."

"I don't know," Maggie said. "They have all these rules in court about things you're not supposed to say."

"No wonder they let all those criminals go scot free."

"Well, at least the lawyer was keeping him from saying things about Howard," Maggie assured her.

Aggie huffed. "I guess you're right."

Mr. Duncan called Helen Sawyer to the stand. "Please tell the court about the relationship between your son Adam and Mr. Barnes."

"When Howard first came here he behaved like a surrogate father to Adam. He visited us several times for dinner, and he seemed greatly interested in everything Adam was doing. And Adam always seemed quite happy to be around him and talk to him."

"Did there come a time when that relationship changed?"

"Yes. It seemed to change."

"Please tell us about that."

"Adam kind of retreated into his own world. He got to be really quiet and brooding. About that time Howard started turning down invitations to dinner, and Adam acted quite upset about that."

"Did Adam talk to you about his relationship with Mr. Barnes?" Mr. Duncan asked.

"No. All he'd say was that he wanted Howard to come and visit again. I told him to go to Howard's apartment and visit him there if he wanted to see him."

"Did he do that?"

"I don't know. I don't think so."

"Did Adam show any other changes in behavior?"

"Yes."

"Tell us about that."

"Adam got a whole new group of friends. Mostly they were older boys, strange looking types. One of them had a car and drove Adam home a few times. I was concerned because if he had a driver license I knew he had to be at least four years older than Adam. They'd come to the store where I work and they'd talk close together, kind of secretively. I thought these changes were because he was in middle school, but these other kids were old enough to be in high school. I was afraid they were into drugs."

"Did you have any discussion with Adam about his involvement with these new friends?"

"All he'd ever say is that they were just hanging out."

"You were obviously concerned about Adam. What did you do to deal with his behaviors?"

"I didn't have much time to do anything," Helen explained. "He'd only been hanging out with these new kids for a couple of weeks when he began brooding and asking to see Howard again. At the same time he began slacking off on his homework. I was going to talk to the counselor at school, but then the police came along asking about him. So I let them talk to him."

Helen seemed not to know anything substantial about Adam's activities with either his new friends or with Howard.

But Clay had a couple of questions. "Did you ever, at any time, suspect Adam of having an improper relationship with Mr. Barnes?"

"Never."

"Did you ever suspect Adam had become involved in homosexual activities with anyone?"

"No."

When Helen had been excused, Mr. Duncan called Adam to the stand. He was small for his age, but he stepped up to the stand briskly and sat straight up to answer questions. He had a cocky air about him.

"Tell me about your relationship with Mr. Barnes," Mr. Duncan said.

"He was a servant – a preacher. He kind of ran our religion and came to our house to visit sometimes."

"How did you get on with him? What did you think of him personally?"

"He was kind of cool. Maybe a bit flakey."

"Did there come a time when things changed between you and Mr. Barnes?"

"Yeah."

"Tell the court about that, please."

"Okay. I met him on my way home from school one day and he asked me to go with him to his studio. When we got there he wanted me to take my pants off."

"What do you mean by studio?"

"That's the place he lives."

"You mean something like an apartment?"

"Yeah."

"And then what happened?"

"He wanted to see under my underwear, so I showed him." He hesitated, then continued. "I knew he'd want to do that because my friend Jason had told me he would."

"And is that all he wanted?"

"No. Well, I don't know really what he wanted. He just told me he was surprised that I had hair down there. And he told me I should shave it because he liked it nice and smooth. He asked me how old I was and I said I was 12. He said he thought I was only nine or ten."

"Did Mr. Barnes want to touch you?"

"I think so. He did, too. He asked me if anyone had ever touched me there, and I said no."

"So what happened then?"

"I was getting hard, so I told him I wanted him to put his mouth on it. He didn't want to, but I told him if he didn't do it I'd tell the police on him. So he did."

"Did Mr. Barnes object?"

"No. Not really. I guess he was scared I'd tell the police. But I just wanted to know what it was like to fuck someone."

There were gasps throughout the courtroom.

Mr. Duncan finished, and Clay began.

"Whose idea was it for you to have oral sex with Howard?" Clay asked.

"Mine."

"How many times did this happen with you and Howard?"

"Only once. But I wanted some more. I went to his house again but he was never there. I was going to take my friends to see him too, but then he moved away somewhere. And it wasn't long before the police came and asked me what was going on."

With that the prosecution rested their case, and Clay promptly announced that he would not be calling any witnesses. Then, after a recess, the jury began hearing closing arguments.

First to address the jury with his closing arguments was Mr. Duncan. There was nothing surprising about his conclusions, of course. All the witnesses called were his own, and what he told the court was basically a summary of all they'd heard. He reiterated his request that Howard be convicted as a means of preventing him from preying on any more children.

More anticipated were Clay's closing arguments. More than a few wondered what he could possibly say to defend his client.

"Ladies and gentlemen," Clay began. "You've heard many people come here to testify about my client, but the very best you've heard of testimony against my client is typical hesaidshesaid testimony. The evidence presented has been woefully inadequate to convict my client."

He continued in a stern, steady voice. "Iris MacLean found a little girl's panties in her front yard. No one witnessed them being put there. Mrs. MacLean never asked anyone in her neighborhood if the panties belonged to them, and where she lives she's surrounded by families with young children.

"Ana Castro told us about her daughter not wearing panties when she came home from school. Yet she did nothing about it other than to ask Maria what had happened. Ladies and gentlemen, Ms. Castro is an elementary school teacher and she's bound by law to report even a suspicion of abuse or neglect to the appropriate authorities, and she did nothing to either verify Maria's story or report the incidents. What credibility can this court give to such testimony in these circumstances?

"Ms. Castro did not even tell Olga Berger, the lady who operated the latchkey program, that it was a man who was bothering Maria. Why would she automatically conclude that it was my client or even a man? In fact, Mrs. Berger said that Maria did not even show any signs of being abused. Such testimony cannot lead us to conclude that it was my client she was talking about.

"Mrs. Berger also gave testimony concerning Sally Fitch. Remember that Mrs. Berger noticed Sally was shy – but she identified nothing about Sally that would indicate she'd been suffering from abuse. In fact, Mrs. Fitch didn't identify anyone to Mrs. Berger, not even that it was a man. We are still no closer to any indisputable evidence that Mr. Barnes had any improper contact with Sally.

"We heard from Mrs. Kennedy that Sally had made comments about improprieties to other students, yet she admitted that Sally had said nothing to her either. There are two problems with Mrs. Kennedy's assuming it had anything to do with Sally being molested. First of all, who is to know that Sally wasn't telling a story to impress her friends and go along with the lesson of the day? Is it not expected at that age level that some student in the class will tell some wild story of a personal experience – not just about this topic but about any topic the teacher's discussing? Furthermore, Sally did not identify any person that Mrs. Kennedy could recall. How can it be concluded from that that Mr. Barnes had any involvement with Sally Fitch?

"Mrs. Fitch, Sally's mother, told us Sally had made numerous complaints about Mr. Barnes, yet she did nothing about it. How is it that a parent would allow her child to be subjected to such treatment as Mr. Barnes has been accused of, and not go to the proper authorities for help?"

Everyone's attention was momentarily diverted to a shuffle that had erupted at the back of the courtroom. Sharon Fitch, in tears, had stood up and Herb was accompanying her out of the room. When they had disappeared, the judge said, "You may continue, Mr. Shipman."

"We had further testimony from David Goldstein. Interestingly, Jason also did not identify to Mr. Goldstein who may have had any improper contact with Mr. Barnes. Jason, himself, gave testimony that would cause one to doubt him. He admitted that he had at first told his mother it was Mr. Barnes who had peed in the corner of the garage, and then he changed the story later on. We also heard that Adam Sawyer had been warned about Mr. Barnes, but he had been warned by Jason Gomez. Who is to know that they weren't drawing suggestions from each other that they could later use in their testimony about Mr. Barnes?

"The school nurse told us about abuse inflicted upon Joey Patten. Joey, we may conclude, was indeed physically abused, but no one has even suggested that Mr. Barnes had anything to do with that abuse. The social worker from Child Protective Services testified about Joey being removed short term from his home, but it was not because of Mr. Barnes. It was because of Mr. Patten. This trial is not about Mr. Patten, it's about Mr. Barnes. Considering the environment of fear that Joey allegedly lives in because of his father, is it not logical to suspect that such a child would blame anyone other than his parent in an effort to prevent any further physical abuse? Joey himself expressed concern that he'd get his father in trouble.

"The only person who gave any indication that Joey may have been sexually assaulted was Dr. Hung, but on cross examination he admitted that Joey had sustained no injuries that gave positive indication of sexual assault.

"We heard from Marian Patten, Joey's mother that she didn't want to take Joey to the doctor. Interestingly, it wasn't Mr. Barnes that she was afraid of, it was her husband who intimidated her into not reporting the abuse.

"Mr. Stokely testified about Adam Sawyer, or Spike, as he prefers to be called. Despite all Adam's sexual discussion, Mr. Stokely could not offer any suggestion that Adam had actually had any sexual contact with anyone. And Helen Sawyer, Adam's mother, admitted she had no suspicion at all that Adam had been assaulted.

"When you consider what Adam told this court, his testimony should of itself raise doubts. Child molesters have patterns of behavior, and what Adam reported to this court does not fit the pattern of the previous alleged victims. Considering that he had already discussed Mr. Barnes with Jason Gomez, what is to prevent him from inventing his own story about what transpired between him and Mr. Barnes? If he is to be believed, it would be simple enough to conclude that it was perhaps Mr. Barnes who was assaulted, not Adam.

"I suggest that Adam is a 12 year old beginning to feel his oats. He's become a concern to his mother because of the friendships and the secretive attitude he's been displaying. Indeed, he gave no indication to this court that he's shy about discussing what he wanted to do with my client, whether it happened or not. What is to prevent anyone from concluding that he was bragging about his imagined conquests?

"Ladies and gentlemen, I suggest that this whole trial has been about frivolous and ill proven accusations. It's not the responsibility of Mr. Barnes to prove his innocence, it's the responsibility of Mr. Duncan to prove beyond a reasonable doubt that Mr. Barnes has committed all or any of these offences. I submit that Mr. Barnes' accusers have not presented proof beyond a reasonable doubt, and I implore you, the jury, to do your duty in this case and find Mr. Barnes not guilty of the charges against him."

Clay finished, and sat down.

When he had finished, Aggie said, "Let's get out of here. I've heard enough of this garbage. What a dirty rat!"

"You mean Mr. Shipman?"

"Yes. I thought he was one of us. He just called every one of us a liar. I've never heard of the likes."

"I don't know," Maggie said. "It sounds to me like he doesn't believe Howard did anything."

"Well I think he did," Aggie asserted.

"So now you think he did?" Maggie was amazed.

"Yes. I changed my mind. He's a dirty rotten scoundrel and he's a shame to the Way. It's not nice to say this, but I think they ought to do something to him."

"Don't be surprised if they do," Maggie said. "I think he did it. But I don't understand why that lawyer would say such things about our friends. Is he really one of us?"

"They said he was, but I'll bet he doesn't show up at assembly while he's here. It's too bad Uncle Floyd wasn't in here to hear what he said. He'd expel him on the spot, I'm sure."

"Are you going to Carl's funeral this afternoon?" Maggie asked.

"Yes. I think it would be a much better place to be than here."

CHAPTER 18

Thursday afternoon there was a quiet funeral for Carl Waterman at the Oak Grove Funeral Home. Compared to everything else that had happened that week, the funeral was uneventful. There were no demonstrators, just a young man with a clipboard and pen who skirted the area before the funeral began. He somehow made the clipboard disappear before he slipped into the funeral home himself. No one in the congregation knew who he was.

Amy was surprised at the number of people in attendance. The chapel was full. Many of the students were there, as were Maggie, Aggie, the Pattens, the Spinners, and the Fitches. Even Pablo was there. But they scarcely made up a quarter of those assembled. Jesse told Amy the rest were all Way friends from other towns – Sacramento, Yuba City, even Chico and San José.

After the service the congregation followed the ornate hearse to an open grave in the cemetery that gently swept into an Oak Grove surrounding the funeral home. And Carl Waterman was laid to rest there.

At dinner time that evening all the students of the Way met at the SUB.

"Did you hear where assembly's going to be now?"

"Yeah. It's going to be at Patten's house."

"Tonight?"

"Yeah, starting tonight."

"Why at Patten's house?" Amy wanted to know.

"Carl died," Jesse explained. "George is the new bishop, I guess."

"Why isn't it at your house, Marty?" someone asked. "What's wrong with your father?"

"Dan Spinner would make a much better bishop."

"He can't control his kid," Marty laughed. "Payback for raising someone like me."

"I wouldn't brag about that," Janet said.

"From what I heard in court George isn't any great example of raising children," Amy commented.

"Why did all you guys go to court anyway?" Janet asked.

"Janet, you should have been there."

"I'm sure Howard will behave himself from now on," Jenny suggested.

"You guys are so crude," Janet observed.

"Even the Baggy Sisters were there," Marty joked.

"Well Bart wasn't there," Janet said.

"He should've been there too. He should've heard what it was he was trying to cover up."

"Hey!" Marty said. "I like that Shipman guy. He's one cool dude. I liked his closing argument. I've just decided I'm going to be a criminal defense attorney."

"The servants might not approve of that," Janet warned.

"Does it matter to Marty what the servants think?"

"They didn't expel *him* for becoming an attorney," Marty noted.

"I really don't think he's going to get poor old Howard off though, Marty."

"Probably not," Marty agreed. "But he made a really good argument for him, and the jury's still out."

"You don't think the jury's going to let him off, do you?"

"No," Marty agreed. "But you're not supposed to win them all. I lost an argument myself just yesterday in class, but I got my point across anyway."

"What were you arguing about this time?" Melissa asked.

"We had an argument about the death penalty," Marty said.

"And what did you say?"

"I said keep him alive so he can repent."

"Yeah. Repent and confess," someone mocked.

"Confess to whom?" Janet asked. "The servants don't go to prisons."

"You don't need a servant to confess to," Marty objected.

"Oh yes you do."

Marty protested. "The Apostle Paul didn't need a servant when he confessed."

"Who told you that?"

"No one. I read it in the Bible."

"That figures! I didn't think a servant would tell you such a thing."

"I even told a servant what I'd read," Marty said. "I don't think he liked it, though."

"What did he say?"

"He told me I was being a smart ass."

"No he didn't."

"But that's what he meant," Marty laughed.

"Then what do you do with the murderers?" Armstrong asked.

"I don't know," Marty shrugged. "That wasn't the question. I suppose you lock them up and feed them, or something. As long as you allow them a chance to save their souls. How can you save someone's soul and kill him at the same time? What kind of hope do you offer a poor guy when you consider him such a piece of crap that you just want to kill him?"

Suddenly Janet burst into tears. "Now you know how poor Pablo must feel."

"What's the situation with Pablo anyway?" Amy pondered.

"Come on guys, the chow line's open. I'm starved."

Amy didn't find out about Pablo, but the conversation was a seminal moment for her. She saw a sensitivity and soberness in Marty behind his reckless facade. She saw a concern and compassion for apparently disadvantaged people behind the inflexibility in Janet's attitude. It led her to conclude that there was something about the Way that made these seemingly incompatible individuals come together in a very fundamental brotherhood.

When Amy got a chance she asked Jesse privately, "What does Marty do that's so bad, anyway?"

"Nothing. It's just his attitude, I guess. He asks people questions they don't want to answer."

"And that's bad?"

"I know it sounds stupid, but yeah, you have to learn the right questions to ask. I think when kids ask questions some of the servants think they're just being argumentative. I just don't ask questions. It keeps me out of trouble."

"Weird."

As advised, most of the Way friends showed up that evening at the Patten's for assembly. Howard, of course, was not there. Neither was Clay Shipman, though everyone knew he was still in town.

It was strange having George in the role of bishop. Amy was secretly glad she didn't have to let George wash her feet. She was still disturbed by what she'd heard about him in court.

Floyd Toner was there too. Amy wanted to see how everyone would behave around such an important person as the head servant. Scott was there too, and he looked as stressed as he had the time Bart had called everyone together at Dan and Shirley Spinners'. While they all sat waiting for assembly to begin, Amy thought how ironic it was that Bart's appeal for silence concerning Howard had suffered the ultimate of defeats – a court case with embarrassing newspaper headlines.

Sharon Fitch wasn't there, but Herb and Sally were. Maggie gave Amy a greeting smile, and then lowered her eyes in meditation. Marian was there of course, and Joey was sitting bolt upright between her and George.

Amy studied all the faces, and was surprised at how calm everyone looked. They all behaved like nothing had ever happened among them. A lot of them quietly lowered their eyes and waited. Except Marty, as Amy had come to expect. Marty's eyes quietly darted around the room as though he were assessing everyone's skill at being at ease in the circumstances. Amy knew Marty would have an insightful observation to make about the gathering, and it amused her.

Floyd began the service, and they sang a hymn. Then there were prayers, and they were about to sing again when there came a hard knock on the door. George got up to answer it, but the congregation began to sing anyway.

They'd hardly sung the first verse when George came back into the room, followed by two policemen. The singing died abruptly, and George said, "That's him." He pointed at Floyd.

Shocked faces turned to Floyd, who feebly responded, "What can I do for you, sir?"

"Are you Floyd Toner?" one of the officers asked.

"Yes."

"Sir, I have a warrant for your arrest. Can I have you stand, please?"

Floyd rose slowly to his feet, and the second officer moved deftly behind him and began applying handcuffs to him.

Floyd asked, "What have I done?"

"You're being charged with a couple of things. One of them is failure to report a suspected child molester under your supervision, and the other is tampering with witnesses."

"I don't understand, sir. What's this all about?"

"I can't discuss the details with you. All I have is a warrant for your arrest. You'll have to discuss it with your attorney and the judge."

"I have to go to Bakersfield in the morning," Floyd protested.

"Are you going to come with us voluntarily, sir?"

"Why yes, sir. I don't understand this. We're in the middle of a religious service."

The officer turned and looked at everyone sitting around the room. "I'm sorry, folks. I thought you were just visiting ... and singing."

No one responded.

Floyd left, an officer holding each of his elbows. When George closed the door, Marian jumped up and ran from the room. Joey began crying, jumped up, and ran after her.

"I'm scared," Maria said, and grabbed her mother.

Sally saw what Maria did, and she jumped into her father's lap.

"I'm getting out of here," Carla Sturm said, and got up to leave. Her children got up to leave with her, and Rodney followed.

"What do we do now?" someone asked.

"We have to finish the hymn," Aggie said.

Marty laughed aloud, then choked it back.

"Maybe we should all just go home," Herb suggested.

Slowly everyone started getting up and preparing to leave.

"What's going on now?"

"I don't know."

"How can they arrest an old man like him?"

"What were they talking about, anyway?"

"This is really stressful."

Someone said, "This is what he gets for not reporting Howard in the first place." And everyone immediately became silent.

"We should all go home and pray about this."

George Patten looked stunned. Before long the last person had left the room, and he was standing alone at his door, watching them go.

"Poor George," Amy observed. "He looks like someone hit him in the guts."

"His first assembly took a rather bad turn, didn't it?" Jesse commented.

Next morning the Sacramento Bee carried another embarrassing headline.

Cult Bishopric Passes to Extremist Member

ESPADÍN — The late bishop of the religious cult commonly called the Way was laid to rest yesterday afternoon in the Oak Grove

Cemetery in Espadín. His funeral was attended by approximately 100 people, most apparently members of the Way congregations throughout northern California. Bishop Carl Waterman died of a heart attack earlier this week as a trial was getting under way for Howard Barnes, one of the ministers of that religion. Barnes is accused of several counts of child molestation and sexual assault. Prior to his passing, Waterman's home was the scene of a demonstration against Barnes, who was staying at the Waterman residence.

Waterman has been replaced as bishop for the Way in the town of Espadín by another town resident who is of much more questionable reputation than Waterman. The new bishop's name is being withheld in an effort to protect the identity of his son, who was a witness at Barnes' trial and an alleged victim of Barnes. Testimony at the trial revealed that the new bishop is himself the subject of an investigation by Child Protective Services into allegations that he also abused his son physically. He was depicted in court by witnesses as an extremist who believes in strict corporal punishment, submissive obedience of wives to husbands, avoidance of physicians, and extreme loyalty to the hierarchy of his sect. During the trial, Judge Charles Pulsifer had him removed from among the spectators because of his efforts to communicate with his son while his son was on the witness stand.

Closing arguments in the trial of Howard Barnes were presented in the courtroom yesterday, and the jury is now deliberating. Speculation is that a verdict will be returned to the court as early as today. A small number of protesters continue to picket outside the courthouse in an effort to inform the public of their displeasure with Barnes' presence in their community.

That day all the Way students went to class. Who could predict when a verdict would come? And they were all concerned about their final exams.

Late in the morning Amy and Jesse met at the SUB. They had just sat down to talk when Marty stormed in and came straight to their table. "There's a verdict!" he announced.

"What is it?"

"Guilty on all counts."

"Wow," Jesse said.

"Poor Howard," Amy said. "What's going to happen to him now?"

"He's going to prison," Marty said. "They took him away in handcuffs. I have to go to class for a change." And he was off as fast as he came in.

That same morning Aggie and Maggie showed up together at the Del Rio County Jail in Espadín.

"Can I help you?" the lady behind the window asked.

"Yes," Aggie said. "We're here to see Mr. Floyd Toner."

"Who's he?"

"He was arrested last night. We'd like to see him."

The lady turned to someone else in the office and asked if they knew who Floyd Toner was. No one knew.

"Are you sure he was arrested?" the lady asked Aggie.

"Yes. I was there when he was arrested."

"We don't have him here. If he was arrested last night he's maybe still in the holding cell over in the police station."

"We'll go there," Aggie said.

On their way to the police station Aggie said, "I feel like a criminal now myself, walking into a jail and wanting to talk to a prisoner."

Maggie chuckled. "They're probably in there laughing their heads off at two old ladies coming in to talk to a prisoner who isn't there."

Aggie even laughed at that comment.

At the police station Aggie asked, "Where do we go to see someone who was arrested last night?"

"Who are you looking for?"

"Floyd Toner."

The receptionist turned to a police officer sitting at a desk. The officer said, "Mr. Toner was released. He went to court earlier this morning and Judge Harewood released him on his own recognizance."

"What does that mean?" Maggie asked.

"It means he was allowed to go without posting bail."

"Oh. So he went home?"

"I presume so, if he lives in town. Whatever the judge ordered."

"Okay. Thank you," Aggie said.

When they left the building, Maggie said, "They never let Howard go so easily."

"No, they didn't. Half a million dollars, can you imagine? I wonder where the money came from."

"Who knows?"

"I hope this means they're not going to do anything with Uncle Floyd. At least he didn't do anything. I still can't believe Howard did all the things they said he did."

"Well, it gives us occasion to visit a couple of jails, anyway," Maggie joked.

"This is so embarrassing," Aggie said. "I thought this would be all over when they finished with Howard. This is outrageous, really. Poor old Uncle Floyd doesn't need to go through this. Imagine, requiring him to report Howard to the police. What's this world coming to? I think they're making this law up just to cause God's people problems. I think we must be coming into the last days."

"You may be right," Maggie said. "I wish we'd thought to come and look for Howard when he was arrested."

"Maybe it's better we didn't," Aggie said. "I don't think Bart wants us dwelling on him any longer."

"What difference? The only thing that's changed is that we now know what was going on all along."

"As does the whole town," Aggie lamented.

"Well, if they'd reported him to the police in the beginning he'd never have come to Espadín to start with."

"You're probably right. But how could anyone ever have imagined the things he was doing?"

"Aggie! That's what people do when they molest children. And kids can talk."

"You mean that's what goes on every time they say a servant had a problem…? You know… You know what I mean."

"Yes, Aggie. What do you think they'd be doing, holding hands?"

"Well, I wouldn't know, Maggie. I guess I have to be told these things."

"Well, that's what goes on. Frankly I was surprised Howard hadn't done a lot more. Of course, he was only here for a couple of months before he got stopped. He'd probably have done a lot more when he found out what all he could get off with."

"Do you really believe that?" Aggie was horrified. "I can't imagine anyone even touching someone." She shivered in disgust.

"Aggie, you never had a boyfriend, did you?"

"No."

"That would help you understand what happens."

Aggie thought for a while, then said, "This makes me sick."

"Me too."

Aggie was quiet for a long time. Then she said, "Did you get an invitation to the reception at the Spinners' for Jenny and Gilmore?"

"Yes. I think it's wonderful they're doing that for them. All the other young kids will be leaving town soon, so they can all be there with them before they go."

"I don't think Bart likes what they're doing."

"I get quite weary of the things Bart doesn't like," Maggie said. "Why on earth did he expel them anyway? I don't understand."

"They say it's because they didn't consult with anyone ahead of time."

"That's ridiculous! Who ever heard of someone being expelled for that reason?"

"Well, you know," Aggie stammered. "I don't know. I guess he had a reason."

"Yeah. He just wants to be in everyone's business."

"Maggie," Aggie exasperated. "He's a servant."

"And if he were a little kid we'd consider him a spoiled brat."

"Maggie ... !"

Saturday morning Amy met Jesse in the SUB after his swim. She was agitated. Jesse asked her what was going on.

"You want the good news or the bad news first?" Amy asked.

"Let's do the bad news first," Jesse suggested.

"The good news is easier. I changed my mind. I'm going to stay here for the summer. I have a job here in the library filling in for all the librarians when they go on vacation."

"Hey, that's great."

"Well, the bad news is ... Wait! I need a newspaper. I'll be right back." She ran across the hall and bought a newspaper and returned. She said, "My father's not pleased with the news from Espadín at all."

"Oh no!"

"He wants me to come home immediately. But I don't want to go. And he said there's more in the paper this morning about the Way, and he wants me to get out of it." She was frantically turning pages of the newspaper trying to find what her father had been talking about.

"Oh oh!"

"Here it is," she announced and began reading.

Verdict and Further Arrest in Espadín Cult Sex Abuse Case

ESPADÍN — Yesterday proved an eventful day for the members of the religious group in Espadín known as the Way. Late in the morning the jury returned its verdict in the trial of Howard

Barnes. Barnes, 47, was charged with the sexual molestation of five child members of the group, and the jury found him guilty on all counts.

Judge Charles Pulsifer sentenced Barnes to one year on each of the two charges of lewdness with a minor. On a third charge of committing a lascivious act on a minor, Barnes was sentenced to three years. On the fourth count, sexual penetration of a minor, Barnes was sentenced to six years. Judge Pulsifer also sentenced Barnes to eight years for performing oral copulation on a person under the age of 14 years. All sentences, except one for lewdness with a minor, are considered felonies and are to be served consecutively in the state prison system. The remaining count of lewdness with a minor is considered a misdemeanor and the sentence for that crime is to be served concurrently with the other four. Barnes is expected to spend a total of 18 years in prison for these crimes.

The Espadín congregation of the Way has also been confronted with another legal problem. Floyd Toner, the leader of all congregations of the Way in California was himself arrested on Thursday evening on two charges in connection with the Barnes case. He is charged with tampering with witnesses in the Barnes trial, and with failing to report Barnes suspected child molestations, as required by California law. Toner, 93, is a resident of Bakersfield. Law enforcement officers in Espadín inadvertently interrupted a service of the Way congregation to make their arrest.

"That's a pretty rough article," Jesse commented.

"And my father reads this stuff and he believes all of it," Amy complained.

"Well, unfortunately all of that was true," Jesse reminded her.

"But my father thinks it's typical of everyone in the Way."

"That's why you have to be careful about what you read in the newspaper."

"What am I going to do?" Amy asked.

"He didn't disown you, so I guess you can just hang on and show him the Way isn't all like that."

"You're awfully cool with this."

"I've known all my life that people react like this to the Way. People are just automatically afraid of people who are different. I guess it's called persecution that we sometimes have to face."

"I hope so," Amy said. "Because, you know, I think the Way is right."

"Yeah?"

"Yeah. I do. All the kids who come here to school talk like they have no doubts whatsoever about it. And every time I ask a question I get an answer right from the Bible. And I can tell they consider Bart kind of, you know, nasty. I don't like him."

"I agree with you. I try to avoid servants like him. It keeps me out of trouble."

Amy laughed. "You told me that yesterday too."

"I'm glad you're staying for the summer," Jesse said. "I won't be left alone in Espadín."

"You wouldn't be left alone anyway," Amy reminded him. "Marty lives here. He'll be here anyway."

"Well, yeah, but that's different." He blushed.

Amy liked his reaction.

CHAPTER 19

It was like a sweet, exciting dream. Clay felt fingernails lightly caressing his chest, and he breathed heavily. When they drifted across his abdomen he felt himself responding, and he stretched to relax and enjoy. He put his arms over his head as the fingers softly grazed his erection, and then the face appeared.

He'd seen it many times. It was always that middle aged man with the black messy hair and unshaven face. He wore thick glasses that magnified his leering eyes, and he always had the same wide grin. The beautiful moment was shattered. The panic came when the man moved to kiss Clay's lips.

Clay struggled to free himself, but as always happened in the dream he found it impossible to make his arms move to defend himself. This time he resisted with more effort, and he struggled to free himself from the man's advance. He woke up and heard himself yelling, "No! No! Stop it!"

Suddenly awake, he had control over his arms and legs, so he pushed his tormenter away and leaped out of bed. The lecherous face disappeared, but he was reeling with revulsion.

He almost lost his balance. He headed to the living room and he thought he heard Nancy say his name.

In a couple of minutes Nancy came out and sat beside him on the couch. "What happened?"

Clay didn't respond.

"Did you have a nightmare?"

"Yeah."

"I was afraid it was me. I was touching you."

"No, it wasn't you" he assured her. "Your touch is beautiful."

"What happened?"

"I don't think I can tell you. It might shock you too much."

"Is it the same one you have all the time?"

"Yes, I have it a lot. And every time it gets worse." He sighed.

Nancy hugged his neck. "Talk about it."

He thought for a long while. He'd hid it from everyone for so many years, but there was no way to get rid of it.

"It's a dream about the man who molested me when I was a kid," he began. "It only happens when I don't know you're going to touch me. I just wish it would go away – I love it when you touch me."

Nancy listened with concern.

"It happened in the dorm at retreat in Nebraska."

"In the dorm?"

"Yes. It makes me feel sick. He waited until all the lights were out. He got down beside my cot while I was asleep and reached under my blanket. Then he grabbed me and stroked me."

"What did you do?"

"Nothing. I was only 12 and he was a middle aged man. And an exservant as well. I didn't dare make a noise or move because someone would've turned on the light and seen me." He paused. "I've never told anyone."

"It's okay. Tell me."

"Once he started I couldn't tell him to stop. As soon as he finished, I felt totally disgusted and dirty. I couldn't sleep the rest of the night. I could hardly wait for morning to take a shower. I even turned my sleeping blanket inside out."

Nancy hung on every word and rubbed his back.

"The worst part was that he made me promise to keep it a secret. There were people around so he whispered it in my ear and I felt his beard scratching my cheek. I was so disgusted. I wish it hadn't felt good."

"He was a sick old man," Nancy said.

"He's still alive and going to retreats," Clay said. "The nauseating part was that it felt good. I couldn't deal with that."

"You were 12 years old. It feels good, whether you like it or not."

He sighed. "It was the first time I ever came. I didn't want to learn that from him." He sobbed. "I wanted to ... to learn about it when I knew what was going on, with someone I liked. He just used me like some kind of farm animal and then left me alone. He hasn't spoken to me since. I had no way to find out what had happened to me.

"I could never figure out why he picked me to do that to. For years I thought there was something wrong with me that made him pick me.

He really didn't need to worry about me telling my parents because I didn't want them to know there was something wrong with me. I'd never heard of a child molester, so I didn't have any other explanation for what happened."

"I don't know what I'd have done," Nancy said. "They should be ashamed of themselves. They expect little kids to shut up and heal themselves, and they especially don't want the kids to tell their parents – the very people who could help them the most." She hugged him. "They don't care that the kids feel guilty about what they did."

"They don't even know that the kids feel anything. They have no rapport with them. Kids are just ... sex objects to them. They treat them like a piece of crap and leave them to deal with it alone where they left them."

"You know, I watched you freak out with this case of Howard's. It was a lot more than the slipperiness of the servants that got to you, wasn't it?"

Clay couldn't answer.

"You'd come home and sit with your eyes glazed over like you were in a really bad daydream for a long time. This is why, isn't it?"

Clay nodded.

"And I have a little secret to share with you."

"What?"

"Nathan saw it happening to you too."

"Oh! He told you?"

"It's okay. He just knew there was something about the case that was really bothering you."

"I knew he did."

"And now you're this big time tough criminal attorney who isn't supposed to be a human being underneath it all. You know what? The servants don't care what you feel like on the inside as long as you can shut up and look good. It stokes their reputation when their flock looks good. If you were to say anything about this to them they'd just say you were whining for attention. Someone has to shove these things right in their face or they'll never get it."

"You sound as angry as I feel."

"That servant should've been reported to the police. Look what it's done to you and me. I want to be able to touch you and make you feel good." She began to cry. "That's why I married you."

Clay hugged her tightly. "You know, I always wondered if he did the same thing with some of the other kids at retreat. I could see something funny in the looks on their faces when he'd walk by us in the yard in the day time. I've always wondered if he went from one cot to another in the dark."

"That's disgusting. He probably did."

"This case in Espadín has really made me go back over this again and reevaluate what went on with me. I can't believe the evil that comes from the actions of those people. I'm crying, ain't I?"

"It's okay," Nancy assured him.

Clay had wondered for years what Nancy would think of him if he were to tell her about the incident. It was a great weight off his mind to suddenly realize that she understood more than he'd ever allowed himself to realize. "Hug me some more," he said. "This has ruined so many good moments for us." A wave of relief swept over him. All he could think was, *She understands.* He let her talk.

"I used to think there was something wrong with me," Nancy confessed. "It seemed like every time I'd come up on you you'd get turned off. You never told me what was going on."

"I'm sorry," he said. "There wasn't anything wrong with you."

"There isn't anything wrong with you either."

"Thanks."

Clay was wiping tears from Nancy's face when Dennis appeared. "Are you crying, Mommy?"

"Just a bit," she replied.

"We had a really bad nightmare," Clay explained.

"You both had a nightmare?" Dennis asked.

"Yeah."

"You're funny!" Dennis said. "Is it better now?"

"Much better, Dennis. Nightmares are only scary while you're still asleep."

"And when they keep coming back," Dennis said.

"That's true, isn't it?" Nancy agreed.

"You're so right," Clay confirmed.

Later that morning the phone rang in Clay's office. His secretary said, "There's a Mr. Bart Stanley on the telephone and he wants to talk to you."

Clay felt sick in the pit of his stomach.

"I'm sorry to bother you," Bart began. "But we're wondering if you could help Uncle Floyd."

What can I do for him?"

"He was arrested last Thursday night."

"What for?"

"They said he was bothering the witnesses in Howard's trial, and they said he neglected to tell the police about Howard."

"How come I didn't know about this? I was in Espadín at the time."

"But you didn't go to assembly here."

"But I was in the courtroom on Friday morning."

"Well, he was in the other courtroom, and we didn't want any more people to know about this than necessary."

Clay was shocked. "Where is he now?"

"He's asleep here at the studio. In Espadín."

"Did someone post bail for him?"

"No. They let him out without bail. But he's not supposed to leave the county without permission. He has to go to court tomorrow morning, and he needs an attorney."

There was a lengthy silence. "We were wondering if you could come and help him," Bart continued.

"I can't be there by tomorrow morning."

"If you left now you could be here by dinner time tonight," Bart said.

Clay had still not recovered from his early morning nightmare, and the insistence in Bart's voice angered him. He felt like saying, *Don't tell me what I can do*, but thought better of it. "I think it would be better if you found a local attorney to help Uncle Floyd."

"Uncle Floyd felt you'd be the best person to help him out of this predicament."

"You know, you should also consider the fact that Uncle Floyd actually did what they say he did. He'd probably be better off if he just admitted that to whatever attorney you hire for him."

Bart was quiet for a minute. "Well, I guess I'll have to take your advice on this."

"I'm sorry I can't be of any more help to you," Clay assured him.

"I'm sure in any case that God will help him," Bart said, and hung up.

Clay sat stunned, still staring at the telephone when Nathan came in and said, "How about a walk around the block. I have to stretch."

"So do I."

That evening at dinner Clay said, "I was approached today to represent another servant in court?"

"What?" Nancy was horrified.

"Yeah."

"Who this time?"

"Uncle Floyd."

"Oh, no!" Nancy said. "For molesting kids?"

"Not that serious. He's being charged with tampering with the witnesses in Espadín."

"What the little birdie told me was true, huh?"

Clay smiled. "Yes, the little birdie was right on."

"So are you going to represent him?"

"No."

"Good," Nancy said.

"But Daddy," Dennis interrupted. "You need to make sure he gets treated properly in court."

Clay had momentarily forgotten they were talking in front of Dennis. "He'll be okay, Dennis. They'll have another good attorney to represent him."

"Will they get him off?" Dennis was curious.

"Only if he did do nothing wrong," Clay assured him.

"Howard did something bad, didn't he?" Dennis asked.

"Yes, he did."

"I know," Dennis said. "I heard them talking about it at assembly last night."

"Really?"

"Yeah."

"Mona was whispering to me after assembly," Nancy said. "She was horrified that Howard had been convicted. At least she was appreciative of the fact that you'd represented him. I think she has a slightly higher opinion of you right now."

Clay laughed.

"But I won't tell anyone about it," Dennis assured his father. "I'll only tell people like you and Mom and whoever you say is okay."

"Now you're a really smart kid," Clay said. "You'll be a really good attorney someday."

Dennis smiled broadly.

It was just a few days later that Clay came home from work again with news for Nancy. "You'll never guess who showed up in my office today."

"Who?"

"Chester."

"You mean the servant Chester?"

"Yeah."

"Dare I ask what he wanted?"

"Yeah," Clay sighed, and slid his briefcase into the closet. "I've been caught lying."

"Lying?"

Clay was returning to his office from the jail that morning when he noticed Chester sitting in the waiting area. "Good morning, Chester."

Chester stood up. "Good morning. Can I talk to you a minute?"

"Uh, yeah," Clay said. He turned to his secretary and told her he'd be busy until after lunch. "Come with me, Chester."

"I thought I'd call on our friendship to ask you a favor," Chester began.

"Yes?"

"I told Bart I'd ask you to help Uncle Floyd with his problems."

"I told Bart I couldn't do anything for him."

"I know. I thought maybe I could take advantage of our friendship and ask for a favor."

Clay studied him a minute. *You picked the wrong day to call me your friend*, he thought. Suddenly Clay felt like he could vomit. "No, I'm sorry. I can't help you."

"It would be best if you could."

"I didn't do so well for Howard."

"We'd like to have one of our own working with us."

"Why?"

"We feel a lot more comfortable with them."

Clay hesitated, then said, "Well, I felt very uncomfortable working for Howard."

"Yes, I suppose," Chester said. "But I guess he actually committed crimes, didn't he?"

"I'm afraid Uncle Floyd has actually committed some crimes too."

"But don't you defend people who commit crimes?"

"Yes, I do. But, you know, I have to be frank with you. I investigate my clients and I like it when they aren't hiding anything from me." He was going to say more, but changed his mind. He wondered who Chester may report their conversation to.

"Uncle Floyd won't be hiding anything from you," Chester assured him.

"I'd prefer not to work with him this time," Clay stated.

Chester looked frustrated. "Well, it's just unfortunate that you treated our friends in Espadín the way you did."

"How's that?"

"I've been told that you made them all out to be liars in court."

"Really?"

"They didn't appreciate that. Were you lying in court? It didn't help the Way at all."

"Why are we having this conversation?" Clay asked.

"I was hoping to impress upon you the need for some loyalty among God's people," Chester stammered.

"No, no," Clay corrected. "You were trying to impress upon me the need to convince the rest of the world about a righteous loyalty we have among us. But we have a problem, the rest of the world knows that two members of our ministry have committed crimes, some of them serious crimes against the rest of us. Everyone calls that abuse."

"Abuse?"

"Yes, abuse."

"Abuse of whom?"

"Servants abusing the congregation. I expect the rest of the world is watching to see if we're going to put up with that."

"I'd hope you wouldn't report a servant to the police."

"You should ask me what I'd do if I caught any living creature abusing my child!"

"I'm shocked."

"I've had a few shocks myself recently," Clay said. "Anyway, I see that no matter whose side I take in a legal case involving two of the Way friends, I run the risk of offending to the point of being expelled."

"Oh, surely not," Chester assured him.

"Maybe you wouldn't expel me, but someone else might. And then what recourse would I have?"

Chester didn't know what to say. When he was leaving, he said, "I hope we don't have to deal with this kind of thing again."

"I hope so," Clay agreed.

"I get it," Nancy said. "He was trying to make you feel guilty about Howard being convicted."

"I think he was trying to turn the screws on me and blackmail me into working for Uncle Floyd. It didn't work."

"You should have told him it was the servants who were twisting the truth."

"I could have told him a lot of things, but who knows whom he'd repeat it to? I just want to have nothing more to do with their legal problems."

"I agree. Dinner's ready, and we have to go to assembly."

"Yes," Clay remembered. "I also told Chester that assembly should be on Friday night, because Easter was on Sunday. If Sunday was the third day, then Friday was the day of the Last Supper. I don't think he liked it a bit."

"You can't behave yourself, can you?"
Clay laughed, and felt a bit better for it.

CHAPTER 20

When the last Wednesday of the college year came, a reception was held at the Spinners' house for Jenny and Gilmore. Shirley had a head table and other tables through the dining room and living room for a sit down dinner. A neighbor lady was in the kitchen with her preparing dinner, and Marty was setting the tables when the guests started arriving. Dan was pinning the last of the trimmings around the room. A tiered wedding cake sat on a small table in the corner. Amy recognized it as the table they normally used for the bread and wine ritual at Sunday fellowship potlucks. The atmosphere was festive.

"We can put the gifts here," Shirley said to each person who arrived.

As requested, Jenny and Gilmore arrived right on time, and they were greeted with cheers, hugs, and congratulations. The old ladies all wanted kisses, and the children were quite fascinated by the first wedding reception they'd ever seen.

Gilmore's mother and father were there. So were Jenny's mother and father. Someone whispered, "I guess Jenny's mother decided she'd at least show up for her daughter's wedding reception. Dear little Jenny!"

When they were all seated, Dan asked a blessing, and Shirley began serving salads.

"What a great party!" someone commented.

"Marty makes a good waiter, doesn't he?"

"We should send him in to the city to wait in one of the high class restaurants down there."

When the salads were about finished and Marty was gathering up the plates; Dan circulated, filling each person's glass from bottles of sparkling drinks. Floyd Armstrong proposed a toast. He cracked a few tame jokes and expressed great wishes that the new couple would live a long and happy life together. Everyone clinked their glasses and sipped.

"Sparkling wine!" Amy commented.

"Yeah. No real wine for dinner," Jesse explained.

"Why not?"

"People might get drunk."

"But the people who've been baptized can have wine."

"Only if it's been, you know, prayed for, and blessed, whatever."

"I thought all the kids at college weren't drinking because they weren't old enough to drink legally."

"Well, that too," Jesse said. "But wine is a sacred drink and it's supposed to be a blasphemy or something to just drink it like a beverage."

"Oh!"

Marty and his mother began serving the main course – plates laden with generous slices of prime rib, rice pilaf, and mixed vegetables. There was a chorus of ahhs as each person got his plate, and the joyful conversation continued.

There was a large burst of laughter from the table where Maggie, Aggie, and Marge Waterman were sitting. "The old ladies are acting up," one of the students commented.

When the dinner plates had been cleared from the tables, it was time for Jenny and Gilmore to cut the cake. Out came the cameras, and Gilmore was warned not to upset the cake on the floor. That accomplished, Shirley and the neighbor lady began cutting the rest of the cake and Marty was assigned to serve.

At that point the door bell rang, and before Dan could answer it Bart walked in. Someone said, "Hi Bart." But Bart just stood there, examining the whole scene.

"Have a seat," Dan invited. "We can even get you a plate of prime rib if you'd like."

"No thank you," Bart said. "I'll just have a seat in the kitchen until you're all done."

Everyone acted like something was wrong, but it only dampened the mood slightly. As the cake disappeared, the tables were cleared and folded up so people could sit and visit.

The visiting didn't last as long as Amy had expected.

"I think they're worried about what Bart's going to think of this," Jesse whispered to her.

"What's wrong?" Amy asked.

"Oh, who knows? I'm glad I can go home right away."

A few people helped Jenny and Gilmore carry the gifts to their car, and when they left the others went home too.

"What a wonderful evening!" Maggie said as she was leaving.

"Yes," Mrs. Waterman said. "What a sweet young couple! Too bad they can't come to assembly anymore."

"Good night everyone," another said.

"Let's have lunch at the SUB tomorrow," Marty said quietly to Jesse as he and Amy were leaving.

"Will do!" Jesse said.

On their way home, Jesse said to Amy, "We'll hear all about Bart's disapproval tomorrow."

Amy agreed. "And you can trust Marty to tell all!"

The SUB was almost deserted when Marty, Amy, and Jesse arrived. There wasn't even a line at the cafeteria.

"So what was Bart's mood last night?" Jesse asked.

"Ah!" Marty began. "He was quite wound up. You should've stayed around and heard him. He started with, 'What's going on here, Dan?'"

"We were having a bit of a wedding reception for Jenny and Floyd Gilmore," Dan replied.

"Really!" Bart said.

"Yeah."

"Why didn't I know about this?"

"We organized it rather quickly, and we only invited the people Gilmore and Jenny had asked for."

"I see. An ungodly affair, I'm sure."

"How so?" Dan asked.

"I saw wine bottles on every table."

"That was sparkling drinks," Dan explained. "There was no alcohol."

"So you didn't have the bread and wine either."

"No. I didn't think it would be appropriate to have that when the guests of honor weren't allowed to participate."

"An ungodly gathering. I'd have thought better of you."

"Well, I apologize," Dan said.

"I'd have thought you'd have consulted with me before you decided to honor such people as them in your home."

"I didn't really know...."

"You surely know not to use your home to honor immoral people."

"Immoral?" Marty interjected. "They're not doing anything immoral."

"Sonny," Bart admonished. "You listen to me. They were fornicating."

"How do you know?" Marty asked.

"How do you know they weren't?" Bart asked. "I don't have to know they weren't. They made it look obvious."

"So are they still fornicating?" Marty asked.

"It makes no difference. God's servants have an unction about such things and they have the authority to make final decisions on such matters."

"Marty, take it easy," his mother cautioned.

"Sure. I have to go to my room and do some studying."

"Studying?" Amy asked. "You were studying last night? Exams are all over"

Marty laughed. "It was a good excuse to make a quick exit. And Bart didn't know any different."

"And you left your parents alone with him," Jesse said.

"Yeah. They can handle him a lot better than I can."

"I don't like him," Amy said.

"He'll go away," Marty said.

"I liked Howard a lot better," Amy commented.

"Yeah. It's too bad he like playing with little kids," Jesse added.

"He was a cool dude otherwise," Marty said. "I think Scotty's going to be a servant like him."

"Where is Scotty these days?" Jesse asked.

"Bart doesn't allow him out much," Marty laughed. "I think he's having a really bad time with Bart."

"Why don't we go over to my place and play Monopoly or Scrabble or something," Jesse suggested.

"Let's go," Amy said. "It's getting too hot to hang around outside."

They had no sooner gone into Jesse's apartment than Marty looked out the window and said, "Here comes Bart!"

"Oh no," Amy said. "Let's hide." She laughed.

"That only prolongs the agony," Marty said. "I'll stay here with you. We can gang up on him." He laughed.

Jesse quickly put his small portable television behind the couch.

"What did you do that for?" Amy asked.

"I don't want to get any more criticism from Bart than necessary," Jesse said. "I expect he'd dump all over me if he saw it here."

"For sure," Marty confirmed.

"Wow," Amy said. "Brutal Bart is a good name for him."

The rap came on the door, and Jesse opened it. "Come in, Bart."

"Thank you," Bart said. He stepped in and looked all around the room. "Have a seat."

"Thank you. What are you all doing here today?"

"We were going to have a game of Monopoly."

"Monopoly," Bart repeated.

"Yes."

"I thought that was a kid's game."

"It probably is," Jesse said. "But we like to play it sometimes."

"I see." Bart said. "Well, I'll get right to the point."

No one spoke, so Bart continued. "I have a couple of things that I'd like to talk to you about today. You and Amy both."

"Okay," Jesse replied.

"Yes," Bart continued. "I was quite disappointed to see you at the Spinners' house last night. It wasn't a very godly gathering."

No one responded, so he continued. "It's not appropriate to honor such immoral people in the homes of God's people."

"Immoral people?" Amy asked.

"Amy," Bart cautioned. "You'll have to listen to me and I'll tell you how it has to be. We cannot have people going around behind the servants' backs and honoring such people. Yes, they're immoral. They were fornicating."

"Baloney," Amy said.

"Amy, I'm attempting to get you in line with God's laws. You'll have to be respectful and take some advice."

"Okay," Amy consented.

"When people are expelled from the Way, there's a very serious reason for it. And to continue to associate with them as usual does two things that are very harmful. First of all, it gives the expelled people the notion that you support what they're doing, and they get the notion they're just the victims of some stubborn servant. That's very dangerous, because it makes it much more difficult for them to confess again at some time in the future.

"The second reason is that it gives people a terrible impression of you. You know the old saying birds of a feather flock together. To be seen with such people is to do great damage to your own reputation. What would people think of you if they saw you associating with them?"

No one replied. Amy looked ready to do verbal battle with him. Jesse was being guardedly silent. Marty looked like a laugh was just under the surface.

Bart continued. "The other matter I wanted to bring up with you, Jesse, is your association with Amy. You're seeing far too much of her."

Jesse shrugged his shoulders, and said nothing.

"You know, Jesse, you have an extremely good reputation among the Way friends, and I'd hate to see you damage that reputation because of her."

"And what do you mean by that?" Amy was furious.

"I'll explain," Bart continued. "Jesse, you're good material for the service, and if you're seen too much with her you'd never be considered acceptable."

"But Bart," Jesse protested. "We're not even boyfriend and girlfriend."

Bart ignored him, and continued. "People will begin thinking that you two are fornicating. And you, Amy, have got to learn to be ashamed of yourself for being alone in an apartment with two men. This gives a very shameful testimony about the Way."

"And do you think Howard's trial did anything to help the image of the Way?" Amy was controlling her tone of voice.

"No, that was shameful too. But that doesn't mean we can't clean up this area. It's become like Sodom and Gomorrah, and I plan to do some house cleaning while I'm here. I'd like to speak highly of all of you to Uncle Floyd, but I'll need to see some improvement in your behaviors before I can do that."

No one responded.

"Can I depend on you folks to comply with that?"

"I'll do the best I can," Jesse assured him.

"And what about you, Amy?"

"I'll see," she said. "I'm a little... Nothing."

"What's that?"

"Oh, nothing," she said. "I'll try."

"I'll be very pleased with you when I see some improvements."

Bart looked like he was going to have some advice for Marty too, but changed his mind.

The business out of the way, Bart made an attempt to change the subject – somewhat. "So have you considered going in the service?" he asked Jesse.

"No. I'm going to be a high school science teacher."

"Will you be teaching evolution?"

"I don't know."

Bart studied Jesse for a long time, then looked all around the room again. No one said anything. Then suddenly he excused himself, said he also needed to visit some other people that afternoon, and left.

When he was gone, Marty said, "Cleaning house! Now there's a man I could have a tremendous lot of fun with. I could bait him until he lost his mind. Do you suppose he snorts when he gets really mad?"

"You better be careful," Jesse said. "He's got a lot of pull with Uncle Floyd."

"If we can keep Uncle Floyd locked up he won't have anyone to report us to," Marty speculated.

"You still better be careful anyway," Jesse cautioned. "If they lock up Uncle Floyd, Bart might just become Uncle Bart, and then you'll really have a problem."

"No," Marty explained. "The next head servant is supposed to be Mark Volpe. I've heard he's a cool dude."

"Let's play Monopoly," Amy said. "I'm about to get either raging mad or extremely depressed."

"Okay." They agreed.

CHAPTER 21

That night at assembly Amy sat nervously waiting for the service to start. Bart was there, and cast darting glances around the room as though checking each person's attitude. Suddenly Amy remembered his admonishment of earlier that morning, and she abruptly stood up and moved to a seat apart from Jesse. Jesse looked confused, until Amy glanced from him to Bart, and then back to Jesse. He nodded that he understood.

All the students were gone, except Amy, Marty, and Jesse. Sharon and Sally Fitch were not there, and neither were Ana and Maria Castro. Helen Sawyer was there with Spike, and Spike looked very subdued. The Sturms were all there, as were the Pattens – of course. Maggie and Aggie were there too. Marge Waterman looked so lonely. She'd never been seen anywhere without her husband for as long as anyone could remember.

For the most part the assembly went as usual, except that Marian Patten didn't pray. Bart was the last person to speak, and he had a very long sermon.

The first point he made was about the sin of men, especially young men, being lured into immorality by seductive women. Amy guessed the sermon was part of Bart's housecleaning project, and it became apparent that Jesse's sin would be first to be addressed. Bart read:

> ... *keep thee from the evil woman, from the flattery of the tongue of a strange woman. Lust not after her beauty in thine heart; neither let her take thee with her eyelids. For by means of a whorish woman a man is brought to a piece of bread; and the adulteress will hunt for the precious life.*

Bart spoke at length about various men he had met who had come to spiritual disaster because of the women they spent time with. One of the women had confessed just to get the man, and that had been a disaster. Another man married a woman whom he later found to be unfaithful, and that was a disaster. Another man thought he could live in a mixed marriage, and that was a disaster too.

Amy was not sure exactly what he meant by spiritual disaster, but she did consider that the sermon was as much about her as about Jesse. She caught Marty giving Jesse a wink, and she wished she could be as unaffected by Bart as Marty seemed to be.

Then Bart moved on to another housecleaning target, and Amy was cautiously relieved. As expected, the Spinners were a concern. And he read:

> *... ye have brought into my sanctuary strangers, uncircumcised in heart, and uncircumcised in flesh, to be in my sanctuary; to pollute it, even my house, when ye offer my bread, the fat and the blood, and they have broken my covenant because of all your abominations.*

Bart expounded on the theme of one's home being God's sanctuary. The list of things that could pollute God's sanctuary proved interesting: immoral and uncircumcised guests, the brawling of celebrations, pretensions of blasphemous drinking, lounging in lascivious garments, indulging in worldly media, and lascivious activities in private.

Ah, Amy thought. I heard the Lword twice.

Everyone present could probably be included in the next reproof. The passage:

> *Let us walk honestly, as in the day; not in rioting and drunkenness, not in chambering and wantonness, not in strife and envying. But put you on the Lord Jesus Christ, and make not provision for the flesh, to fulfill the lusts thereof. And be not drunk with wine, wherein is excess; but be filled with the Spirit; Speaking to yourselves in psalms and hymns and spiritual songs, singing and making melody in your heart to the Lord...*

Bart explained that when God's people are together they shouldn't be discussing the news, talking about anyone not present, or making plans for a future that might not be theirs. Neither should they get together to play or party, because those activities are spiritually unprofitable. Rather, the Way friends should discuss Godly things such as what God expects from them, and the work of the servants. He suggested that when they're together they should sing at least one hymn for each person present.

Amy checked, and Marty was counting heads. Jesse rolled his eyes. Everyone else was studying whatever was in their laps.

On their way outside after assembly Marty started giggling. "Now I know what Gilmore's problem is. He's uncircumcised."

Jesse laughed. "So is Howard, apparently."

"I have an idea," Marty said. "Tomorrow when Bart comes over I'm going to say to him, 'Bart, I enjoyed your sermon very much last night. I learned things I never knew before. And it explained to me why Howard could be so evil – he's uncircumcised. Did you know that, Bart?'"

"Shh," Amy cautioned. "Here comes Aggie."

"Let's go to the Ice Cream Palace."

Once there, Marty announced, "Bart's going to get rid of the studio."

"Why?"

"He says it's not needed anymore because there are enough houses in the area that he can rotate from one to the other without being a bother to anyone."

Amy laughed and almost choked. "You are crazy!"

"No," Marty said. "I'm serious."

"Oh, help!" Amy said.

"He can really clean house then," Jesse observed. "Literally."

"You got it," Marty said. "It's kind of funny, though. I happen to know the landlord asked him to give his notice. I guess he's had it with demonstrations in front of his house and servants molesting kids in the apartment."

"So now the servants will move in with the kids!" Amy was shocked.

"They do that most places anyway," Jesse explained. "Anywhere there are a lot of friends around, they just stay with them."

"It's supposed to be more scriptural," Marty said.

Amy studied him. She didn't know whether he was serious or joking. "You're joking, right?"

"No," Marty said. "Would I joke?"

"So this thing about being circumcised – do you have to be circumcised too?"

"I don't know," Marty said, and looked at Jesse. "Are you?"

"I don't know," Jesse laughed, and blushed profusely.

"You're a trouble maker," Jesse said.

Marty laughed.

"I am too," Amy confessed. "I might as well tell you what I did. I reported George to the police."

"You did?"

"What for?"

"Didn't you see that bump on the side of Marian's head last Thursday night?" Amy asked.

"No."

"I thought she'd been hit on the head so I called the police."

"Wow!" Marty said, and thumped the table. "You rebel! What did they say?"

"I didn't talk to them at first," She explained. "Friday night I wrote up a thing about what I'd seen and suspected, and I went over to the police station and I dropped it in the mail slot at the front desk."

"Did you sign it?"

"Yeah. And I put my address and telephone number on it."

"What happened?"

"About an hour later a couple of policemen came knocking on my door, and they wanted to ask me some more questions. I suppose they also wanted to make sure I was a real person. I never heard anything else until the next afternoon. One of them came back and told me they'd arrested George, and he was out on bail. And he wasn't supposed to go back to his house for seven days. They called it a cooling down period."

"But that was only last weekend?" Marty said.

"It hasn't been seven days yet."

"I know," Amy said.

"Where was he in the meantime?"

"My Dad said he saw George leaving the servants' studio the other day," Marty said. "Do you suppose he was staying there?"

"He shouldn't have been at his own house tonight." Amy said. "And when I get home tonight I'm going to call the police station and leave a little message. That officer told me to call him if I ever noticed anything else. George still has to go before the judge again tomorrow morning."

"We're going to end up with everyone in jail," Jesse said. "This is getting out of hand."

"Are there any other completely dead towns in California where we can send this girl?" Marty asked. "You sure know how to stir things up."

"What's going to happen to Uncle Floyd?" Jesse asked.

"I haven't heard a thing," Marty said. "No one's said anything about him."

"Do you want to go to court in the morning and see what's going on?" Amy asked.

"Sure," Marty said. "I like this stuff. Court is fun."

"It's not so much fun for the people on trial," Amy said.

"No. But the adrenaline!" Marty said. "Can you imagine what it would be like to be in a courtroom before a judge and some man's life was at stake depending on what you could do for him. Man, I have to have some of that! I'm going to be an attorney."

"You can have it," Amy said. "I got so nervous just sitting in that courtroom. I hope I never need to sit anywhere in that room in my lifetime."

"Where's Howard now?" Jesse asked.

"They took him to the State Prison in Sacramento," Marty said. "We should go see him."

"Are we allowed?" Amy asked.

"Sure," Marty said, "unless you're another criminal."

"But what about Bart? What will he think?"

"Who cares? Forgiveness is a lot easier to get than permission. Let's go anyway and see what happens."

"I was going to go home for the long weekend," Amy said. "But court tomorrow and State Prison on Sunday – that could be more fun."

"What about fellowship on Sunday?" Jesse asked.

"We'll have fellowship with Howard," Marty said.

"But Howard was expelled when he was convicted," Amy reminded him.

"Who cares?" Marty said. "Play stupid."

"Marty," Jesse said. "How many good kids have you gotten into trouble so far in your lifetime?"

Marty laughed. "Maybe a few."

They all laughed.

When they arrived at court the next morning they found both George Patten and Floyd Toner on the docket.

"Did you call the policeman last night?" Jesse asked.

"I sure did."

"What did he say?"

"He thanked me. He said he was going to be here this morning."

"All rise."

The business of the day began rather slowly. There was a traffic incident that needed to be dealt with. There was a truant student whose punishment had to be assigned by the court. And there was a dizzy acting high school student who was sent with the bailiff to submit to a urine test somewhere in the bowels of the building.

Then it was time for Floyd Toner's matter to be dealt with.

"Your honor," his attorney said. "My client wishes to plead guilty to all charges brought against him."

Judge Pulsifer questioned Floyd about his understanding of his guilty pleas, and asked him some specific questions about each of the victims he had attempted to influence. He then asked Floyd and his attorney if they had any comments to make before he pronounced sentence.

Floyd's attorney had some requests. "Your honor, I'd request that you respect my client's advanced age and consider that to confine him would be an undue hardship for him. Furthermore, it's unlikely that he'll reoffend. Also, I'd ask you to consider that Mr. Toner has a residence in Bakersfield, and if he were granted probation he'd like the convenience of living there."

In a further attempt to soften the punishment for Floyd, the attorney offered another consideration. "You honor, considering that in almost any other jurisdiction in this state the courts are far to busy to even consider such charges as were brought against Mr. Toner, I'd ask that you exercise generous leniency in your sentencing."

The judge thanked him for his concerns. Then he addressed Floyd.

"Mr. Toner, concerning the five charges against you for attempting to influence witnesses in the trial of Mr. Howard Barnes, I must take into account the egregious nature of the crimes perpetrated on the victims you were attempting to influence. I find it unconscionable of a person in your position to attempt to deprive those young victims of justice for their abuser. To be perfectly frank with you, Mr. Toner, a ministry that would deprive justice in child molestation cases is not family friendly. The state of California will not allow your ministry to abuse our children and deny them the protections this state provides in law.

"Also, it is appropriate and good that those young victims witnessed justice being served. They will better understand that they are indeed victims of serious crimes and have done nothing wrong in exposing their abuser in this courtroom.

"For those reasons, I am sentencing you to the maximum period of one year of confinement for each of the five charges. These terms are to be served consecutively.

"Now concerning the five charges of failing to report the suspicions of child abuse by a minister under your supervision, I sentence you to the period of six months confinement allowed by statute for each offense. You will serve these sentences consecutively. Further, I order you to pay a fine of $1,000 for each of these five offences.

"This amounts to a total of ten sentences, but I am ordering that the two series of consecutive sentences be served concurrently."

"He's gone for five years," Marty whispered.

But the judge had not finished. "Normally, because of the accumulation of time involved in these sentences, they would be served in the state prison. However, I take full note of your age, Mr. Toner, and I am ordering that all sentences of confinement be suspended and that you be placed on probationary supervision. I also expect that you are unlikely to reoffend. The total of $5,000 in fines, however, must be paid.

"Now concerning the terms of your probation, I will satisfy the request that you be allowed to leave this county. In fact, I am ordering that you maintain a residence outside Del Rio County and to refrain from returning to Del Rio County without the permission of the supervisor of your probation officer. Further, concerning the terms of your probation, I order that you register with the probation office in the county where you will be residing within 72 hours. Do you have any questions concerning these instructions?"

Floyd's attorney replied, "We do not, you honor."

The judge continued. "It was interesting, counsel, that you mentioned that in many larger jurisdictions in this state the court's time would not be used for the prosecution of these offences. However, this court believes it is a distinct advantage to the citizens of Del Rio County to live in a jurisdiction that does have the time to prosecute such offences in an effort to maintain the low crime rate that is so much appreciated by the citizens of this community."

And Floyd was escorted through a door by the bailiff, accompanied by his attorney.

"Amazing!" Amy remarked.

"I can't believe this," Jesse said. "I've never heard of a servant being arrested in my life, and now two of them have been sentenced."

"Here comes George," Marty said.

"How do you respond to these charges, Mr. Patten?" Judge Pulsifer asked.

"No contest, your honor."

The judge then asked George some questions about the incident for which he'd been arrested.

"My wife was being quite defiant," George said. "She wasn't pleased that I wanted to take my son out of public school and have her teach him at home."

"Is your wife a teacher, Mr. Patten?"

"No, but she knows a lot more than the teachers do."

"So how was it that she sustained an injury to her head?"

"I didn't hit her, your honor. I was going to work and she was following me out of the house and I didn't want her following me, so I slammed the door and it hit her head."

"Were you angry with her, Mr. Patten?"

"Yes, I was."

"When you slammed the door, were you aware that she was standing in the doorway?"

George thought for a while. "Yes, I guess I was. I was looking right at her."

"Is there anything more you'd like to tell me before I move on, Mr. Patten?"

"Yes. I'm hoping you'll give me some support in managing my household in an appropriate manner."

"Is that all you have to say now?"

"Yes, your honor."

The judge asked the district attorney if he had some comments to make, and he did. "Your honor, it's been brought to my attention that Mr. Patten was present in his home last evening. This, you will note, was a violation of the instructions you gave him at his first appearance in this court, at which time you warned him he was not to return home until tomorrow evening. I'd ask that you take this into consideration when you pronounce sentencing."

"Do you have any further comments?"

"No, your honor."

Judge Pulsifer turned to George. "Mr. Patten, did you in fact return home last evening?"

"I only went home for a short period in the evening. I left later last night."

"Tell me why you chose to return home for that period of time."

"I, well, you see, we have a religious assembly that gathers at my house every Thursday night, and I have to be there to conduct that. I didn't sleep there."

"Thank you, Mr. Patten." The judge turned to George's attorney and asked, "Do you have any comments to make before I pronounce sentence, sir?"

"Yes, your honor. I would recommend that any punishment you give Mr. Patten not exceed a brief period of probation. The court will know that Mr. Patten has never had any previous convictions, and appears to have learned from this experience that his behavior during the incident in question was inappropriate."

The judge listened carefully to George's attorney. Then he said, "Mr. Patten, I am not convinced that you have learned sufficiently from this experience. I note that you have requested some support in managing your household, which I interpret as more precisely to mean that you want some support in controlling members of your family. Though you have no prior convictions, I must consider that I very recently issued an order that your son be closely monitored by Child Protective Services because of suspicions of physical abuse in your home. So to accommodate your request of support in managing your family, I am ordering you to register and complete a 6 month program in anger management. Your attorney can help you register for such a program in the Clerk's Office. This program requires that you attend a three hour session each Saturday for a period of six months. It will help you better understand your anger and your impulses to violence. I'm sure the program will be very beneficial for you.

"The fact that you have already violated this courts previous instructions gives me great concern, and it must not be overlooked. Therefore I am ordering you confined in the Del Rio County Jail for 100 hours, which is to be followed by 50 weeks of probation. I have inquired about the date on which the next anger management program will begin, and that date is two weeks from tomorrow. Considering the fact that you are a working man, and considering the fact that domestic violence is more prevalent on weekends than on work days, I am ordering that you be immediately remanded to the County Jail for a period of 52 hours, after which you will arrange to be further confined for a period of 48 hours next weekend in the County Jail."

The judge turned to George's attorney and said, "Since Mr. Patten will momentarily be in custody, I would recommend that you register him today for his anger management program. That will assure that he will be able to complete this portion of his sentence without delay."

"I will do that, your honor."

"Are there any questions concerning this sentence?" Judge Pulsifer asked. There were none.

The judge nodded to the bailiff, who approached George and quickly handcuffed him and led him away.

"Where are they taking him?" Amy asked.

"Down stairs to the slammer," Marty said.

"Aren't they going to let him tell Marian where he went?" she asked.

"She'll figure it out," Jesse said.

"They don't let people go home and tidy up their closets," Marty said. "I think they're afraid they might not come back to get locked up."

"No kidding!" Jesse laughed.

"You want to stay for more, or will we leave now?" Marty asked.

"Let's go."

CHAPTER 22

The Sunday following Floyd's sentencing the Shipmans were at fellowship in El Segundo. As usual, Dennis was outside playing with the other children, and Clay was deep in a discussion about the latest automobile market with some of the men. Nancy was helping the women arrange the dining room for the pot luck dinner.

The women's conversation turned to the latest astounding news among the Way friends throughout California.

"Did you hear what happened with Howard Barnes?"

"Yes. Isn't that terrible!"

"I just can't even imagine him molesting children, but he must have done something."

"And I heard it was all in the newspapers too. Just terrible!"

"It's too bad they hadn't just warned him and moved him somewhere else."

"At least it could have all been kept quiet."

"Who on earth reported him to the police anyway?"

"I heard that it was teachers at school who reported him."

"Isn't that shameful. This is what the school system has come to – policing the parents."

"How would teachers know such things to begin with? Ridiculous!"

"Can you imagine how the parents feel about this?"

"I sure wouldn't want to think a child of mine was the means of putting a servant in prison."

"I know. I'd feel guilty for the rest of my life."

"It'll be a hard thing for the mothers up there to live down, I'm sure."

Diane turned to Nancy and said, "But Nancy, I have to tell you how much we all appreciate Clay's help in all of this."

"Oh, thank you," Nancy said.

There followed a chorus of appreciation for Clay. It was something Nancy was not used to hearing.

And the conversation went on.

"But when you end up in court they can really throw the book at you."

"And these days everyone's so much more aware of all the abuse that goes on in other religions. You can't be surprised that they think we're just the same."

"Did you hear they also arrested Uncle Floyd?"

"No!"

"Oh no! Whatever for?"

"I was told they arrested him because he didn't report Howard to the police."

"That's ridiculous."

"Poor old Uncle Floyd."

"What did they do with him?"

"Oh, he's okay. They let him go."

"Of course. How could they arrest him for something like that? Isn't that harassment or something?"

"Sounds like they're having a witchhunt against the Way to me."

"I should say so."

"But what a blessing they actually realized Uncle Floyd was innocent. It's just proof again that God sees to it there's proper justice for His people."

"Yes, we have to remember that God will always defend His own. It really helps to make us patient with those who'd try to persecute us, doesn't it?"

"We have so much to be thankful for."

"This must have been so hard on Uncle Floyd."

"I know. He's such a dear old man."

"We're lucky no one else was arrested. If they'd arrest poor old Uncle Floyd it's a wonder they didn't try and find someone else to arrest."

"I can imagine that once Uncle Floyd got in court his spirit would convince the judge that we aren't people to harbor a child molester."

"You're right. Once people find out what the Way friends are like, they change their mind and often will come forward and defend us when we're being persecuted."

"It's a wonderful example we can be to the world, isn't it?"

"I should say. It really makes one feel terribly responsible, doesn't it?"

"It really does. It's hard to grasp sometimes just how much responsibility we have in being an example to the whole world."

"It boggles the mind, doesn't it?"

"Well, it looks like all the damage has been done now. It can all be left behind us."

"When you think about it, there was some good to come by having Uncle Floyd arrested."

"How do you mean?"

"When you think of all the people who'd be pointing fingers at the Way because of Howard, it was really good for Uncle Floyd to make the Way look so good to everyone. No doubt God had a hand in that."

"I never thought of that."

"We just can't imagine what the hand of God can accomplish."

Nancy had heard enough. Suddenly, on impulse, she said, "Uncle Floyd was not found innocent. He pleaded guilty to 10 charges in court."

Everyone became silent, and all eyes and open mouths turned to Nancy.

Finally someone said, "Really?"

"Yes."

"Why did they let him go?"

"He's on probation for five years," Nancy said.

Being Clay's wife, no one would question her on that.

Someone said, "How horrible! He'll be 100 years old by then."

"And he'll have to report to a probation officer," Nancy said. It occurred to her that she may have said too much, but couldn't stop herself. She said, "And Uncle Floyd wasn't the only other person arrested either."

"That's horrible!"

"Who else was arrested?"

Nancy decided she better not tell anything more. "I can't tell you."

"Was it a servant?"

Nancy hesitated, and decided she wouldn't say a thing. "I can't say. I just know that much."

By then it was time for people to begin eating, and everyone was gathered by the table. The women were all very sober. By contrast the men were all in a jovial mood. *Maybe they just look that way because the women are so sober,* Nancy thought. *I'll bet all these men get a bit of sobering news on their way home from here today.*

Monday morning Clay's secretary called him in his office and said, "I have Victor Bergman on the line, and he says he'd like to see you this afternoon if he can. I told him you were in court this morning, but I'd check with you about this afternoon."

"Tell him I'll work him in, but it might not be until about three o'clock."

A minute later the secretary confirmed that Victor was happy with that arrangement.

I wonder what he wants now, Clay thought. Not another servant arrested, hopefully. What I need right now is a good honest murder suspect to represent – or maybe a good vacation.

He grabbed his briefcase and left the office.

It was nearly four o'clock when Victor arrived. Clay was deeply engrossed in a case he was working on, but asked to have Victor sent in anyway. *For some finality to all this*, he thought.

"Good afternoon."

They shook hands and Victor sat down. "Clay," he began. "I'm disappointed that you wouldn't help Uncle Floyd with his case."

"I apologize for that, but I've been working on another very difficult case ever since Howard was sentenced. I couldn't possibly have done anything for him at the time."

"I believe we were thinking you'd put the matters of the Way ahead of other matters."

"Unfortunately I have deadlines to meet when I'm representing people in court, and if I don't meet those deadlines I could be risking the welfare of my clients, if not their lives."

"I see," Victor said, as though he reluctantly understood. "We could have used you again in Espadín."

"I appreciate that. But I understand Uncle Floyd was exonerated by the court."

"You heard that?"

"Yes. It was all the good news at Sunday fellowship down here yesterday."

"Well, I guess that's good – that you heard that, I mean. But you know, Uncle Floyd pleaded guilty and the judge put him on ten years' probation and fined him $5,000."

"Oh! Where would people get the idea he was exonerated?"

"I told Bart he was let go," Victor explained. "He said he'd let people know."

"I see. Well, what can I do for you today?"

"I was quite upset to learn that your wife contradicted the news yesterday that Uncle Floyd was let go."

Now aren't you a sly fox! Clay thought. "Who told you that?"

"Never you mind."

"But I do mind, actually," Clay said. "I'll need to know who said that."

"Why?"

"Because I want to blame the right person. I'd be devastated to ever learn I'd been blaming the wrong person."

"In that case then, it was Chester who told me."

"Thank you."

"I think it would be big of you, since you can't help the servants, to at least stop spreading negative talk about them."

"What have I told anyone?"

"How did people learn that Uncle Floyd pleaded guilty?"

"It's public record, Victor. I don't understand your concern."

"You're going to undermine everything the servants are trying to do."

"It sounds to me like someone has attempted to deceive the Way friends with misleading information."

Victor hesitated. "That's a terrible thing to say about any servant."

"But you told me it was you who told Bart what went on in court. What did you want Bart to tell everyone?"

Victor began to fluster. "You know, the servants have a difficult time keeping order in the Way. We have to support them in the work they're attempting to accomplish."

"What are they trying to accomplish?" Clay asked.

Victor didn't answer.

"Is there something I can do for you today?" Clay asked.

"I just came here to tell you that I expect you to present the right impression about the servants."

"All the way from Bakersfield."

Victor didn't reply.

"Victor, I tried to do that in Howard's case. I'm in the business of sorting out the truth, and frankly I wasn't greatly impressed with the understanding a few of the servants have of the concept of 'truth'. In court, you see, they expect to not only hear some truth, but to hear the whole truth and nothing but the truth."

"You didn't even let Uncle Floyd speak in court."

"I understand Uncle Floyd did get to speak in court. What did he say?"

Victor sat looking stunned. Then he said, "I realize I didn't pay the last bill you sent me for Howard's case. I wasn't going to pay that until we got the verdict, but ...."

"Victor, it's too late now. The case is over, and I'd prefer that you didn't pay that last bill I sent you."

"I don't understand."

"Don't worry about it. I understand that Howard is now officially expelled not just from the service but from the Way. But I intend to continue to visit him as a personal friend and not as a client in the future."

"So what's wrong with my money?"

"Nothing, Victor. I only expect payment from clients. Now that Howard's no longer a client I'd like to leave the business part behind."

"I don't understand what you're coming at."

"Just don't worry about it," Clay said. "If you're satisfied, then we're square."

Victor was angry. "I should sue you for dereliction of representation. I spent a lot of money on Howard."

"Well, that's up to you. And if you feel that way about how I represented Howard, then I'd invite you to seek some redress through the justice system."

Victor studied Clay for a long moment. Clay said nothing.

Then Victor said, "You know, you're one arrogant son of a ..." Then suddenly stopped.

Clay said nothing.

Victor's tone changed. Calmly, he said, "Well, I must be going now." He stood up and left.

Clay was sitting at his desk sorting through his thoughts when Nathan burst into his office.

"Are you okay?" Nathan asked.

"I think so," Clay said. "You're really concerned about how I'm getting on with this Howard Barnes matter, aren't you?"

"Yes, I am. You don't need any more cases like that again for a long time."

"I think you're right."

"Is Bergman satisfied now?"

"Who knows? He says he's going to sue me now for dereliction of representation."

Nathan laughed loudly.

"You know, I don't think this is the end of my involvement with this mess," Clay said. "Can I call on you to represent me when I end up in court?"

"Pro bono," Nathan assured him.

Clay sighed deeply, then mostly to himself he said, "I feel cleansed, in a way, for having refused that man's money."

Nathan studied him for a while. "You're a man of principle. That's good."

CHAPTER 23

That Sunday fellowship in Espadín was at Rodney and Carla Sturm's house, and the number of attendees had diminished greatly. There were no students at all, and a few people asked where Amy, Jesse, and Marty were. If Marty's parents knew where they'd gone, they gave no indication.

Sharon Fitch wasn't there. But by then it had become known among the Way friends that Sharon was having problems with her nerves, so no one asked Herb where she was. Sally was there, and was playing happily with the other children.

"Where are the Pattens?"

"I have no idea," Bart snapped. It shocked everyone, so no one mentioned them again.

And Maria and her mother were also absent. "Where's Ana Castro today?" someone asked.

"I don't know."

"Is one of them sick?"

"Do you know where she is, Bart?"

"I don't know where she is," he replied. "I assume she's looking for another place to live."

"Really! Why?"

"She was fired from her job, you know," Bart explained.

"Oh no!"

"Do you know why?"

"I have no idea," Bart said. "I guessed it wasn't my business to ask why."

"What a pity! Poor Ana has such a difficult situation to deal with. I'm sure it didn't help to have Maria involved as she was with Howard."

"I understand Maria's doing very well," Bart said. "No permanent damage, of course. The courts usually overreact to such things anyway these days."

A few people glanced at Rodney Sturm to see whether he was going to respond. No one could forget his outburst when he first learned the news about Howard; but Rodney showed no interest in the topic and said nothing.

"I have to say I'm very well pleased at how everyone has come together and put this whole matter of Howard behind us," Bart bragged. "And it's really wonderful to learn that Uncle Floyd has been allowed to go free."

There was a gasp, or sigh, that echoed through the room.

"Isn't that wonderful?"

"I knew they'd let him go. What a ridiculous thing to have him arrested."

"You have to understand," Bart explained, "the justice system is really an agent of Satan, and it can't be expected that they'll understand the righteousness of the Way friends and servants. Their eyes have been darkened so they can't see the light that leads the lives of God's people. And with all the terrible things happening in some other churches it's no wonder they think we're just the same."

"Isn't that so!" someone commented.

Bart continued. "Uncle Floyd has gone back to Bakersfield, and he directed me to let people know that he was released. So I notified as many of the servants in the state as I could so they could pass the good news on to all the friends. It'll be such a relief to everyone."

"I'm sure it will."

"It was good of you to tell everyone, Bart. I'm sure they'll appreciate that."

"And it's good to have this whole matter over with before summer retreats come around."

Then Friday came.

"I'm so glad to see you," Maggie said. "I missed you two last Sunday at fellowship, and then I didn't see you last night at assembly, Amy. And thanks again for the groceries, Jesse. I don't know what I'd do without you two."

"I was glad when Jesse came by and told me you wanted us for dinner," Amy said.

When they were settled down, Maggie asked, "I suppose you went home for the weekend after your finals."

"No, we didn't," Amy said. "Jesse, can we tell her where we were?"

"Sure," Jesse said. "You can tell Maggie anything, can't we, Maggie?"

"I hope so," Maggie said.

"We went to see Howard," Jesse said.

"Really! Poor Howard. How's he doing?"

"He seemed okay to us," Amy said.

"We took Marty with us," Jesse added.

"You're good young kids, but don't bother telling anyone what you did. Aggie tells me that Howard's now expelled and Bart doesn't think we should have anything to do with him. But I don't see anything wrong with you visiting him. In fact, I think it's admirable of you to care about people, no matter what they've done."

"I wouldn't want him around my kids," Jesse said. "But it's not up to me to throw him away."

"You're a good boy, Jesse."

"Did you hear what happened to Ana?" Maggie asked.

"No."

"Bart said she was fired, but I don't think that's what happened. She came here the other day and talked to me. She was crying. She told me that the principal at her school put her on something called administrative leave because she hadn't reported Howard to the police. Do you know what that could be about?"

"Yeah," Jesse said. "Putting someone on administrative leave means that they have to stay home while they decide whether to fire her or not."

"Can they fire her for that?" Maggie asked.

"Maybe," Amy said. "According to the law any teacher who suspects a student has been abused or molested has to report it to the authorities."

"Oh!" Maggie was surprised. "So I suppose this is because Maria is a student at her school."

"It could be," Jesse agreed. "I don't know how that works."

"I hope she doesn't get in big trouble," Maggie said. "She's such a sweet little person, and Maria's a wonderful little girl."

While they were eating, Amy asked, "Was George at assembly last night?"

"Oh yes, dear. He was there," Maggie assured her.

"I don't care for that man," Amy said.

"He's a severe man, I think." Maggie shook her head.

"I'm surprised he's allowed to have people come to his house for assembly," Amy said.

"George is in trouble too," Jesse explained.

"I know that Child Protective Services were checking on Joey," Maggie said.

"But he's in more trouble than that," Jesse said. "He was arrested for domestic battery. He slammed a door on Marian's face."

Maggie was horrified. "That's horrible. Did she call the police?"

"Someone else called the police," Jesse said. "He was sentenced the same day Uncle Floyd was sentenced."

But Bart told everyone Uncle Floyd was let go."

"That's not true, Maggie. Uncle Floyd pleaded guilty to a total of ten charges and he's on probation for the next five years."

"Oh!" Maggie was shocked. "That's terrible. Oh my! What are we going to do now?"

"Maybe carry on as usual," Jesse said. "Uncle Floyd doesn't have to go to jail."

"That's good. Poor old man! He's so old!" Maggie thought a minute. "And you said George was sentenced too?"

"Yeah, he's on probation for a year. And he was in jail last weekend. We saw them taking him away."

"George and Marian are having problems," Maggie said. "Aggie told me Bart was upset with Marian. I guess she called Bart and wanted to ask him if she should leave George because she was afraid of him. And Bart told her she couldn't leave him. He told her she just had to obey him willingly and everything would be okay."

"I'm sorry," Amy said. "But someone has to tell Bart to mind his own business. First he doesn't want anything done with Howard for molesting kids, and now he thinks Marian should just let George do whatever he wants to her."

"I know," Maggie said wearily. "I was lucky. My husband was a really kind man, and he'd never treat our children like George treats poor Joey. And as far as I know no one ever molested our kids. I heard of such things happening, but I never had to do anything about someone like that."

"You were lucky, weren't you?"

"I was. Oh, this is so terrible! You know, I've been worrying about Bart coming here for a visit. I don't think I want to have him confront me with anything. He seems to be so rough on people."

"That's why they call him Brutal Bart," Jesse explained.

"That's funny!" Maggie mused.

"Why does Bart hang out all the time in Espadín anyway?" Amy asked. "He should give the other assemblies a visit sometime," Amy said.

Maggie laughed. "I like your frankness, Amy. You're an honest kid, I can tell."

Jesse laughed too.

"I get myself in trouble sometimes too for saying what I think."

"Don't worry," Maggie assured her. "It's always better when people know what you think. Then they don't try to play tricks on you."

Amy realized she and Jesse trusted Maggie with all their thoughts, and she felt good.

"Are we being gossips today?" Jesse asked.

"No, my dear," Maggie assured him. "We're only gossips when we want to learn things that we won't forgive."

They sat quietly for a moment. Then Amy said, "Maggie, you are a beautifully wise old lady. I'm just so glad I got to know you."

"I'm glad I got to know you too, dear. And Jesse too, of course." They laughed together.

On the way to the next Thursday assembly Amy reminded Jesse, "Don't sit beside me tonight."

"Okay." He laughed

Bart, of course, was there again and had another lengthy sermon.

"I'm going to talk about the place of the servants in the Way," Bart began. "It's the servants' place to care for the flock. It's the wise person who understands that the servants are God's gift to the church.

"The servants are expected to examine the people to know what's been going on, to be sure that no abominations are being practiced among the people. The servants have to see if there's any infection in the Way, and to rule over everyone to prevent anything that could cause shame to the Way. The servants will deal with people who've done wrong. They have to see that appropriate punishments are given, and to determine the severity of the punishment. God commanded in the Scriptures that even death was to be prescribed. In the book of Deuteronomy it says, *Then shalt thou bring forth that man or that woman, which have committed that wicked thing, unto thy gates, even that man or that woman, and shalt stone them with stones, till they die.* Unfortunately, we can't do this to people today because we have a government that won't allow us to do such things. But we can demonstrate the spirit of this punishment.

"Now it's not normal for people to want to submit to servants like this. People protest, and they speak against the servants. It's the history of the world that people will curse the servants of God, but the servants meditate in the Lord's statutes and know how to enforce them. The Bible tells us in Exodus 22 that *Thou shalt not revile the gods, nor curse the ruler of thy people.* It's an abominable thing to criticize a servant.

"And the Bible tells us what's wrong with these people. They're proud, and pride is the end of them. But no matter that such a person thinks he knows something! His pride is blinding and he will not see righteousness.

"The problem is that people don't want instruction," Bart explained. "They can't accept that the souls of men are wicked. So how do they find favor in God's eyes? People learn from being disciplined. The servants keep them on track. And the reaction to the servants' discipline is an indication of the favor they'll find with God. Someone once said, Wise people learn from the mistakes of others. I don't have to tell you that we've had a recent example of someone who's had to be banished from the Way. It would be foolish of any of us to ever think that the same thing couldn't happen to us."

But Bart has something heartwarming to add. "But remember, there are people who bring great pleasure to the servants. It encourages servants to continue their work. These people remember God warns that if the servants aren't around it will be the end of the Way. This is why the servants continuously discipline the people so that they'll not involve themselves in the evil things they'd do if left alone.

"And I repeat, there's a simple way to know whether you're in the favor of the Lord or not. If you take discipline, you've demonstrated your fear of the Lord. It's good when people live their lives as the servants tell them.

"Some people here in Espadín know Edith Kite in Los Angeles. What a wonderful example she was of a good Christian woman. She always did what she was told. She took advice from the servants on whom to marry. And she made her children obey her husband and the servants. And I must also add that it never crossed Edith's mind to ever report her husband to the police for any reason.

"The Bible explicitly says this:

> *Dare any of you, having a matter against another, go to law before the unjust, and not before the saints? Do ye not know that the saints shall judge the world? And if the world shall be judged by you, are ye unworthy to judge the smallest matters?*

"Imagine what God must think of a wife who'd complain to the police about her husband. What pride must be in such a woman's heart that she'd ever do such a thing! And I've found that, worst of all, they have their minds made up about things, and it's very difficult for servants to instruct such women when they're like that."

Marian was sitting stone faced and pale, staring straight ahead. Amy felt like going over and hugging her. She decided she'd do that as soon as assembly was over.

Bart went on. "It's been laid on my heart that I must also remind you about the dangers of keeping company with people of bad influence. We've had a recent example of how such people end up. We have to remember that unsaved people exert an evil influence on us, and it doesn't please the Lord for us to be found socializing with them.

"Let me remind you that abominations come from the hearts of people. Foul and abominable conversation comes from the hearts of these evil people. Let me read some scripture for you from Proverbs 26.

> *Burning lips and a wicked heart are like a potsherd covered with silver dross. He that hateth dissembleth with his lips, and layeth up deceit within him; When he speaketh fair, believe him not: for there are seven abominations in his heart. Whose hatred is covered by deceit, his wickedness shall be shewed before the whole congregation. Whoso diggeth a pit shall fall therein: and he that rolleth a stone, it will return upon him. A lying tongue hateth those that are afflicted by it; and a flattering mouth worketh ruin.*

"Imagine the folly of a child of God attempting to even have a conversation with a person of such evil influence! Everyone needs to recognize such a person and avoid him.

"And not only should we avoid such a person, we have to refrain from speaking about him, or even mentioning his name. There's nothing good to be said about such people – only lies. Let me read this scripture to you from Proverbs 6.

> *These six things doth the LORD hate: yea, seven are an abomination unto him: A proud look, a lying tongue, and hands that shed innocent blood, An heart that deviseth wicked imaginations, feet that be swift in running to mischief, A false witness that speaketh lies, and he that soweth discord among brethren.*

"Christians need to refrain from a lot of lies and mischief. It's been brought to my attention that this has been taking place among the Way friends, as far away as southern California. Some people we know have gone so far as to contradict the servants' report that Uncle Floyd was set free by the courts. Lies and mischief, all of it! Let me read this scripture about people who spread such evil conversations.

> *He is proud, knowing nothing, but doting about questions and strifes of words, whereof cometh envy, strife, railings, evil surmisings, Perverse disputings of men of corrupt minds, and destitute of the truth, supposing that gain is godliness: from such withdraw thyself.*

"I encourage everyone to refrain from such gossiping, and to avoid people who engage in it.

"I guess that's all the time I should take for tonight. I'll have even more good advice for you when the next assembly time comes."

When assembly was over, Amy went quickly to hug Marian. "You're having some rough days, aren't you?" Amy said quietly.

"Yes," Marian murmured.

"If I can help you, let me know."

"Thank you," Marian said. She paused a moment, then said, "Can I call you tomorrow morning?"

"Can you remember my number?" Amy asked.

"No." She looked around the room, then said in a low voice, "Come here after nine o'clock tomorrow morning. Promise me?" She looked desperate.

"I'll do that," Amy assured her. She kissed Marian on the cheek and left the room. She felt Bart's eyes follow her out the door.

CHAPTER 24

Amy checked her watch and made sure she didn't go to see Marian before nine o'clock. When she knocked on the door, she saw Marian peek out the living room window before she answered. She welcomed Amy in with a hug.

"I'm so ashamed," Marian began. "I'm losing my mind here."

"You don't have to tell me about it. I just happened to be in court the day they took George off to the jail. You poor lady. Can I do something for you?"

"I don't know what to do. I called Bart to ask his advice and he only made me feel worse." Marian began to cry.

"It's okay," Amy comforted her.

"He's such a mean man," Marian complained. "I called him over yesterday morning to talk to him and I knew when he came in the door I was going to be in trouble."

"Good morning," Marian said. "Come in."

"So what's your problem today, Marian?" Bart asked before she had a chance to offer him a seat.

"I have a terrible problem, Bart. I really can't bear the way George has been treating me and Joey. I'm afraid I'm going to lose my mind. I can't take it anymore."

"I know exactly what your problem is, Marian."

"You do?"

"Yes. You're not submitting properly to your husband."

"I do everything he says, and I can't please him."

"I understand how you feel. But, it's pride working in you. When a woman is properly submissive to her husband she experiences the beauty of obeying him. And it's begun to show in Joey. He's learned from you to be defiant of his father."

"Bart, that's not true."

"Marian, I have to tell you that it is. I happen to know that you've already called the police on him and caused him great shame. Fortunately none of the Way friends know about that. He's now the bishop here. How would all our friends feel if they thought their bishop had been taken to court by his own wife?"

"Bart, that's not true. I never called the police on him."

"You shouldn't lie to me, Marian. Lying to a servant is like lying to God."

"But I didn't call the police."

"Marian. Listen to me. A wife who has behaved as you have has only one way to redeem herself. She must learn she's not running the household by herself. It's God's order that the husband run his household. You must learn not to even complain about this, because you're only tormenting yourself with thoughts of what George is keeping you from doing."

"I don't understand…"

"I have to warn you. If you don't accept what God has planned for your life, you may soon lose your salvation, and then you'll have a much greater thing to worry about. It's quite simple, really."

Marian began crying. She was frustrated, afraid, and desperate. And she had Bart sitting in her kitchen berating her about things she'd not done. The only thing good about the visit had been that Bart had quickly excused himself and left when he saw that Marian had nothing more to discuss with him.

"And then he came here last night and he preached at me in front of the whole assembly," Marian cried. "I'd be really angry with him if I weren't so afraid."

"You don't have to put up with that treatment," Amy said. "You've tried to help, but it's not working. You have to do something else. Have you thought of leaving him?"

"Oh yes, I have. My sister in Oregon wants me to go and live with her."

"Maybe you should do that. You need a break so you can help yourself settle down and think more clearly about your situation."

"I think you're right," Marian said, then added almost in a whisper, "I think I'll call my sister right now and ask her what to do."

So she did. When she hung up, she asked, "Can you help me with this? I'm too nervous to do it by myself."

"Sure. I don't have to go to work until this afternoon. What can we do?"

"First I have to pack a suitcase for me and Joey. Then I have to go to school and get Joey. And then I have to go to the supermarket and get some money that my sister's going to wire to me there."

"Your sister knows where to have the money wired to?" Amy asked.

"Yeah. Last year when she was here she checked in the supermarket to see if she could send money to me there. I told her not to give me the cash then because George would find it and ask too many questions."

"This has been going on for a long time, it sounds like."

"Well, yeah. But I can't keep people from finding out about it anymore."

"You poor dear lady," Amy said.

"You're so kind to me," Marian said. "Can you help me do this? I mean, just be here with me. It helps me think more clearly. I don't know if I can remember all I have to do before he comes home for lunch."

"Sure. Let's do it."

While they were packing, Amy asked, "Where does your sister live?"

"Portland."

"How are you going to get to Portland?"

"I'm going to take a taxi to Sacramento. It's the closest place for me to get a bus to Portland."

"Does your sister know what a bus ticket is going to cost?"

"I don't know," Marian sighed. "She told me that after she wires me the money she's going to the bus station in Portland and buying a ticket for me to pick up in Sacramento. Two tickets, one for me and one for Joey."

"She's a good sister," Amy commented.

"I don't know what I'd do without her. I just can't figure anything out right now. I hope I don't get you in trouble."

"Don't worry about me," Amy assured her.

"But George is going to be really mad when he finds I'm gone."

"He'd just be mad about something else if he came home and you were still here."

"Yes. He would be. He's always mad about something."

They put two suitcases in the back seat of Amy's car, and went to Joey's school. Marian showed her identification, and Joey was quickly brought to the office to meet her. Not unexpectedly, a couple of ladies working in the office watched Marian skeptically. Her agitated state was apparent.

In the car, Joey asked, "Where are we going?"

"We're going to live in Oregon," Marian said.

"Is Daddy going too?"

"No."

"Does he know where we're going?"

"No. I didn't tell him."

"What will he say when he finds out?"

"We won't know what he says because we won't be here."

"He'll be really mad," Joey warned.

"But we won't be here."

"He'll come and get us and I don't want to get another beating," Joey said, and began to cry.

Marian began to cry.

Amy said, "No Joey. Your father won't be able to beat you this time. We're going to see to that."

"Are you sure?" he whimpered.

"Yes, we're sure," Amy assured him. And Joey settled down.

At the supermarket, Marian had to wait nearly 20 minutes until the moneygram arrived. She signed the check, took the cash, and went directly to a taxi company.

"I need to go to Sacramento," Marian said.

"Right now, ma'am?"

"Yes. It's an emergency."

"I'll have to call in one of our nighttime drivers."

"I'm sorry."

"No problem, lady. But you'll have to show me the money before I call him."

"Okay. How much is it going to be?"

The man thought a minute. "One hundred and fifty dollars. It's overtime for him, you know."

"That's okay," Marian said, and reached into her pocket for the money.

Surprisingly, the driver arrived in just a few minutes, and in short order Joey and Marian were loaded into the taxi. Amy kissed Marian and Joey before they left, and they waved to her as the taxi drove out of sight.

Wow, Amy thought. When Bart finds out about this there'll be hell to pay. And then she wondered whether she should tell anyone about it, or just let it be a secret between her and Marian.

When Amy suggested they invite Maggie for dinner that night, Jesse agreed quickly. So while Amy prepared the meal in Jesse's kitchen, Jesse went to get Maggie.

When she arrived at Jesse's apartment, Maggie said, "I'm getting to spend a lot of time with you two. It's fun."

"It is," Amy agreed.

Amy had made spaghetti and meatballs, and a green salad. Jesse and Maggie complimented her profusely on it, and Amy beamed with delight.

"You could win a man's heart with this meal," Maggie commented.

"I'll have to try that someday."

Maggie winked at Jesse. He felt himself blushing, and he hoped Amy hadn't noticed.

"Aggie came by my place again this morning," Maggie said.

"What's Aggie's news today?"

Maggie laughed. "Poor Pablo came for assembly last night and went to Waterman's instead."

"No one told him where to go," Jesse guessed.

"No," Maggie said. "Poor Pablo. They forget about him all the time."

"What's the story on Pablo anyway?" Amy asked. "I think I've only seen him twice since I came to the Way."

"I think I've only seen him four times," Jesse said.

"Pablo's wife divorced him about 15 years ago," Maggie said. "He was working in the fields for a big time farmer up near Marysville, and I guess she started having an affair with Pablo's boss. And she told the servants that Pablo was abusing her, so they said it might be good for her to separate from him for a time.

"So she went to live in the house with Pablo's boss. I guess it was a really big house, and the boss had a wife there, and it all looked okay to the servants. But before long she complained to the servants that Pablo wasn't giving her any living expenses. So the servants told Pablo he couldn't participate in assemblies or have bread and wine any more – or at least until his wife was satisfied that he'd caught up with his support payments.

"But while this was happening, the boss' wife was filing for divorce from her husband and she was claiming in court that it was because she'd caught him cheating on her with Pablo's wife. Everyone knew about it because the boss was really rich and the whole thing was in all the newspapers – a real scandal for a while."

Did the servants change their mind about Pablo when they found out about her?"

"Oh no," Maggie said. "Servants don't change their minds when they do something like that. It would look bad for a servant to change his mind, Aggie says, but I don't agree. But there's another thing, the servants don't all read newspapers either. They wouldn't believe anything like that from a newspaper."

"I get it now," Amy said. "Bart expects no one to read the newspaper, so he thinks we're all ignorant enough to believe what he told us about Uncle Floyd."

Maggie chuckled. "I like you, Amy. You're straightforward. I like that."

Amy laughed. "You mean the servants don't want us reading the newspapers?"

"Most of them won't say anything to you," Jesse said. "But Bart probably would. He'd tell anyone anything that crossed his mind. I just wouldn't tell Bart I read something in the newspaper."

Amy rolled her eyes. "So what became of Pablo's wife?"

"Oh yeah," Maggie said. "She complained to the servants that it was upsetting to her to have Pablo in the same assembly with her, so they told him he couldn't go to assembly any more in Marysville. He's been supposed to come here to Espadín ever since."

"Poor guy," Jesse said. "It's a long way from Marysville on a week night."

"And then they complained because he didn't come down here every Thursday," Maggie added. "But they soon had to expel Pablo's wife anyway. She got a divorce from Pablo and went straight up to Tahoe and got married to his boss."

"And the servants still kept Pablo on probation?" Jesse asked.

"Oh yes," Maggie sighed. "They just kind of forgot about him. I think he was so discouraged by everything that he didn't dare ask them if he could get his probation lifted. And, you know, if he didn't ask to be taken off probation, the servants would never come to him and offer. They never do that."

"I have a question," Amy said. "How come Bart hasn't treated Marian like the servants treated Pablo's wife?"

"How do you mean?" Jesse asked.

"Well, they sympathized with Pablo's wife even though she wasn't desperate. But look at poor Marian. She's virtually a battered woman and Bart just hammered her down and told her she had to do exactly as George says."

"He did?" Jesse asked.

Maggie raised her eyes in curiosity.

"Oh," Amy said. "Since I'm in good company, I have a bit of a confession to make. I went to see Marian this morning before I went to work."

"Yeah?"

"I helped her run away with Joey after George left for work."

"Where did she go?"

"She went to Sacramento in a taxi and she was going to Portland on a bus from there."

Maggie and Jesse were too surprised to speak.

"She told me what Bart had said to her, and I think she was smart to leave before she lost her mind. She was so confused she couldn't even think straight to pack her suitcases."

"So right now she's on a bus with Joey headed for Portland?" Jesse asked.

"Yeah."

"This is going to be hard on George," Maggie said. "But I can't say I didn't expect it."

"I never thought George was such a brute," Jesse said. "The first year I was here everyone all seemed to be so ... normal. You know, not stressed out or anything."

"George isn't the brightest guy in town," Maggie said. "He's something like Bart – he doesn't understand when something doesn't make sense to people who can think. All he can do is know the rules and try to make everyone follow them. He's always been a bossy guy with poor little Marian. He's just been showing his stuff a bit more now that he's got Bart here to impress. And you know, he's well connected with the servants from away back."

Maggie paused, then whispered, "And Pablo's a Mexican."

"Ah," Amy said. "So the Way's not all that straight after all."

"No," Maggie replied. "Not when the *who's who* has to be considered."

"That's how it works?"

"I'm afraid so."

"So will there still be assembly at George's house now?" Jesse asked.

"They'll have to change that if Marian won't come back," Maggie confirmed. "There has to be a wife in the house to have assembly there."

"I've never heard of so much scandal in one place at one time in the Way," Jesse said.

"No," Maggie agreed. "I never have either. But you know, I have to say something. If they'd been honest about Howard and tried not to cover it up, most of this mess wouldn't have happened. All these people stressed and upset because they've been expected to pretend something outrageous never happened.

"Think about it. All Uncle Floyd had to do was call the police like the law says. But he never did. Now look what comes of it. Ana gets in trouble at work because she took his example. And George gets frustrated and takes it all out on his wife and son. It was enough that Howard was messing up little kids, but everyone else is getting in trouble one way or another because they wouldn't hold Howard properly accountable." Maggie looked like she might cry. "They just have to deflect as much blame away from the service as they can, and it's shameful."

"And they've stressed you seriously, haven't they?" Amy asked Maggie.

"Yes, they have," Maggie agreed. "And poor Sharon. There wasn't anything wrong with her until Bart or Uncle Floyd or whoever started trying to straighten out Herb. I'm afraid she's had a nervous breakdown over this."

"This stresses me," Jesse admitted. "When Bart came here he said he was going to clean up this area."

"And now he's taking advantage of the situation to impress Uncle Floyd with a cleanup, like the Way friends in Espadín had such a bad reputation. There was nothing wrong with anyone here except Howard. It's just all wrong."

"I guess we'll all have to kind of hide and do what he says until he goes away?" Jesse said. "He will leave, you know, sooner or later."

"Hopefully sooner," Amy said.

"Yes," Maggie agreed. "Hopefully."

Bart did indeed give Maggie a visit. Interestingly he arrived with Aggie, and that caused Maggie some concern.

"Come in," Maggie greeted them.

"Thank you," Bart said. "I brought Aggie with me so there'd be no appearance of impropriety."

"Thank you," Maggie said, "but you don't have to worry. You won't get off with any impropriety here."

Aggie chuckled, then got very sober.

"Have a seat," Maggie said.

Bart and Aggie accepted coffee, and then Bart began his conversation. "Maggie, I feel there's something I have to talk to you about."

"Yes?"

"I understand you were seen going to visit Jesse at his apartment."

"Who saw me?" Maggie asked.

"I'd prefer not to tell you," Bart said.

"But I want to know."

Aggie was startled. Her eyes darted from Maggie to Bart.

"Well then I'll tell you," Bart said. "It was me. I saw Jesse drive up to his apartment with you in the car and he helped you out of the car and into his apartment."

Maggie didn't respond.

"And that's not an appropriate thing for you to be doing."

"Why not?"

"It's not appropriate for you to be alone in a house with a young single man."

"Bart! This is ridiculous. I wasn't there alone with him."

"Who else was there?"

"Amy."

"Amy?"

"Yes."

"I didn't see her," Bart said.

"Well, she was there. If you'd have come to the door you'd know that."

"So that girl is living there with him," Bart concluded.

"No, Bart. Why would you say that?" Maggie asked.

"Why else would she be in that house without him?" Bart said.

"She was cooking dinner for us."

"This is a terrible thing. What you're telling me doesn't make any sense to me."

"But you have to take my word for it, Bart, don't you?"

Aggie's mouth dropped open.

"To begin with," Bart said, "that girl should not even be in that apartment without another woman there. I'm beginning to see that this girl is something of a tramp."

"Bart," Maggie interrupted. "Shame on you!"

"She's become a serious trouble maker for the Way friends here in Espadín."

Bart seemed to wait for Maggie to respond, but she said nothing. So he continued. "She's already succeeded in breaking up the Patten's marriage. I saw how she was treating Marian at assembly the last time, and the next thing I heard Marian had disappeared and George doesn't know where she went."

"George is in jail," Maggie said.

"And that's because Marian called the police on him. She ought to be ashamed of herself, reporting her husband to the police. What kind of Christian attitude is that?"

Maggie didn't respond.

"I think it would be better if that Amy girl would just move on and leave us alone. She's nothing but trouble. She got it from her father. I met her father. It was her father who influenced both her and Jesse to go to court while the Way was being scandalized there."

Much to Maggie's surprise, Aggie said, "They were prosecuting Howard."

Bart paused, then gathered his thoughts. "What an ungodly place for God's children to be found – in a worldly court where the Way was being scoffed at."

Maggie decided to say nothing more.

"I have to have a talk to Jesse too. That young man's going to be carried away from the Way by the influence of that woman, and he'll never know what happened to him. Oh the evil that young men can fall prey too!"

He paused, then said, "I'd like you to have nothing more to do with that girl Amy. We're in a very serious situation here in Espadín, and I have to visit everyone and tell them what they're going to have to do to make all this settle down.

"Now if Marian won't come back, we'll have to find another bishop in Espadín, and I don't think there's anyone qualified."

Neither Maggie nor Aggie responded.

"We can't make Spinner bishop because he has that wild kid of his living in the house. And we can't make Herb Fitch bishop because his wife thinks she's had some kind of nervous breakdown. She's just upset because she didn't get her way about something, probably, but she thinks she's had a nervous breakdown and won't come to assembly. Women do that. Herb won't let me talk to her, whatever his problem is."

Again Maggie and Aggie said nothing, so Bart talked on.

"The only person left is Rodney, and he's a novice. But he seems to be the only person worthy. I thought when I first came here that he'd been corrupted like everyone else in this town, but he's really turned himself around and has confessed how much he's going to support the servants from now on. No doubt Howard had a bad effect on him at the time.

"It'll be good to get all these people straightened out before retreat time so we can start another season on good footing. Wouldn't it be good if Marian came home from wherever she went so assembly can still be at George's house?"

Neither woman said a word.

"Are you going to be able to go to retreat this time?" Bart asked.

"I haven't decided yet," Maggie said. "It's difficult for me."

"The Lord can provide a way," Bart assured her. "I'm sure you're going, Aggie."

Surprisingly, Aggie didn't say a word. She just nodded her head.

There was a long pause. The silence was probably getting to Bart, so he stood up and said, "Well, I guess I should be going now. You ladies have a good visit."

"We will," Aggie said.

As soon as Bart was gone, Aggie said, "That man doesn't care for women."

"You may be right," Maggie agreed.

"In fact I think he hates women. I'm beginning to think he makes as much trouble as Howard. How long is he going to be here?"

"Who knows? Sometimes a servant will be in an area for a long time."

"Someone should tell Uncle Floyd on him."

"I don't think that would do any good," Maggie said. "Uncle Floyd owes Bart for saving his reputation among the Way friends."

"What do you mean by that?" Aggie asked.

"Uncle Floyd pleaded guilty in court and is on probation for the next five years. But Bart told everyone Uncle Floyd went free."

"No!" Aggie was horrified. "And what is this about George being in jail?"

"George is in jail this weekend. He was in jail last weekend too."

"What for?"

"For beating on Marian."

"How do you know that?"

"I just know," Maggie said.

Aggie paused, then said, "I'll believe you."

"Poor Sharon."

"She's a nice person. I knew something was wrong the last couple of times I went to see her. The last time she wouldn't even answer the door. And the time before that she wouldn't talk to me. She must be upset about Howard."

"I think everyone in Espadín is hurting. We just have to start being as kind to everyone as we can."

"Yes," Aggie agreed. "But I wonder what happened to Rodney Sturm. He used to be always arguing about everything, and now he's the only one Bart seems to like."

"You'll have to pardon me," Maggie said, "but maybe he just learned how to cozy up to the servants."

"Oh dear," Aggie sighed. "I wish you weren't right so often."

"I've never heard you talk like this about a servant before," Maggie observed.

"He just went too far with this women stuff," Aggie said. "I have my limits, you know."

Maggie always found it amusing when Aggie showed a flare of temper.

CHAPTER 25

One day before the summer weekend retreat was to take place in Auburn, Jesse ran into Jenny and Gilmore in the supermarket. When talk of retreat came up, the Gilmores said how bad they felt that they couldn't go – for the first time in their lives. But Jesse had a suggestion. They should all sneak off to southern California that weekend and go to retreat there, where no one knew the Gilmores. Gilmore called it a coup, and they easily enlisted Amy and Marty in the daring adventure. So it was the plan.

As they drove into the orchard in Rancho Cucamonga, Jesse announced, "Here we are."

"So your folks come here all the time, huh?" Marty asked.

"Twice a year for as long as I can remember."

"Nice place," Gilmore commented.

The Rancho Cucamonga retreat was held in a sprawling orchard.

"Lots of girls here," Marty noted.

Amy laughed. "Marty, do you go to retreat to find girls?"

"Of course," he said. "Bart used to do that too."

"Yeah, I bet!" Amy mocked.

"He was a teenager once, they tell me."

"That sounds like ancient history," Jesse said.

"Hey, look!" Amy said. "There's that attorney from Howard's trial. Right there! Look!"

"Oh great!" Marty said. "I gotta get a chance to talk to him."

They parked and took their sleeping bags to the dormitories to reserve places to sleep. They met again under a big spreading shade tree in the center of the orchard.

"Why doesn't everyone just go and sleep at home at night?" Amy asked. "It's not that far from here to San Bernardino."

"They don't like for us to leave," Jesse explained. "It's supposed to be more of a retreat from the rest of the world if we just stay here for the full time."

"Oh."

Before long Jesse's parents found them, and Jesse introduced them all. "Mom and Dad, this is Amy and Jenny and Gilmore. And my Mom and Dad are Linda and Ryan."

That afternoon Jesse was having a quiet chat with Ryan. "Dad," he said. "Amy and Marty and I went to see Howard in prison."

"Good! How's he doing?"

"Not too bad."

They talked about Howard for a while, then Jesse asked, "Have you ever heard of John Campbell?"

"No. Who's he?"

"Howard told me that was the person who started the Way."

"I never heard of him."

"I thought the Way was from all the way back to, you know, the Bible, I guess."

"Where did Howard get that?"

"I don't know. I didn't ask," Jesse said. "Doesn't the Way go back to the Bible?"

Ryan thought a while. "I thought so. I don't know. No one ever told me it didn't."

"I'm sure I've heard some of the servants tell us the Way started with Jesus."

"I'm sure they have."

"Were they lying?"

"Well," Ryan thought. "Who knows? I heard a rumor once about someone who started the Way, but no one seemed to believe it so I didn't pay any attention to it."

"Then how could the Way be the only right religion if it didn't start in the Bible times?"

"That's a good question." Ryan looked worried.

"Should I ask Howard some more about that?"

"Yeah, if you're going to see him again, ask him. I'd like to hear what he says about that."

"I'm really afraid Amy'll start asking me about that. What should I tell her?"

"I don't know," Ryan said. "I always wondered why no one knew anything about the past."

"You know, Howard told us you didn't necessarily have to be a member of the Way to be saved."

"He did?"

"Yeah. He told us he still believed he could be saved even though the servants wouldn't have anything more to do with him."

"He's probably right."

"You think so?" Jesse asked.

"It's important to remember that it's our own relationship with God that saves us. Some of the people the servants won't have anything to do with have nothing wrong with them. When you have a servant around like Bart you always have a few casualties."

"Can't anything ever be done about people like him?"

"No," Ryan sighed. "I know a lot of people who've been expelled for some really bad reasons. People should just avoid servants like Bart, as far as I'm concerned. I don't see any other way to cope with them." Then he said, "Bart's here, you know?"

"No!" Jesse was shocked.

"Yeah. His name is on the program."

"Gilmore and Jenny better hide."

Ryan was going to say something to him, but Marty came along and interrupted them.

"Guess what? I found Mr. Shipman," Marty announced.

"Yeah?" Jesse asked.

"He's a really cool guy. I like him."

"So what did you talk to him about?"

"I told him I wanted to be a criminal defense attorney."

"What makes you want that profession?" Clay asked.

"I was in court every day in Espadín, and I thought it was fascinating what you did," Marty explained.

"I remember seeing you there," Clay said. "But I wouldn't call what I did there good lawyering. And I didn't win, you know."

"I know. But Howard needed someone to help him."

"Do you think Howard was guilty?"

"Oh yeah," Marty said. "I thought he was."

"So you know you'd run the risk of having a lot of clients being found guilty."

"I know that," Marty said. "But I thought it was kind of awesome the way you made people think about the possibility that Howard was ... you know, framed, or something."

"Could Howard have been framed?" Clay was intrigued.

"Oh yeah," Marty chuckled. "Bart Stanley can frame someone without even knowing he's doing it."

"You know Bart well, I see."

"Yeah. He's a classic loose cannon. Constantly cocked and waiting to fire."

They both laughed.

"Have you consulted with the servants about being an attorney?"

"No."

"Why not?" Clay was curious.

Marty shrugged. "I don't ask the servants for advice about things I'm sure of."

"They might not approve, you know."

"That wouldn't be the first time they didn't approve of me," Marty said. "They've just kind of given up on me."

"You think so? Maybe they're scared of you," Clay suggested.

Marty was surprised. "Scared of me?"

"Let me guess," Clay said. "They can't depend on you to agree with them."

"No, they can't."

"They're probably worried that you'll embarrass them or someone else."

"I try to say what I think," Marty laughed. "They get mad at me a lot when I ask them questions."

Clay laughed. "Sit here and talk for a while."

And they talked until they were interrupted.

"Take my card," Clay said. "I'd like to talk some more with you."

"Me too," Marty said.

Next time you come to L.A., call me ahead of time and we can get together for a while. I'd like you to meet Nancy and my son Dennis, too."

"I'll do that."

Well!" Ryan exclaimed. "I guess if you want to be a criminal defense attorney he's the right guy to talk to."

"He's the guy who defended Chen in that big trial in L.A.," Marty said.

"I know," Ryan said. "He's a local guy for us."

"There was a lot of talk going around down here about him during that trial," Jesse said.

"I bet," Marty agreed. "I'm not sure everyone in Espadín knew he was one of us at the time."

"Everyone down here knew who he was, and all the little old ladies were horrified and scared to say anything about him."

"I wish now I'd paid more attention to that trial," Marty admitted. "I should've been watching the court channel on TV.... Oops, shouldn't have said that."

"You don't have to worry about my Dad," Jesse said. "He's kind of a liberal thinking guy."

"Good," Marty said. "I don't want to damage my reputation with him the first time I meet him."

Ryan laughed. "Here come the girls."

Amy, Jenny, and Linda came to join them.

"Where's Gilmore?" Jenny asked.

"He hasn't come back from the men's room," Marty said.

"I have to talk to him," Jenny said. "You'll never guess who's here."

"I know," Jesse said. "Bart's here."

"What am I going to do now?" Jenny asked.

"You'll be all right," Linda said. "Just stay close to me and he won't say anything."

"You have the coolest parents," Jenny said to Jesse. "They're a lot more sensible than that lady we met in the restroom."

"What happened in the restroom?"

"This little old lady asked me if I was all ready to listen to Bart this afternoon."

"Hello dear," the lady said. "I haven't seen you before. I'm Mildred."

"Hi. I'm Jenny."

"Where are you from, dear?"

"I'm from Espadín."

"Oh," Mildred said. "Isn't that the place up north, you know, where there was a problem?"

"Yes," Jenny said.

"Are these your friends?"

"Yes," Jenny said. "This is my friend Amy, and this is Linda."

"Oh yes," Mildred said. "I've known Linda for years. How's Jesse been doing?"

"Just fine, Mildred."

"I'm glad to hear that." She turned back to Jenny. "What a terrible time it must have been for all our friends in Espadín."

"It was interesting," Jenny agreed.

"My husband and I just had a little visit with Bart Stanley yesterday," Mildred said. "He was telling us that everyone in Espadín is doing so well. Everyone has recovered like nothing happened. Isn't that wonderful?"

No one responded.

Mildred continued. "I'm sure Bart had something to do with that. He has such a sweet mellow nature. My husband and I just love his humble spirit. He always comes to see us when he's in our area, but we don't get to see him so much since he went to northern California."

Still no one responded, so Mildred continued. "He promised me that today he'll talk on modern morality? And – oh my goodness, look at the time! It starts in only about 15 minutes."

"Modern morality?" Amy said.

"Yes, dear. He has such a kind way with young people. I can hardly wait to hear what he has to say. Why don't you come along with my husband and I?"

"I don't think so," Amy said. "I don't want to hear anything Bart has to say about anything."

Mildred was horrified. "Oh," she moaned. "You don't want to hear Bart?"

Amy realized she had shocked poor Mildred. She said, "No, Mildred. Not right now. I have recently been exposed to his thoughts on morals and I don't think I could face it again right now. I'm sorry."

"I understand," Mildred smiled. She patted Amy's arm. "I have to go. I don't want to be late. I'll see you later." And she left.

"Modern morality!" Marty remarked. "I'd like to hear that."

"You want to check it out and tell us all about it?" Amy asked. "I'm not going."

"On second thought," he said, "I think I've heard enough about his thoughts on morality for a while too."

"Here comes Gilmore," Jenny said. "Let's just sit here until Bart's done."

"Let's."

Later in the day, after his sermon was over, Bart went looking for Gilmore and Jenny in the orchard.

"I need to talk to you," Bart said.

"Okay."

"Come over here." Bart indicated an area out of the way of others who were milling around. Gilmore and Jenny followed him.

Bart started talking, and from where Jesse and Amy were standing they could tell it wasn't exactly a cordial conversation.

"What's he talking to them about?" Amy asked.

"Who knows? He's probably upset they're here," Jesse replied.

"So what really is going on here?" Amy asked. "Are they supposed to be here or not?"

"I don't know," Jesse said. "I've never heard of anyone chasing people away from a retreat."

Linda came up to them. "What's Bart doing?" she asked.

"It looks like he's giving Gilmore and Jenny the old one two three," Jesse said.

"I'm going to investigate," she said, and headed off in Bart's direction.

Jesse and Amy followed her at some distance, and they heard what was said.

"What's the problem, Bart?" Linda asked.

"I was just telling these people they shouldn't be here. They've been expelled."

"They're not causing a problem for anyone, Bart."

"That's not the point," Bart protested. "They've just come here to flaunt themselves in the face of the servants. They didn't even come inside for the service this afternoon."

"Bart, Bart! Listen to yourself! Are you not concerned about the welfare of these young folks?" She gestured toward Gilmore and Jenny.

"I am concerned about their souls. But they can't be so shameless as to come here and make themselves a bad influence on the other young people."

"What influence, Bart? What influence are you talking about?"

"They ran off and got married secretly. Everyone knows what that looks like, and we can't condone that kind of example...."

"Bart!" Linda interrupted. "No one here will know that unless you're going to tell people. Anyway, who cares? Other young people here are married. You have to leave them alone. You should appreciate the fact that they even want to be here. Why are you trying to chase them away?"

Bart stared at her for a minute, then said, "I guess I can't make any headway with you folks. I have to be going." And he turned and walked away.

"Ignore him," Linda said.

Jenny was in tears. "I can't ignore him. He just doesn't want us around."

"Darling," Linda said. "He's just an egotistical old man, and he's more interested in having his way than anything else. I wouldn't take a thing he says seriously."

"But what's going to happen when we go back to Espadín? He's never going to let us go back to assembly."

"Probably not," Ryan agreed. "All you have to do is just hang on until he's not around and some other servant will restore you."

"He told us all the servants have been warned that we can't be restored until we apologize to the assembly for what we did," Gilmore said. "I don't understand."

"I want to go home," Jenny said.

"It's kind of late tonight," Gilmore said. "Maybe we can leave first thing in the morning." He turned to Amy and Jesse. "Do you mind if we leave in the morning?"

"Fine with me," Amy said.

"Me too," Jesse agreed.

"Fine with me," Marty said. "Bart needs someone with backbone to stand up to him."

"Well, don't get yourselves in any more trouble than you have to," Ryan advised. "Bart has enough influence here to make your lives miserable."

Next morning as they were packing the car to leave, an elderly man came over to them and asked, "Are you folks leaving already?"

"We have to," Gilmore replied. "Bart doesn't want us here."

"Oh my," the man said. He stared at them for a minute, and then walked away.

"Hopefully he'll tell someone," Marty said.

"Marty!" Amy said. "You're not sounding like your jovial self this morning."

"Frankly, no," Marty said. "I'm just a little bit ticked off, in a manner of speaking. I'll settle down soon."

A couple of hours later on the freeway, they were passing Fresno. Very little had been said, and Jesse spoke up. "What's wrong with us that we can't handle all this?"

After a minute, Marty replied. "We're handling it," he said. "There's nothing wrong with being smart enough to know when someone's screwing you over." He paused. "And there's nothing wrong with expecting someone to forgive you, especially if you've done nothing wrong."

After a few more miles, Marty spoke up again. "Gilmore, Jenny, don't apologize to anyone just to appease that egotistical old man. We'll hang out with you until Bart goes away."

"Don't worry, Marty," Gilmore said. "I don't feel guilty about anything. The way Bart acted back there just helps me understand that he's the problem, not Jenny and I."

"Good," Marty said.

"And Jesse," Jenny said. "Be sure to tell your mother I appreciate her sticking up for us."

"I'll do that," Jesse assured her.

"I'm glad to be with you all," Amy said.

"We like you too," Marty assured her.

CHAPTER 26

Jesse slept in as long as he could that Monday morning. He'd registered to take an afternoon summer course, but classes didn't started until Tuesday.

When he did get up, he thought all day about what had happened at retreat. Over and over in his mind he asked himself if there was something he misunderstood about what had been going on in the last months, and he couldn't get a grip on it. He couldn't imagine that so many negative events could occur in such a short time, and he worried that it was going to adversely affect Amy's regard for the Way.

So the next evening he was immediately fearful when Bart appeared at his door while he was preparing himself dinner. He invited Bart in, and offered him something to eat, but Bart declined the invitation.

Instead, Bart launched right into his reasons for the visit. "I have to talk to you about something."

Jesse felt the tension in himself increase. *I'm in trouble now*, he thought. *And here I am alone with him.*

"I'm concerned that you took the Gilmores to Cucamonga."

Jesse appreciated that Bart was not using the critical tone of voice he was so noted for.

"You should not have taken them there," Bart said.

"Well," Jesse said, "they actually took me there."

"They took you?"

"Yeah. They went and I rode with them."

"I see. Whose idea was that?"

Jesse didn't know what the best answer would be, so he said, "I don't know, exactly. We just all went together."

"I have a request to make of you," Bart said.

"Yeah?"

"You'll have to restrict your contact with the Gilmores."

Jesse did not reply.

"You see, they're a bad influence."

"They want to be allowed to go to assembly, though," Jesse said.

"It'll be a long time before they get to go to assembly. We just can't have them giving the wrong example to our other young people."

"What are they doing that's wrong?"

"They're being disrespectful of God's servants. I told them not to go to any gatherings, and they continue to show up."

What can I say? Jesse thought.

"If you continue to treat them as though everything is okay all the other young people will begin to think they can do the same thing. Do you realize that this all started when they ran off and got married secretly?"

"Uh, no."

"See, this is the problem. If nothing is done about them running off and doing drastic things on their own everyone else will be doing the same."

"Well I don't have any plans to run off and get married," Jesse assured him.

"I should hope not. I'm glad to see that girl's not here tonight."

"She lives on campus, you know."

"Yes, I know," Bart said. "But I also know what college students are like. They're exposed to the worst kind of immorality at college and it rubs off on them and they have a terrible struggle to keep it from affecting their own lives. You'll have to heed my warning, because the first thing you know you'll end up having her here all the time, and you know what happens when girls begin visiting boys in their apartments."

"Amy only comes here when she needs help with her homework," Jesse protested.

"She has to get someone else to help her," Bart said. "If she doesn't stop coming here, before you know it she'll have you sleeping with her."

Now this offends me!

"Can I get you to promise not to have her here again?" Bart asked.

"Well, I'll see what I can do," Jesse hedged.

"See! She already has you considering the possibility that it'll be okay for her to come back here."

I'm NOT going to treat Amy like that.

Not getting a response, Bart went on to the next item of business. "I hear that you went to visit Howard in prison."

"Yes, I did. But Marty went with me." Jesse was immediately sorry he had implicated Marty in this apparent error.

"I know. And I'll be speaking to Marty about this too."

You really don't like anything about any of us, Jesse thought.

"As long as people keep visiting him we'll never be able to put the shame of him behind us. You know, as long as people keep seeing him everyone is going to think that we believe it's okay to behave immorally with children. Are you planning to go and see him again?"

"I have no plans to," Jesse said.

"That's good. I'm glad to hear that. And I hope if Marty asks you to go with him that you'll refuse to go."

I don't have the courage to argue with you, but I don't dare lie to you either.

"Can you promise me that?"

It startled Jesse that Bart would put it so bluntly. "Well, maybe I can."

Bart studied Jesse for a while.

He's not happy with that answer. I wish I weren't here alone with him.

"You know, Jesse. I'm worried that you aren't more ready to accept instruction from me. I'm afraid I'm going to have to spend some more time with you to help you shrug off some of the bad influences you've been under recently. I'd be really disappointed if I had to report to your family that you became an apostate. And even worse, that I had to expel you. I'm sure you'd be disappointed with yourself if that happened."

I can't take much more of this.

Apparently Bart had completed his spiel; or maybe he concluded that he was wasting his time on Jesse. In any case, he made an abrupt exit.

Jesse felt himself shaking when he reached to accept Bart's handshake as he was leaving.

When Bart was gone, Jesse paced in his apartment. *What am I going to do now? He isn't going to let up on me. I can't call Amy. I don't want her to know about this. I'd like to call Marty, but Bart's probably over there right now. I'd like to call Dad, but I don't want to upset Mom.*

Suddenly he noticed he'd not eaten his dinner. He decided he had no more appetite for it and threw it into the garbage can.

Lacking anything better to do, he went outside and walked for an hour. By the time he returned to his apartment he'd decided to tell Maggie what had happened.

"I'm scared of Bart," Jesse said.

"Yes," Maggie responded. "So am I."

"Is this something new, or am I dreaming? Do people get afraid of the servants like this very often?"

"I don't know. I've never been afraid of a servant before. But I'm sure some other people have been."

"I've started thinking there's something wrong with me," Jesse sighed. "I never thought it was appropriate to feel this way about a servant."

"Normal people don't feel afraid without a reason."

"Well, I was thinking I wasn't normal."

"Of course you're normal. You feel threatened. There'd be something wrong with you if you didn't feel afraid. It's just that simple."

"I guess what I'm confused about, then, is why a servant should make me so afraid."

"What are you afraid of?" Maggie asked.

"I don't know," Jesse said. "Well, I do know. I'm afraid that if he expels me I'll go to hell."

"So you really believe that?"

"My mind tells me no," Jesse said. "But I can't let myself believe it. I guess I can't understand how come the only way to get to heaven can be screwed up by people like Bart."

"I think we have to get over that notion," Maggie said. "I'm sure most of the servants want us to think that way, but I can't believe that."

"What should I do?" Jesse asked.

"I don't know," Maggie sighed. "I've never talked to anyone like this before."

Jesse was surprised. "Am I making you uncomfortable?"

"Oh no, my dear. I'm glad you trust me to talk this way. I don't know anyone else who'd talk to me like this. You know, one time I asked a servant if someone who was mistreated and expelled by a servant was going to be saved anyway. And the servant told me that it was impossible to bypass the servants to get to salvation."

Jesse didn't reply.

"It was then I decided I wouldn't believe just everything the servants say."

"Why?"

"Because... well, I just couldn't figure out how people for hundreds of years could not get salvation when there were no Way servants around. When you ask them about that, they have a lot of different answers, like *Well God will look after them.* Or, *There wasn't anyone in the world who was worthy of salvation at the time.* You see, when I confessed the servant never talked about anything like this. All he'd ever speak about was believing in Jesus. Now we have servants telling us that we have to be approved by them to get saved. Either that's new, or I've been missing something for years. I'm not sure I can believe both those things at the same time."

"I see your point," Jesse agreed. And he was puzzled. He remembered Howard telling him about John Campbell.

"And here's something else that I find intolerable," Maggie confessed. "I don't think I should be telling you this because the servants don't want us to know about it. But I think it's terrible for the servants to create a religion and then try to make us believe they never did that." She stopped abruptly, as though she had made some kind of mistake.

Jesse was surprised. "When we went to see him, Howard told us that the Way was started by a guy called John Campbell. Is that true?"

"Yes, it is," Maggie said. "I'll bet no one's ever told you that."

"No. I always thought the Way must have been forever. I guess I should have asked."

"I think they expected no one would ever find out about it."

"This is really confusing."

"Don't be confused," Maggie advised. "Just trust what you believe. Just stay that way."

"I'm worried about Amy," Jesse said. "How can I explain all this to her?"

"I don't know," Maggie said. "I don't know. I think you'll just tell her the right things. I trust you."

"Thank you. Hopefully Bart will soon be done cleaning up Espadín."

"Hopefully. Helen Sawyer was talking to me and told me what Bart did to her. Poor lady."

"Helen," Bart said. "I'm disappointed you let your son testify against Howard in court."

"Why are you disappointed?" Helen asked.

"Because it made the servants look bad."

"Do you think Howard was innocent?"

"No. He was a shame to the service."

"Then why would you expect me to protect him?"

"I wouldn't expect you to protect him," Bart explained. "But I would expect you to protect the rest of the servants from shame."

"How would it protect the servants if I didn't let Adam testify against Howard?"

"It's not really to protect the servants," Bart said. "It's really about preserving the reputation of the servants. How can we expect to attract converts to the Way if all the newspapers are saying that the servants aren't perfect?"

"The newspapers never said that."

"But you know very well that the purpose of the newspapers is to make people think that. Newspapers are only interested in bad news."

"I guess you can think what you want about that."

"But Helen, why on earth would you allow your son to be involved in such a trial? As a mother, aren't you concerned that you protect your son from such exposure? What good did you expect to come from having him do such a thing?"

"This is how I feel about it," Helen began. "I was really pleased that the prosecutor came and asked Adam to testify. And here's the reason why.

"Adam's just old enough that he doesn't need anyone to encourage him to experiment with sexual matters. And this is what happened. Howard exposed him to something I didn't want him exposed to. Aside from the fact that I think it was immoral, it's also illegal. And I don't want my son to end up going to prison for years like Howard.

"If you'd been in court you'd have heard that Adam wasn't so sure what Howard had done was so bad – simply because it was a servant who introduced him to it. How do you discourage a boy who has reached puberty from experimenting with something he's intensely curious about if some servant promotes it?

"I was quite thankful Adam got to see first hand what happens to people who commit sex crimes. I'm sure his experience in court did more to deter him from trying that again than anything anyone else could do for him."

Bart was startled by her frankness. "But think about the servants looking for converts!"

"Do you think I'm going to let my son be sexually molested and do nothing about it just to make you look good? Not on your life. I only have one chance to raise my son, and you have the rest of your life to work on your reputation. You know what I think?"

"What?" Bart stuttered.

"I think you should be a bit more concerned about caring for and protecting the friends you've been assigned to minister to and let us decide whether to recommend you to your prospective converts. I'd gladly recommend you to others if you weren't so ready to expel people."

"Well, I guess I'd better be going," Bart said. "It was nice talking to you."

When he left, Helen went to her bedroom and cried for a long time. When she heard Adam coming in from school she washed her face in the bathroom and came out to meet him.

"I like that woman a lot," Maggie said. "She's a wise mother."

"Does everyone come to talk to you?" Jesse asked.

"Oh, some people do," Maggie smiled. "I can't do much for anyone, but there's one thing I've learned I can do for everyone who comes to talk to me."

"What's that?"

"I can tell them to trust their heart. They're all good hearted people, and they don't deserve to be beaten up by some egotistical kook."

Jesse smiled. *Maggie knows how to talk to kids.*

Maggie smiled back.

Jesse hugged her warmly and kissed her cheek when he left to go home.

Yes, even Aggie came to talk to Maggie. It was only a few days later that she showed up at Maggie's apartment.

"Bart wants me to let people know that assembly from now on will be at the Sturms'."

"Oh," Maggie said. "What do you suppose George will think of this?"

"Poor George," Aggie said. "He's taking it really well, considering what happened to him."

"What happened to him?"

"They found out where Marian went, and she's refused to come back to him," Aggie informed her.

"Was George really surprised?" Maggie asked.

"I expect so. I don't think any man would expect his wife to leave him and never come back."

"I think he abused her a lot."

"But Maggie, wives are supposed to be in submission to their husbands."

"Oh, I know all about that," Maggie said. "But George wasn't doing what the Bible tells him about how to treat his wife. A man is supposed to love his wife as he loves his own body."

"Where did you get that notion?"

"It says that in the Bible."

"You read the Bible too much," Aggie said. She apparently thought better of her admonition, and added, "Who said that was in the Bible?"

"I read it."

"Well, the servants don't talk about that."

"I think they should," Maggie said.

"Maybe you're right," Aggie agreed. "I think that would be good."

"They put too much emphasis to how women are supposed to behave with their husbands."

"But what right does a woman have to tell her husband he's wrong?" Aggie wondered.

"Who needs the right?" Maggie asked. "What women really need to do is grasp onto their freedom to think and believe for themselves. There's nothing more confusing than trying to figure out what some man thinks is right and wrong. I get weary of women thinking they're not supposed to know anything on their own. If women were intended to be stupid their heads would be smaller."

"Maggie, you need to be careful who you say these kinds of things to." Aggie giggled.

"I think I'm too old to worry much about that anymore."

"I hope so," Aggie said. "And Marian has been put on suspension."

"Oh really?" Maggie was surprised.

"Yes. She left George. They can't let her continue, because she won't come back to Espadín."

"I suppose they don't care to consider why she left."

"She had a bad life with him, didn't she?"

"Aggie, I think you agree with me most of the time."

"Unfortunately, yes, Maggie, I do. But you see, it's not about what you and I think. We just have to accept that the men are going to have more spiritual insight than we."

"I'm not big on respect for spiritual insight at the moment," Maggie said. "Remember that Howard had a lot of spiritual insight. And what do you think of Bart's spiritual insight on women?"

Aggie thought for a while. "You know, every time I come here for a visit I go home and it takes me days to think about everything you tell me."

"I'm sorry," Maggie chuckled.

"Oh, don't worry," Aggie assured her. "I won't tell Bart anything."

They both laughed.

CHAPTER 27

"Are they staying overnight?" Nancy asked.

"No," Clay said. "Just a short visit."

"What do they want?"

"I don't know. Chester just said they wanted to talk to me."

"You know what that means, don't you?"

"What do you think?"

"It means you're in trouble for something," Nancy said.

"Maybe so."

"Maybe so? Does Uncle Floyd come down here for just a friendly little visit? And does Uncle Floyd go anywhere with another big gun if he's not about to shoot off about something?"

Clay smiled. "Rough talk for a cute little lady."

"I think I'll just be busy and go out somewhere when they come here," Nancy said.

"You better stay. They'll not like it that you took off. And you don't have to say a word."

"I can't deal with them when they get like that."

"I'd like you to stay," Clay said. "Don't say anything. I just think it might be good to have someone on my side to hear the conversation."

Nancy thought for a while, then said, "You don't trust them, do you?"

"Let's just say I don't trust them to hear me correctly."

"Okay. I'll listen, very carefully."

When Chester and Floyd arrived they were somber. Chester was not his jovial self. Floyd looked around the apartment as though he were inspecting it.

"Can I get you something to drink?" Nancy offered as they were sitting down.

"That won't be necessary," Chester said. "Perhaps later."

So Nancy sat down.

Floyd began. "Clay. I've been told you've gone to visit Howard in prison."

"That's true."

"I've also been told you've refused to accept payment for representing him in court."

"Yes, I did refuse to accept part of the payment."

"So we are concerned about why you continue to see him."

"Why are you concerned?" Clay asked.

Nancy cast him her warning eye. It said, *There you go again, cross questioning someone.*

"We're wondering what your interest is in Howard if you're not accepting payment for representing him."

"I don't understand."

Chester was saying nothing.

"You know," Floyd explained. "Howard's no longer one of us. He's been expelled."

"I know."

"We don't look kindly on people going out of their way to befriend those who've had to be expelled."

"I know," Clay said.

"So I'm curious about why you continue to befriend him."

"Why do you use the word befriend?" Clay asked. "I've visited dozens of people in prison and I don't consider it befriending them. They're clients."

Floyd was flustered. "But I've been told that you consider Howard your friend, and I was very disappointed to learn that?"

"Who told you that?"

"Why, it was Victor, I think."

"I know it was," Clay asked. "He's the only one of our friends who knows that I went to see Howard."

"So what friendship do you have with Howard?"

Clay felt his adrenaline kicking in. He would never forget the visit he'd with Howard. He believed it precipitated a turning point in his life.

"Thank you for coming," Howard said.

"My pleasure," Clay said. "Has anyone else come to see you?"

"Yes. Three college kids came in. They're good kids. One of them was the girl who confessed in my gospel services in Espadín."

"I'm glad. A lot of people come in here and never see anyone they know again."

"I know," Howard said thoughtfully. "I've been talking to some other inmates. That's what they say."

"How are your accommodations?"

"Good, I guess. As good as can be expected. They put me in a special part of the prison where I'm supposed to be protected from people who might want to beat me to death."

"That's good."

"I think I know why they'd do that to me, though." A desperate sadness came over Howard's face.

"But they have no moral or legal right to murder you," Clay said. "One thing we have to say for the prison system is that they try to keep prisoners from murdering each other."

"Yeah," Howard agreed. "But I'm a bit depressed."

"Do you have a counselor to talk to?"

"Yeah. He's pretty good, really. I'd like to have a Bible. That would help. I need to read something positive."

"Won't they let you have a Bible?"

"They would, but I didn't have a chance to go back to the studio to get mine. I wrote to Bart and asked him to send my Bible to me, but I've never heard from him."

"I'll go get it for you," Clay promised.

"Would you?"

"I sure will."

They talked for a long while about how Howard spent his days in the prison. Howard asked all about Clay and his family. Then the conversation went to Howard's offenses.

"I have a confession to make," Howard said. "I really did all those things to those kids."

"Well, the jury thought so, didn't they?"

"But I really did. Are you upset to know that?"

"No."

"But I was really trying to lie about it, wasn't I?"

"You didn't lie in court. You didn't say a word."

"But I really did lie to you, didn't I?"

"Well, maybe," Clay conceded. "But when a person pleads not guilty, the prosecution is required to prove their accusations. That's their job. I can defend anyone without lying in court."

"But did I lie when I pleaded not guilty?"

"I can't say you did."

Howard looked like he didn't understand.

"The concern in a courtroom is not about moral guilt," Clay explained. "The court's concern is about legal guilt. And according to the law you must be allowed to confront your accusers. The civilized way to confront your accusers is to plead not guilty. So no, you did not lie in court."

"But I did lie to you."

"Well," Clay said. "We've all lied – for a lot of reasons. But we're past that now."

After a long pause, Howard said, "You know, I'm kind of relieved to be here."

"Yeah?"

"I couldn't stop."

"I've been wondering about that."

"I was let off too long," Howard confessed. "They should have reported me a long time ago."

"Does it get to be like an obsession?"

"I don't know if that's the word," Howard said. "It's like this. I've done this ever since I went into the service. When you're a servant, people just push their kids at you, especially when you treat the kids nicely. They give you every opportunity to indulge your curiosity. The hardest part is when the kids climb all over you and you can't keep from touching them. It's like some normal man having an attractive woman climbing all over him and he's not supposed to recognize that that's what he really wants to get his hands on."

"I can understand that."

"And everyone thinks its so cute when the kids do it. It kind of makes me sick to my stomach now to think about it.

"But there's something else. Most of the time when one of the kids tells on you, the parents won't do anything about it. They'll just make excuses and try not to let you go to their house again. Once in a while they'll tell the head servant about it, and that's really no help at all. Normally what the head servant does is tell everyone to keep quiet and never say a word about it. If it gets so they think a lot of people know about it, they'll send you to another state where no one knows you. What else can they do? They don't want adverse publicity and they certainly don't want police scrutiny."

"What does the head servant say when he talks to you about it?"

"Oh, you get really chewed out for an hour or so maybe, but that soon ends and then they try to be nice to you, especially when other people are around. But you know, that's not so hard to take, because servants get used to getting told off all the time. It's one of the on the job training techniques they use. When I was first in the service I used to get depressed about it, but I got used to it."

"Couldn't they just put you out of the service?" Clay asked.

"Yeah, they do, if they have no place to send you. But it's really better for them to send you somewhere else. Then they won't have to admit to anyone that they've got a servant who bothers children. They can say the servant was needed somewhere else and everyone accepts that."

"Do they really think our friends in one state don't talk to friends in other states?"

"I don't know. They act like they do. I think what really happens is that they expect when they tell people not to say anything that they just won't say anything to anyone."

"But some people do."

"Of course they do," Howard said. "Our friends are just like servants. They learn who they can trust to tell things to and they say what they want to them. Word gets around.

"The worst part was that I couldn't stop," Howard said. "I knew what was wrong with me, but I couldn't get any help for it. It's kind of like going completely crazy and not being allowed to let anyone know about it. Can you imagine what would happen if I asked for permission to go to a psychiatrist? They'd never let me do a thing like that. They're paranoid about psychiatrists."

"But a psychiatrist wouldn't have to tell the police."

"But he'd need to get paid. They don't believe in paying psychiatrists. They don't even believe in psychiatrists. They just think I could turn myself off because I wanted to."

"How did it start with you?" Clay asked.

"I was a kid. A servant wanted to play around with me, and he asked me not to tell anyone. Every time he came around it was the same thing. My parents loved him, and they thought it was so great that he was paying attention to me. He never got in trouble that I know of. In the beginning I thought there was something wrong with what we were doing, but over time I decided it couldn't be all that wrong as long as no one knew anything about it. I remember thinking that probably that servant or some other servants were doing the same thing with other kids."

"You know, a servant did that to me too," Clay said.

"Oh?"

"Yeah. I was 12 years old."

"Then I want to know something," Howard said. "What did it do to you?"

Clay was startled.

"Can you tell me?" Howard persisted. "I want to know if I could. I never knew what it might do to someone."

"But someone molested you," Clay said. "You know what is does."

"No, I don't. You and I are not the same. You're normal, and I'm… What can I say?"

"Tell me."

"I could never be married." Howard's voice was faltering. "I have an aversion to naked adult bodies."

"A lot of people would say that."

"But with them it's posturing their morals," Howard explained. "For me it's a spontaneous, sickening revulsion. I might know why, but I can't tell you – at least just not yet. I haven't been able to confront it yet. I'll get there, maybe. But it won't make any difference. I can't be fixed."

Clay listened intently.

"It hurts," Howard said. "I haven't been able to think about it since I was …" He stopped, as though he feared what he might say.

"Since you were molested?" Clay asked.

"No." He thought for a while. "It was … something else."

"Worse?"

"Yes." Then he changed the topic. "Tell me what it did to you."

"Well, I have nightmares," Clay confessed.

"I'm sorry," Howard said.

"I didn't think it affected me until I was married. And even then I didn't think it affected me. But one day I realized that Nancy couldn't touch me when I wasn't expecting it, you know, when I was asleep. I'd have this nightmare and see that same servant trying to come onto me like he did at retreat when I was 12 years old. It ruins a beautiful expression – being touched by my wife. I'm sorry, you didn't need to hear that."

"I did," Howard said. "I always wondered. You know, they tell people that these kids get over it and forget it. That always excused me in a way – the idea that the only damage I was doing was to the reputation of the servants. They didn't know it, but they were doing everything they could to make it easy for me to continue."

"Where all have you been?" Clay asked.

"I was in a couple of states back in the Midwest, and they kept moving me around. Then they sent me to Colorado, and I was only there for a year and a half and they sent me here to California. I've only been here a little more than a year. I've got a bad record."

They visited for a couple of hours. When it was time to go, Clay said, "I'll go over to Espadín and get your Bible for you. Anything else you want?"

"No."

"I'll be back to see you again."

"I'm glad. Thanks for coming. And I'm so sorry for what this has done to your marriage. I've never had that kind of a relationship."

"You're helping me understand this," Clay said.

"I hope so. I'm glad you told me, because I don't think most of the servants would even want to know what you told me."

"I'll take your word for what goes on inside the service."

As Clay was leaving the visiting area, he looked back in time to see the guard escorting Howard out another door. Howard was looking back, watching Clay leave, and when he saw Clay looking at him he smiled.

"I don't know what to tell you about the friendship I have with Howard," Clay said.

"What kind of friendship can you have with anyone who rejects God's will and brings such shame on God's people?" Floyd asked.

"It's the kind of friendship that can help me understand the damage a child molesting servant can do to a child."

"I don't understand," Floyd said.

"It's like this," Clay explained. "You wanted me to defend Howard in court. It was okay to have me defend him in court, but what you really wanted me to do was to save the reputation of the service. If you were really concerned about Howard, you wouldn't have expelled him when it became evident he was going to be a public scandal to the Way."

Floyd just stared back at Clay.

"You know, Howard really shouldn't have been brought here to California at all. But since you had him come here, your big mistake was not reporting him to the police when you heard what he was doing. Howard would have ended up in prison anyway, but you wouldn't have five years of probation ahead of you. It's really that five years of probation that brings scandal on the Way. It means that you tried to shelter a child molester from prosecution. This society doesn't care too much for religious people who protect child molesters in their ministry."

"Be easy on Uncle Floyd," Chester said.

"Those children never suffered anything," Floyd protested. "People these days are just looking to make trouble for whoever they can."

Clay continued. "I was molested by an exservant myself. I was 12 years old, and it was in the dormitory at retreat. And no, I wasn't traumatized by it. As far as I knew there were no ill effects. No one else knew anything about it, so of course no one else thought there were any ill effects to me. And as far as causing me to be a pervert or something, no, that never happened either. But I'll tell you what did happen to me. After I was married it caused problems for me in my intimate relationship with my wife. Do you want me to tell you how?"

"Oh, uh, well, that won't be necessary?" Floyd said. "We don't need to know things like that. Anyway, you have a child, so there can't be a serious problem in that respect."

"Floyd," Clay said. "People don't have sex just to have children. People have sex for the pleasure of a loving, intimate relationship. That's what a marriage is. It's supposed to be a beautiful thing, and here you are trying to protect people who do damage to that kind of relationship. Do you have any idea how much damage is done to marriages in this country because of child molestation? We're always being told by the servants about the evils of divorce. Well, here's something servants can do to help people have better marriages. Report child molesters to the police so they won't contaminate the future marriages of every child in the area."

"I think you're overreacting," Chester interrupted.

Clay continued in a calm, even voice. "No, I'm not overreacting. Do you sleep every night of your life with someone with whom you're expected to have a sexual relationship and find yourself unable to perform because it causes you to have nightmares about the person who molested you when you were a child?"

"It sounds to me like you need psychological help," Floyd said.

"You're right. I do," Clay agreed. "I should have had help years ago, but I knew perfectly well that no one wanted to hear about it then. Do you have any help to offer me now?"

"This is outrageous," Chester protested.

"Yes. It is outrageous," Clay agreed. "But you need to seriously think about this. You ought to be very thankful that none of the parents in Espadín have tried to sue you personally for what was done to their children."

"I didn't do anything." Floyd said.

"You sent a known child molester to them and didn't warn a single one of them. And then you tried to protect him when he was molesting their children."

"They'd have to sue Howard," Chester said. "Anyway, how would we pay? We're basically penniless."

"No one would ask if you're penniless," Clay explained. "But when the judge decides you have to pay, it's your responsibility to pay."

"And what if we can't pay?"

"You wouldn't pay. You'd just have a legal judgment against you."

"Fortunately we just have the five years of probation for Floyd to deal with this time," Chester said.

"Not too fast," Clay warned. "The five years' probation is only for the criminal charges. Parents still have the right to sue in civil court for damages."

Floyd and Chester just stared at him.

I wish I knew what you two are thinking, Clay thought.

"Maybe we better go," Floyd said.

"Yes," Chester agreed. "This isn't a productive conversation at all."

Floyd and Chester stood, shook hands with Clay and Nancy, and left.

When they were gone, Nancy said, "You scare the life out of me."

"I scare the life out of them too," Clay said.

"I can't believe you said all that stuff to them."

Clay smiled nervously.

"How can you be so calm about this?"

"I'm not calm. I just let it escape in a way that will do what I want it to do. Like a steam engine, you know."

"I have to remember that," Nancy said. "So about this problem you have with your marriage. Are you really that psychologically damaged?"

"How should I know?" Clay laughed. "I just know how I feel. Anyway, what difference? They couldn't care less what anything does to me. I had a point to make and they didn't like it."

"I was afraid you were going to get expelled on the spot."

"They weren't prepared to do that. They came here to make me agree not to see Howard again and I changed the topic on them. They weren't prepared to discuss the problems of our marriage, so they didn't have any expulsion discussion prepared for that topic."

"You do live dangerously," Nancy said.

"But it's not boring."

"You'll give yourself an ulcer."

"Ulcers are caused by a virus, I've heard."

"That's not the end of your dealings with those two, you know."

"Then, in the meantime, let's work on the marriage problem," Clay said, and reached to hug her.

Nancy giggled.

CHAPTER 28

That afternoon when Jesse came home from work he found Scott sitting with a suitcase on the steps outside his apartment. He looked distressed.

"Hi," Jesse greeted him.

"Hi. I hope I'm not bothering you."

"Not at all. I'm glad to see you. I haven't seen you for a long time. Where've you been?"

Scott looked pained. "Bart's kept me hidden."

"Come in."

"I was wondering if you'd mind if I stayed overnight here."

"Yeah, sure." As he unlocked the door, he asked, "Are you okay?"

"No," Scott said. He looked like he might cry. "I have to go home."

"You mean to Yreka?"

"Yeah." Scott put his suitcase on the floor. "I'm sorry to bother you, but I just can't deal with it anymore."

"With what?"

"With Bart. With the service. I just need to go home."

"Okay," Jesse said. "You want to talk about it?"

"Yeah, I do. I can't take Bart any longer," Scott began. "I've started hoping I'm not going crazy. I have to get away and clear my head. I'm afraid I can't think straight."

"What does he do?"

"It's hard to say. I can't really pinpoint it. I just can't stand his mind. I never thought being a servant would mean dealing with the likes of Bart."

"Not all the servants are like Bart," Jesse assured him.

"I know," Scott agreed. "But I just realized that I could lose it completely before I get away from him. I have to get out of here."

"This is big! Suppose he'll be mad?"

"Oh, for sure. That's why I brought my suitcase. I've heard so much of what he thinks of other people that I don't want to be around when he starts to talk about me. Can I use your telephone to call my parents?"

"Sure."

"I have to get them to come and get me so I can go home. Do you mind if I stay here until they can send me some money?"

"I'll give you some money," Jesse offered.

"You're a student, you can't afford to do that."

"Better yet, I'll take you home."

"Let me call my Dad. He'll be home from work by now."

Jesse tried not to listen to Scott's conversation with his father, but while Scott was talking Jesse detected a tremble in his voice. At one point he heard him say, "I just want to go home as soon as I can."

Then Scott called to Jesse, "Can you talk to my Dad for me?"

Jesse and Scott's father decided to meet at a truck stop near Red Bluff.

On the way north, Scott poured out his woes.

"What really finished me off with Bart was what he did to Marian."

"Really?"

"Yeah. A servant in Oregon called Bart to ask him about Marian, and I heard Bart's side of the conversation. He called her down to the lowest, and told him she was no good. She just secretly packed up and sneaked out of town with Joey one day. He told him she reported George to the police just because he was trying to make the kid behave, and that she complained about George in court. He told him she should under no circumstances be permitted to have her feet washed again until she repents and comes back home to George. So Marian's on suspension for leaving George. I couldn't stand sitting there listening to him get off with a spiel like that, but I didn't dare say a word to stop him."

"Between you and me," Jesse said, "George has a violent temper and he's physically abusive. He was even physically abusive to Marian."

"I know."

"You should have been in court during the trial," Jesse said. "It wasn't Marian who gave all the details about George in court. George got himself in trouble. The judge had to throw him out during Howard's trial."

"I always thought George was a bit of a nut case."

"So I suppose Bart thinks George is quite all right?"

"Oh yeah," Scott confirmed. "He praises George up the highest. He says Marian has shamed the whole Patten family. He thinks George's only mistake was marrying Marian."

"I say Marian's only mistake was marrying George. And staying with him so long."

"Bart can make you feel like a worthless piece of trash," Scott said.

Jesse smiled. "I've never heard a servant talk like that."

"Well, I'm not a servant anymore."

"You're sure?"

"Yeah, I'm sure. I suppose when Bart finds out where I've gone he'll want me slapped around a bit too, but I don't care. I'm going to stay at home until I can get myself straightened out."

"What can he do about it that you're going home?"

"Oh," Scott sighed. "It'll go like this. I'll need to be reminded that I had made a lifetime commitment to the Lord, and I've broken my vows."

"Do you think a lot of people will confront you with that?"

"It'll only take one," Scott said. "And the way I feel right now, I don't even want to hear one person tell me that."

"How does Bart get off with being so rude to people?"

"Who'd correct him?"

"Wouldn't Uncle Floyd be able to tell him not to be so rude?"

"Don't expect that. Bart's all kissup with Uncle Floyd. From what I can figure out, Uncle Floyd only deals with something when it annoys him. As long as Bart doesn't ruffle Uncle Floyd's feathers, Bart will do just what Bart wants."

"But Uncle Floyd seems like a really kind person."

"Don't fool yourself," Scott said. "People just think that because he doesn't batter people around publicly. He just sends the likes of Bart to carry out his wishes."

"Oh!" Jesse sounded surprised.

"That's how it works, unfortunately."

"So what does Bart really think of Howard?" Jesse asked. "In the beginning he sounded like he was going to protect him at all cost, and now he doesn't want anyone to even mention his name."

"Bart never liked him," Scott said. "Or that's what he told me. He told me Howard never was on the right track anyway. At least Howard would let me get out of the house and get some fresh air once in a while. All Bart ever let me do was go visiting old women and men with him. I didn't mind the visits, but I was locked up all the rest of the time."

"I suppose he doesn't think a whole lot of me either," Jesse said. "I went to visit Howard in prison."

"Really?" Scott sounded surprised. "I didn't know that."

"Bart never told you?"

"No. Bart has you picked out to be a servant. Did you know that?"

"Oh no!"

"And he wants to get Amy out of town so you can concentrate on going into the service."

"Oh really?" Jesse said. "I'm not surprised that he wants to get rid of Amy. I don't think he ever liked Amy."

"And he doesn't like Marty either. He talks about him all the time. Marty has a silly look on his face. Marty moves his head back and forth too much. Marty asks too many questions. Marty won't stay in the room very long when Bart goes to visit the Spinners."

"I won't tell Marty, but I'm sure it wouldn't bother him a bit."

"And he really doesn't like Gilmore and Jenny. He told me she's pregnant and they're pretending she's not. Is that true?"

"I don't think so," Jesse said. "I've not heard anything, and I've not noticed anything. I think if they had to get married there'd be some visible evidence of that by now."

"The man has a really bad mind. He suspects people of everything. And I hate to talk about him this way, but it's true."

"Let it out, Scott."

"Yeah, I guess so."

"I suppose he doesn't like the attorney who defended Howard in court either."

"Oh, he thought Shipman was really great," Scott said.

"You're kidding."

"No. I think it must have been because the guy was one of our friends and didn't charge them anything. Bart used to talk for hours about how much money the Way was going to have to waste on Howard, and Howard wasn't worth it."

"The attorney didn't take any pay?"

"I don't think so. Well, I shouldn't say so for sure because they'd never tell me anything about what it cost or who paid. All Bart ever said about money to me was to ask how much I had on me and take some from me if I had too much."

"I couldn't live like that," Jesse confessed. "I mean, I understand it's supposed to be that way, but I think I'd feel like a slave if I had to live the rest of my life with someone else controlling my livelihood."

"Oh! Servants live on faith," Scott explained.

"Personally, I'd sooner have a job and no faith."

Scott was quiet for a while. "Yeah. Me too. Actually, the living on faith part went well for me. I was well supported by a lot of kind gifts. I just got kind of panicky when Bart would take away what I got by faith. I'll never forget the day he told me I didn't need to buy new underwear yet and took a twenty dollar bill from me."

"No kidding!"

"I bought my own clothes since I was twelve years old. It was just creepy having an old man tell me how much to spend and what kind of boxer shorts to buy."

"Gross."

Scott laughed, then was sober again. "But he really likes Rodney Sturm."

"You're kidding me."

"No, I'm serious. Remember that big flareup at fellowship where Rodney blew his top and made a really big scene?"

"Yeah."

"Bart took me over to the Sturms' house a couple of days later and he read the riot act to Rodney. Oh, you should've heard it! He told him he was going straight to hell for talking like that to a servant and Rodney was almost in tears. Before it was over Rodney was on his knees on the floor begging for Bart's forgiveness."

"What?"

"Yeah, he scared Rodney so bad that he slid off his chair and onto his knees. I never saw anything like that in my life."

"Come on, Scotty! For real?"

"For real. I couldn't believe what I was seeing. Bart loved it."

"This boggles my mind. So now Bart likes him."

"Oh yes. Now he's the best man in Espadín. It wasn't any surprise to me that Rodney became bishop."

"But he's just new in the Way," Jesse said. "I thought a bishop had to have some history."

"Or a brown nose," Scott said dryly.

Jesse considered the comment, then looked over at Scott and said, "Did you really say that?"

Scott started to laugh. "Yes, I did."

Jesse laughed.

"Boy, that felt good!" Scott said. "I haven't been able to talk like that for a long time."

They laughed hysterically for a few minutes.

"I wish Amy were here to hear that," Jesse said.

The Straight Way

"I wish I could just get together with all the kids in Espadín and have a good time with them without some cranky old man watching my every move and correcting my every sentence," Scott said soberly.

"I know what I'm going to do," Jesse said. "When I can I'm going to get as many young people together as possible and we'll all go to Yreka and visit you and we'll not tell anyone what we're doing. How about that?"

"That would be good," Scott said.

Jesse saw him wipe a tear from his eye.

"I want to see you all again," Scott said.

"You'll see us," Jesse assured him.

Scott had a tearful reunion with his father in Red Bluff, and then Jesse was on his way back to Espadín. It was a long way home, alone, with endless troubling concerns revolving in his mind. It was after midnight when he got into bed. His last thought before he dropped off to sleep was about Scott, and he hoped Scott was going to sleep comfortably that night. He decided he'd call Scott the next afternoon to see how he was doing.

But the next afternoon, Bart showed up where Jesse worked. Jesse was shocked.

"Good afternoon," Bart began.

"Good afternoon."

"Can we have a few minutes to talk?"

"Well, I'm sorry. I'm the only person here to look after the cash register," Jesse explained.

"Where's your boss?"

"She's in that office over there."

"Thank you," Bart said. "I'll go talk to her."

The boss had been watching the brief conversation and she was waiting for Bart.

"Is it possible for me to talk to Jesse privately for a while?"

"Is this an emergency?" she asked.

"Not a lifeordeath emergency," Bart admitted. "But I need to talk to him."

"Can it wait until after work?"

"I'd like to talk to him now."

"I think it would be better if you waited until some other time."

Bart stared at her for a minute, then turned and left without saying a word to Jesse.

The boss approached Jesse. "Who's that?"

"My minister."
"What does he want?"
"I don't know."
"He looks mad about something."
"Yeah, he does."
"And you turned green while he was talking to you. That's why I didn't let him talk to you."
"Thank you," Jesse stammered. "I didn't know it showed that much."
"I think you should reconsider your relationship with your minister," she said. "He's got a poor attitude for a minister."
"Maybe you're right."

The encounter threw Jesse into more turmoil. While he waited on customers, be remained preoccupied with what Bart could have on his mind. He couldn't imagine what Bart could need to talk about immediately. He knew he'd find out, soon.

An hour later Jesse's boss sent him for a break. At the picnic table outside he indulged himself by shedding a few tears. All he could think was: *How did I get into this situation? If I'd done something wrong I could understand. I wish I knew how to get Bart off my back.*

When Jesse went back to work, his boss patted his shoulder. *She knows something's wrong*, Jesse thought. *I hope she doesn't ask any questions. This is so embarrassing. I never thought I'd be ashamed of a servant, but Bart isn't allowing me to get around this.*

As Jesse was leaving work, his boss said, "Have a good evening."
"Thank you. You too."
"And I want to tell you this. You're a good kid. Don't let that minister tell you anything to the contrary."
"I'll try."

When Jesse arrived home, Amy was waiting at his door with a fried chicken dinner for each of them.
"Thanks," Jesse said. "I don't feel like cooking anything right now."
"You look like you've seen a ghost."
"Bart came to the store this afternoon and wanted to talk to me immediately in private."
"And what's his problem this afternoon?"
"I don't know what he wanted. My boss wouldn't let me talk to him."
"Oh!"
"No. She took one look at him and decided she didn't like him."
"Perceptive lady!" Amy remarked.

"I was showing distress, I guess. But I have to tell you what I did last night."

"Do tell."

"I helped Scott escape Bart's clutches. He was sitting on my doorstep when I came home yesterday, so I took him to Red Bluff to meet his father."

"You mean Scott ran away from the service?"

"Yeah. He said he was sick of Bart's mentality."

"Wow! Smart kid. But couldn't he just say I'm leaving and go?"

"He's all tied up with the idea that he's breaking his vow to stay in the service for life."

"Forgive me, but isn't that a bit unrealistic?"

"Well, I agree. But I guess official doctrine has it that once a servant always a servant. I guess I won't become a servant."

"Smart guy. Why don't we go see a good movie tonight? You need to get your mind off this whole mess."

"Good idea."

As they were throwing the remains of dinner into the garbage there came a hard knock on the door. Jesse opened the door, and there was Bart.

"Good evening," Bart said.

"Hi." Jesse froze.

Bart was impatient. "Can I come in?"

"Uh, yes."

Bart stepped in, as though brushing Jesse aside, and took a quick investigatory glance about the apartment. "I see you have the girl here again," Bart said.

Jesse didn't reply.

So Bart continued. "I told you once about consorting with her."

Jesse was still quiet.

Bart turned to Jesse. "I know what you did last night."

"Yeah?"

"Yes, I do. You went to Red Bluff."

"Yes, I uh ..."

"And you took Scott with you."

Jesse didn't reply.

"And you didn't speak to me about that before you did it."

"Does he have to get permission from you to go to Red Bluff?" Amy interrupted.

"Young lady," Bart fired at her. "I don't need to hear any of your opinions."

Amy's mouth gaped open.

Bart turned to the portable television on the table and pointed at it. "And what is this?"

Amy laughed aloud. "That's a television."

"I know that," Bart shot back. He turned to Jesse. "What's that doing in your apartment?"

"It has a tape player in it so I can watch anything I have to watch ...."

"Young man," Bart interrupted. "You don't have to watch anything on TV. I want you to get rid of it today. I'll come back tomorrow to make sure you've disposed of it."

Amy grabbed the television from the table and headed into Jesse's bedroom with it. "I'll hide it for you, Jesse," she said.

"You little hussy," Bart said. "You get yourself out of this young man's bedroom. You ought to be ashamed of yourself. First you come in here with dinner for him, then you walk uninvited into his bedroom. I think you should just get out of here and go home. I'll catch up with you later."

Amy glared at him, then picked up her purse and headed for the door.

"And Jesse," she said. "I'll catch up with you later."

"Yeah," Jesse said.

And Amy was gone.

"Young man," Bart said. "You have a long list of offences to consider. You refused to stop having that young woman in your apartment. Shameful! You have a television sitting on your table. You know television is an instrument of the Devil. And you conspired with Scott to run away from his vows to the service. Shame on you! In fact, I now also think you conspired to get Marian out of town and away from her husband. Unfortunately it appears that you're unworthy to have fellowship with us anymore. I don't want you to have your feet washed again until I permit it. Better yet, I don't think you should appear at any assembly either. You should come only to the gospel services. They're going to start up again in the Greek Theater, and I'll have services there until I have this whole town straightened out again. This place is no better than Sodom and Gomorrah. Do you understand me?"

"Yes." *But I'm not getting down on my knees and beg you for anything,* Jesse thought.

"Good. I'll be on my way."

As soon as Bart left, Jesse's phone rang.

"Hello."

It was Amy. "Hi. I'm across the street on my cell phone."

"Yeah. What are you doing?"

"I'm watching Bart."

"What's he doing?"

"He's sitting in his car watching your apartment."

Jesse sighed. "I can't take this anymore. I'm sick to my stomach."

"I'm going to watch him until he leaves," Amy said.

"Maybe you should just go home, Amy. You don't want him to catch you spying on him, do you?"

"I'd be delighted," she said. "In fact, I may just go over there and confront him if he doesn't leave in a timely manner. Better yet, maybe I'll call the police and tell them he's stalking you in your apartment."

"Oh, don't do that."

"It's okay, Jesse. What did he say after I left?"

"He expelled me."

"Oh!" She paused. "I'm so sorry. It's all because of me."

"No, it's not."

"I think it is."

"No, Amy, it's not. It's Bart. You and I didn't do anything wrong. Bart's just trying to find fault with everyone he can to cover up for what happened with Howard."

"Well, maybe ..."

"It's true."

"I'll call you when he leaves, okay?"

"Okay."

It was eleven o'clock when Amy called back.

"He's gone," Amy said.

"When did he leave?"

"Two minutes ago."

"You're kidding."

"No, I'm not."

"Where are you?"

"I'm on my way back to my dorm."

"I'll walk you back. It's too late for you to be out there alone."

"Don't worry. I'm so mad right now I could tear anyone's eyes out. You're in bed. Don't get dressed."

"How did you know?"

"Bart left when you turned out your light."

This is like being in prison, Jesse thought.

CHAPTER 29

Aggie came again to visit Maggie with news. "Bart's going to have gospel services again at the Greek Theater," she announced.

"I hope I'll be able to go."

"I'll see that you can make it," Aggie assured her.

"I'll tell you if I'm able to make it."

"I hope you can. Bart's going to be straightening out the young people in town."

"Well then maybe I won't be going," Maggie said.

"Why not?"

"I don't care for Bart's ranting at the immorality of our good young people."

"Maggie, don't talk like that."

"It's true. Why does he call them gospel services? He's not preaching gospel. He's just putting people down. Gospel is supposed to mean good news. I don't mind listening to that. As far as I'm concerned Bart has done enough damage around here already."

"I think it was Howard who caused all the problems," Aggie corrected.

"Oh no," Maggie said. "Granted, Howard did his share, but the only reputation he ruined was his own. Bart has slandered everyone else in his effort to make the servants look good. I say shame on him. Have you counted the number of people missing from assembly since he came here?"

"He's just cleaning up a bit."

"Humph." Maggie wasn't impressed.

"You know, Maggie, you have to have a bit of sympathy for Bart. Did you know what happened to him this week?"

"No."

"Scott ran away on him."

"What?"

"Yeah, it's true. The evening before last Bart went back to the studio and Scott wasn't there. He'd packed his bags and left town."

"Where did he go?"

"He went home, I think. Bart said his father went to Red Bluff to meet him."

"How did he get to Red Bluff?" Maggie wondered.

"Bart thinks the Weber kid took him there."

"Jesse?"

"Yes. I don't think he's such a great kid, Maggie. Bart's been disappointed with him."

"I guess you don't question anything Bart tells you."

"Why should I? My dear, Bart's our salvation these days. We have nothing else. I'd have to meet my maker and explain why I didn't.... you know, believe everything he says."

"That's one way to feel about it," Maggie conceded.

Then there was a knock on the door. It was Jesse.

"I'm so glad to see you," Maggie said.

Aggie said nothing.

"I'm glad to see you," Jesse said.

"How've you been?" Maggie asked.

"Not too well."

"I'm sorry to hear that."

Aggie said nothing.

"I've been expelled," Jesse blurted.

"No!" Maggie was horrified.

"I told you so," Aggie said.

"Why?" Maggie asked.

"You took Scott to Red Bluff, didn't you?" Aggie accused.

"Yes, I did."

"So what's wrong with that?" Maggie asked.

"Young man, you should've been encouraging him to stay in the service, not run away from it. No wonder you were expelled," Aggie said.

"But Aggie? Do people get expelled for such a thing?" Maggie asked.

"I'm sure there was more than that," Aggie replied.

"Well," Jesse offered, "I had a portable television on my ...."

"See, Maggie, I told you there was more. Jesse, did you think you were going to get off with that?"

"Aggie," Maggie protested. "People don't get expelled for that either. This is shameful."

"All I can say is that there's more," Aggie said. "Bart wouldn't do such a thing without a good reason."

"Well, dear," Maggie tried to comfort Jesse. "You just come to assembly as usual tomorrow night and we'll show all kinds of support for you."

"I'm not allowed to go to assembly anymore," Jesse said.

Neither Maggie nor Aggie said anything.

Jesse continued. "The only place I'm allowed to go is to gospel services."

"Then you should go there, starting this Sunday," Aggie advised. "Bart's going to be able to tell you everything you've been doing wrong. He has your best interest at heart, you know. The reason he's having this series of services is to help you young people get back on track."

Jesse didn't reply.

"What about Amy?" Maggie asked.

"I don't know. Bart doesn't like her at all. He's really rude with her."

"He must have a good reason," Aggie assured him.

"I think his only reason is to put all us young people down."

They were all quiet for a while.

"I think I want to go," Jesse announced and stood up.

"Come back again," Maggie said.

"I will," Jesse promised. And he left.

Maggie turned to Aggie. "He's been crying, you know."

"Well he might," Aggie said.

"I can't believe you're so heartless, Aggie. You never had a younger brother, did you?"

"No."

"Well, that's too bad. Your mother could have taught you that you don't whip your brother when he's down."

Aggie sat silently for a while. "Maybe you're right," she finally admitted.

"There've been too many people getting beaten up in this town lately. It's a shame. I don't recall that Jesus beat anyone into submission. I always find it amazing how people can be so welcoming of people into the Way and then once they confess they start analyzing them and criticizing them like they're stupid because they don't figure out all the rules at once. Why don't they just compile a list of these crazy rules and hand them out to people before they confess so they'll know what they're getting into?"

"Maggie, I'm horrified," Aggie said. "If I didn't know better I'd think you've lost your spirit altogether."

"I've not lost anything," Maggie assured her. "I just remember the kind of gospel services I was at before I confessed, and Bart doesn't remind me of them at all."

"Well, we'll just have to go along with it because we have to be in the Way, and we have to obey the servants."

"I don't know," Maggie mused. "I worry about what's happening. Something's gone seriously wrong."

Aggie changed the topic, and soon decided it was time to go.

Maggie thought, *I wonder who she's going to visit next. Now she has me to talk about as well as all the young kids in town. Oh well!*

A couple of hours later Maggie's telephone rang. It was Jesse.

"Maggie, do you have a minute to talk?"

"Yes, I do."

Jesse sighed deeply. "I feel terrible."

"Jesse, don't let Aggie get you upset."

"It's not Aggie. It's Amy. She's gone home because she can't deal with ... us ... anymore."

"Oh my," Maggie said. "She's upset with me and you?"

"No, it's not you and me. I think it's mostly Bart." And he proceeded to tell her what had transpired between him and Amy after he'd gone home from her house.

There was a knock on the door, and it was Amy. Her eyes were red.

"What's the matter?" Jesse asked.

"I've never felt so dirty in my life," she began. "I'm going home. I have to get out of this town."

"Why?"

"I can't take any more of this religion."

Jesse didn't know what to say.

"That man makes me feel like a dirty tramp. All I wanted to do was be a good Christian and be like everyone I met in college who's in the Way, and all I ever got from him was putdowns and insults. I can't take any more of that."

"I... I'm sorry. Did I do something...?"

"It's not you and it's not Maggie and it's not anyone at the college. It's just that man and his religion. I got all my stuff in my car and I'm going home."

"Oh," Jesse said, shocked. "Can I do something... ?"

"No, you don't have to do anything." She burst into tears. "I have to go home."

She threw her arms around his neck and kissed him on the cheek. "I love you but I need to get away from here."

She turned to leave. "I'll keep in touch with you, I promise."

And she was gone.

Jesse stood there, stunned, looking at the door for a long while after she left.

He sat down, and realized he was still savoring the smell of Amy's perfume. But she was gone and he sensed he wouldn't see her again. She was going home.

He stood up and paced. He felt lost. He'd never thought of their relationship as boyfriend and girlfriend, but now he felt like his best friend had died. And he was going to have to mourn the loss. *I have to mourn losing her before ever we were able to ....* He couldn't even think of what their relationship would have developed into if she'd not been driven away by that man.

He continued to pace. And he felt even more lost. *I'm no longer a part of the Way. What can I do now? I never wanted to leave the Way.* He tried to remind himself that it wasn't Bart's approval that would save his soul, but he found he was quite incapable of reconciling that belief with his lifelong understanding that the Way was perfect. For all of his life the servants had been the guardians of the Way, and there was no bypassing them to get into the Way.

He felt alone. And he couldn't figure out how he had so suddenly come to this end. He knew he'd disagreed with Bart on a lot of things, but it had never occurred to him that he could actually be expelled for anything he'd done in Espadín. *I wish Dad were here for me to talk to.* But his father was in San Bernardino. *I could call him, but I'm afraid he'd cry and Mom would be too worried about me.* Anyway, he knew he couldn't call his father and tell him calmly that he had been expelled because his father might think he'd done something deserving of being expelled. *I don't want him to think I'd lie to him.*

He didn't know how long he paced. Then suddenly he grabbed his telephone and called Maggie.

"Ah, Jesse. I'm so sorry," Maggie said. "I'm going to have to think of something to do for you. Do you want to come over and talk?"

"I don't think I can," Jesse said. "I so confused I feel dizzy."

"I want you to just try to relax and I'll get back to you," she said. "Are you going to be okay?"

"Yeah, I'll be okay. Right now I'm too confused to do anything."

"That's good," Maggie assured him. "Can you call me back in a couple of hours?"

"Yeah."
"Don't forget."
"I won't," Jesse assured her.
And they hung up.

Jesse had just dozed off into an uneasy sleep when there came another knock at the door. It startled him, and he considered ignoring it. Then he decided that it might be Amy coming back, so he jumped to answer it.
It was Marty.
"Hey, buddy, let me come in," Marty said.
"Okay," Jesse agreed.
"Maggie told me you need a friend tonight."
Jesse hesitated, then said, "Yeah, I guess I do."
"What's happening?"
"I've been expelled."
"What for?"
"A bunch of things, I guess. Bart came by and found my television, and he was also mad because Amy was here. He called her everything but a tramp. And he just told me I can't go to assembly anymore."
"Bart needs to be touched up," Marty said.
"Don't get yourself in trouble," Jesse warned.
"I'm always in trouble. Don't worry about me."
"How do you get off with things?" Jesse asked.
"I think I'm just a bit more obnoxious than Bart and he has to defer to my superiority in that department."
Jesse tried to laugh. "And Amy left too, you know."
"Where'd she go?"
"She went home. She told me she couldn't stand being here anymore. I don't think she's going to come back. She..."
"You liked her, didn't you?"
"Well, like a friend."
"No, you were in love with her."
"I don't know. You know, I never kissed her or anything."
"Don't matter. You were in love with her and she was in love with you. She'll be back."
"I don't know."
"Trust me."
"She's not coming back to Espadín."
"Would you blame her?"
There was a long pause. "What am I going to do now?" Jesse asked.

"Move to Texas, or Florida, or who knows where. Go to Mexico or Canada. Anywhere where Bart can't find you."

"That's easier said than done."

"You don't have to decide right now," Marty said. He threw an arm over Jesse's shoulder and said, "Let's go for a walk. You have to vent."

"Okay."

They walked and talked, and ended up at the Spinners' house.

"Stay here tonight," Mrs. Spinner suggested. And Jesse did.

The next morning he woke up an hour after he was supposed to be in class, and panic struck him again. "I missed my exam," he said.

Go over there right now and the prof'll probably let you take it if you start before the others leave."

"No, I can't. I never studied for it. I was going to do that last night." He decided he had to be alone. "I think I'll go home and decide what to do."

Jesse went home and spent the morning wondering what he'd do about his situation. He went to work in the afternoon, and drew the curiosity of his boss.

"What's bothering you today?" she asked.

"It's that minister again," Jesse said.

"You have to get rid of him. He's certainly not ministering to you."

"You're probably right." If she only knew.

CHAPTER 30

Sunday evening came, and with it the first of Bart's new series of gospel services in the Greek Playhouse. Jesse had struggled with the prospect of appearing at such a service after he'd been absent from assembly and Sunday fellowship. He decided he could go, swallow his pride, and face the music. After all, it was his soul's salvation that was at stake, and in his lifetime he couldn't recall having done anything that would put that salvation in jeopardy.

He reasoned that his only problem was his pride. After all, salvation was available to everyone who'd pursue it. All his life he'd heard about the cost of one's salvation, and it had always made sense that it was worth giving even one's life for salvation. What then, would be unreasonable about accepting a bit of shame in order to secure it? He could chalk it up to the cost.

But then salvation was supposed to be free. He understood and accepted the concept of persecution from unbelieving people, but he never expected the cost of salvation would involve tolerating and accommodating injustice and personal grudges from his brothers and sisters in the Way. People in the Way bragged that no one ever had that problem in the Way. They were supposed to be known by the great love and care they had for one another.

He remembered the stories he'd heard of others who'd fallen into disfavor with some servant and the difficulties they had experienced in being allowed to confess again. He knew of some people who never returned – they'd given up on waiting for permission to reconfess.

And he thought about all the things that had been said about those people. Because they never returned they were usually said to have developed a wrong spirit. Their fate was easily explained with others' recollections of their pride, stubbornness, and other attitudes that disrupted the unity of the Way. Jesse wondered what people would be saying about him these days.

He reasoned that attending the gospel services would prove that he'd not fallen deeply into a bad spirit condition. But he also reasoned that the only person, or people, who needed that kind of proof were the likes of Bart and people like Aggie who never believed what anyone said until a servant said it was true.

He thought of calling on Gilmore and Jenny, but he feared the possibility that Bart would still be watching him. To be caught consorting with other expelled people would definitely smack of a conspiracy. What he needed to do was make every attempt available to associate with the acceptable Way friends, despite the fact that they'd have been warned against associating with him. This predicament, in fact, made it impossible for him to consult with anyone who'd show any empathy with him. He was not afraid to talk to Marty – Marty took full responsibility for everything he did. But he was afraid to contact Maggie because he thought it was not beyond Bart to chastise her for talking to him.

It gnawed at him that he really believed he'd been selected for this treatment to provide yet another deterrent example for any other young person who dared to disagree with Bart in any way.

What distressed him most was how his conscience guided him. It told him that he should be ready to forgive, and he'd done that with Howard. It told him that he should be kind, and he'd done that with Gilmore and Jenny. It told him he should be honest, and he had been honest about his relationship with Amy – despite his suspicions that Bart didn't believe him. It told him he shouldn't sacrifice his own integrity for the reputation of a selfish old man. He regretted thinking that Bart was a selfish old man, but he couldn't find any evidence to convince himself to the contrary.

And no matter what happens, I'm not getting down on my knees to anyone, especially that mean old man.

He dressed for the service and drove to the Greek Theater.

He parked around the corner where he could watch to see who was going into the hall, but behind a small tree so people would probably not see him. He'd decided he'd wait until just time for the service to start and then go in. The closer the time came for the service to start the easier he thought it would be for him to slip in and take a seat without many people noticing.

The first people to arrive were the Sturms, Rodney and Carla and their children. A few minutes later Marty arrived with his parents.

Aggie arrived with Mrs. Waterman. Maggie wasn't with them. Helen and Spike showed up, as did Herb Fitch and Sally. Gary and Melissa arrived together, and Jesse wondered if Bart would be suspicious of their arriving in the same vehicle. George Patten came, and then Lidia and Jason Gomez arrived.

No one from outside Espadín had come. That meant no one else had been invited. Of course! The services were intended to straighten out the wild college students in Espadín.

Interestingly, of all the students who were there at the beginning of the school year, only Marty, Gary, and Melissa had come to this service. Maggie wasn't there, Jesse feared she wanted to miss the service more than she wanted to be there. Marian and Joey were in Oregon, and Ana Castro and Maria had left town. Sharon Fitch hadn't appeared among any of the Way friends since Howard's arrest, and Pablo rarely appeared at any gathering. And, of course, Scott and Howard had left Espadín as well.

Jesse counted those missing, and found the number only three less that the number in attendance. *And I'm one of the ones left on the outside*, he thought.

But I'm not going in there, he thought. *I can't.* He realized a sick feeling had been creeping into his stomach. He looked at his watch and it was one minute to time for the service to start, and another sick wave swept over him.

He thought for a minute he might vomit. When he'd swallowed down the sick feeling, he heard the first echoes of the opening hymn emerging from the open door to the theater. *Tell me the story of Jesus. Write on my heart every word.* It sounded beautiful, nostalgic, even inviting.

He felt guilty, but he didn't feel any urge to get out of his car and go into the hall. *I just can't face them anymore*, he decided.

He started his car and went back to his apartment.

He called his father and said he was going home.

Next morning Aggie was again at Maggie's door.

"We missed you at the gospel service last night," Aggie said.

"What did you hear?" Maggie asked.

"It was so good. Bart has such care for everyone."

"What did he talk about?"

"It was so uplifting. It would make anyone want to confess – all over again."

"What did he tell you?"

"What did he tell us?" Aggie asked.

"Yeah. I want to know what he talked about."

"Well, he talked about ... you know, sins and how slack everyone is getting about morals, and how they have to start taking the advice of servants again."

"Again?" Maggie asked.

"Yes, Maggie. You know people have been getting slack. Look at the number of people who have just gone away in the past few months."

"Did he tell you anything about gospel?"

"Gospel?"

"Yeah, gospel. You know? Good news."

"Well yes. What do you mean?"

"The gospel of forgiveness," Maggie explained.

"Maggie. You have to tell people how to earn their forgiveness."

"No, no," Maggie said. "That's nonsense, earning your forgiveness. Forgiveness is a gift."

"You know Maggie," Aggie admonished. "If the servants used your approach people would think they could do anything at all and be saved."

"I know differently."

"How can you say that?"

"Because that was my experience. I was forgiven first, then I started being concerned about what I should be doing and what not to be doing. I don't think I'm any different from anyone else."

Aggie looked at her for a long time. Then she changed the topic. "The Weber boy didn't show up last night."

"I know," Maggie said.

"You know?"

"Yes. He was here earlier this morning. He came in to say goodbye. He's gone home."

"Why did he go home?"

"He can't take any more of Bart's nonsense."

"Did he tell Bart?"

"Of course not."

Aggie got quiet again. Then she said, "There were only about twenty people at the service last night."

Maggie didn't say anything.

"But Bart has assured us that number will soon increase quite a bit."

"How's that going to happen?"

"He said he's got three families to move here from the Bay Area. They have a number of kids each and he says they'll be a good example for everyone else here."

"We'll see," Maggie responded.

"You're not feeling well this morning," Aggie tendered a guess.

"No, I'm not," Maggie agreed. "I'm seriously disturbed about what Bart's done to all my good friends in this town. How long is he going to stay around here?"

"I'm horrified," Aggie said. "Don't tell me you're going to leave the Way too."

"No, I'm not," Maggie said. "I'm just not going to have anything more to do with Bart until it comes time for him to leave."

"Maggie, we're not getting any younger, you know."

"Neither is Bart," Maggie said.

"You'll miss a lot of fellowship."

"I've never worried about fellowship," Maggie said. "People don't come to visit with me because Bart sent them. They come to see me if they share something with me, and that's worth a lot more to me. All those kids Bart expelled are still my good friends."

"Oh dear," Aggie sighed. "It must be nice."

"I wouldn't trade it for anything. There's nothing like a nice warm heart to cheer me up any time."

Aggie thought for a long time. "Maggie, what if Bart gets upset with you and tells me to stop coming here to visit you?"

"Then you'll have to decide for yourself what to do about it," Maggie said.

"That would put me in a pretty difficult position."

"I know, Aggie. But you'll always be welcome here. I'm just not going to do anything different."

Aggie pondered that thought for a long time. "Thank you," she said. "I think I'd come back and visit you anyway."

"I'd like that." Maggie smiled.

"Are you serious about not going to assembly again?"

"No. I'll go to assembly. I'm just not going anywhere again just to hear Bart."

"But he might expel you."

"If I were expelled, I could visit with you or anyone else all I wanted. It would be you who'd have to worry about visiting me."

"Oh! I never thought of it that way."

"I'd feel free," Maggie said.

CHAPTER 31

"This is a surprise," Howard said. "I didn't expect you to come back so soon."

"Nancy has a cousin in Santa Rosa," Clay explained. "We come up here quite often."

"Thanks for coming. I really appreciate this."

"How've you been?"

"I'm okay. I get to the library a lot. And I'm going to tutor other inmates in the prison school."

"That's great," Clay said. "I went to get your Bible for you."

"Thank you."

"Bart gave me one, but he said there was another one that he threw out. He said it wasn't fit for anyone to read."

Howard laughed. "That would be my New International Version."

"Oh."

"I'm sure Bart doesn't believe in reading that version."

"Come to think about it, he did tell me the King James version was the original Bible," Clay said. "He had a long and convoluted explanation about the reliability of that version. I think he fancies himself somewhat of a scholar."

"He does, doesn't he?"

"I indulged him. I let him think I was impressed with his explanation. I'll buy you a new NIV Bible to go with your King James version."

"That's great. Thank you."

They talked for a long time, about a lot of different topics.

At one point Clay said, "I had a dream."

"Not a nightmare, I hope."

"I don't know. I wasn't really frightened, but it really shook me up."

"What was it about?"

The Straight Way

"I was about to have my usual nightmare again. You know, the one where the servant comes onto me. This time, in the dream, I really fought back. I told him to get his filthy fingers off me, and I sat up. Strange! He turned into Uncle Floyd when I sat up and I really told him off. I forget what all I said to him, but I was raging mad and quite abusive. I used a bit of foul language, too."

Howard laughed.

"I don't really know how the dream ended. I just woke up and all I could feel was relief. I was totally exhausted. Then I couldn't get back to sleep. It was like I'd broken out of some cage deep in my psyche."

He paused for a while, then continued. "I feel different since then – like I don't care so much anymore about the servants dogging me. It's like I got rid of a huge weight, or something."

"Have you had your nightmare since then?" Howard asked.

"No."

"Maybe you got rid of it."

"That simply?"

"Who knows?"

"Maybe so," Clay agreed. "To be so lucky! Maybe I shouldn't tell you this, but it's made a difference in my private life. Nancy can... I better not tell you." He felt a rush of excitement through his whole body. *I get carried away thinking about what she can do to me now*, Clay thought.

"I'm glad," Howard said.

And Clay realized that in that instant his mind had wandered away. "I'm fortunate to have a good and understanding wife."

"I'd like to be able to have that," Howard said.

Clay wondered what to say. "I'm sorry. That doesn't help you much, does it?"

"It's okay. It would never have worked for me, you know. I knew that a long time ago. That's one of the reasons I went into the service – so I wouldn't have to confront my identity problem."

"I've wondered if guys go into the service for that reason."

"I'm sure some do. A lack of interest in mature females gets interpreted as a sign of commitment to the Lord and the service."

"In high school the lack of a girlfriend makes people think you're gay. I got that a few times. I wanted a girlfriend who was in the Way."

"The service is a very attractive place for people who feel they need some external control in their lives to keep them from acting out their offbeat fantasies. It's kind of a double blessing. It saves you from yourself and gives you the blessing of being a servant. It's kind of a good deal if you're screwed up in your sexual identity. But it's not the solution."

"What's the solution?" Clay asked.

There was a long pause. "I don't know. As far as I know the only thing that works is locking us up." A great sadness came over him.

"But your life could be so productive outside these walls."

"Yeah, I know. But people like me have nowhere to go for help. The first thing we learn about ourselves is that there's something wrong with us and that other people don't want to know anything about it. We think we can handle it until we get in trouble and then all people can do is either punish us or enable us."

"Do you ever feel that people don't really care?"

"Sometimes. But really, we're not any concern to anyone else until it affects them adversely." He thought for a while. "In a way I feel safer in here. I don't have to worry about temptation here. It's a terrible burden to live with."

"I can appreciate that."

"And I know why it's wrong?" Howard said.

"Why?"

"It's because the kids don't give their consent. They can't, neither legally nor spontaneously. And we don't expect them to. We're always in control and everything that happens is at our direction. If they were to consent it would abort the, uh, assault."

After a pause, he continued. "I know that's true. The very second Adam started telling me what to do I was totally revolted by him. It was disgusting. I'm totally incapable of having a truly intimate relationship with anyone. I mean, a sharing relationship. I know I can't have that. Why am I like that? How come you're not like that?"

"I don't know. I've never thought about that. It sounds like you'd make a good spokesperson for child molesters."

Howard shrugged. "There aren't many people to listen to this aspect of the problem, are there?"

"That's true."

Then Howard asked, "Is it possible for you to send me a picture of you and Nancy?"

"Sure. I can do that."

"But not your little boy."

"I'd send you one if ..."

"No, Clay. Don't send a picture of him. I don't think they'd let me have that in here anyway."

"You're right."

"How's Nancy doing?"

"Nancy had a rough week. Chester has a new young protégé, Norman."

"Oh, Norman," Howard remarked. "I've met Norman."

"I think little Norman has to be reined in. He stopped assembly Thursday night to scold Nancy in front of everyone and she was totally embarrassed."

The service had proceeded smoothly. People in the Santa Monica assembly had been waiting for Norman to visit their assembly ever since he'd come to Los Angeles. He'd only been in the service a couple of years and there was speculation that he was almost ready to be sent somewhere on his own.

The first time they'd seen him, Nancy said to Clay, "He acts like a take charge kind of guy."

"I agree," Clay said. "No lack of confidence."

"A bit too confident for a young kid, if you ask me."

"I expect Chester will clip his wings a bit when he gets out of hand," Clay assured her.

So it was not surprising that Norman made commanding remarks at the beginning of the service for everyone to be prompt and brief in their prayers and testimonies. And everyone complied.

Norman was the last person to stand and speak. Ironically, he was not so brief himself. After he'd been speaking for possibly ten minutes, Dennis turned and whispered to Nancy, "Is he almost done?"

"I don't know, dear. Just be patient and he'll soon finish."

"I want to go home real soon."

"Don't worry, he won't speak much longer. It'll be okay."

Abruptly Norman stopped speaking and said, "Do you have something to say to me?"

Everyone was surprised, and they were all looking around to see who Norman was talking to.

Then he repeated, "Do you have something to say to me?"

He was looking directly at Nancy. Much to Nancy's horror the whole assembly was looking at her, and she had no idea what to do, much less say. Clay looked shocked, and Dennis looked afraid.

When no one said anything, Norman began studying the page in his Bible that he'd been discussing, and he took all of a minute before he started to speak again. "I have completely lost my train of thought. Perhaps we should just proceed directly to the bread and wine. And tonight I want Parker and Everett to bless them before we partake of them."

Clay watched Nancy to see if she was okay. She looked more confused than anything else. Dennis was watching her too, knowing instinctively that she'd been embarrassed by the incident.

As people were milling about the room following the service, both Diane and Mona made obvious moves to avoid shaking Nancy's hand before they left. A couple of others shook her hand but said nothing.

At the door, Nancy extended her hand to Norman and said, "I'm sorry. I think it was me who upset you."

"Yes, it was," he replied. "You're going to have to learn to keep your child from distracting you during assembly." That was all he said.

Clay shook his hand. Norman said nothing, so Clay said nothing.

"What a rude soandso," Clay said when they were in the car.

"What did I do?" Nancy asked.

"Were you whispering to Dennis?"

"Yes, I was, but I thought I was being quiet."

"I didn't hear anything," Clay said.

Dennis spoke up. "I couldn't even hear you. I don't like that man."

"We'll have to be polite to him," Clay admonished.

"I don't think we should let him come to our house," Dennis concluded.

Nancy and Clay smiled at each other.

"Ah," Howard said. "Another Bart in the making."

"Aren't young servants in training supposed to be a bit more mousy than that?" Clay asked.

Howard laughed. "Yeah, they are. Well, they should be mousy around the older servants. But remember, they're in training to be able to herd the flock around, so the sooner they can display a take charge attitude the faster they can advance."

"I guess you'd know better about that than me."

"And I guess I can say what I want now that I'm in here."

They both laughed heartily.

"Have you heard anything about Marty and Amy and Jesse?"

"I don't think I know Amy and Jesse. But I've met Marty. Nancy's cousin told us Bart has expelled as many as four or five of the college kids in Espadín."

"The three of them came and visited with me one Sunday. They're the only ones I've heard from, except you."

"That's hard."

"But I understand. I quite probably wouldn't come here myself if I were in their position. Not everyone has the courage to buck the system, you know."

"Marty came to me and introduced himself at retreat in Rancho Cucamonga. He wanted to tell me that he's going to be a criminal defense attorney."

"That sounds like Marty," Howard said. "Come to think of it, he'd probably be a good one. He's a really good kid. But everyone knows they can't tell him what to do or think. I was a bit surprised to see Jesse and Amy here, but Marty – never. He's a rebel. Jesse was always careful not to hurt anyone's feelings. Some of the servants take advantage of people like him, just because they won't push back when they're pushed around. I hope Amy and Jesse aren't among the ones Bart's expelled."

"I'll find out for you."

"Could you?"

"Sure."

"If I could have their addresses I'd write to them."

Before he left Clay said, "I have to tell you my visits with you are good for me."

"That's good. But it's mostly you doing something for me, I think."

"In my business it's a joy to talk to someone who's totally honest about his problems."

"I wasn't always all that honest with you," Howard confessed.

"That's okay."

"You're a good man."

"So are you," Clay said. "We're all guilty of something."

"That's why we need the gospel, isn't it?"

"I've come to the conclusion that what people don't understand is the difference between the truth and the gospel."

"What's that?" Howard asked.

"We turn to the courts in our pursuit of the truth, but there's no forgiveness in the law. There is forgiveness in the gospel."

"That's very well put," Howard agreed.

CHAPTER 32

When Clay came home from the office Monday night, Nancy said, "Chester wants to talk to you."

"Chester?"

"Yes, Chester."

"What for?"

"I don't know."

"And you didn't ask?"

"No, I didn't ask," Nancy said. "I don't want to know. Actually, I do know, but I didn't want him to tell me what it was, so I didn't ask."

"Smart girl," Clay said.

"I've learned a few things being a lawyer's wife. But just because you'll take on anyone doesn't mean I want to deal with a disgruntled servant."

He laughed. "How can I find out what he wants to talk about?"

"He's going to call back tonight."

"Okay."

"But I don't want to talk to him, and I don't want you to let him come here."

"You're sure?"

"Yes, I'm sure," she said. "I was totally mortified last Thursday night and I can't imagine there's any apology forthcoming. If there were, I'd have gotten it over the telephone."

When the phone rang, Nancy said, "You answer it."

"Hello."

"Clay." It was Chester. "How are you tonight?"

"I'm fine."

"You had a good day at work today?"

"The usual."

"Well, I was calling to ask if I could have a little talk with you. Norman has a concern that he's brought to my attention."

"Okay."

"Well, uh, when can we come over to your house?"

"That wouldn't be a good idea," Clay said. "Nancy's somewhat indisposed to company right now."

"Well, it wouldn't have to be tonight. How about tomorrow night or Wednesday night. As long as it's before assembly on Thursday."

"Can we meet somewhere else? Nancy'll still be indisposed on those days."

"We, uh, we'd like to have both Nancy and Dennis with us for our talk."

"That won't be possible."

"Oh." There was a long pause.

"Can I treat you to coffee at a nice shop down the street tonight?" Clay asked.

"That wouldn't be a good place for it," Chester said. "Let me check with Henry and see if we can have a visit at his house." Henry was the bishop of the Santa Monica assembly.

"Okay."

"I'll call you back," Chester said.

When the telephone rang again, Clay didn't answer it.

"Aren't you going to answer?" Nancy asked.

"No. He can talk to the answering machine."

After the introduction had played through, Chester spoke. "Hi Clay. I called Henry and we can have a visit tomorrow evening at his house about seven o'clock. We'd still like to have Nancy and Dennis with us."

"Nancy and Dennis!" Nancy said. "And why Dennis?"

"I have no idea," Clay said.

"He's not going."

"Definitely not."

"Are you going?"

"I'll go and see what they want, and take it from there."

"And don't tell Dennis."

"No, we won't tell Dennis," Clay agreed.

On Tuesday afternoon, Clay's secretary said, "A Mr. Chester Rose called to remind you of his meeting with you tonight at seven."

"I'm remembering," Clay said.

"He said he might call back to make sure you'll be there."

"Tell him I'll be there. But don't put him through to my office."

"Whatever you say."

When Clay arrived at Henry's house, it was Norman who answered the door. He looked a bit nervous. "Come in, Clay."

"Thank you."

Henry and his wife were nowhere to be seen. The only others there were Chester, and Mona and Marcel, Alexander's mother and father from El Segundo. That increased Clay's curiosity greatly.

There were five chairs set in a circle in the living room, and they all sat down.

"Clay," Chester began. "Norman has a concern about what happened at assembly last week. Can you tell me what happened?"

"No, I can't. All I know is that Norman was upset with Nancy for some reason and he stopped the service. Nancy was very embarrassed."

"Yes," Chester said. "We were hoping Nancy and Dennis could be here tonight."

"Why do you need to talk with Nancy and Dennis?" Clay asked.

"We've noticed that the Shipmans are disturbing the assembly," Chester said. He made a serious attempt to sound kind.

"Oh really?" Clay asked. "In what way?"

"Nancy was talking to Dennis during the service last Thursday night," Chester said. "It was very disruptive."

Clay looked at Norman. "Did you say that?"

Norman winced. "Well, yes, I did."

"And you were disturbed by that?"

"Yes, I was."

"She was whispering!" Clay said. "Like all parents do with their children when they're restless in assembly."

"Other parents take their children out to correct them," Norman said.

"And some of them take their kids out to beat them," Clay said. "We don't."

"It's disruptive to the meeting," Chester said.

Mona and Marcel were staring at Clay.

"So that's disruptive." Clay said. "Is that all?"

"Well, no," Chester said. "Dennis has been a bad example to the other children in the assembly, and we're very concerned about that."

"How so?" Clay asked.

"You can tell him." Chester nodded to Marcel.

Marcel blinked, then said, "Yes, I'm upset that your son's been telling Alexander that you're going to have me arrested."

"Whatever for?" Clay asked.

"For beating my son."

"Why would Dennis tell him something like that?"

"I don't know, but it's caused some problems for Alexander."

"I don't understand," Clay said. "To begin with, I don't arrest anyone. In fact, if you do get arrested for beating your son, I might be the one who could come to your help."

Marcel stared at him like he didn't understand. "Well, I don't appreciate it that your son told my son that I could get arrested for beating him."

"You could, you know," Clay warned.

"Clay," Chester said. "It's not your son's place to be informing Alexander of things like that."

"And this meeting is about that?" Clay asked.

"Well, there's more," Chester said. "It's been brought to our attention that you've also taught your son that he shouldn't do whatever the servants tell him."

"Where did you get that?"

Marcel jumped out of his chair and approached Clay, pointing his finger at him. "Your son told my son that it's not necessary to do everything the servants say. He told him that you don't ask the servants for advice. Are you going to deny that?"

"No," Clay said.

"No?" Marcel said, his voice rising.

"No, I'm not going to deny that."

"What do you mean by that?" Marcel thundered.

"I mean that I don't ask the servants for advice unless I think I need it and I don't do anything the servants tell me that I think is not the right thing to do."

Marcel looked at Chester, then back at Clay. "What did you say?"

"I said I don't ask the servants for advice unless I think I need it. And neither do I do what the servants say when I think it's wrong."

Marcel sat down, a look of complete frustration on his face. He looked to Chester to continue the conversation.

"So you don't obey the servants?" Chester said.

"Not always. I've told Dennis that if a servant asks him to take his pants down and show him his private parts he's to refuse to do that. Should I be teaching Dennis to do something like that just because a servant says so?"

"Well, of course not in that case," Mona huffed.

"My point exactly," Clay said. "Do you agree, Marcel? Would you expect Alexander to show a servant his private parts just because the servant asked?"

"Well, I can think of a good reason for that," Marcel said.

"No," Clay said. "There's no good reason for that. People call the police when that happens." Clay turned to Chester. "Do you object to my telling my son to refuse to show his private parts to a servant?"

"This is ridiculous," Chester said. "I wasn't talking about that."

"But Marcel was," Clay corrected, "and you brought his concern to me."

Chester didn't know what to say.

"What else has Dennis done?" Clay asked.

No one said a word.

Then Chester said, "We have a concern about Nancy's attitude toward the rest of the women in the assembly."

"And what's her attitude?" Clay asked, looking at Mona.

Mona said not a word.

"Mona tells us that Nancy doesn't associate with the women in the assembly," Chester said.

"Nancy's been complaining to me for some time that Mona and Diane don't speak to her," Clay said. "Actually, she's been quite hurt by it."

"We can't have people treating each other disrespectfully at assembly," Norman said.

"And I shook Nancy's hand at assembly last Thursday night," Mona averred.

"But you didn't say hello, did you?" Clay said.

Mona did not reply.

"Nancy said Diane didn't speak to her either." Clay looked at Norman. "Nancy also cried after the last assembly because of how you embarrassed her in front of the whole assembly."

"But she interrupted me," Norman protested.

"But you were rude," Clay said. "You said we shouldn't be rude to each other at assembly."

Norman just stared silently back.

"So is this what you wanted to talk to me about?" Clay asked.

"Well, we have something else," Chester said. "Actually, this is about you."

"Okay."

"We missed you at fellowship on Sunday."

"Yes." Clay did not elaborate.

"It's not wise to miss fellowship," Chester said.

"We didn't miss fellowship," Clay said.

"Did you go to fellowship somewhere else?"

"Yes."

"Where did you go for fellowship?"

"Why are you asking me that?" Clay asked.

"We're concerned that you're visiting Howard in prison."

"The servants were quite happy to have me defend him in court," Clay responded.

"But he's no longer one of us."

"And?"

"It's not appropriate to have fellowship with him anymore," Chester explained.

"Oh, so you're telling me that I'm having fellowship with Howard."

"Well, you know..."

"No," Clay said. "I don't know. Tell me. Why do you assume I'm having fellowship with Howard?"

"We have to assume that if you're going to see him that ..."

"You don't have to assume anything," Clay said. "You can ask me. I'd tell you."

"We'd prefer that you not have fellowship with Howard."

"I know."

"Are you going to visit Howard again?"

"Probably. Why?"

"I was just wondering what you'd do with my advice."

"Why?" Clay asked.

"Why?" Chester questioned.

"Yeah. Why do you want to know if I'm going to see Howard again? Do you have something for me to take to him?"

"Well, no," Chester stammered.

"You know, if you ever were locked up in jail I'd go to visit you too. Would you call that fellowship?"

Chester didn't know what to say.

Norman spoke up. "One of your problems, Clay, is that your profession brings you in contact with so many unsavory people."

"True," Clay agreed.

Norman nodded.

Clay looked at Chester. "Are you going to suggest that I find another profession?"

"Well, no, we..."

"Okay," Clay said. "What else?"

"I don't know how to say this, but aren't you spending too much time with people you take to court?"

"I beg your pardon."

"Well, you know, everyone needs a defense when they're accused of a crime," Chester conceded. "But to keep on visiting them after they're convicted and put away! What good can that do for your testimony among the Way friends?"

"I don't understand your concern," Clay said. "That's my job."

"But don't you spend just a bit too much time with them .... socializing?" Chester asked.

"I don't ever socialize with my clients," Clay said. "No more than Nancy socializes with the public at the art gallery where she works."

"But if I remember correctly," Chester said, "Nancy was thinking about asking one of those people to come to gospel services."

"I could ask one of my clients to a gospel service too," Clay said. "I could ask a total stranger to come to a gospel service. Would that be okay?"

"Well, yes," Chester agreed.

"But it wouldn't be okay if I asked the likes of Howard to come to a gospel service." Clay proposed.

Chester and Norman both stared at him for a while. Mona looked from one to the other to see who was thinking what. Marcel looked confused, or frustrated.

"What else?" Clay asked.

Chester was becoming annoyed by Clay's assertiveness. "We're not pleased that you tell Nancy about things that happen in court," Chester said. "You're either going to have to stop telling her things like that or find some way to make her stop repeating them."

"What are you referring to now?"

"It was Nancy who told all the women at fellowship that Uncle Floyd is on probation."

"Really?"

"Yes, she did," Mona said.

"So what's the problem?" Clay asked.

"She shouldn't be telling things like that," Chester said.

"But it's true." Clay protested.

"But why was she telling that to everyone?"

"How should I know?" Clay asked. "I didn't even know she was aware of that."

"It was you who told her that," Chester said.

"How do you know that?" Clay asked.

"Well, we have to assume..."

"Chester," Clay interrupted. "You don't have to assume anything. I'd advise you not to assume anything. As a matter of fact, I was not in court when Uncle Floyd was sentenced. A lot of people knew about that before I ever heard about it."

"Well where did Nancy hear about that?" Norman asked.

"You'll have to ask her," Clay said.

"But she's not here," Chester said. "We wanted her to be here."

Is this ever going to end? Clay thought.

When Clay wouldn't respond, Chester continued. "To return to our concern about you and your fellowship. We feel you don't value the friends in the assembly where you have fellowship."

"How could you know that?"

"We sense that you're looking for fellowship elsewhere."

"Really?" Clay repeated.

"Yes," Chester said.

Clay turned to Marcel. "How frequently in my prayers do I express my thankfulness for the people that I have the privilege of having fellowship with?"

"I hear you say that a lot," Marcel said.

"And that means I don't appreciate my fellowship?" Clay was frustrated.

"But we know who it is you're being thankful for," Marcel protested. "We know you're not being thankful for us. You're thankful for all those other people out there that you're having fellowship with."

"I don't believe this!" Clay said.

"Well, we have to assume, you know ..." Marcel said.

"You don't have to assume anything," Clay said. "Look what happens when you assume."

Chester changed the topic. "Clay, we're also concerned that you're postponing buying a house for so long."

"What do you mean?"

"Our friends all want to buy houses for the convenience of fellowship gatherings," Chester explained. "And you're still living in an apartment. It makes it difficult for people to gather there for fellowship."

"What's the difficulty?" Clay asked. "There's lots of parking, no stairs to climb with the elevator, and we've always had lots of room to visit. The kids even have the whole playground when they want it."

"But it's not your home," Chester said. "It belongs to someone else, and it's difficult for us to have appropriate fellowship in a house that's owned by an unsaved person."

"But I own the place," Clay said.

"You own the whole building?" Marcel asked. He looked surprised.

"No, I bought my apartment. I own it. It's convenient for our lifestyle."

"But your lifestyle should be more accommodating for our friends when they come for fellowship," Chester explained.

"But you just acknowledged that no one was inconvenienced."

"We prefer to have our married friends living in private houses."

"I don't have a million dollars to buy one I'd care to live in," Clay protested. "This is Santa Monica. You know how much a private house costs in this city now."

"You're of a very different mind than the rest of our friends," Chester said. "I remember that you also questioned why we have our assemblies on Thursday night."

"I only asked a hypothetical question?" Clay said. "I wasn't disputing the correctness of Thursday evening for assembly."

"But the very fact that you asked the question means you put some effort into finding a reason to ask the question," Chester explained. "People who are well grounded in the Way don't go looking for contradictions to the Way."

"I didn't go looking," Clay said. "I just read my Bible and I find these things. Did you also know that Jesus was not crucified on the same day in all of the four Gospels?"

"I've never heard of such a thing."

"You should see if you can find which one has it happening on a different day of the week," Clay suggested.

"Clay," Chester interrupted. "We can't spend all night like this. You don't agree with us, but I have to tell you this. Your disturbing the assembly has to stop or else. We just can't have this going on among our friends."

"Yes," Clay agreed. "I have to be going."

As he was leaving, Chester extended his hand. "I hope you'll be able to talk to Nancy and Dennis about these things."

"I assure you," Clay said. "I'll discuss it with them."

"We're hoping for the best," Chester assured him.

"So what exactly did I do wrong?" Nancy asked when Clay arrived back home.

"I don't remember," Clay said. He scratched his head.

"You can't remember?" Nancy asked.

"It wasn't just you," Clay said. "It was all of us, including Dennis."

"What did we do?"

"Everything. Nothing. We are just all disturbing the assembly."

Nancy studied him for a while. "You really aren't going to tell me all about it, are you?"

"No, I can't. It was all mean and really quite ridiculous. I have to decide what I think about it myself before I can talk about it."

"Okay."

By the time Thursday assembly came that week Nancy had decided she wasn't going back to that assembly again. Clay understood, but decided he'd go to check the atmosphere, as he described his purpose.

When he entered the room both Norman and Chester gave him the widest of smiles, followed by puzzled looks when they discovered he was alone. When prayer time came he didn't pray, remembering that they'd made such a petty criticism of his other prayers. He decided he wouldn't share any of his thoughts with them, either. In fact, he was sure they wouldn't appreciate any of his thoughts from that week.

When it came time to partake of the bread and wine, he declined. When the assembly was over he shook a few hands and made a quick exit. Norman pushed a couple of people aside to get to him for a handshake. He thought he heard Chester call his name as he was leaving the house, but he didn't look back to see who it was.

Late the next afternoon Clay was trying to finish up what he was working on so he could go home for a full two day weekend. He was interrupted by a call from his secretary.

"A Mr. Chester Rose is here to see you," she said.

"Send him in."

When Chester came in, Clay was a bit abrupt. "Hi."

"Hi Clay."

Clay didn't respond.

"I'd like to talk about last night."

"Okay."

"We were disappointed that you didn't have any part in the assembly."

"I didn't want to disturb anyone."

Chester sat for a while, and Clay said nothing.

"We may have to rethink the suitability of having fellowship at your house if you refuse to have any part in assembly," Chester warned.

"Let me get back to you on that," Clay said.

"Pardon me."

"Let me get back to you on that."

Chester didn't respond.

"Anything else?" Clay asked.

"No," Chester said. "I'll be going."

"See you." Clay didn't extend his hand.

"Yes," Chester said awkwardly. "I'll be seeing you." And he left.

When he was safely outside, Clay called Henry and asked if Chester was there.

"No, Clay, he isn't. But we're expecting him for dinner."

"Can I get you to give him a message for me?"

"Sure."

"It's about fellowship at our place on Sunday."

"Yeah. Looking forward to it."

"He doesn't have to tell all the people who don't like us to stay away this Sunday. They're still welcome to come."

"I... I don't understand," Henry said.

"You know, all those people we've been disturbing at assembly."

"No, I don't know," Henry said. "I didn't know you were disturbing anyone."

"Oh yes," Clay said. "All of us, Nancy, Dennis, and myself – we've been disturbing a lot of people. Chester can tell you all about it."

"I don't know what to say."

"Just tell him that," Clay said. "He'll know exactly what I mean."

"Okay."

That Sunday no one showed up at the Shipmans' house for fellowship. Neither did anyone call to say they wouldn't be there.

Dennis was greatly disappointed. He had plans for his visit with Alexander.

"You're not surprised," Nancy said. "What did you do?"

"I told Henry to tell Chester he could still invite all the people who don't like us to come here for fellowship today. I guess they didn't accept the invitation."

"I know what he did," Nancy said. "He told everyone to go somewhere else."

"Of course."

"So I guess we're off the fellowship list now."

"Just that simple," Clay agreed.

CHAPTER 33

Late in August, one Saturday evening, Jesse came home from his job at a nearby supermarket and noticed a strange car sitting by the curb in front of his parents' house. When he opened the back door he found a little boy playing with the old Lego blocks he hadn't seen in years.

"Hi," Jesse said.

"Hi," the boy replied.

"Who are you?"

"I'm Dennis. Are you Jesse?"

"Yes, I am."

The boy turned and called loudly, "Amy, Jesse's here!"

And Amy came bounding from the living room. She flung her arms around Jesse's neck, and he dropped his keys to hug her.

"I love you," he whispered, and kissed her.

"I love you too," she said. "I'm sorry I left when I did."

"It's okay."

They were still kissing when Linda appeared in the doorway.

Dennis was staring at them, quite fascinated at the show of affection. "They're kissing," he said to Linda.

"I see that." She laughed.

"How did you find your way here?" Jesse asked.

"I found Mr. Shipman's office in Santa Monica and he brought me here."

"And we're all staying for dinner," Dennis chirped.

"And dinner's all ready," Linda announced.

"Good," Jesse said. "I'm hungry."

"Can I sit with them at the table?" Dennis asked.

"Sure," Amy said. "Isn't he the cutest little boy!" she asked Jesse.

"What grade are you in, Dennis?" Jesse asked.

"I'm in the sixth grade at the César Chávez Leadership Academy."

"Good for you."

There was a long discussion about how Amy had determinedly found her way to Clay's law office, and how Clay had found Jesse's address in San Bernardino.

"I called Chester to get your address," Clay explained. "But he told me he'd lost his membership book."

"I doubt that," Linda said. "Servants guard their membership book like I guard my bank card."

"He just didn't want to be of any help to you," Ryan said.

"Probably not," Nancy agreed. "So I just called my cousin in Santa Rosa and she asked the servant up there for your address, and he gave it to her, no problem."

"He didn't know what she was going to do with the address," Linda laughed.

"And here I am!" Amy said.

Jesse was smiling from ear to ear.

"This is so romantic!" Nancy said.

EPILOGUE

From the day Amy showed up at Jesse's home in San Bernardino, it was no secret to anyone that they were very much in love. They both enrolled at the state college in Orange County for the winter semester, where they continued their education. Neither of them attempted to return to the Way. To Jesse's surprise, his parents didn't attempt to encourage him to return. Their attitude toward him hadn't changed at all. It was then he began to understand what good friends his parents were.

Clay, of course, kept the luxury condominium near the ocean in Santa Monica. To their delight, Nancy discovered she was pregnant again in January. No one from the Santa Monica assembly made any contact with them, and Clay and Nancy replaced the Gameboy that Alexander was unable to return to Dennis.

And another event that fall brought yet another much unexpected client to Clay's office. Jerry Hollander, the bishop of the assembly in Costa Mesa, had been arrested on an accusation of molesting a child in his assembly. Jerry claimed he was absolutely innocent, and the servant in Orange County claimed he believed him, but suggested he plead guilty to avoid the publicity of yet another child sexual abuse trial. Jerry wouldn't accept that he should sacrifice his career and live the rest of his life as a registered sex offender just because someone wanted to blame it on him, so he pleaded *not guilty*. So the servant in Orange County panicked and announced that Jerry was expelled and the Costa Mesa assembly would be moved to another home.

Clay employed a private detective, who discovered by the time the trial was about to go forward that Jerry was not the offender – the child who'd accused him later went missing and was found three days later in a cabin in the San Bernardino National Forest. The man who had abducted the child lived next door to Jerry. Ironically, this turn of events proved far more embarrassing for the servant than he could ever have imagined, because the media discovered he'd actually advised Jerry to plead guilty to save the reputation of the group, and Jerry and Clay became the heroes of Jerry's neighborhood.

Bart Stanley would continue as the servant in Del Rio County for several more years. He was quite proud of what the assembly in Espadín had become while he was there. Four new families of Way friends moved there from the Bay area, and he spoke widely about how satisfied they were with their move away from the rush of the big city and into such a peaceful assembly.

Rodney continued to be the bishop. George became Bart's right hand man, but Marian never came back; and George failed to have Joey returned to his custody from Oregon. A few new college students came to Espadín, but none of them ever intended to stay permanently.

Herb and Sharon Fitch moved away. Bart was visibly annoyed upon hearing that Sharon began going to assembly again after she'd moved to Oregon. Maggie moved to Orange County beyond Bart's jurisdiction and scrutiny. Aggie reluctantly approved of Maggie's decision.

Adam began showing an improved attitude. Bart advised against it, but Helen had Adam see a counselor. She was pleased when Adam began unloading his worries on her. Despite his cocky stance in the courtroom, when he learned what Howard's fate was he became greatly concerned that he'd ever again get himself in any kind of trouble and have to go to court.

Lidia and Jason Gomez stayed in town; and Pablo continued to come to assembly a couple of times a year and to fellowship a bit more frequently.

Ana and Maria Castro moved to Calexico where they moved in with Ana's brother and his family. Ana got a job as a teacher's aide, and was looking forward to the day when she could get another job as a contracted teacher. The school district in Del Rio County dropped their efforts to fire her when she tendered her resignation.

Floyd and Jenny Gilmore graduated after the fall semester and moved to Orange County to do post graduate studies at the University of California Irvine. Marty had to stay in Espadín for another four semesters, but he had his heart set on law school in Los Angeles.

When Gilmore and Jenny arrived in Orange County, they approached the servant there about returning to assembly. When he discovered they'd come there from Espadín he immediately consulted with Bart, and within 24 hours denied their request to be reinstated in the Way. He did, however, invite them to attend gospel services.

Gilmore wasn't pleased with the implication that they should come back to the Way as repentant sinners, so they declined the gospel invitation. Jerry Hollander heard about their plight, so he contacted them and suggested they have their own independent assembly, and he'd join them. The three settled on Friday evening as the usual time. They met at Gilmore and Jenny's apartment, because Jerry's wife continued at the new servant sanctioned assembly in Costa Mesa.

When Jesse and Amy found out what they were doing, they arranged their schedules so they could go to Irvine every Friday evening for the assembly as well. And the numbers grew.

When Clay learned Jerry was having unsanctioned assemblies with the students on Friday nights, he told Nancy about it, and they decided to go together for those gatherings. When Clay adjusted his work schedule to have Friday evenings free, Nathan commented, "Friday night now, huh? You're getting more Jewish all the time." They had a good laugh about that.

"You should come with us some time," Clay said.

"You know, I think I will," Nathan said. "After the events of this past year I think I have to find out what it is you're into now that you're minus your religious attachments."

Then Maggie made her surprise move to Orange County too. Maggie sold her apartment in Espadín and went to an inlaw suite in her daughter's house. More surprisingly, when Maggie learned of the unsanctioned assemblies she decided to meet there with the others. And she brought an old family friend with her, Mr. Ortiz. He'd confessed in Espadín when Maggie's husband was alive, but shortly before her husband died Mr. Ortiz disappeared. Apparently no one ever knew what happened to him either, except Maggie and her husband, and they apparently never told anyone.

For Floyd Toner and the rest of the servants, the sketchy rumors of an unsanctioned assembly in Orange County was a distressing development. There was a lot of hushed discussion about it. A number of official explanations were given for what had happened to each suspected attendee at those assemblies – mostly claims that they'd been offended and overcome by a bad spirit. Anyone who knew firsthand about the unsanctioned assemblies was afraid to say anything about them for fear of being suspected of having attended one themselves.

Then, in the summer of the following year, Floyd Toner's health took a drastic turn for the worse, and after a brief illness passed away. Mark Volpe was called to his side, and they spent Floyd's last week together.

"What about these people who've gone off on their own?" Mark asked.

"They can never be saved," Floyd replied. "You can't have an assembly without a bishop, and you can't have a bishop without the servants' sanction. This is how all the false religions of the world began – people who wouldn't submit to the authority of the Way, so they made their own way."

"What can we do about them?"

"We'll have to ignore them," Floyd said, "and hope our friends do too. I'm sorry to be leaving you with such a problem."

"I've been told that some of them wanted to come back," Mark said.

"This is a straight Way, Mark. We have to keep it straight."

"How do we keep it straight, Uncle Floyd?"

"We keep it straight by weeding out the dissenters. We cannot tolerate their heresies and disobedience."

"Yes, I think you're right."

"Yes, Mark. I'm sure of that."

Look for these sequels to

The Straight Way
The Unworthy Servant
The Handmaiden's Diary